## PRAISE FOR NERO WOLFE

"It is always a treat to read a Nero Wolfe mystery. The man has entered our folklore. . . . Like Sherlock Holmes . . . he looms larger than life and, in some ways, is much more satisfactory."
—*New York Times Book Review*

"Nero Wolfe towers over his rivals . . . he is an exceptional character creation." —*New Yorker*

"The most interesting great detective of them all."
—Kingsley Amis, author of *Lucky Jim*

"Nero Wolfe is one of the master creations." —James M. Cain, author of *The Postman Always Rings Twice*

## AND FOR REX STOUT

"Rex Stout is one of the half-dozen major figures in the development of the American detective novel." —Ross Macdonald

"I've found Rex Stout's books about Nero Wolfe endlessly readable. . . . I sometimes have to remind myself that Wolfe and Goodwin are the creations of a writer's mind, that no matter how many doorbells I ring in the West Thirties, I'll never find the right house." —Lawrence Block

"Fair warning: It is safe to read one Nero Wolfe novel, because you will surely like it. It is extremely unsafe to read three, because you will forever be hooked on the delightful characters who populate these perfect books." —Otto Penzler

## AND FOR ARCHIE GOODWIN

"Archie is a splendid character." —Dame Agatha Christie

"Stout's supreme triumph was the creation of Archie Goodwin."
—P. G. Wodehouse

"If he had done nothing more than to create Archie Goodwin, Rex Stout would deserve the gratitude of whatever assessors watch over the prosperity of American literature. . . . Archie is the lineal descendant of Huck Finn." —Jacques Barzun

## PRAISE FOR *FER-DE-LANCE*

"*Fer-de-Lance* will be welcomed by the legions of Rex Stout fans, and serve as welcome introduction to a whole new generation of mystery buffs." —*Midwest Book Review*

"A 1934 period mystery that is remarkably fresh."
—*Roanoke Times*

# The Rex Stout Library

# REX STOUT

## Fer-de-Lance
### &
## The League of Frightened Men

*Introduction to* Fer-de-Lance
*by Loren D. Estleman*

*Introduction to* The League of Frightened Men
*by Robert Goldsborough*

BANTAM BOOKS

FER-DE-LANCE/THE LEAGUE OF FRIGHTENED MEN
A Bantam Book / July 2008

Published by
Bantam Dell
A Division of Random House, Inc.
New York, New York

ISBN 978-0-553-38545-8

Printed in the United States of America
Published simultaneously in Canada

www.bantamdell.com

OPM 10 9 8

# Fer-de-Lance

# Introduction

Series are seldom read in order. By the time the average reader discovers a continuing character the chronicle is usually well advanced, and except in the case of those dreary series whose titles are numbered prominently on the covers, he has no way of knowing at what point in the saga the book he has just acquired takes place. This can cause confusion, particularly if the *next* book he reads is an earlier entry in which the hero he knows as widowed appears with his wife, or having quit smoking and drinking is seen puffing and guzzling happily away with no explanation for his relapse.

Rex Stout avoided this situation through the simple expedient of never changing his characters. The Nero Wolfe and Archie Goodwin of *A Family Affair*, the 46th (and last) book in the epoch of West 35th Street, are essentially the same thought-and-action team we meet for the first time in *Fer-de-Lance*. And therein lies the secret of the magic.

Under the present technocracy, when even the nine-to-five ethic is threatened, we can find peace in the almost Edwardian order of life in the old brownstone: Plant-rooms, nine to eleven A.M. and four to six P.M.; office, eleven A.M. to 1:15 P.M., six P.M. to dinnertime and after dinner if necessary, day in and day out (except Sunday). Like Sherlock Holmes's corpulent brother Mycroft—an uncle, perhaps? Stout is coy on this point—Wolfe "has his rails and he runs on them." Nothing short of a major catastrophe, such as a submachine gun assault on the plant-rooms (*The Second Confession*), can persuade him to alter that comfortable routine or, worse, leave home on business. Barring extreme circumstances, he will be found in those places at those hours in 1975 and 1934 and all the years between with all his virtues and vices intact.

The reader new to Wolfe and Goodwin may be surprised upon reading *Fer-de-Lance* to learn that it represents their debut. So many references are made to earlier adventures in such an offhand, familiar way by narrator Archie, and his abrasive relationship with his eccentric employer fits them so much like a beloved and well-worn suit of clothes, that the newcomer may be excused the assumption that he has encountered the canon in mid-stride. Throughout the book, and indeed throughout the series, the sense is acute that these two fixed planets and their satellites— laconic Theodore Horstmann of the orchids; Fritz Brenner the unflappable cook and major domo; loyal and efficient bloodhounds Saul Panzer, Fred Durkin, and Orrie Cather; and the volcanic Inspector L. T. Cramer—exist beyond the margins of the pages and that their lives do not start and stop with the first and last chapters. Has any other saga begun with a statement as casual as "There was no reason why I shouldn't have been sent for the beer that day . . ."?

When *Fer-de-Lance* appeared, popular crime literature was divided between the manorial "English School" of puzzle mysteries and the two-fisted American urban variety that took its inspiration from the headlines of Prohibition and Depression. Now, nearly six decades later, that division still exists, but there is evidence that the two camps are drifting closer together as both the grim butler and the sadistic bootlegger pass into history. From the start, Stout wedded the two forms. Nero Wolfe, the eccentric genius swathed in his one-seventh of a ton, is a combination of Sherlock Holmes in his more comtemplative moments and Baroness Orczy's sedentary Old Man in the Corner. Archie Goodwin exemplifies the hardboiled, wisecracking "private dick" prevalent in pulp fiction. Consider this exchange:

WOLFE: "Your errand at White Plains was in essence a primitive business enterprise: an offer to exchange something for something else. If Mr. Anderson had only been there he would probably have seen it so. It may yet materialize; it is still worth some small effort. I believe though it is getting ready to rain."

GOODWIN: "It was clouding up as I came in. Is it going to rain all over your clues?"

WOLFE: "Some day, Archie, when I decide you are no longer worth tolerating, you will have to marry a woman of very modest mental capacity to get an appropriate audience for your wretched sarcasms."

Not exactly the Holmes-Watson relationship, but a symbiotic one. Without Goodwin's badgering, Wolfe would certainly starve, collapsing under the weight of his own sloth. Without Wolfe—well, learn from *In the Best Families* that Goodwin can get along only too well without any oddball geniuses around the coddle, but we may assume by how readily he takes up his old post when Wolfe returns from his enforced sabbatical that for all Archie's grousing he prefers the status quo, as do we.

We read Nero Wolfe because we like a good mystery. We *re*read him not for the plots, which have neither the human complexity of Raymond Chandler's nor the ingenuity of Agatha Christie's, but for the chemistry between the orchid-fancying *enfant terrible* and his optimistic-cynical amaneuensis and all-around dogsbody, and for the insular complacency of life in the old townhouse where world-class meals are served three times daily; the Cattleyas Laelias continue to get on splendidly with the Laeliocattleya Lustre; a peek through the tricked-up waterfall picture in Wolfe's office may provide a glimpse of the Great Man relaxing in his custom-built chair with some arcane volume or pushing his lips in and out with his eyes closed over some dense pattern of facts while his legman sits by the telephone, waiting for his cue to gather all the suspects and other interested parties for the *denouement*.

This is a world where all things make sense in time, a world better than our own. If you are an old hand making a return swing through its orbit, welcome back; pull up the red leather chair and sit down. If this is your first trip, I envy you the surprises that await you behind that unpreposessing front door.

—**Loren D. Estleman**

# Chapter 1

There was no reason why I shouldn't have been sent for the beer that day, for the last ends of the Fairmont National Bank case had been gathered in the week before and there was nothing for me to do but errands, and Wolfe never hesitated about running me down to Murray Street for a can of shoe-polish if he happened to need one. But it was Fritz who was sent for the beer. Right after lunch his bell called him up from the kitchen before he could have got the dishes washed, and after getting his orders he went out and took the roadster which we always left parked in front. An hour later he was back, with the rumble seat piled high with baskets filled with bottles. Wolfe was in the office—as he and I called it, Fritz called it the library—and I was in the front room reading a book on gunshot wounds which I couldn't make head or tail of, when I glanced through the window and saw Fritz pull up at the curb. It was a good excuse to stretch my legs, so I went out and helped him unload and carry the baskets into the kitchen, where we were starting to stow the bottles away in a cupboard when the bell rang. I followed Fritz into the office.

Wolfe lifted his head. I mention that, because his head was so big that lifting it struck you as being quite a job. It was probably really bigger than it looked, for the rest of him was so huge that any head on top of it but his own would have escaped your notice entirely.

"Where's the beer?"

"In the kitchen, sir. The lower cupboard on the right, I thought."

"I want it in here. Is it cold? And an opener and two glasses."

"Mostly cold, yes, sir. Very well."

I grinned and sat down on a chair to wonder what Wolfe was doing with some pieces of paper he had cut into little discs and was pushing around into different positions on the desk blotter. Fritz began bringing in the beer, six at a time on a tray. After the third trip I had another grin when I saw Wolfe glance up at the array on the table and then around at Fritz's back going through the door. Two more trays full; whereupon Wolfe halted the parade.

"Fritz. Would you inform me when this is likely to end?"

"Very soon, sir. There are nineteen more. Forty-nine in all."

"Nonsense. Excuse me, Fritz, but obviously it's nonsense."

"Yes, sir. You said one of every kind procurable. I went to a dozen shops, at least that."

"All right. Bring them in. And some plain salt crackers. None shall lack opportunity, Fritz, it wouldn't be fair."

It turned out that the idea was, as Wolfe explained to me after he had invited me to draw my chair up to the desk and begin opening the bottles, that he had decided to give up the bootleg beer, which for years he had bought in barrels and kept in a cooler in the basement, if he could find a brand of the legal 3.2 that was potable. He had also decided, he said, that six quarts a day was unnecessary and took too much time and thereafter he would limit himself to five. I grinned at that, for I didn't believe it, and I grinned again when I thought how the place would be cluttered up with empty bottles unless Fritz ran his legs off all day long. I said to him something I had said before more than once, that beer slowed up a man's head and with him running like a brook, six quarts a day, I never would understand how he could make his brain work so fast and deep that no other man in the country could touch him. He replied, also as he had before, that it wasn't his brain that worked, it was his lower nerve centers; and as I opened the fifth bottle for him to sample he went on to say—not the first time for that either—that he would not insult me by acknowledging my flattery, since if it was sincere I was a fool and if it was calculated I was a knave.

He smacked his lips, tasting the fifth brand, and holding up the glass looked through the amber at the light. "This is a pleasant surprise, Archie. I would not have believed it. That of course is the advantage of being a pessimist; a pessimist gets nothing but pleasant surprises, an optimist nothing but unpleasant. So far, none of this is sewage. As you see, Fritz has marked the prices on the labels, and I've started with the cheap ones. No, here, take this next."

It was at that moment that I heard the faint buzz from the kitchen that meant the front door, and it was that buzz that started the ball rolling. Though at the time it appeared to be nothing interesting, just Durkin asking a favor.

Durkin was all right up to the neck. When I

consider how thick he was in most respects I am
surprised how he could tail. I know bull terriers are
dumb, but good tailing means a lot more than just
hanging on, and Fred Durkin was good. I asked him
once how he did it, and he said, "I just go up to the
subject and ask him where he's headed for, and then if
I lose him I know where to look." I suppose he knew
how funny that was; I don't know, I suspect him.
When things got so Wolfe had to cut down expenses
like everybody else from bankers to bums, Saul Panzer and I got our weekly envelopes sliced, but Durkin's was stopped altogether. Wolfe called him in when
he was needed and paid him by the day, so I still saw
him off and on and knew he was having hard sledding.
Things had been slow and I hadn't run across him for
a month or more when the buzzer sounded that day
and Fritz brought him to the door of the office.

Wolfe looked up and nodded. "Hello, Fred. Do I
owe you something?"

Durkin, approaching the desk with his hat in his
hand, shook his head. "How are you, Mr. Wolfe. I wish
to God you did. If there was anybody owed me
anything I'd be with him like a saddle on a horse."

"Sit down. Will you sample some beer?"

"No, thanks." Fred stayed on his feet. "I've come
to ask a favor."

Wolfe looked up again, and his big thick lips pushed
out a little, tight together, just a small movement, and
back again, and then out and back again. How I loved
to watch him doing that! That was about the only time
I ever got excited, when Wolfe's lips were moving like
that. It didn't matter whether it was some little thing
like this with Durkin or when he was on the track of
something big and dangerous. I knew what was going
on, something was happening so fast inside of him and

so much ground was being covered, the whole world in a flash, that no one else could ever really understand it even if he had tried his best to explain, which he never did. Sometimes, when he felt patient, he explained to me and it seemed to make sense, but I realized afterward that that was only because the proof had come and so I could accept it. I said to Saul Panzer once that it was like being with him in a dark room which neither of you has ever seen before, and he describes all of its contents to you, and then when the light is turned on his explanation of how he did it seems sensible because you see everything there before you just as he described it.

Wolfe said to Durkin, "You know my failing on the financial side. But since you haven't come to borrow money, your favor is likely granted. What is it?"

Durkin scowled. Wolfe always upset him. "Nobody needs to borrow money worse than I do. How do you know it's not that?"

"No matter. Archie will explain. You're not embarrassed enough, and you wouldn't have brought a woman with you. What is it?"

I leaned forward and broke in, "Damn it, he's alone! My ears are good anyhow!"

A little ripple, imperceptible except to eyes like mine that had caught it before, ran over Wolfe's enormous bulk. "Of course, Archie, splendid ears. But there was nothing to hear; the lady made no sound audible at this distance. And Fritz did not speak to her; but in greeting Fred there was a courtesy in his tone which he saves for softer flesh. If I should hear Fritz using that tone to a lone man I'd send him to a psychoanalyst at once."

Durkin said, "It's a friend of my wife's. Her best friend, you know my wife's Italian. Maybe you don't know, but she is. Anyway, this friend of hers is in trouble, or thinks she is. It sounds to me like a washout. Maria keeps after Fanny and Fanny keeps after me and they both keep after me together, all because I told Fanny once that you've got a devil in you that can find out anything in the world. A boob thing to say, Mr. Wolfe, but you know how a man's tongue will get started."

Wolfe only said, "Bring her in."

Durkin went out to the hall and came right back with a woman in front of him. She was little but not skinny, with black hair and eyes, and Italian all over though not the shawl kind. She was somewhere around middle age and looked neat and clean in a pink cotton dress and a black rayon jacket. I pulled over a chair and she sat down facing Wolfe and the light.

Durkin said, "Maria Maffei, Mr. Wolfe."

She tossed Fred a smile, showing little white teeth, and then said to Wolfe, "Maria Maffei," pronouncing it quite different.

Wolfe said, "Not Mrs. Maffei."

She shook her head. "No, sir. I'm not married."

"But in trouble anyhow."

"Yes, sir. Mr. Durkin thought you might be good enough—"

"Tell us about it."

"Yes, sir. It's my brother Carlo. He has gone."

"Gone where?"

"I don't know, sir. That's why I am afraid. He has been gone two days."

Where did he—no, no. These are not phenomena, merely facts." Wolfe turned to me. "Go on, Archie."

By the time he had finished his "no, no" I had my notebook out. I enjoyed this sort of business in front of Wolfe more than at any other time because I knew damn well I was good at it. But this wasn't much of a job; this woman knew what to get down as well as I did. She told her tale quick and straight. She was housekeeper at a swell apartment on Park Avenue and lived there. Her brother Carlo, two years older than her, lived in a rooming-house on Sullivan Street. He was a metal-worker, first class she said; for years he had made big money working on jewelry for Rathbun & Cross, but because he drank a little and occasionally didn't turn up at the shop he had been one of the first to go when the depression came. For a while after that he had got odd jobs here and there, then he had used up his small savings, and for the past winter and spring he had been kept going by his sister. Around the middle of April, completely discouraged, he had decided to return to Italy and Maria had agreed to furnish the necessary funds; she had, in fact, advanced the money for the steamship ticket. But a week later he had suddenly announced that the trip was postponed; he wouldn't say why, but he had declared that he would need no more money, he would soon be able to return all she had lent him, and he might stay in this country after all. He had never been very communicative, but regarding the change in plans he had been stubbornly mysterious. Now he was gone. He had telephoned her on Saturday that he would meet her Monday evening, her evening off, at the Italian restaurant on Prince Street where they often dined together, and had added gaily that he would have enough money with him to pay back everything and lend her some into the bargain if she needed it. Monday evening she had waited for him until ten o'clock, then had gone to his rooming-house and been told that he had left a little after seven and had not returned.

"Day before yesterday," I observed.

Durkin, I saw, had his notebook open too, and now he nodded. "Monday, June fourth."

Wolfe shook his head. He had been sitting as still and unobservant as a mountain with his chin lodged on his chest, and now without moving otherwise his head shook faintly as he murmured, "Durkin. Today is Wednesday, June seventh."

"Well?" Fred stared. "Okay with me, Mr. Wolfe."

Wolfe wiggled a finger at Maria. "Was it Monday?"

"Yes, sir. Of course. That's my evening off."

"You should know that evening. Durkin, annotate your notebook, or, better perhaps, throw it away. You are a full twelvemonth ahead of your times; next year Monday will be June fourth." He turned to the woman. "Maria Maffei, I am sorry to have to give you a counsel of desperation. Consult the police."

"I have, sir." A gleam of resentment shot from her eyes. "They say he has gone to Italy with my money."

"Perhaps he has."

"Oh no, Mr. Wolfe. You know better. You have looked at me. You can see I would not know so little of a brother as that."

"Do the police tell you what boat your brother sailed on?"

"How could they? There has been no boat. They do not investigate or even consider. They merely say he has gone to Italy."

"I see, they do it by inspiration. Well. I'm sorry I can't help you. I can only guess. Robbery. Where is his body then? Again consult the police. Sooner or later someone will find it for them and your puzzle will be solved."

Maria Maffei shook her head. "I don't believe it,

Mr. Wolfe. I just don't believe it. And there was the phone call."

I broke in, "You mentioned no phone call."

She smiled at me with her teeth. "I would have. There was a phone call for him at the rooming-house a little before seven. The phone there is in the downstairs hall and the girl heard him talking. He was excited and he agreed to meet someone at half-past seven." She turned to Wolfe. "You can help me, sir. You can help me find Carlo. I have learned to look cool like the grass in the morning because I have been so long among these Americans, but I am Italian and I must find my brother and I must see anyone who has hurt him."

Wolfe only shook his head. She paid no attention.

"You must, sir. Mr. Durkin says you are very tight about money. I still have something left and I could pay all expenses and maybe a little more. And you are Mr. Durkin's friend and I am Mrs. Durkin's friend, my friend Fanny."

Wolfe said, "I am nobody's friend. How much can you pay?"

She hesitated.

"How much have you got?"

"I have—well—more than a thousand dollars."

"How much of it would you pay?"

"I would pay—all of it. If you find my brother alive, all of it. If you find him not alive and show him to me and show me the one who hurt him, I would still pay a good deal. I would pay first for the funeral."

Wolfe's eyelids lowered slowly and raised slowly. That, as I knew, meant his approval; I had often looked for that sign, and frequently in vain, when I was reporting to him. He said, "You're a practical woman, Maria Maffei. Moreover, possibly, a woman of honor. You are right, there is something in me that can help you; it is genius; but you have not furnished the stimulant to arouse it and whether it will be awakened in search of your brother is problematical. In any event, routine comes first, and the expense of that will be small."

He turned to me.

"Archie, go to Carlo Maffei's rooming-house; his sister will accompany you as authority. See the girl who heard the phone call; see others; examine his room; if any trail is indicated phone here for Saul Panzer any time after five; returning here bring with you any articles that seem to you unimportant."

I thought it was unncessary for him to take that dig at me before a stranger, but I had long since learned that there was no point in resenting his pleasantries. Maria Maffei got up from her chair and thanked him.

Durkin took a step forward. "About that being tight with money, Mr. Wolfe, you know how a man's tongue will get started—"

I rescued him. "Come on, Fred, we'll take the roadster and I might as well drop you on the way."

# Chapter 2

When I parked the big shiny black roadster in front of the number on Sullivan Street Maria Maffei had given me I felt that I might never see it alive and happy again—the roadster I mean—for the street was littered with rubbish and full of wild Italian kids yelling and dashing around like black-eyed demons. But I had had the roadster in worse places than that, as for instance the night I chased young Graves, who was in a Pierce coupé with a satchel of emeralds between his knees, from New Milford all over Pike County, up and down a dozen mountains in a foot of mud and the worst rain I ever saw. It was Wolfe's orders that after every little rub the roadster should be fixed up as good as new, and of course that pleased me just as well.

It was just another rooming-house. For some reason or other they're all alike, whether it's a high-hat affair in the Fifties or a brownstone west of Central Park full of honest artist girls or an Italian hangout like this one on Sullivan Street. With, of course, a difference in details like garlic. Maria Maffei took me first to the landlady, a nice fat woman with wet hands and a pushed-in nose and rings on her

fingers, and then upstairs to her brother's room. I
looked around a little while Maria Maffei went to get
the girl who had heard the phone call. It was a
good-sized room on the third floor with two windows.
The rug was worn and the furniture old and sort of
broken, but it was clean and really not a bad room
except for the noise from the hoodlums below when I
opened the window to see if the roadster was still on
its feet. Two large traveling bags were stacked in a
corner, one flimsy and old and done for, the other one
old too but sturdy and good. Neither was locked. The
flimsy one was empty; the good one contained a lot of
small tools of different shapes and sizes, some of which
had pawnshop tags hanging on them, and some pieces
of wood and metal and odds and ends like coil springs.
The closet contained an old suit of clothes, two overalls, an overcoat, two pairs of shoes, and a felt hat. In
the drawers of the bureau which stood between the
windows was an assortment, not scanty for a man who
had been living on his sister for a year, of shirts, ties,
handkerchiefs, socks, and a lot of miscellaneous junk
like shoestrings, lead pencils, snapshots, and empty
pipe-tobacco cans. In an upper drawer was a bundle of
seventeen letters in envelopes all with Italian postage
stamps, fastened with a rubber band. Scattered
around in the same drawer were receipts and paid
bills, a tablet of writing-paper, a few clippings from
newspapers and magazines, and a dog collar. On top of
the bureau, along with comb and brush and similar
impedimenta as Wolfe would say, were half a dozen
books, all in Italian except one that was full of pictures
and designs, and a big stack of magazines, different
monthly issues for three years back all with the same
name, *Metal Crafts*. In the corner by the right window was a plain rough wood table with its top scarred

and cut all over, and on it was a small vise, a grinder and buffer with an electric cord long enough to reach the lamp socket, and some more tools like those in the traveling bag. I was looking over the grinder to see how recently it had been used when Maria Maffei came in with the girl.

"This is Anna Fiore," the woman said.

I went over and shook hands with her. She was a homely kid about twenty with skin like stale dough, and she looked like she'd been scared in the cradle and never got over it. I told her my name and said that I had learned from Miss Maffei that she had heard Mr. Maffei answering the phone call before he went out Monday evening. She nodded.

I turned to the woman. "I expect you'd like to get along back uptown, Miss Maffei. Anna and I will get along."

She shook her head. "If I'm back by dinner it will be all right."

I got a little gruff. The truth was that I agreed with Durkin that it was a washout and that there was nothing to be expected from it but fanning the air. So I told Maria Maffei that I could easily do without her and she'd better trot along and she'd hear from Wolfe if there was anything to hear. She shot a glance at the girl and showed her teeth to me, and left us.

I pulled a couple of chairs face to face and got the girl deposited on one in front of me, and pulled out my notebook.

"You've got nothing to be scared of," I told her. "The worst that can happen to you is that you'll do a favor to Miss Maffei and her brother and she might give you some money. Do you like Miss Maffei?"

She seemed startled, as if surprised that anyone should think it worth the trouble to learn her likes and dislikes, but the answer was ready behind the surprise. "Yes, I like her. She is nice."

"Do you like Mr. Maffei?"

"Yes, of course, everybody does. Except when he drinks, then a girl should stay away from him."

"How did you happen to hear the phone call Monday evening? Were you expecting it?"

"How could I be expecting it?"

"I don't know. Did you answer the phone?"

"No, sir. Mrs. Ricci answered it. She told me to call Mr. Maffei and I called upstairs. Then I was clearing the table in the dining-room and the door was open and I could hear him talking."

"Could you hear what he said?"

"Of course." She looked a little scornful. "We always hear everything anyone says on the telephone. Mrs. Ricci heard him too, she heard the same as I did."

"What did he say?"

"First he said *hello.* Then he said *well this is Carlo Maffei what do you want.* Then he said *that's my business I'll tell you when I see you.* Then he said *why not here in my room.* Then he said *no I'm not scared I'm not the one to be scared.* Mrs. Ricci says it was *it's not me that's scared,* but she don't remember right. Then he said *sure I want the money and a lot more.* Then he said *all right seven-thirty at the corner of.* Then he said *shut up yourself what do I care.* Then he said *all right seven-thirty I know that car.*"

She stopped. I said, "Who was he talking to?"

I supposed of course that the answer would be that she didn't know, since Maria Maffei had not known, but she said at once, "The man that called him up before."

"Before? When?"

"Quite a few times. In May. One day twice. Mrs. Ricci says nine times before Monday altogether."

"Did you ever hear his voice?"

"No, sir. Mrs. Ricci always answers."

"Did you ever hear this man's name?"

"No, sir. After Mrs. Ricci got curious she asked it, but he always just said *never mind tell him he's wanted on the phone.*"

I began to think there might be some fun in this somewhere, possibly even some money. Not that the money interested me; that was for Wolfe; it was the fun I was after. Anyway it might not be just a stick-up and a stiff in the East River. I decided to see what I could get, and I went after that girl. I had heard Wolfe do it many a time, and while I knew most of his results came from a kind of feeling that wasn't in me, still a lot of it was just patience and hit-or-miss. So I went after her. I kept at it two hours, and collected a lot of facts, but not one that meant anything to me. Once I thought I might be getting warm when I learned that Carlo Maffei had two different women with whom he appeared publicly on different occasions, and one of them was married; but when I saw that wouldn't tie up with the phone call I threw it out. Maffei had mentioned going to Italy but had given no details. He had pretty well kept his business in his own bosom. He had never had callers except his sister and a friend from his old prosperous days with whom he had occasionally gone to dine. I pumped her for two hours and couldn't see a gleam anywhere, but something about that phone call kept me from calling it a dull day and putting on my hat. Finally I said to her:

"You stay here a minute, Anna, while I go down and see Mrs. Ricci."

The landlady confirmed the girl's version of the

phone call and said she had no idea who the caller was though she had tried on several occasions to find out. I asked her a few questions here and there, and then requested permission to take Anna with me uptown. She said no, she couldn't be left alone with the dinner to get, so I produced a dollar bill, and she asked what time she might expect the girl back, saying that it must not be later than nine o'clock.

After taking my dollar! I told her, "I can make no promises, Mrs. Ricci, when my boss gets started asking questions nights and days are nothing. But she'll be back safe and sound as soon as possible."

I went upstairs and got Anna and some of the stuff from the bureau drawer and when we got to the street was relieved to find that the roadster hadn't lost a fender or a spare tire.

I moseyed along uptown taking it easy, not wanting to reach Thirty-fifth Street too soon, since Wolfe was always upstairs with the plants from four to six and it wasn't a good idea to disturb him during those two hours unless you had to. Anna was overwhelmed by the roadster; she kept her feet pulled back against the seat and her hands folded tight in her lap. That tickled me and I felt kindly toward her, so I told her that I might give her a dollar if she told my boss anything that would help him out. It was a minute or two after six when I pulled up in front of the old brownstone less than a block from the Hudson River where Wolfe had lived for twenty years and where I had been with him a third of that.

Anna didn't get home that night by nine o'clock. It was after eleven when Wolfe sent me to the *Times* office for the papers, and it was well past midnight when we finally hit on the spot that Anna recognized. By that time Mrs. Ricci had telephoned three times, and when I got to Sullivan Street with the girl a little before one the landlady was waiting out in front, maybe with a knife in her sock. But she didn't say a word, only glared at me. I had given Anna her dollar, for something had happened.

I had reported to Wolfe up in the front plant-room, the sun-room, leaving Anna down in the office. He sat there in the big chair with a red and tan orchid eight inches wide tickling the back of his neck, looking not interested. He really wasn't interested. He barely glanced at the papers and things I had brought with me from Maffei's room. He admitted that the phone call had a dash of possibility in it, but couldn't see that there was anything to bother about. I tried to persuade him that since the girl was already downstairs he might as well take it up and see what he could get; and I added with malice:

"Anyway, she cost a dollar. I had to give the landlady a dollar."

"That was your dollar, Archie."

"No, sir, it was an expense dollar. It's down in the book."

I went with him to the elevator. If he had had to do his own lifting and lowering I don't think he would ever have gone upstairs, even for the plants.

He began on Anna at once. It was beautiful. Five years earlier I wouldn't have appreciated it. It was beautiful because it was absolutely comprehensive. If there was anything in that girl, any bit of knowledge, any apparently forgotten shred of feeling or reaction, that could show us a direction or give us a hint, it simply could not have kept away from him. He questioned her for five hours. He asked her about Carlo Maffei's voice, his habits, his clothing, his meals, his temper, his table manners, his relations with his

sister, with Mrs. Ricci, with Anna herself, with everyone Anna had ever seen him with. He asked her
about Mrs. Ricci, about all the residents of the
rooming-house for two years, about the neighbors,
and about the tradesmen who delivered things to the
house. All this he did easily and leisurely, careful not
to tire her—quite different from the time I watched
him with Lon Graves; him he wore down and drove
halfway crazy in an afternoon. It seemed to me he got
only one thing out of the girl, and that wasn't much,
only an admission that she had removed something
from Maffei's room that very morning. Wednesday.
Little pieces of paper from his bureau drawer with
mucilage on the back, and printed on the front S.S.
*LUCIA* and S.S. *FIORENZA*. Of course they were
steamship luggage stickers. From the newspaper file I
learned that the *Lucia* had sailed on the 18th of May
and the *Fiorenza* on the 3rd of June. Evidently Maffei
had decided on Italy not once, but twice, and had
given it up both times. Anna had taken them, she said,
because they were pretty colors and she wanted to
paste them on the box she kept her clothes in. During
dinner, which the three of us ate together in the
dining-room, he let Anna alone entirely and talked to
me, mostly about beer, but with the coffee he moved
us back to the office and went at it again. He doubled
back and recovered the ground, he darted around at
random on things so irrelevant and inconsequential
that anyone who had never seem him pull a rabbit out
of that hat before would have been sure he was merely
a nut. By eleven o'clock I was through, yawning and
ready to give up, and I was exasperated that he
showed not the slightest sign of impatience or discouragement.

Then all at once he hit it.

"So Mr. Maffei never gave you any presents?"

"No, sir. Except the box of chalk I told you about. And the newspapers, if you call that a present."

"Yes. You said he always gave you his morning paper. The *Times*."

"Yes, sir. He told me once he took the *Times* for the classified ads. You know, the job ads."

"Did he give you his paper Monday morning?"

"He always gave it to me in the afternoon. Monday afternoon, yes, sir."

"There was nothing peculiar about it that morning, I suppose."

"No, sir."

Apparently Wolfe caught some faint flicker in her eye, some faint movement that I missed. Anyway he insisted.

"Nothing peculiar about it?"

"No, sir. Except—of course, the cut-out."

"The cut-out?"

"A piece cut out. A big piece."

"Did he often cut out pieces?"

"Yes, sir. Mostly the ads. Maybe always the ads. I used the papers to take the dirt up in and I had to watch for the holes."

"But this was a big piece."

"Yes, sir."

"Not an advertisement then. You will pardon me, Miss Fiore, if I do not say *ad*. I prefer not to. Then it wasn't an advertisement he cut out of Monday's paper."

"Oh no, it was on the front page."

"Indeed. Had there ever been a piece cut out on the front page before?"

"No, sir. I'm sure not."

"Never anything but advertisements before?"

"Well, I'm not sure of that. Maybe only ads, I think it was."

Wolfe sat for a minute with his chin on his chest. Then he turned to me. "Archie, run up to Forty-second Street and get twenty copies of Monday's *Times*."

I was glad for something to wake me up. Not that it was anything to get excited about, for I could see that Wolfe was just taking a wink at the only crack that had shown any chance of light; I wasn't expecting anything and I didn't think he was. But it was a fine June night, cool but soft and pleasant, and I filled my lungs with good air snatched from the breeze I made as I rolled crosstown to Broadway and turned north. At Times Square I saw a cop I knew, Marve Doyle who used to pound the cement down on Fourteenth Street, and he let me leave the car against the Broadway curb while I ran across the street to the *Times* office. The theater and movie mob was slopping off the sidewalks into the street, deciding between two dollars at a speak and two nickles at a Nedick's.

When I got back to the office Wolfe was giving the girl a rest. He had had Fritz bring in some beer and she was sipping at a glass like it was hot tea, with a stripe of dried foam across her upper lip. He had finished three bottles, though I couldn't have been gone more than twenty minutes at the outside. As I came in he said:

"I should have told you city edition."

"Sure, that's what I got."

"Good." He turned to the girl. "If you don't mind, Miss Fiore, it would be better if you did not overlook our preparations. Turn her chair around, Archie; there, the little table for her beer. Now the papers. No, don't rip it off; better intact I think; that's the way

she first saw it. Remove the second sections, they'll be
a find for Miss Fiore, think of all the dirt they'll hold.
Here."

I spread open a first section on the desk before him
and he pulled himself up in his chair to hunch over it.
It was like seeing a hippopotamus in the zoo get up for
a feed. I took out all the second sections and stacked
them on a chair and then took a front page for myself
and went over it. At the first glance it certainly looked
hopeless; miners were striking in Pennsylvania, the
NRA was saving the country under three different
headings, two boys had crossed the Atlantic in a
thirty-foot boat, a university president had had heart
failure on a golf course, a gangster had been tear-
gassed out of a Brooklyn flat, a negro had been
lynched in Alabama, and someone had found an old
painting somewhere in Europe. I glanced at Wolfe; he
was drinking the whole page. The only thing that
looked to me worth trying at all was the painting
which had been found in Switzerland and was supposed to have been stolen from Italy. But when Wolfe
finally reached for the scissors out of the drawer it
wasn't that one he clipped, it was the gangster piece.
Then he laid the paper aside and called for another
one. I handed it to him, and this time I grinned as I
saw him go after the article about the painting; I came
in second anyhow. When he called for a third paper I
was curious, and as he ran the scissors around the
edges of the story about the university president I
stared at him. He saw me. He said without looking up,
"Pray for this side, Archie. If it's this one we shall
have an *Angræcum sesquipedale* for Christmas." I
could spell that because I kept his accounts for him on
orchids as on everything else, but I could no more
have pronounced it than I could have imagined any

connection between the university president and
Carlo Maffei.

Wolfe said, "Show her one."

The last one he had clipped was on top, but I
reached under it and got the next one; the painting
piece had been in a large box in the lower right
quarter of the page. As I held it out, spread open, to
Anna, Wolfe said, "Look at that, Miss Fiore. Is that
the way the piece was cut out Monday morning?"

She gave it only a glance. "No, sir. It was a big
piece out of the top, here, let me show you—"

I snatched it out of the way before she could get
hold of it, tossed it back to the table, and picked up
another. I spread it in front of her. This time she took
two glances, then she said, "Yes, sir."

"You mean that's it?"

"It was cut out like that, yes, sir."

For a moment Wolfe was silent, then I heard him
breathe and he said, "Turn her around, Archie." I took
the arm of her chair and whirled it around with her in
it. Wolfe looked at her and said, "How sure are you,
Miss Fiore, that the paper was cut out like that?"

"I know it was, sir. I'm sure."

"Did you see the piece he had cut out? In his room,
in the wastebasket perhaps, or in his hand?"

"No, I never saw it. It couldn't have been in the
wastebasket because there isn't any."

"Good. If only all reasons were as good as that. You
may go home now, Miss Fiore. You have been a good
girl, good and patient and forbearing, and unlike most
of the persons I avoid meeting by staying inside my
house, you are willing to confine your tongue to its
proper functions. But will you answer just one more
question? I ask it as a favor."

The girl was completely tired out, but there was

enough life left in her to let the bewilderment show in
her eyes. She stared at him. Wolfe said, "Just one
more question. Have you ever at any time seen a golf
club in Carlo Maffei's room?"

If he was looking for a climax he got it, because for
the first time in all these hours the girl shut up on him.
It was funny how plain you could see it happen. For an
instant she just looked, then when the question had
clicked what little color she had left her till she was
dead white and her mouth dropped half open; she
looked absolutely like an idiot, and she began to
tremble all over.

Wolfe bored at her, quiet. "When did you see it?"

All of a sudden she shut her lips tight, and her
hands in her lap closed into fists. "No, sir." It was just
a mumble. "No, sir, I never did."

Wolfe looked at her a second, then he said, "All
right. It's quite all right, Miss Fiore." He turned to
me. "Take her home."

She didn't try to stand up till I went over and
touched her shoulder. Then she put her hands on the
arms of the chair and got to her feet. He had certainly
got her somehow, but she didn't seem exactly scared,
just caved in. I got her jacket from the back of a chair
and helped her put it on. As she started for the door I
turned to say something to Wolfe, and couldn't believe
my eyes. He was raising himself out of his chair to
stand up! Actually. I had at one time seen him refuse
to take that trouble for the departure from that room
of a woman worth twenty million American dollars
who had married an English duke. But anyway I said
what I had started to say:

"I told her I'd give her a dollar."

"Then you'll have to do it, I'm afraid." He raised his

voice a little to reach the door: "Good night, Miss Fiore."

She didn't reply. I followed her to the hall and took her out to the roadster. When we got to Sullivan Street Mrs. Ricci was waiting in front with a glare in her eye that made me decide not to stop for any amenities.

# Chapter 3

By the time I had garaged the car and walked the two blocks back to Thirty-fifth Street the office was dark and when I went up a flight I saw a ribbon of light under the door of Wolfe's bedroom. I often wondered how he ever got his clothes off, but I know Fritz never helped him. Fritz slept up above, across the hall from the plant-rooms; my room was on the second floor, the same floor as Wolfe's, a fair-sized room in front with its own bath and a pair of windows. I had lived there seven years, and it certainly was home; and seemed likely to remain so for another seven, or even twenty-seven, for the only girl I had ever been really soft on had found another bargain she liked better. That was how I happened to meet Wolfe—but that story isn't for me to tell, at least not yet. There are one or two little points about it that will need clearing up some day. But that room was certainly home. The bed was big and good, there was a desk with plenty of drawer-space and three chairs all roomy and comfortable, and a real carpet all over, no damn little rugs to slide you around like a piece of butter on a hotcake. The pictures on the walls were my own, and I think they were a good selection; one of Mount Vernon, the home of George Washington, a colored one of a lion's head, another colored one of woods with grass and flowers, and a big framed photograph of my mother and father, who both died when I was just a kid. Also there was a colored one called *September Morn*, of a young woman apparently with no clothes on and her hair hanging down in front, but that was in the bathroom. There was nothing unusual about the room, it was just a good room to live in, except the big gong on the wall under the bed, and that was out of sight. It was connected up so that when Wolfe turned on a switch in his room, which he did every night, the gong would sound if anyone stepped in the hall within five feet of his door or if any of his windows was disturbed, and also it was connected with all entrances to the plant-rooms. Wolfe told me once, not as if it mattered much, that he really had no cowardice in him, he only had an intense distaste for being touched by anyone or for being compelled without warning to make any quick movements; and when I considered the quantity he had to move I was willing to believe him. For some reason questions like that of cowardice have never interested me as regards Wolfe, though ordinarily if I have cause to suspect that a man is yellow as far as I'm concerned he can eat at another table.

I took one of the newspapers from the office upstairs with me, and after I had undressed and got into pajamas and slippers, I made myself comfortable in a chair with cigarettes and ashtray handy and read that university president article three times. It was headed like this:

## PETER OLIVER BARSTOW
## DEAD FROM STROKE

### PRESIDENT OF HOLLAND
### SUCCUMBS ON LINKS

### Friends Reach His Side
### With His Last Breath

It was quite a piece, with a full column on the front page, another column and a half on the inside, and in another article a long obituary with comments from a lot of prominent people. The story itself didn't amount to much and there was really nothing to it except another man gone. I read the paper every day and this one was only two days old, but I couldn't remember noticing this. Barstow, 58-year-old president of Holland University, had been playing golf Sunday afternoon on the links of the Green Meadow Club near Pleasantville, thirty miles north of New York, a foursome, with his son Lawrence and two friends named E. D. Kimball and Manuel Kimball. On the fairway of the fourth hole he had suddenly pitched forward and landed on his face, flopped around on the ground a few seconds, and then lay still. His caddy had jumped to him and grabbed his arm, but by the time the others got to him he was dead. Among the crowd that collected from the clubhouse and other players was a doctor who was an old friend of Barstow's, and he and the son had taken the body in Barstow's own car to the Barstow home six miles away. The doctor had pronounced it heart disease.

The rest was trimmings, all about Barstow's career and achievements and a picture of him and this and that, and how his wife had collapsed when they brought him home and his son and daughter bore up

well. After the third reading I just yawned and threw
up the sponge. The only connection that I could see
between Barstow's death and Carlo Maffei was the
fact that Wolfe had asked Anna Fiore if she had seen
a golf club, so I tossed the paper away and got up
saying to myself aloud, "Mr. Goodwin, I guess you
haven't got this case ready for the closed business
file." Then I took a drink of water and went to bed.

It was nearly ten o'clock when I got downstairs the
next morning, for I need eight hours' sleep when I can
get it, and of course Wolfe wouldn't be down till
eleven. He arose always at eight, no matter what time
he went to bed, had breakfast in his room with a
couple of newspapers, and spent the two hours from
nine to eleven in the plant-rooms. Sometimes I could
hear old Horstmann, who tended the plants, yelling at
him, while I was dressing or taking a bath. Wolfe
seemed to have the same effect on Horstmann that an
umpire had on John J. McGraw. Not that the old man
really disliked Wolfe, I'm sure he didn't; I wouldn't
wonder if he was worried for fear Wolfe's poundage,
having at least reached the limit of equilibrium, would
topple over and make hash of the orchids. Horstmann
didn't think any more of those plants than I do of my
right eye. He slept in a little room partitioned off of a
corner, and I wouldn't have been surprised if he had
walked the floor with them at night.

After I got through in the kitchen with a dish of
kidneys and waffles and a couple of glasses of milk—
for I absolutely refused to let Fritz dress up the dining-
table for my breakfast, which I always had alone—I
went out for ten minutes' worth of air, hoofing it down
around the piers and back again, and then settled down
at my corner desk in the office with the books, after
dusting around a little and opening the safe and filling

Wolfe's fountain pen. His mail I left on his desk unopened, that was the custom; there wasn't any for me. I
made out two or three checks and balanced my expense
book, not much to that, things had been so quiet, and
then began going over the plant records to be sure
Horstmann had his reports up to date. I was in the
middle of that when I heard the buzzer in the kitchen,
and a minute later Fritz came to the door and said a man
named O'Grady wanted to see Mr. Wolfe. I took the card
and looked at it and saw it was a new one on me; I knew
a lot of the dicks on the Homicide Squad, but I had never
seen this O'Grady. I told Fritz to usher him in.

O'Grady was young, and very athletic judging
from his make-up and the way he walked. He had a
bad eye, conscientious and truculent; from the way he
looked at me you might have thought I had the
Lindbergh baby in my pocket.

He said, "Mr. Nero Wolfe?"

I waved at a chair. "Have a seat." I glanced at my
wrist. "Mr. Wolfe will be down in nineteen minutes."

He scowled. "This is important. Couldn't you call
him? I sent in my card, I'm from the Homicide Squad."

"Sure, I know, that's all right. Just have a seat. If
I called him he'd throw something at me."

He took the chair and I went back to the plant
records. Once or twice during the wait I thought I
might try pumping him just for the fun of it, but a
glance at his face was enough; he was too young and
trustworthy to bother with. For nineteen minutes he
sat as if he was in church, not saying a word.

He got up from the chair as Wolfe entered the
office. Wolfe, as he made steady progress from the
door to the desk, bade me good morning, asked me to
open another window, and shot a glance at the visitor.
Seated at the desk he saw the card I had laid there,

then he took a look at the mail, flipping the corners of
the envelopes with his quick fingers the way a bank
teller does the checks when he is going over a deposit.
He shoved the mail aside and turned to the dick.

"Mr. O'Grady?"

O'Grady stepped forward. "Mr. Nero Wolfe?"

Wolfe nodded.

"Well, Mr. Wolfe, I want the papers and other
articles you took yesterday from Carlo Maffei's room."

"No!" Wolfe lifted his head to see him better.
"Really? That's interesting, Mr. O'Grady. Have a
chair. Pull him up a chair, Archie."

"No, thanks, I've got a job on. I'll just take those
papers and—things."

"What things?"

"The things you took."

"Enumerate them."

The dick stuck his chin out. "Don't try to get funny.
Come on, I'm in a hurry."

Wolfe wiggled a finger at him. "Easy, Mr. O'Grady."
Wolfe's voice was clear and low, with a tone he didn't use
very often; he had used it on me only once, the first time
I had ever seen him, and I had never forgotten how it
sounded; it had made me feel that if he had wanted to he
could have cut my head off without lifting a hand. He
went on with it, "Easy now. Sit down. I mean it, really,
sit down."

I had a chair shoved behind the dick's knees, and
he came down onto it slowly.

"What you are getting is a free but valuable
lesson," Wolfe said. "You are young and can use it.
Since I entered this room you have made nothing but
mistakes. You were without courtesy, which was
offensive. You made a statement contrary to fact,
which was stupid. You confused conjecture with

knowledge, which was disingenuous. Would you like me to explain what you should have done? My motives are entirely friendly."

O'Grady was blinking. "I don't charge you with motives—"

"Good. Of course you had no way of knowing how ill-advised it was to imply that I made a journey to Carlo Maffei's room; unfamiliar with my habits, you were not aware that I would not undertake that enterprise though a *Cattleya Dowiana aurea* were to be the reward. Certainly not for some papers and—as you say—things. Archie Goodwin," a finger circled in my direction, "doesn't mind that sort of thing, so he went. What you should have done was this. First, answered me when I wished you good morning. Second, made your request courteous, complete, and correct as to fact. Third—though this was less essential—you might as a matter of professional civility have briefly informed me that the body of the murdered Carlo Maffei has been found and identified and that the assistance of these papers is required in the attempt to discover the assassin. Don't you agree with me that that would have been better, Mr. O'Grady?"

The dick stared at him. "How the hell—" he started, and stopped, and then went on, "So it's already in the papers. I didn't see it, and his name couldn't have been for it's only two hours since I learned it myself. You're quite a guesser, Mr. Wolfe."

"Thank you. Neither did I see it in the papers. But since Maria Maffei's report of her brother's disappearance did not arouse the police beyond a generous effort at conjecture, it seemed to me probable that nothing less than murder would stir them to the frenzy of discovering that Archie had visited his room and removed papers. So. Would you mind telling me where the body was found?"

O'Grady stood up. "You can read it tonight. You're a lulu, Mr. Wolfe. Now those papers."

"Of course." Wolfe didn't move. "But I offer a point for your consideration. All I ask of you is three minutes of your time and information which will be available from public sources within a few hours. Whereas—who knows?—today, or tomorrow, or next year, in connection with this case or another, I might happen upon some curious little fact which conveyed to you would mean promotion, glory, a raise in pay; and, I repeat, you make a mistake if you ignore the demands of professional civility. Was the body by any chance found in Westchester County?"

"What the hell," O'Grady said. "If I hadn't already looked you up, and if it wasn't so plain you'd need a boxcar to get around in, I'd guess you did it yourself. All right. Yes, Westchester County. In a thicket a hundred feet from a dirt road three miles out of Scarsdale, yesterday at eight P.M. by two boys hunting birds' nests."

"Shot perhaps?"

"Stabbed. The doctor says that the knife must have been left in him for a while, an hour or more, but it wasn't there and wasn't found. His pockets were empty. The label on his clothes showed a Grand Street store, and that and his laundry mark were turned over to me at seven o'clock this morning. By nine I had his name, and since then I've searched his room and seen the landlady and the girl."

"Excellent," Wolfe said. "Really exceptional."

The dick frowned. "That girl," he said. "Either she knows something, or the inside of her head is so unfurnished that she can't remember what she ate for breakfast. You had her up here. What did you think when she couldn't remember a thing about the phone call that the landlady said she heard every word of?"

I shot a glance at Wolfe, but he didn't blink an eyelash. He just said, "Miss Anna Fiore is not perfectly equipped, Mr. O'Grady. You found her memory faulty then?"

"Faulty? She had forgot Maffei's first name!"

"Yes. A pity." Wolfe pushed his chair back by putting his hands on the edge of the desk and shoving; I saw he meant to get up. "And now those papers. The only other articles are an empty tobacco can and four snapshots. I must ask a favor of you. Will you let Mr. Goodwin escort you from the room? A personal idiosyncrasy; I have a strong disinclination for opening my safe in the presence of any other person. No offense of course. It would be the same, even perhaps a little accentuated, if you were my banker."

I had been with Wolfe so long that I could usually almost keep up with him, but that time I barely caught myself. I had my mouth open to say that the stuff was in a drawer of his desk, where I had put it the evening before in his presence, and his look was all that stopped me. The dick hesitated, and Wolfe assured him, "Come, Mr. O'Grady. Or go rather. There is no point in surmising that I am creating an opportunity to withhold something, because even if I were there would be nothing you could do to prevent it. Suspicions of that sort between professional men are futile."

I led the dick into the front room, closing the door behind us. I supposed Wolfe would monkey with the safe door so we could hear the noise, but just in case he didn't take the trouble I made some sort of conversation so O'Grady's ears wouldn't be disappointed. Pretty soon we were called back in, and Wolfe was

standing on the near side of the desk with the tobacco
can and the envelope I had filed the papers and
snapshots in. He held them out to the dick.

"Good luck, Mr. O'Grady. I give you this assurance, and you may take my word for what they are
worth: if at any time we should discover anything that
we believe would be of significance or help to you, we
shall communicate with you at once."

"Much obliged. Maybe you mean that."

"Yes, I do. Just as I say it."

The dick went. When I heard the outer door close
I went to the front room and through a window saw
him walking away. Then I returned to the office and
approached Wolfe's desk, where he was seated again,
and grinned at him and said:

"You're a damn scoundrel."

The folds of his cheeks pulled away a little from the
corners of his mouth; when he did that he thought he
was smiling. I said, "What did you keep?"

Out of his vest pocket he pulled a piece of paper
about two inches long and half an inch wide and
handed it to me. It was one of the clippings from
Maffei's top bureau drawer, and it was hard to believe
that Wolfe could have known of its existence, for he
had barely glanced through that stuff the evening
before. But he had taken the trouble to get O'Grady
out of the room in order to keep it.

*METAL-WORKER, must be expert both de-
sign and mechanism, who intends returning to
Europe for permanent residence, can get lucrative commission. Times L467 Downtown.*

I ran through it twice, but saw no more in it than
when I had first read it the afternoon before in Maffei's

room. "Well," I said, "if you're trying to clinch it that he meant to go for a sail I can run down to Sullivan Street and pry those luggage stickers off of Anna's wardrobe. And anyway, granting even that it means something, when did you ever see it before? Don't tell me you can read things without looking at them. I'll swear you didn't—" I stopped. Sure, of course he had. I grinned at him. "You went through that stuff while I was taking Anna home last night."

He waited till he was back around the desk and in his chair again before he murmured sarcastically, "Bravo, Archie."

"All right," I said. I sat down across from him. "Do I get to ask questions? There's three things I want to know. Or am I supposed to go up front and do my homework?" I was a little sore, of course; I always was when I knew that he had tied up a nice neat bundle right in front of me without my even being able to see what was going in it.

"No homework," he said. "You are about to go for the car and drive with reasonable speed to White Plains. If the questions are brief—"

"They're brief enough, but if I've got work to do they can wait. Since it's White Plains, I suppose I'm to take a look at the hole in Carlo Maffei and any other details that seem to me unimportant."

"No. Confound it, Archie, stop supposing aloud in my presence; if it is inevitable that in the end you are to be classed with—for instance—Mr. O'Grady, let us at least postpone it as long as possible."

"O'Grady did a good job this morning, two hours from a coat label and a laundry mark to that phone call."

Wolfe shook his head. "Cerebrally an oaf. But your questions?"

"They can wait. What is it at White Plains if it's not Maffei?"

Wolfe gave me his substitute for a smile, an unusually prolonged one for him. Finally he said, "A chance to make some money. Does the name Fletcher M. Anderson mean anything to you without referring to your files?"

"I hope so." I snorted. "No thanks for a bravo either. Nineteen-twenty-eight. Assistant District Attorney on the Goldsmith case. A year later moved to the country and is now District Attorney for Westchester County. He would admit that he owes you something only if the door were closed and he whispered in your ear. Married money."

Wolfe nodded. "Correct. The bravo is yours, Archie, and I shall manage without the thanks. At White Plains you will see Mr. Anderson and deliver a provocative and possibly lucrative message. At least that is contemplated; I am awaiting information from a caller who is expected at any moment." He reached across his rotundity to remove the large platinum watch from his vest pocket and glance at it. "I note that a dealer in sporting goods is not more punctual than a skeptic would expect. I telephoned at nine; the delivery would be made at eleven without fail; it is now eleven-forty. It really would be well at this point to eliminate all avoidable delay. It would have been better to send you— Ah!"

It was the buzzer. Fritz passed the door down the hall; there was the sound of the front door opening and another voice and Fritz's in question and answer. Then heavy footsteps drowning out Fritz's, and there appeared on the threshold a young man who looked like a football player bearing on his shoulder an enormous bundle about three feet long and as big around as Wolfe himself. Breathing, he said, "From Corliss Holmes."

At Wolfe's nod I went to help. We got the bundle onto the floor and the young man knelt and began untying the cord, but he fumbled so long that I got impatient and reached in my pocket for my knife. Wolfe's murmur sounded from his chair, "No, Archie, few knots deserve that," and I put my knife back. Finally he got it loose and the cord pulled off, and I helped him unroll the paper and burlap, and then stood up and stared. I looked at Wolfe and back again at the pile on the floor. It was nothing but golf clubs, there must have been a hundred of them, enough I thought to kill a million snakes, for it had never seemed to me that they were much good for anything else.

I said to Wolfe, "The exercise will do you good."

Still in his chair, Wolfe told us to put them on the desk, and the young man and I each grabbed an armload. I began spreading them in an even row on the desk; there were long and short, heavy and light, iron, wood, steel, chromium, anything you might think of. Wolfe was looking at them, each one as I put it down, and after about a dozen he said, "Not these with iron ends. Remove them. Only those with wooden ends." To the young man, "You do not call this the end?"

The young man looked amazed and superior. "That's the head."

"Accept my apologies—your name?"

"My name? Townsend."

"Accept my apologies, Mr. Townsend. I once saw golf clubs through a shop window while my car was having a flat tire, but the ends were not labeled. And these are in fact all varieties of a single species?"

"Huh? They're all different."

"Indeed. Indeed, indeed. Plain wooden faces, inset faces, bone, composition, ivory—since this is the head I presume that is the face?"

"Sure, that's the face."

"Of course. And the purpose of the inset? Since everything in life must have a purpose except the culture of Orchidaceæ."

"Purpose?"

"Exactly. Purpose."

"Well—" The young man hesitated. "Of course it's for the impact. That means hitting the ball, it's the inset that hits the ball, and that's the impact."

"I see. Go no further. That will do nicely. And the handles, some wood, really fine and sensitive, and steel— I presume the steel handles are hollow."

"Hollow steel shaft, yes, sir. It's a matter of taste. That one's a driver. This is a brassie. See the brass on the bottom? Brassie."

"Faultless sequitur," Wolfe murmured. "That, I think, will be all, the lesson is complete. You know, Mr. Townsend, it is our good fortune that the exigencies of birth and training furnish all of us with opportunities for snobbery. My ignorance of this special nomenclature provided yours; your innocence of the elementary mental processes provides mine. As to the object of your visit, you can sell me nothing; these things will forever remain completely useless to me. You can reassemble your bundle and take it with you, but let us assume that I should purchase three of these clubs and that the profit on each should be one dollar. Three dollars? If I give you that amount will it be satisfactory?"

The young man had, if not his own dignity, at least

that of Corliss Holmes. "There is no obligation to purchase, sir."

"No, but I haven't finished. I have to ask a favor of you. Will you take one of these clubs—here, this one—and stand there, beyond that chair, and whirl it about you in the orthodox manner?"

"Whirl it?"

"Yes; club, strike, hit, whatever you call it. Pretend that you are impacting a ball."

Beyond snobbery, the young man was now having difficulty to conceal his contempt. He took the driver from Wolfe, backed away from the desk, shoved a chair aside, glanced around, behind, and up, then brought the driver up over his shoulder and down and through with a terrific swish.

Wolfe shuddered. "Ungovernable fury," he murmured. "Again, more slowly?"

The young man complied.

"If possible, Mr. Townsend, more slowly yet?"

This time he made it slow motion, a cartoon, derisive, but Wolfe watched it keenly and soberly. Then he said:

"Excellent. A thousand thanks, Mr. Townsend. Archie, since we have no account at Corliss Holmes, will you please give Mr. Townsend three dollars? A little speed now, if you don't mind. The trip I mentioned is imminent and even urgent."

After the quiet weeks that had passed it made my heart jump to hear Wolfe ask for speed. The young man and I had the package together again in no time; I went to let him out the front door, and then back to the office. Wolfe was sitting there with his lips fixed to whistle, but with no sound that could be heard six feet away; you only knew the air was going in and out by his chest rising and falling. Sometimes, when close enough to him, I had tried to hear if he really thought he was doing a tune, but without success. He stopped as I came in and said:

"This will only take a minute, Archie. Sit down. You won't need your notebook."

# Chapter 4

When I'm driving I don't see much of anything except the road, for I have the type of mind that gets on a job and stays there until it's time for another one. That day I hit a good clip, too; on account of the traffic it took a long while to get to Woodlawn, but from there to White Plains my clock covered just twenty-one minutes. But in spite of my type of mind and the hurry I was in I enjoyed the Parkway out of the corner of my eye. Lots of the bushes were covered with flowers, the new crop of leaves on the trees was waving easy in the breeze like a slow dance, and the grass was thick and green. I thought to myself that they couldn't make a carpet if it cost ten thousand dollars that would be as nice to walk on as that grass.

The hurry didn't help any. When I got to the courthouse there was nothing but bad luck. Anderson was away and wouldn't be back until Monday, four days. In the Adirondacks, they said, but wouldn't give me his address; it wouldn't have been a bit unpleasant to head the roadster for Lake Placid and step on it. His chief assistant, whose name, Derwin, I had never heard before, was still out to lunch and wouldn't be back for half an hour. No one around seemed to care about being helpful.

I went down the street to a phone and got Wolfe in New York. He said to wait for Derwin and try it on him; and I didn't mind having time for a couple of sandwiches and a glass of milk before he was expected back. When I returned Derwin was in his office, but I had to wait for him twenty minutes, I suppose for him to finish picking his teeth. The place was certainly dead.

When I consider the different kinds I've seen it seems silly to say it, but somehow to me all lawyers look alike. It's a sort of mixture of a scared look and a satisfied look, as if they were crossing a traffic-filled street where they expect to get run over any minute but they know exactly the kind of paper to hand the driver if they get killed and they've got one right in their pocket. This Derwin looked like that; otherwise he seemed very respectable, well-dressed and well-fed, somewhere around forty, under rather than over, with his dark hair brushed back slick and his face happy and pleased-looking. I laid my panama on a corner of his desk and took a chair before I said:

"I'm sorry to have missed Mr. Anderson. I don't know if you'll be interested in my message, but I'm pretty sure he would."

Derwin was leaning back in his chair with a politician's smile. "If it is connected with the duties of my office, I certainly will, Mr. Goodwin."

"It's connected all right. But I'm at a disadvantage since you don't know my employer, Nero Wolfe. Mr. Anderson knows him."

"Nero Wolfe?" Derwin wrinkled his forehead. "I've heard of him. The private detective, you mean of course. This is only White Plains, you see, the provinces begin a little farther north."

"Yes, sir. Not that I would call Nero Wolfe a private detective. As a description—well, for one thing it's a little too active. But that's the man I work for."

"You have a message from him?"

"Yes, sir. As I say, the message was for Mr. Anderson, but I telephoned him half an hour ago and he said to give it to you. It may not work out the same, for I happen to know that Mr. Anderson is a rich man, and I don't know that much about you. Maybe you're like me, maybe your salary is the only rope that holds Saturday and Sunday together for you."

Derwin laughed, just a trick laugh, for in a second his face was solemn and businesslike. "Maybe I am. But although I am not particularly rushed this afternoon, I am still waiting for the message."

"Yes, sir. It's like this. Last Sunday afternoon, four days ago, Peter Oliver Barstow, president of Holland University, died suddenly while playing golf on the links of the Green Meadow Club over toward Pleasantville. You know about that?"

"Of course. It was a loss to the community, to the whole country in fact. Of course."

I nodded. "His funeral was Tuesday and he was buried at Agawalk Cemetery. Mr. Nero Wolfe wants to bet you—he would rather bet Mr. Anderson but he says you'll do—that if you'll have the body lifted and an autopsy made you'll find proof of poison. He will bet ten thousand dollars and will deposit a certified check for that amount with any responsible person you name."

I just grinned as Derwin stared at me. He stared a long time, then he said, "Mr. Nero Wolfe is crazy."

"Oh no," I said. "Whatever you bet on, don't bet on *that*. I haven't finished yet with Nero Wolfe's bet. The rest of it is that somewhere in Barstow's belly, probably just below the stomach, somewhere between one and three inches in from the skin, will be found a short, sharp, thin needle, probably of steel but possibly of very hard wood. It will be pointing upward, approximately at an angle of forty-five degrees if not deflected by a bone."

Derwin kept staring at me. When I stopped he tried his trick laugh again, but it didn't work so well. "This is about as big a bunch of nonsense as I've ever heard," he said. "I suppose there is a point to it somewhere, if you're not crazy too."

"There's a point all right." I reached in my pocket for the check Wolfe had given me. "There are very few people in the world who would risk ten thousand on a bunch of nonsense, and you can take it from me that Nero Wolfe isn't one of them. Peter Oliver Barstow was murdered, and he's got that needle in him. I say it, Nero Wolfe says it, and this ten grand says it. That's a lot of testimony, Mr. Derwin."

The lawyer was beginning to look not nearly as happy and pleased as he had when I went in. He got up from his chair and then sat down again. I waited. He said, "It's preposterous. Absolutely preposterous."

"Wolfe isn't betting on that." I grinned. "He's just betting that it's true."

"But it can't be. It's merely preposterous and—and monstrous. Whatever the stunt may be you're trying to pull, you've hit the wrong man; I happen to be acquainted with the Barstow family and therefore know the facts. I won't recite them to you; such idiotic nonsense. Do you know who signed the death certificate? I don't suppose—"

"Sure," I put in, "Dr. Nathaniel Bradford. Coronary thrombosis. But if all the doctors in the world were as good as him, and if they all said coronary thrombosis, Nero Wolfe's money is still right here ready to talk."

I had seen the change come over Derwin's face; he had got over his shock and was now ready to be clever. His voice was sharp. "See here, what's your game?"

"No game at all. None. Except to win ten grand."

"Let me see that check."

I handed it to him. He looked it over thoroughly and then pulled his desk telephone over, took off the receiver and in a moment spoke to someone: "Miss Ritter, please get me the Thirty-fourth Street branch of the Metropolitan Trust Company." He sat and looked at the check and I folded my arms and got patient. When the bell rang he took the phone again and began asking questions, plenty of them; he certainly made sure there could be no mistake. When he hung up I said pleasantly:

"Anyway we're getting started, now that you know it's real dollars."

He paid no attention, but just sat frowning at the check. Finally he said in a shrewd voice, "Do you mean that you are actually empowered to wager this money on that proposition as you stated it?"

"Yes, sir. That check is made out to me, and certified. I can endorse it just like that. If you want to phone Wolfe, the number is Bryant nine, two-eight-two-eight. In order to avoid any misunderstanding, I would suggest that you have your stenographer type a memorandum of the details for us to sign. I should tell you that Wolfe undertakes to furnish no reasons or suggestions or clues and will not discuss the matter. It's a bet, that's all."

"Bet, hell. You're not expecting any bet. Who do you expect to bet with you, Westchester County?"

I grinned. "We hoped for Mr. Anderson, but lacking him we're not particular. Anyone with ten thousand dollars; Wolfe wouldn't care; a chief of police or a newspaper editor or maybe some prominent Democrat with a strong sense of civic duty."

"Indeed!"

"Yes, sir, indeed. My instructions are to do my best to get the money covered before dark."

Derwin got up, kicking his chair back. "Hah! Bet? Bluff."

"You think so, sir? Try me. Try covering it."

Evidently he had decided something, for with my words he was crossing the room. At the door he turned to say, "Will you wait here for me ten minutes? I imagine you will, since I have your check in my pocket."

It wasn't endorsed. He was gone before I could toss a nod at him. I settled down to wait. How was it going, I wondered. Had I passed up any advantages? Would it have been better to postpone my last threat for more stubbornness if he had it in him? How could I force him to act quick? And after all, did this third-rater have the authority or the guts to undertake a thing like this with his boss gone? What Wolfe wanted was quick action; of course I knew he no more expected a bet than I expected him to give me the ten grand for my birthday; he was after an autopsy and that needle. I could see now how he had guessed the needle, but how he had ever connected it with Carlo Maffei in the first place—I stopped myself to switch back to the immediate job. If this Derwin laid down and played dead on me, where would I go next? Between four and six I would have to use my own judgment; I wouldn't dare to interrupt Wolfe with a phone call while he was upstairs with the damn plants. It was now two-fifty. Derwin had been gone ten minutes. I began to feel silly. What if he left me sitting there holding my fingers all afternoon, and him with the check? If I let a third-rate brief-shark do that to me I'd never be able to look Wolfe in his big fat face again. I should never have let him out of my sight, certainly not without getting the check back. I jumped out of my chair and crossed the room, but at the door I calmed down and took it easy; softly I turned the knob and pulled and stuck my head out. There was a dinky hall leading to the outer office, and I could hear the girl on the telephone.

"No, operator, person-to-person. No one but Mr. Anderson will do."

I waited till she had hung up, then I went on out and over to her desk. "Would it be much bother to tell me where Mr. Derwin has gone to?"

She seemed interested in me; she took a good look. But she answered straight enough. "He's in Mr. Anderson's room telephoning."

"You wouldn't lie to me just for practice?"

"I don't need any practice, thanks."

"All right. If you don't mind, I'll try one of these chairs. It was awful in there all alone."

I sat down within three feet of the entrance door, and I had no sooner got disposed than the door opened and a man came in, a husky, busy-looking man in a blue suit and black shoes, with a stiff straw hat. From where I sat, as he went toward the girl with his back to me, it was easy to see that he had a gun on his hip. The girl said, "Howdedo, Mr. Cook, Mr. Derwin's in Mr. Anderson's room." When the man had gone on through another door I said to the girl, "Ben Cook maybe?" She nodded without looking at me, and I grinned, and sat and waited.

It was all of fifteen minutes more before the door of Anderson's room opened again and Derwin appeared and called to me, "Come in here, Goodwin."

I went. When I got inside and saw that they had actually staged me it was too funny not to laugh. Ben Cook was in a chair that had been drawn alongside the one by the desk—that one of course for Derwin—and one had been placed just right for me, quite close and facing them and the light.

"Amused, huh," the husky man grunted. Derwin waited till he was back in his chair to inform me. "This is the chief of police."

I was pretending to blink at the light. "Don't tell me," I said. "Do you think Ben Cook's reputation stops at Bronx Park?"

Derwin went stern on me. Lord, it was funny. He even went so far as to shake a finger at me. "Goodwin, I've been pretty busy for half an hour, and now I'm ready to tell you what comes next. You'll tell us what you know, if anything, while we're waiting for Wolfe. What reason have you—"

I hated to interrupt the show, but I couldn't help it. It was involuntary. "Waiting for Wolfe? Here?"

"Certainly, here. If he knows what's good for him, and I think I made that plain on the telephone."

I didn't laugh. I just said, "Listen, Mr. Derwin. This is one of your bad days. You never had a chance at so many rotten bets in your life. Nero Wolfe is about as apt to come here as I am to tell you who killed Barstow."

"Yeah?" It was Ben Cook. "You'll tell us plenty. Plenty."

"Maybe. But I won't tell you who killed Barstow,

because I don't know. Now if you want to ask about roads, for instance—"

"Cut it out." Derwin got sterner. "Goodwin, you have made a most startling accusation in a most sensational manner. I won't pretend that I have a lot of questions ready for you, because I obviously have nothing to base them on. I have just one question, and I want a prompt and complete answer. For what reason and for what purpose did your employer send you here today?"

I sighed and looked solemn. "I've told you, Mr. Derwin, to get a bet down."

"Come on, act as if you had some sense. You can't get away with that, you know damn well you can't. Come on. Let's hear it."

Ben Cook said, "Don't try to be bright. You'd be surprised how we treat bright boys up here some-times."

I could have kept it going all night, I suppose, if I had wanted to, but time was passing and they gave me a pain. I said, "Listen a minute, gentlemen. Of course you're peeved and that's too bad, but I can't help it. Let's say I tell you to go to hell and get up and walk out, what are you going to do—? Yes, Chief, I know it's only a short distance to the station, but I'm not going that way. Honest, you're acting like a pair of dumb flatfeet. I'm surprised at you, Mr. Derwin. Nero Wolfe offers to let you in right at the beginning of a big thing, and the first thing you do is spill it to Ben Cook and the next is to drive me to take it away from both of you and toss it to the wolves. You can't touch me, don't be silly. Nero Wolfe would love a suit for false arrest, and I never go to police stations except to visit friends unless you can show me a warrant, and think how funny it would be after the reporters got my story

and then the proof followed of Barstow's murder. As a
matter of fact, I'm beginning to get a little bit sore and
I've got half a mind to demand that check back and
walk out on you. Get this: I'll tell you exactly nothing.
You understand that maybe? Now you can give me
that check or talk sense yourself."

Derwin sat with his arms folded and looked at me
without making any effort to open his mouth. Ben
Cook said, "So you've come out to the country to show
the hayseeds how it's done. Sonny, I'm plenty big
enough to take you to the station with nothing at all
but the inclination. That's all I need."

"You can afford to be breezy," I told him. "Derwin
has handed you a firecracker that he might have to set
off himself, and you know it." I turned to Derwin.
"Who did you telephone to in New York? Headquarters?"

"No. The District Attorney."

"Did you get him?"

Derwin unfolded his arms, pulled himself back in
his chair and looked at me helplessly. "I got Morley."

I nodded. "Dick Morley. What did he tell you?"

He told me that if Nero Wolfe was offering to bet
ten thousand dollars on anything whatever he would
appreciate it if I'd take him on for another thousand,
only he would give me ten to one."

I was too sore to grin. I said, "And still you invite
me in here to tea instead of getting a spade and
beating it to Agawalk Cemetery. I repeat that I'll tell
you nothing and Wolfe will tell you nothing, but if ever
you had a sure thing to go on it's right now. The next
thing to do is to give me back that check, and then
what?"

Derwin let out a sigh and cleared his throat, but he
had to clear it again. "Goodwin," he said, "I'll be frank
with you. I'm out of my depth. That's not for publica-

tion, Ben, but it's a fact anyhow. I'm clear out of my depth. Good Lord, don't you know what it would mean—an exhumation and autopsy on Peter Oliver Barstow?"

I put in, "Rot. Any of a dozen excuses is enough."

"Well, maybe I'm not good at excuses. Anyway, I know that family. I can't do it. I've telephoned Anderson at Lake Placid and couldn't get him. I'll have him before six o'clock, before seven sure. He can take a sleeper and be here tomorrow morning. He can decide it then."

"That lets today out," I said.

"Yes. Not a chance. I won't do it."

"All right." I got up. "I'll go down to the corner and phone Wolfe and see if he'll wait that long, and if he says okay I'll head south away from the hayseeds. I might as well have that check."

Derwin took it from his pocket and handed it to me.

I grinned at Ben Cook. "Shall I give you a lift as far as the station, Chief?"

"Run along, sonny, run along."

# Chapter 5

Wolfe was as nice as pie that evening. I got home in time to eat dinner with him. He wouldn't let me say anything about White Plains until the meal was over; in fact, there wasn't any conversation to speak of about anything, for he had the radio going. He was accustomed to say that this was the perfect era for the sedentary man; formerly such a man could satisfy any amount of curiosity regarding bygone times by sitting down with Gibbon or Ranke or Tacitus or Greene but if he wanted to meet his contemporaries he had to take to the highways, whereas the man of today, tiring for the moment of Galba or Vitellius, had only to turn on the radio and resume his chair. One program Wolfe rarely missed was the Joy Boys. I never knew why. He would side with his fingers interlaced on his belly, his eyes half closed, and his mouth screwed up as if there was something in it he would spit out any minute. Frequently I went for a walk at that time, but of course when dinner was a little early so that it came then I was caught. I have my radio favorites all right, but the Joy Boys seem to me pretty damn vulgar.

In the office after dinner it didn't take me long to

report. I hated apologizing to Wolfe because he was so invariably nice about it; he always took it for granted that I had done everything possible and that there was nothing to criticize but the contrariety of the environment, as he put it. He made no comments and didn't seem much interested in the report or the apology either. I tried to get him started, tried for instance to find out if he had really had some sort of wild idea that I might kid a District Attorney into covering a bet of ten thousand dollars just like that, but he only stayed nice and quiet. I asked him if he thought it likely that I could have taken any line at all that would have persuaded Derwin to start the digging that afternoon. He said probably not.

"Frogs don't fly." He was sitting at his desk examining with a magnifying glass the rostellum from a *Cymbidium Alexanderi* that Horstmann had brought down wilty on the stem. "He would have needed a touch of imagination, just a touch, but I would judge from your description that he lacks it. I beg you not to reproach yourself. This affair may prove unprofitable in the end. With Fletcher M. Anderson it might have been different. He is a rich man with professional ambitions, and no fool. He might easily have reflected that if a quiet and unadvertised autopsy proved me wrong he would win ten thousand dollars; if it proved me right he would have to pay me, but he would get a remarkable and sensational case in return, and he might also infer that having pocketed his money I would have further information to be placed at his disposal. Your errand at White Plains was in essence a primitive business enterprise: an offer to exchange something for something else. If Mr. Anderson had only been there he would probably have seen it so. It may yet materialize; it is still worth some small effort. I believe though it is getting ready to rain."

"What are you doing now, changing the subject?" I stuck to the chair near his desk, though I saw that I was being regarded as a mild nuisance, for I had some questions to ask. "It was clouding up as I came in. Is it going to rain all over your clues?"

He was placid, still bent over the magnifying glass. "Some day, Archie, when I decide you are no longer worth tolerating, you will have to marry a woman of very modest mental capacity to get an appropriate audience for your wretched sarcasms. When I mentioned the rain I had your own convenience and comfort in mind. This afternoon it struck me as desirable that you should visit Sullivan Street, but tomorrow will do as well.

It was hard to believe unless you were as well acquainted with him as I was; I knew that he was really serious, he thought that leaving the house at any time was an unpleasant venture, but to go out in the rain was next to foolhardy. I said, "What do you think I am, the Chinese army? Of course I'll go. That was one of my questions. Why do you suppose Anna Fiore closed up so hard on O'Grady? Because he wasn't all grace and charm like you and me?"

"Likely. Excellent conjecture, Archie. The more so because when I sent Panzer for her today she confessed only reluctantly to her name and she would not budge. So your grace and charm will be needed. If it would be convenient have her here in the morning at eleven. It's not of great importance but can do no harm for passing the time, and such stubbornness deserves a siege."

"I'll go get her now."

"No. Really. Tomorrow. Sit down. I would prefer

to have you here, idle and useless, while I purpose-lessly inspect this futile flower. Futile and sterile apparently. As I have remarked before, to have you with me like this is always refreshing because it constantly reminds me how distressing it would be to have someone present—a wife, for instance—whom I could not dismiss at will."

"Yes, sir." I grinned. "Go on with the rest of it."

"Not just now. Not with the rain falling. I dislike it."

"All right, then tell me a few things. How did you know Carlo Maffei had been murdered? How do you know Barstow was poisoned? How do you know he's got a needle in him? Of course I see how it got there since you had the boy from Corliss Holmes show us, but how did you get that far?"

Wolfe laid down his magnifying glass and sighed. I knew I was making him uncomfortable, but aside from curiosity it was a matter of business. He never seemed to realize that while it was all very well for me to feel in my bones that he would never get us committed to a mistake, I could do my part with a little more intelligence if I knew what was making the wheels go round. I don't believe he ever would have opened up once, on any case big or little, if I hadn't kept nudging him.

He sighed. "Must I again remind you, Archie, of the reaction you would have got if you had asked Velasquez to explain why Aesop's hand was resting inside his robe instead of hanging by his side? Must I again demonstrate that while it is permissible to request the scientist to lead you back over his foot-prints, a similar request of the artist is nonsense, since he, like the lark or the eagle, has made none? Do you need to be told again that I am an artist?"

"No, sir. All I need to be told is how you knew Barstow was poisoned."

He took up the magnifying glass. I sat and waited, lighting another cigarette. I had finished it, and had about decided to go to the front room for a book or magazine, when he spoke.

"Carlo Maffei is gone. Common enough, beaten and robbed probably, until the telephone call and the advertisement. The telephone call as a whole does not lack interest, but it is the threat, *I'm not the one to be scared*, that has significance. The advertisement adds a specification; to that point Maffei has been this and that, he now becomes also a man who may have made something intricate and difficult that would *work*. The word *mechanism* made that a good advertisement, but it also offered magnificent suggestions to an inquiring mind. Then, quite by accident just as the creation of life was an accident, Maffei becomes something else: a man who clipped the Barstow news from the paper on the morning of his disappearance. So, read the Barstow news again and find the aspect of it that closely concerned Carlo Maffei. An obscure Italian metal-worker immigrant; a famous learned wealthy university president. Still there must be a connection, and the incongruity of the elements would make it only the more plain if it was visible at all. There is the article; find the link if it is there; stop every word and give it passage only if its innocence is sure. But little effort is required; the link is so obvious that it is at once apparent. At the moment of, and for some time immediately preceding, his collapse, Barstow had in his hands and was using not one, but an entire assortment, of instruments which if they were not intricate and difficult mechanisms were admirably adapted to such a use. It was a perfectly composed picture. But while it needed no justification, nothing indeed but contemplation, as a work of art, if it were to be put to practical uses a little fixative would help. So I merely asked Miss Fiore if she had ever seen a golf club in Maffei's room. The result was gratifying."

"All right," I said. "But what if the girl had just looked and said no, she never saw one anywhere?"

"I have told you before, Archie, that even for your amusement I shall not advise replies to hypothetical questions."

"Sure, that's an easy out."

Wolfe shook his head regretfully. "To reply is to admit the validity of your jargon, but I have learned not to expect better of you. How the devil do I know what I would have done *if* anything? Probably bade her good night. Would I have found varnish for my picture elsewhere? Maybe; maybe not. Shall I ask you how you would have seen to eat if your head had been put on backwards?"

I grinned. "I wouldn't have starved. Neither will you; if I know anything I know that. But how did you know that Maffei had been murdered?"

"I didn't, until O'Grady came. You heard what I said to him. The police had searched his room. That could only be if he had been taken in a criminal act, or been murdered. The first was unlikely in the light of other facts."

"All right. But I've saved the best till the last. Who killed Barstow?"

"Ah." Wolfe murmured it softly. "That would be another picture, Archie, and I hope an expensive one. Expensive for the purchaser and profitable for the artist. Also, one of its characters would be a worthy subject. To continue my threadbare metaphor, we shan't set up our easel until we are sure of the commission.—Yet in point of fact that isn't strictly true. We shall get in a spot of the background tomorrow morning if you can bring Miss Fiore here."

"Let me get her now. It's only a little after nine."

"No—hear the rain? Tomorrow will do."

I knew there was no use insisting, so after a try at a couple of magazines had got me good and bored I got a raincoat from upstairs and went out for an hour at a movie. I wouldn't have admitted to anyone else, but I did to myself, that I wasn't any too easy in my mind. I had had the same kind of experience often before, but that didn't make me like it any better. I did absolutely feel in my bones that Wolfe would never let us tumble into a hole without having a ladder we could climb out with, but in spite of that I had awful doubts sometimes. As long as I live I'll never forget the time he had a bank president pinched, or rather I did, on no evidence whatever except that the fountain pen on his desk was dry. I was never so relieved in my life as I was when the guy shot himself an hour later. But there was no use trying to get Wolfe to pull up a little; I hardly ever wasted time on that any more. If I undertook to explain how easy he might be wrong he would just say, "You know a fact when you see it, Archie, but you have no feeling for phenomena." After I had looked up the word phenomena in the dictionary I couldn't see that he had anything, but there was no use arguing with him.

So here I was uneasy again. I wanted to think it over, so I got my raincoat and went to a movie where I could sit in the dark with something to keep my eyes on and let my mind work. It wasn't hard to see how Wolfe had doped it out. Someone wanted to kill Barstow, call him X. He put an ad in the paper for an expert to make him something, fixing it to get someone intending to leave the country for good so if he had any curiosity later on it wouldn't hurt him any. Maffei answered the ad and got the job, namely to make an arrangement inside a golf club so that when the inset on the face hit a ball it would release a trigger and shoot a needle out of the handle at the other end. Probably X presented it as a trial of skill for the European commission to follow; but he gave the Italian so much money for doing it that Maffei decided not to go back home after all. That started an argument inside a golf club so that when the inset on the face anyhow, X proceeded to use the club for its calculated purpose, putting it in Barstow's bag (it had of course been made identical in appearance with Barstow's own driver). Then Maffei happened to read Monday's *Times* and put two and two together, which wasn't strange considering the odd affair he had been paid to construct. X had telephoned; Maffei had met him, made him a present of his suspicions, and tried blackmail. X didn't wait this time for an expert design and mechanism, he just used a knife, leaving it in Maffei's back to keep from soiling the upholstery of the car. He then drove around the Westchester hills until he found a secluded spot, put the body in a thicket and pulled out the knife and later tossed it into a handy stream or reservoir. Arriving home at a decent hour, he had a drink or two before going to bed, and when he got up in the morning put on a cutaway instead of a business suit because he was going to his friend Barstow's funeral.

Of course that was Wolfe's picture, and it was a lulu, but what I figured as I sat in the movie was this, that though it used all the facts without any stretching, anyone could have said that much a thousand years ago when they thought the sun went around the earth. That didn't stretch any of the facts they knew, but what about the ones they didn't know? And here was Wolfe risking ten grand and his reputation to get Barstow dug up. Once one of Wolfe's clients had told him he was insufferably blithe. I liked that; Wolfe had liked it too. But that didn't keep me from reflecting that if they cut Barstow open and found only coronary thrombosis in his veins and no oddments at all in his belly, within a week everybody from the D.A. down to a Bath Beach flatfoot would be saving twenty cents by staying home and laughing at us instead of going to a movie to see Mickey Mouse. I wasn't so dumb, I knew anyone may make a mistake, but I also knew that when a man sets himself up as cocksure as Wolfe did, he had *always* got to be right.

I was dumb in a way though. All the time I was stewing I knew damn well Wolfe *was* right. It was that note I went to sleep on when I got home from the movie and found that Wolfe had already gone up to his room.

The next morning I was awake a little after seven, but I dawdled in bed, knowing that if I got up and dressed I would have to dawdle anyway, since there was no use bringing Anna Fiore until time for Wolfe to be down from the plant-rooms. I lay, yawning, looking at the picture of the woods with grass and flowers, and at the photograph of my father and mother, and then closed my eyes, not to nap for I was all slept out, but to see how many different noises from the street I could recognize. I was doing that when there was a knock on the door and in answer to my call Fritz came in.

"Good morning," I said. "I'll have grapefruit juice and just a tiny cup of chocolate."

Fritz smiled. He had a sweet sort of faraway smile.

He could catch a joke but never tried to return it. "Good morning. There's a gentleman downstairs to see Mr. Wolfe."

I sat up. "What's his name?"

"He said Anderson. He had no card."

"What!" I swung myself to the edge of the bed. "Well well well well. He's not a gentleman, Fritz, he's a noovoh reesh. Mr. Wolfe is hoping that soon he'll be less reesh. Tell him—no, don't bother. I'll be right down."

I doused some cold water over my face, got on enough clothes for an emergency, and gave my hair a few swipes with a brush. Then I went down.

Anderson didn't get up from his chair when I entered the office. He was so sunburned that on the street it would have taken me a second glance to recognize him. He looked sleepy and sore and his hair hadn't been brushed any better than mine.

I said, "My name's Archie Goodwin. I don't suppose you remember me."

He kept his chair. "I suppose not, I'm sorry. I came to see Wolfe."

"Yes, sir. I'm afraid you'll have to wait a little. Mr. Wolfe isn't up yet."

"Not long I hope."

"I couldn't say. I'll see. If you'll excuse me."

I beat it to the hall and stood there at the foot of the stairs. I had to decide whether this was a case when Wolfe would want to break a rule. It was a quarter to eight. Finally I went on upstairs and down the hall to a point about ten feet from his door where there was a push-button in the wall. I pushed it, and right away heard his voice faintly:

"Well?"

"Turn off the switch. I'm coming in."

I heard the little click and then: "Come."

You would never believe there was such a thing in the world as Wolfe in bed if you didn't see it. I had seen it often, but it was still a treat. On top was a black silk puffy cover which he always used, winter and summer. From the mound in the middle it sloped precipitously on all sides, so that if you wanted to see his face you had to stand well up front, and then you had to stoop to look under the canopy arrangement that he had sticking out from the head of the bed. It was also of black silk, and extended a foot beyond his chin and hung quite low on all three sides. Inside it on the white pillow his big fat face reposed like an image in a temple.

His hand came from beneath the cover to pull a cord that hung at his right, and the canopy folded back against the headboard. He blinked. I told him that Fletcher M. Anderson was downstairs and wanted to see him.

He cursed. I hated to hear him curse. It got on my nerves. The reason for that, he told me once, was that whereas in most cases cursing was merely a vocal explosion, with him it was a considered expression of a profound desire. He did it seldom. That morning he cursed completely. At the end he said, "Leave, get out, go."

I hated to stammer, too. "But—but—Anderson—"

"If Mr. Anderson wishes to see me he may do so at eleven o'clock. But that is unnecessary. What do I pay you for?"

"Very well, sir. Of course you're right. I break a rule and I get bawled out. But now that that's done with may I suggest that it would be a good idea to see Anderson—"

"You may not."

"Ten thousand dollars?"

"No."

"In the name of heaven, sir, why not?"

"Confound it, you badger me!" Wolfe's head turned on the pillow, and he got a hand around to wiggle a finger. "Yes, you badger me. But it is a valuable quality at times and I won't cavil at it. Instead I'll answer your question. I shall not see Mr. Anderson for three reasons: first, being still in bed I am undressed and in an ugly temper. Second, you can do our business with him just as well. Third, I understand the technique of eccentricity; it would be futile for a man to labor at establishing a reputation for oddity if he were ready at the slightest provocation to revert to normal action. Go. At once."

I left the room and went downstairs to the office and told Anderson that if he wanted to wait he could see Mr. Wolfe at eleven o'clock.

Of course he couldn't believe his ears. As soon as he became able to credit the fact that the message was like that and that it was meant for him, he blew up. He seemed especially indignant that he had come straight to Wolfe's place from a sleeper at Grand Central Station, though I couldn't see why. I explained to him several times how it was, I told him it was eccentricity and there was no help for it. I also told him that I had been to White Plains the day before and was acquainted with the situation. That seemed to calm him a little and he began asking me questions. I fed it to him in little pieces, and had the fun of seeing the look on his face when I told him about Derwin calling Ben Cook in. When he had the whole story he sat back and rubbed his nose and looked over my head.

Finally he brought his look down to me. "This is a startling conclusion Wolfe has made. Isn't it?"

"Yes, sir. It is indeed."

"Then he must have some startling information."

I grinned. "Mr. Anderson, it is a pleasure to talk with you, but there's no use wasting time. As far as startling information is concerned, Wolfe and I are the same as two mummies in a museum until that grave is opened and Barstow is cut up. Not a chance."

"Well. That's too bad. I might offer Wolfe a fee as a special investigator—a sort of inquiry and report."

"A fee? That's like saying as long as a piece of string."

"Say, five hundred dollars."

I shook my head. "I'm afraid he's too busy. I'm busy too, I may have to run up to White Plains this morning."

"Oh." Anderson bit his lip and looked at me. "You know, Goodwin. I rarely go out of my way to be offensive, but doesn't it occur to you that this whole thing is fairly nasty? It might be better to say unethical."

I got sore at that. I looked back at him and said, "Look here, Mr. Anderson. You said you didn't remember me. I remember you. You haven't forgotten the Goldsmith case five years ago. It wouldn't have hurt you a bit to let people know what Wolfe handed you on that. But let them go, let's say you needed to keep it for yourself. We wouldn't have minded that so much. But how ethical was it for you to turn it around so that Wolfe got a nice black eye instead of what was really coming to him? You tend to your own ethics maybe."

"I don't know what you're talking about."

"All right. But if I go to White Plains today somebody will know what I'm talking about. And whatever you get this time you'll pay for."

Anderson smiled and got up. "Don't bother, Goodwin. You won't be needed at White Plains today. On information that I have received I have decided definitely on the exhumation of Barstow's body. You will be here throughout the day, or Wolfe? I may wish to get in touch with him later."

"Wolfe is always here, but you can't get him between nine and eleven or four and six."

"Well. Such an eccentric!"

"Yes, sir. Your hat's in the hall."

I went to the front room window and watched his taxi roll off. Then I turned to the office, to the telephone. I hesitated; but I knew Wolfe was right, and if he wasn't, a little publicity wouldn't make it any harder for us. So I called the *Gazette* office for Harry Foster, and by luck he was in.

"Harry? Archie Goodwin. Here's something for you, but keep it so quiet you can hear a pin drop. This morning at White Plains, Anderson, the District Attorney, is going to get a court order for an exhumation and autopsy on Peter Oliver Barstow. He'll probably try to keep it mum, but I thought you might like to help him out. And listen. Some day, when the time comes, I'd be glad to tell you what it was that made Anderson so curious. Don't mention it."

I went upstairs and shaved and did my dressing over. By the time I had finished with that, and with breakfast and a little chat in the kitchen with Fritz about fish, it was nine-thirty. I went to the garage for the roadster and filled up with gas and oil, and headed south for Sullivan Street.

Since it was school hours it wasn't as noisy and dirty around there as it had been before, and it was different otherwise. I might have expected the decorations, but it hadn't occurred to me. There was a big

black rosette with long black ribbons hanging on the
door and above it was a large wreath of leaves and
flowers. A few people were standing around, mostly
across the street. A little distance off a cop stood on
the sidewalk looking uninterested; but when my roadster pulled up some yards short of the door with the
wreath on it I saw him cock an eye at me. I got out and
went over to him to say hello.

I handed him a card. "I'm Archie Goodwin of Nero
Wolfe's office. We were engaged by Maffei's sister to
look for him the day before his body was found. I've
come to see the landlady and check up a little."

"Yeah?" The cop stuck my card in a pocket. "I don't
know a thing except that I'm standing here. Archie
Goodwin? Pleased to meet you."

We shook hands and as I moved off I asked him to
keep an eye on my car.

Mrs. Ricci didn't seem very glad to see me, but I
could understand that easy enough. That dick O'Grady
had probably raked her over for letting me take stuff
from Maffei's room, of course without any right or
reason, but that wouldn't deter O'Grady. I grinned
when I saw the landlady's lips go shut, getting ready
for the questions she thought I had come to ask. It's
never any fun having a murdered man lying upstairs,
even when he was only a roomer. So I sympathized
with her a little before I mentioned that I'd like to see
Anna Fiore.

"She's busy."

"Sure. But this is important; my boss would like to
see her. It would only take an hour or so, here, a
couple of dollars—"

"No! For the love of God can't you let us alone in
our house? Can't you let the poor woman bury her

brother without cackling in her ears to drive her
crazy? Who are you that—"

Of course she would have to pick me to blow up on.
I saw it was hopeless to get any co-operation out of
her, she wouldn't even listen to me, so I removed
myself and went back to the front hall. The door to the
dining-room was open, but the room was empty. After
I had slipped in there I heard footsteps in the hall, and
looking through the crack between the door and the
jamb I saw Mrs. Ricci start upstairs. She went on up,
and I could hear her continue the second flight. I stuck
behind the door and waited, and luck came my way.
Not more than ten minutes had passed before there
were steps on the stairs, and using the crack again I
saw Anna. I called her name, softly. She stopped and
looked around. I called still softly, "In the dining-
room." She came to the threshold and I moved around
where she could see me.

"Hello, Anna. Mrs. Ricci told me to wait here till
you came down."

"Oh. Mr. Archie."

"Sure. I came to take you for a ride. Mrs. Ricci was
angry that I came for you, but you remember on
Wednesday I gave her a dollar? Today I gave her two
dollars, so she said all right. But hurry up; I told her
we'd be back before noon."

I grabbed Anna's hand, but she held back. "In that
car like the other day?"

"Sure. Come on."

"My jacket is upstairs and look at my dress."

"It's too warm for a jacket. Hurry; what if Mrs.
Ricci changed her mind? We can buy you one—come
on."

With my hand on her arm I worked her out of the
dining-room and down the short hall to the entrance

door, but I didn't want to look anxious outside; there was no telling how important that cop might think he was and any interruption might queer it. So I threw the door open and said, "Go on and get in, I'll tell Mrs. Ricci good-bye." I waited only a few seconds before I followed her; she was at the roadster opening the door. I went around to my side and climbed in, stepped on the starter, waved to the flatfoot and shot off down Sullivan Street in second with the engine roaring so that no yelling from an upstairs window could hurt Anna's ears.

She certainly was a scarecrow. Her dress was a sight. But I wasn't ashamed to have her beside me as, headed uptown again, I circled through Washington Square and rolled into Fifth Avenue. Not a bit. The clock on the dash said twenty after ten.

Anna said, "Where are we going, Mr. Archie?"

I said, "You see how it is about your dress in this low seat? Nobody can see you anyway except your face and there's nothing wrong with that. What do you say we drive around Central Park? It's a beautiful morning."

"Oh yes."

I didn't say anything and she didn't either for about ten blocks and then she said again, "Oh yes."

She was certainly having a swell time. I went on up the Avenue and into the Park at Sixtieth. Up the west side to a Hundred and Tenth, across to Riverside Drive, up to Grant's Tomb where I circled around and turned downtown. I don't think she glanced at the trees or the grass or the river once; she kept looking at people in other cars. It was five minutes to eleven when I drew up in front of Wolfe's house.

Mrs. Ricci had already telephoned twice. Fritz had a funny look when he told me about it. I settled that at once by calling her up and giving her a piece about obstructing justice. I didn't know how much of it she heard with her yelling, but it seemed to work; we didn't hear another peep out of her before noon, when I left to take Anna home.

Wolfe came in while I was phoning Mrs. Ricci. I watched him stopping to tell the girl good morning on his way to the desk. He was elegant with women. He had some sort of a perverted idea about them that I've never caught the hang of but every time I had ever seen him with one he was elegant. I couldn't describe how he did it because I couldn't make it out myself; it was hard to see how that enormous lump of flesh and folds could ever be called elegant, but he certainly was. Even when he was bullying one of them, like the time he sweated the Diplomacy Club business out of Nyura Pronn. That was the best exhibition of squeezing a sponge dry I've ever seen.

He started softly with Anna Fiore. After he had flipped through the mail, he turned and looked at her a minute before he said, "We no longer need to indulge in any conjectures as to the whereabouts of your friend Carlo Maffei. Accept my condolences. You have viewed the body?"

"Yes, sir."

"It is a pity, a real pity, for he did not seek violence; he got in its path by misadventure. It is curious on how slender a thread the destiny of a man may hang; for example, that of the murderer of Carlo Maffei may hang on this, Miss Fiore: when and under what circumstances did you see a golf club in Maffei's room?"

"Yes, sir."

"Yes. It will be easy to tell us now. Probably my

question the other day recalled the occasion to your
mind."

"Yes, sir."

"It did?"

She opened her mouth but said nothing. I was
watching her, and she looked odd to me. Wolfe asked
her again, "It did?"

She was silent. I couldn't see that she was a bit
nervous or frightened, she was just silent.

"When I asked you about this the other day, Miss
Fiore, you seemed a little upset. I was sorry for that.
Would you tell me why you were upset?"

"Yes, sir."

"Was it perhaps your memory of something unpleasant that happened the day you saw the golf club?"

Silence again. I saw that something was wrong.
Wolfe hadn't asked the last question as if it meant
anything. I knew the shades of the tones of his voice,
and I knew he wasn't interested; at least, not in that
question. Something had him off on another trail. All
at once he shot another question at her in another
tone.

"When did you decide to say *Yes, sir*, to anything I
might ask you?"

No answer; but without waiting Wolfe went on:
"Miss Fiore, I would like to make you understand this.
My last question had nothing whatsoever to do with a
golf club or with Carlo Maffei. Don't you see that? So
if you have decided to reply nothing but *Yes, sir*, to
anything I may ask about Carlo Maffei that will be all
right. You have an absolute right to do that because
that is what you decided to do. But if I ask you about
other things you have no right to say *Yes, sir*, then,
because that is not what you decided to do. About
other things you should talk just as anyone would. So,

when you decided to say nothing but *Yes, sir*, to me, was it on account of anything that Carlo Maffei had done?"

Anna was looking hard at him, right at his eye. It was clear that she wasn't suspecting him or fighting against him, she was merely trying to understand him. She looked and he looked back. After a minute of that she said:

"No, sir."

"Ah! Good. It was not on account of anything he had done. Then it had nothing to do with him, so it is all right for you to tell me anything about it that I may ask. You see that of course. If you have decided to tell me nothing of Carlo Maffei I won't ask you. But this other business. Did you decide to say *Yes, sir*, to Mr. O'Grady, the man that came and asked you questions yesterday morning?"

"Yes, sir."

"Why did you do that?"

She frowned, but said, "Because something happened."

"Good. What happened?"

She shook her head.

"Come, Miss Fiore." Wolfe was quiet. "There is no reason on earth why you shouldn't tell me."

She turned her head to look at me, and then back at him again. After a moment she said, "I'll tell Mr. Archie."

"Good. Tell Mr. Archie."

She spoke to me. "I got a letter."

Wolfe shot a glance at me and I took it up. "You got a letter yesterday?"

She nodded. "Yesterday morning."

"Who was it from?"

"I don't know. There was no name, it was on a

typewriter, and on the envelope it said only Anna and the address, not the rest of my name. Mrs. Ricci gets the mail from the box and she brought it to me but I didn't want to open it where she was because I never get a letter. I went downstairs where I sleep and opened it."

"What did it say?"

She looked at me a moment without replying, and then suddenly she smiled, a funny smile that made me feel queer so that it wasn't easy to look at her. But I kept my eyes on hers. Then she said, "I'll show you what was in it, Mr. Archie," and reached down and pulled her skirt up above her knee, shoved her hand down inside of her stocking, and brought it out again with something in it. I stared as she unrolled five twenty-dollar bills and spread them out for me to see.

"You mean that was in the letter?"

She nodded. "One hundred dollars."

"So I see. But there was something typewritten."

"Yes. It said that if I would never tell anyone anything about Mr. Maffei or anything he ever did I could keep the money. But if I would not do that, if I told about him, I would have to burn it. I burned the letter, but I will not burn the money. I will keep it."

"You burned the letter?"

"Yes."

"And the envelope?"

"Yes."

"And you think you won't tell anyone about Mr. Maffei or about that golf club?"

"I never will."

I looked at her. Wolfe's chin was on his chest, but he was looking at her too. I got up from my chair. "Well, of all the damn fairy stories—"

"Archie! Apologize."

"But good heavens—"

"Apologize."

I turned to the girl. "I apologize, but when I think of all the gas I burned up riding you around the park—" I sat down.

Wolfe said, "Miss Fiore, did you happen to notice the postmark? The little round thing on the envelope that tells where it was mailed?"

"No, sir."

"Of course not. By the way, that money did not belong to the man who sent it to you. He took it from Carlo Maffei's pocket."

"I will keep it, sir."

"No doubt you will. You may not be aware that if the police knew of this they would take it from you ruthlessly. But do not be alarmed; your confidence in Mr. Archie is not misplaced." He turned to me. "Grace and charm are always admirable qualities and sometimes useful. Take Miss Fiore home."

I protested. "But why not—"

"No. Get her to burn those bills by replacing them from your expense book? No. She would not do it; but even if she would, I would not see money burned to save beauty herself from any grave that might be dug for her. The destruction of money is the only authentic sacrilege left us to abhor. Possibly you don't realize what that hundred dollars means to Miss Fiore; to her it represents the unimaginable reward for a desperate and heroic act. Now that she has it safely back in its crypt, take her home." He started to get himself out of his chair. "Good day, Miss Fiore. I have paid you a rare compliment; I have assumed that you mean what you say. Good morning."

I was at the door telling her to come on.

Going back downtown I let her alone. I was pretty

sore, after kidnapping her and driving her around in style for nearly an hour to have her go moron on us, but there was no use wasting breath on her. At Sullivan Street I just dumped her out on the sidewalk with a good deal of satisfaction, thinking that Wolfe had been elegant enough for both of us.

She stood there. As I pulled the gear shift lever to go on she said, "Thank you, Mr. Archie."

She was being elegant! She had caught it from Wolfe. I said, "You're not welcome, Anna, but good-bye and no hard feelings," and rolled off.

# Chapter 6

It was during the half-hour that I was gone taking Anna Fiore home that Wolfe had a relapse. It was a bad one, and it lasted three days. When I got back to Thirty-fifth Street he was sitting in the kitchen, by the little table where I always ate breakfast, drinking beer with three bottles already gone, arguing with Fritz whether chives should be used in tomato tarts. I stood and listened a few minutes without saying anything, then I went upstairs to my room and got a bottle of rye from the closet and took a drink.

I had never really understood Wolfe's relapses. Sometimes it seemed plain that it was just ordinary discouragement and funk, like the time the taxi driver ran out on us in the Pine Street case, but other times there was no accounting for it at all. Everything would be sailing along and it would look to me as if we were about ready to wrap up the package and deliver it C.O.D., when for no reason at all he would lose interest. He was out and that was all there was to it. Nothing that I could say made the slightest dent on him. It might last anywhere from one afternoon up to a couple of weeks, or it was even possible that he was out for good and wouldn't come back until something new turned up. While it lasted he acted one of two different ways: either he went to bed and stayed there, living on bread and onion soup, refusing to see anyone but me and forbidding me to mention anything I had on my mind; or he sat in the kitchen telling Fritz how to cook things and then eating them on my little table. He ate a whole half a sheep that way in two days once, different parts of it cooked in twenty different ways. At such times I usually had my tongue out from running all over town from the Battery to Bronx Park, trying to find some herb or root or maybe cordial that they needed in the dish they were going to do next. The only time I ever quit Wolfe was when he sent me to a Brooklyn dock where a tramp steamer from China was tied up, to try to buy some badden-root from the captain. The captain must have had a cargo of opium or something to make him suspicious; anyway he took it for granted that I was looking for trouble and filled my order by having half a dozen skinny savages wrap things around my skull. I quit the next afternoon, phoning from the hospital, but a day later Wolfe came and took me home, and I was so astonished that he actually came himself that I forgot I had quit. That finished that relapse, too.

This day I knew it was a relapse as soon as I saw him sitting in the kitchen arguing with Fritz, and I was so disgusted that after I had gone upstairs and had a couple of drinks I came down again and went out. I started walking, but after a few blocks the appetite from the drinks was quite active and I stopped at a restaurant for a meal. No restaurant meal was much after seven years of Fritz's everyday cooking, but I wouldn't go home to eat; in the first place I was disgusted and in the second place those relapse menus couldn't be depended on—sometimes it was a feast for an epicure, sometimes it was a dainty little taste good for eighty cents in Schrafft's and sometimes it was just a mess.

But after the meal I felt better, and I walked back to Thirty-fifth Street and told Wolfe what Anderson had said that morning and added that it looked to me as if there would be something doing before the full moon came.

Wolfe was still sitting at the little table, watching Fritz stir something in a pan. He looked at me as if he was trying to remember where he had seen me before. He said, "Don't ever mention that shyster's name to me again."

I said, hoping to get him sore, "This morning I phoned Harry Foster at the *Gazette* and told him what was up. I knew you'd want plenty of publicity."

He didn't hear me. He said to Fritz, "Have boiling water ready in case it should disunite."

I went upstairs to tell Horstmann he'd have to nurse his babies alone that afternoon and maybe for a week. He would be miserable. It was always funny how he pretended to be annoyed when Wolfe was around but if anything happened to keep Wolfe from showing up on the dot at nine or four he was so worried and anxious you might have thought mealy bugs were after him. So I went upstairs to make him miserable.

That was two o'clock Friday afternoon, and the first sane look I got from Wolfe was eleven Monday morning, sixty-nine hours later.

In between things happened a little. First was the telephone call from Harry Foster Friday around four. I'd been expecting it. He said they had dug Barstow up and done the autopsy but wouldn't make any announcement. It wasn't his story any more; others had got wind of it and were hanging around the coroner's office.

A little after six the second phone call came. This time it was Anderson. I grinned when I heard his voice and glanced at my wrist; I could see him fuming around waiting for six o'clock. He said he wanted to talk to Wolfe.

"I'm sorry, Mr. Wolfe is busy. This is Goodwin."

He said he wanted Wolfe to come to White Plains. I laughed at him. He rang off. I didn't like it, he struck me as a bad guy. After thinking it over a little I called up Henry H. Barber at his apartment and got all the dope on things like accessories and arrests of material witnesses. Then I went to the kitchen and told Wolfe about the two phone calls. He wiggled a spoon at me.

"Archie. This Anderson is a disease. Cleanse the telephone. Did I forbid mention of his name?"

I said, "I'm sorry, I should have known better. You know what I think, sir. A nut is always a nut even when it's you. I want to talk to Fritz."

Wolfe wasn't listening. I told Fritz that for dinner I would come and get sandwiches and take them to the office, and then I told him that when the buzzer rang, until further notice, he was not to go to the door, I would attend to it. Under no circumstances was he to open the door.

I knew it was probably uncalled-for precaution, but I was taking no chances on anyone busting in there with Wolfe in one of his Bloomingdale moods. I was glad he hadn't tried to send me for anything and I hoped he wouldn't, for I wouldn't have gone. If it was a washout, all right, but I wasn't going to let them make ninnies of us if I could help it. Nothing happened that night. The next morning I stayed out of Wolfe's way, mostly in the front room, opening the door to a gas man and an expressman, and once to a slick youth that wanted to get helped through college. I helped him as far as the bottom of the stoop. It was around eleven when I obeyed the buzzer by opening the door again and found a big husky standing against it, coming in with it, his foot sliding along. I gave him a good solid stiff-arm and pushed him back, and went on out, shutting the door behind me.

I said, "Good morning. Who invited you?"

He said, "It wasn't you anyhow. I want to see Nero Wolfe."

"You can't. He's sick. What do you want?"

He smiled, being smooth, and handed me a card. I looked at it.

"Sure. From Anderson's office. His right-hand man? What do you want?"

"You know what I want," he smiled. "Let's go in and talk it over."

I didn't see any sense in trying to be coy. Anyway I had no idea when Wolfe might kick out of it, and that made me sick. So I covered it all in as few words as possible. I told him that Wolfe didn't know one thing that they didn't know, at least nothing that applied to Barstow, and that what he did know came to him in a dream. I told him that if they wanted Wolfe on the case at a price to say so and name the price and he would take it or leave it. I told him that if they wanted to try any funny warrants they would be surprised how funny they'd turn out to be before Wolfe got through with them. Then I told him that I could see that he weighed twenty pounds more than I did and that therefore I wouldn't attempt to go back in the house until he had departed, and that I would appreciate it if he would get a move on because I was

reading an interesting book. He inserted a few remarks as I went along, but when I finished all he said
was:

"Tell Wolfe he can't get away with it."

"Sure. Any other message?"

"Just go to hell for you."

I grinned, and stood on the stoop watching him as
he walked off, headed east. I had never heard of him
before, but I didn't know Westchester very well. The
name on the card was H. R. Corbett. I went back to
the front room and sat and smoked cigarettes.

After lunch, some time around four, I heard a
newsy out in the street calling an extra. I went out
and called him and bought one. There it was taking up
half of the front page: BARSTOW POISONED—
DART FOUND IN BODY. I read it through. If ever
I had a pain in the neck it was then. Of course Wolfe
and I weren't mentioned; I hadn't expected that; but to
think of what that piece might have meant to us! I
kicked myself for bungling with Derwin, and again
with Anderson, for I was sure it could have been
handled somehow to let us in, though it was hard to
see how. And I kicked Wolfe for his damn relapse. At
least I wanted to. I read it again. It wasn't a dart at
all, it was a short steel needle, just as Wolfe had said,
and it had been found below the stomach. Sore as I
was at Wolfe, I handed it to him. There was his
picture.

I went to the kitchen and laid the paper on the
table in front of Wolfe without a word, and went out
again. He called after me, "Archie! Get the car, here's
a list for you."

I pretended I didn't hear. Later Fritz went.

Next day the Sunday papers were full of it. They
had sent their packs running around sniffing all over

Westchester County, but they hadn't found a thing. I read all the articles through, and I learned a lot of details about the Green Meadow Club, the Barstow family, the Kimballs who had been in the foursome, the doctor who had pulled a boner, and a lot besides, but nobody really knew any more than Wolfe had known Wednesday evening when he had asked Anna Fiore if she had ever seen a golf club in Carlo Maffei's room. Not as much, for there was no accepted theory as to how the needle got in Barstow's belly. All the papers had pieces by experts on poisons and what they do to you.

Sunday evening I went to a movie, telling Fritz to open the door to no one. Not that I expected anything; it looked as if Anderson was playing his own hand. Possibly, through motive or discoveries he had made, he was really lining it up. I would have got drunk that evening if it hadn't been Sunday. When I got back from the movie Wolfe had gone up to his room, but Fritz was still in the kitchen washing up. I fried a piece of ham to make myself a sandwich and poured a glass of milk, for I hadn't had much dinner. I noticed that the *Times* I had put there in the morning for Wolfe was still on top of the refrigerator just as I had left it. It was ten to one he hadn't looked at it.

I read in my room until after midnight and then had trouble going to sleep on account of my mind working. But apparently there was no trouble about it after I once got started, for when I pried my eyes open in the morning enough to glance at the clock on the stand it was after nine. I was sitting on the edge of the bed yawning when I heard a noise overhead that woke me up good. Either that was two pairs of footsteps and I knew both of them or I was still

dreaming. I went out in the hall and listened a minute
and then ran downstairs. Fritz was in the kitchen
drinking coffee. "Is that Mr. Wolfe up with Horstmann?"

"And how." That was the only slang Fritz ever
used and he always welcomed a chance to get it in. He
smiled at me, glad to see me excited and happy. "Now
I will just get a leg of lamb and rub garlic on it."

"Rub poison ivy on it if you want to." I went back
up to dress.

The relapse was over! I was excited all right. I
shaved extra clean and whistled in the bathtub. With
Wolfe normal again anything might happen. When I
got back down to the kitchen a dish of figs and a fat
omelet were ready for me, and the newspaper was
propped up against the coffeepot. I started on the
headlines and the figs at the same time, but halfway
through a fig I stopped chewing. I raced down the
paragraphs, swallowing the mouthful whole to get it
out of the way. It was plain, the paper stated it as a
fact. Although no confirmation was needed, I turned
the pages over, running my eyes up and down and
across. It was on page eight toward the bottom, a neat
little ad in a neat little box:

I WILL PAY FIFTY THOUSAND DOLLARS REWARD
TO ANY PERSON OR PERSONS WHO WILL FUR-
NISH INFORMATION RESULTING IN THE DISCOV-
ERY AND RIGHTEOUS PUNISHMENT OF THE
MURDERER OF MY HUSBAND PETER OLIVER
BARSTOW.

ELLEN BARSTOW

I read it through three times and then tossed the
paper away and got calm. I finished the fruit and

omelet, with three pieces of toast and three cups of coffee. Fifty grand, with the Wolfe bank balance sagging like a clothesline under a wet horse blanket; and not only that, but a chance of keeping our places on the platform in the biggest show of the season. I was calm and cool, but it was only twenty minutes after ten. I went to the office and opened the safe and dusted around and waited.

When Wolfe came down at eleven he looked fresh but not noticeably good-humored. He only nodded for good morning and didn't seem to care much whether I was there or not as he got himself into his chair and started looking through the mail. I just waited, thinking I would show him that other people could be as hard-boiled as he was, but when he began checking off the monthly bill from Harvey's I popped at him:

"I hope you had a nice weekend, sir."

He didn't look at me, but I saw his cheeks folding. "Thank you, Archie. It was delightful; but on awakening this morning I felt so completely water-logged that with only myself to consider I would have remained in bed to await disintegration. Names battered at me: Archie Goodwin, Fritz Brenner, Theodore Horstmann; responsibilities; and I arose to resume my burden. Not that I complain; the responsibilities are mutual; but my share can be done only by me."

"Excuse me, sir, but you're a damn liar, what you did was look at the paper."

He checked off items on the bill. "You can't rile me, Archie, not today. Paper? I have looked at nothing this morning except life, and that not through a newspaper."

"Then you don't know that Mrs. Barstow has

offered fifty thousand dollars for her husband's murderer?"

The pencil stopped checking; he didn't look at me,
but the pencil was motionless in his fingers for seconds. Then he placed the bill under a paperweight,
laid the pencil beside it, and lifted his head.

"Show it to me."

I exhibited first the ad and then the first page
article. Of the ad he read each word; the article he
glanced through.

"Indeed," he said. "Indeed. Mr. Anderson does not
need the money, even granting the possibility of his
earning it, and only a moment ago I was speaking of
responsibilities. Archie, do you know what I thought
in bed this morning? I thought how horrible and how
amusing it would be to send Theodore away and let all
those living and breathing plants, all that arrogant
and pampered loveliness, thirst and gasp and wither
away."

"Good God!"

"Yes. Just an early morning fantasy; I haven't the
will for such a gesture. I would be more likely to
offer them at auction—should I decide to withdraw
from responsibilities—and take passage for Egypt.
You know of course that I own a house in Egypt
which I have never seen. The man who gave it to me,
a little more than ten years ago—yes, Fritz, what is
it?"

Fritz was a little awry, having put on his jacket
hurriedly to go to the door.

"A lady to see you, sir."

"Her name?"

"She had no card, sir."

Wolfe nodded, and Fritz went out. In a moment he
was back on the threshold, bowing in a young woman.

I was on my feet. She started toward me, and I inclined my head in Wolfe's direction. She looked at him, stopped, and said:

"Mr. Nero Wolfe? My name is Sarah Barstow."

"Be seated," Wolfe said. "You must pardon me; for engineering reasons I arise only for emergencies."

"This is an emergency," she said.

# Chapter 7

From the newspapers I was pretty well up on Sarah Barstow. She was twenty-five, popular, a graduate of Smith, and prominent both in university society at Holland and in various groups in summer Westchester. Of course beautiful, according to the papers. I thought to myself that this time that detail was accurate, as she arranged herself in a chair in front of Wolfe and sat with her eyes on him. She wore a tan linen dress with a coat to match and a little black hat on sideways. Her gloves showed that she was driving. Her face was a little small but everything on it was in place and well arranged; her eyes were too bright in the pupils and too heavy around the edges from tiredness, and from crying perhaps, and her skin was pale, but health and pleasantness showed through that. Her voice was low and had sense in it. I liked her.

She started to explain herself, but Wolfe wiggled a finger at her. "It is unnecessary, and possibly painful to you, Miss Barstow, I know. You are the only daughter of Peter Oliver Barstow. All you need tell is why you have come to me."

"Yes." She hesitated. "Of course you would know,

Mr. Wolfe. It is a little difficult—perhaps I wanted a preamble." She had a try at a smile. "I am going to ask you a favor, I don't know how much of a favor it will be."

"I can tell you that."

"Of course. First I must ask you, do you know that my mother had an advertisement in the paper this morning?"

Wolfe nodded. "I have read it."

"Well, Mr. Wolfe, I—that is, we, the family—must ask you to disregard that advertisement."

Wolfe breathed and let his chin down. "An extraordinary request, Miss Barstow. Am I supposed to be as extraordinary in granting it, or do I get reasons?"

"There are reasons of course." She hesitated. "It is not a family secret, it is known that my mother is—in some degree and on various occasions—irresponsible." Her eyes were earnest on him. "You must not think there is anything ugly about this or that it has anything to do with money. There is plenty of money and my brother and I are not niggardly. Nor must you think that my mother is not a competent person— certainly not in the legal sense. But for years there have been times when she needed our attention and love, and this—this terrible thing has come in the middle of one of them. She is not normally vengeful, but that advertisement—my brother calls it a demand for blood. Our close friends will of course understand, but there is the world, and my father—my father's world was a wide one—we are glad if they help us mourn for him but we would not want them—Father would not want them—to watch us urging on the bloodhounds—"

She gave a little gasp and stopped, and glanced at me and back at Wolfe. He said, "Yes, Miss Barstow, you are calling me a bloodhound. I am not offended. Go on."

"I'm sorry. I'm a tactless fool. It would have been better if Dr. Bradford had come."

"Was Dr. Bradford considering the enterprise?"

"Yes. That is, he thought it should be done."

"And your brother?"

"Well—yes. My brother greatly regrets it, the advertisement I mean. He did not fully approve of my coming to see you. He thought it would be—fruitless."

"On the theory that it is difficult to call off a bloodhound. Probably he understands dogs. Have you finished, Miss Barstow? I mean, have you any further reasons to advance?"

She shook her head. "Surely, Mr. Wolfe, those are sufficient."

"Then as I understand it, your desire is that no effort be made to discover and punish the persons who murdered your father?"

She stared at him. "Why—no. I didn't say that."

"The favor you ask of me is that I refrain from such an effort?"

Her lips closed. She opened them enough to say, "I see. You are putting it as badly as possible."

"Not at all. Clearly, not badly. Understandably, your mind is confused; mine is lucid. Your position as you have so far expressed it is simply not intelligent. You may make any one of several requests of me, but you may not ask them all at once, for they are mutually exclusive. You may, for instance, tell me that while you are willing that I should discover the murderer, you request me not to expect to be paid for it as your mother has offered. Is that your request?"

"It is not. You know it is not."

"Or you may tell me that I may find the murderer

if I can, and collect the reward if I choose to take advantage of the legal obligation, but that the family disapproves of the offer of reward on moral grounds. Is that it?"

"Yes." Her lip trembled a little, but in a moment she pulled it up firm. Then suddenly she stood up and shot at him: "No! I'm sorry I came here. Professor Gottlieb was wrong; you may be clever—good day, Mr. Wolfe."

"Good day, Miss Barstow." Wolfe was motionless. "The engineering considerations keep me in my chair."

She was going. But halfway to the door she faltered, stood a moment, and turned. "You *are* a bloodhound. You are. You are heartless."

"Quite likely." Wolfe crooked a finger. "Come back to your chair. Come, do; your errand is too important to let a momentary resentment ruin it. That's better; self-control is an admirable quality. Now, Miss Barstow, we can do one of two things: either I can flatly but gracefully refuse your original request as you made it and we can part on fairly bad terms; or you can answer a few questions I would like to ask and we can then decide what's to be done. Which shall it be?"

She was groggy, but game. She was back in her chair and had a wary eye on him. She said, "I have answered many questions in the past two days."

"I don't doubt it. I can imagine their tenor and their stupidity. I shall not waste your time or insult your intelligence. How did you learn that I knew anything of this business?"

She seemed surprised. "How did I learn it? Why, you are responsible for it. That is, you discovered it. Everyone knows it. It was in the paper—not New York, the White Plains paper."

I had a grin at that. Derwin would phone Ben Cook to come and assist me to the station, would he?

Wolfe nodded. "Have you asked the favor of Mr. Anderson that you have asked of me?"

"No."

"Why not?"

She hesitated. "Well—it didn't seem necessary. It didn't seem— I don't know how to express it."

"Use your wits, Miss Barstow. Was it because it appeared unlikely that he would do any discovering worthy the name?"

She was holding herself tight. Her hands—damn good hands with strong fingers and honest knuckles—were little fists in her lap. "No!" she said.

"Very well. But what made you think it likely, at least possible, that my discovering might be more to the point?"

She began, "I didn't think—" But he stopped her:

"Come, control yourself. It is an honest plain question. You did think me more competent at discovery than Mr. Anderson, did you not? Was it because I had made the original discovery?"

"Yes."

"That is, because I had somehow known that your father was killed by a poisoned needle propelled from the handle of a golf club?"

"I—don't—know. I don't know, Mr. Wolfe."

"Courage. This will soon be over. Curiosity alone prompts the next question. What gave you the strange idea that I was so rare a person as to respond favorably to the idiotic request you meant to make of me?"

"I didn't know. I didn't have that idea really. But I was ready to try, and I had heard a professor at the university, Gottlieb, the psychologist, mention your name—he had written a book called *Modern Crime Detection*—"

"Yes. A book that an intelligent criminal should send as a gift to every detective he knows."

"Perhaps. His opinion of you is more complimentary. When I telephoned Professor Gottlieb he said that you were not susceptible of analysis because you had intuition from the devil, and that you were a sensitive artist as well as a man of probity. That sounded—well, I decided to come to see you. Mr. Wolfe, I beg you—I beg of you—"

I was sure she was going to cry and I didn't want her to. But Wolfe brusquely brought her up:

"That's all, Miss Barstow. That is all I need to know. Now I shall ask a favor of you: will you permit Mr. Goodwin to take you upstairs and show you my plants?"

She stared; he went on, "No subterfuge is intended. I merely wish to be alone with the devil. Half an hour perhaps; and to make a telephone call. When you return I shall have a proposal for you." He turned to me. "Fritz will call you."

She got up and came with me without a word. I thought that was pretty good, for she was shaky and suspicious all over. Instead of asking her to walk up two flights of stairs I took her down the hall and used Wolfe's elevator. As we got out on the top floor she stopped me by catching my arm.

"Mr. Goodwin. Why did Mr. Wolfe send me up here?"

I shook my head. "No good, Miss Barstow. Even if I knew I wouldn't tell you, and since I don't know we might as well look at the flowers." As I opened the door to the passage Horstmann appeared from the potting room. "All right, Horstmann. May we look around a little?" He nodded and trotted back.

As many times as I had been there, I never went in the plant-rooms without catching my breath. It was like other things I've noticed, for instance no matter how often you may have seen Snyder leap in the air and one-handed spear a hot liner like one streak of lightning stopping another one, when you see it again your heart stops. It was that way in the plant-rooms.

Wolfe used concrete benches and angle-iron staging, with a spraying system Horstmann had invented for humidity. There were three main rooms, one for Cattleyas Laelias and hybrids, one for Odontoglossums, Oncidiums and Miltonia hybrids, and the tropical room. Then there was the potting room, Horstmann's den, and a little corner room for propagation. Supplies-pots, sand, sphagnum, leafmold, loam, osmundine, charcoal, and crocks were kept in an unheated and unglazed room in the rear alongside the shaft where the outside elevator came up.

Since it was June the lath screens were on, and the slices of shade and sunshine made patterns everywhere—on the broad leaves, the blossoms, the narrow walks, the ten thousand pots. I liked it that way, it seemed gay.

It was a lesson to watch the flowers get Miss Barstow. Of course when she went in she felt about as much like looking at flowers as I did like disregarding her mother's ad, and down the first rows of Cattleyas she tried to be polite enough to pretend there was something there to see. The first one that really brought her up was a small side-bunch, only twenty or so, of Laeliocattleya Lustre. I was pleased because it was one of my favorites. I stopped behind her.

"Astonishing," she said. "I've never seen one like that. The colors—amazing."

"Yes. It's a bigeneric hybrid, they don't come in nature like that."

She got interested. In the next walk were some Brassocattlaelias Truffautianas and I cut off a couple and handed them to her. I told her a little about hybridization and seedlings and so on, but maybe she didn't hear me. Then, in the next room, I had a disappointment. She liked the Odontoglossums better than the Cattleyas and hybrids! I suspected it was because they were more expensive and difficult, but it turned out that she hadn't known that. No accounting for tastes, I thought. And best of all, even after we had been through the tropical room, she liked a little thing I had never looked at twice, a Miltonia bluea-naeximina. She talked about its delicacy and form. I nodded and began to lose interest, and anyway I was wondering what Wolfe was up to. Then at last Fritz appeared. He came down the walk clear up to us and bent himself at the middle and said that Mr. Wolfe expected us. I grinned and would have liked to dig him in the ribs as I went by, but I knew he'd never forgive me.

Wolfe was still in his chair, and there was no indication that he had been out of it. He nodded at Miss Barstow's chair and at mine, and waited till we were arranged to say:

"You liked the flowers?"

"They are wonderful." She had a new eye on him, I could see that. "They are too much beauty."

Wolfe nodded. "At first, yes. But a long intimacy frees you of that illusion, and it also acquaints you with their scantiness of character. The effect they have produced on you is only their bluff. There is not such a thing as too much beauty."

"Perhaps." She had lost interest in the orchids. "Yes, perhaps."

"Anyway they passed your time. And of course you would like to know how I passed mine. First I telephoned my bank and asked them to procure immediately a report on the financial standing of Ellen Barstow, your mother, and the details of the will of Peter Oliver Barstow, your father. I then telephoned Dr. Bradford and endeavored to persuade him to call on me this afternoon or evening, but he will be otherwise engaged. I then sat and waited. Five minutes ago my bank telephoned me the report I had requested. I sent Fritz for you. Those were my activities."

She was getting worked up again. Her lips were getting tight. Apparently she didn't intend to open them.

He went on. "I said I would have a proposal for you. Here it is. Your notebook, Archie. Verbatim, please. I shall use my best efforts to find the murderer of Peter Oliver Barstow. I shall disclose the result of my efforts to you, Sarah Barstow, and if you interpose no objection I shall also disclose them to the proper public authorities, and at the proper time shall expect a check for the sum your mother has offered as a reward. But if my inquiries lead to the conclusion that the murderer is actually the person you fear it is, whom you are now endeavoring to shield from justice, there will be no further disclosure. Mr. Goodwin and I will know; no one else ever will. Just a moment! This is a speech, Miss Barstow; please hear all of it. Two more points. You must understand that I can make this proposal with propriety. I am not a public servant, I am not even a member of the bar, and I have sworn to uphold no law. The dangerous position of an accessory after the fact does not impress me. Then: if your fears prove to be justified, and I withhold disclosure, what of the reward? I find I am too sentimental and romantic to make it part of this proposal that under those circumstances the reward shall be paid. The word blackmail actually strikes me as unpleasant. But though I am handicapped by romance and sentiment, at least I have not pride further to hamper me, and if you should choose to present a gift it would be accepted.—Read it aloud, Archie, to make sure it is understood."

Miss Barstow's voice was first: "But this—it's absurd! It—"

Wolfe wiggled a finger at her. "Don't. Please. You would deny that you came here with that nonsense to shield someone? Miss Barstow! Really now. Let us keep this on a decent level of intelligence. Read it, Archie."

I read it through from my notes. When I had finished Wolfe said, "I advise you to take it, Miss Barstow. I shall proceed with my inquiry in any event, and if the result is what you fear it would be convenient for you to have the protection I offer. The offer, by the way, is purely selfish. With this agreement I shall expect your interest and co-operation, since it would be well for you, no matter what the outcome, to get it over with as speedily as possible; without it I shall expect considerable obstruction. I am no altruist or *bon enfant*, I am merely a man who would like to make some money. You said there was too much beauty upstairs; no, but there is too much expense. Have you any idea what it costs to grow orchids like that?"

Sarah Barstow only stared at him.

"Come," Wolfe said. "There will of course be no signing. This is what is humorously called a gentlemen's agreement. The first step in fulfilling it will be for Mr. Goodwin to call at your home tomorrow morning—it can wait till then—to talk, with your permission, with yourself and your brother and mother and whosoever—"

"No!" she exploded. Then she shut up.

"But yes. I'm sorry, but it is essential. Mr. Goodwin is a man of discretion, common decency, and immeasurable valor. It really is essential.—I'll tell you what, Miss Barstow." He put his hands on the edge of the desk and shoved his chair back, moved his hands to the arms of the chair and got himself to his feet, and stood in front of her. "You go on home, or about your errands, whatever they may be. People often find it difficult to think in my presence, I do not leave enough space. I know you are suffering, your emotions are tormenting you with their unbearable clamor, but you must free your mind to do its work. Go. Buy hats, or keep a rendezvous, or attend to your mother, whatever you may have in mind. Telephone me this evening between six and seven and tell me what time Mr. Goodwin may arrive in the morning, or tell me that he is not to come and we are enemies. Go."

She stood up. "Well—I don't know—my God, I don't know—"

"Please! That is not your mind speaking, it's the foam of churned feelings and has no meaning. I do not wish to be your enemy."

She was right in front of him, facing him, with her chin tilted up so that her eyes could be on his. "I believe you," she said. "I really believe you don't."

"Indeed, I do not. Good day, Miss Barstow."

"Good day, Mr. Wolfe."

I took her to the front door and let her out. I thought she might have handed me a good day too, but she didn't. She didn't say anything. As she went out I saw her car at the curb, a dark blue coupé.

Back in the office, Wolfe was in his chair again. I stood on the other side of the desk looking at him.

"Well," I said, "what do you know about that?"

His cheeks folded. "I know I'm hungry, Archie. It is pleasant to have an appetite again. I've had none for weeks."

Naturally I was indignant; I stared at him. "You can say that, after Friday and Saturday and Sunday—"

"But no appetite. A desperate search for one. Now I'm hungry. Lunch will be in twenty minutes. Meantime: I have learned that there is a person attached to a golf club called a professional. Find out who fills that post at the Green Meadow Club; see if we have any grateful client who might introduce us on the telephone; invite the professional, urgently, to dine with us this evening. There is a goose left from Saturday. After lunch you will pay a visit to the office of Dr. Nathaniel Bradford, and stop at the library for some books I need."

"Yes, sir. Who do you think Miss Barstow—"

"Not now, Archie. I would prefer just to sit here quietly and be hungry. After lunch."

# Chapter 8

At ten o'clock Tuesday morning, June 13, I drove the roadster through the entrance gate of the Barstow place, after it had been opened for me by a state trooper who was there on guard. Another husky was with him, a private watchman of the Barstows', and I had to furnish plenty of proof that I was the Archie Goodwin Sarah Barstow was expecting. It looked likely that many a newspaper man had been sent to climb a tree around there in the past three days.

The house was at the low point of a saddle between two hills about seven miles northeast of Pleasantville. It was built of stone, quite large, well over twenty rooms I should say, and there were a lot of outbuildings. After going through about three hundred yards of trees and shrubbery the drive circled around the edge of an immense sloping lawn and entered under the shelter of a roof with two steps up to a flagged terrace. This was really the side of the house; the front was around the corner looking over the lawn down the hill. There were gardens ahead as you entered, and more gardens at the other edge of the lawn, with boulders and a pool. As I eased the roadster along taking it in I thought to myself that fifty grand was nothing. I had on a dark blue suit, with a blue shirt and a tan tie, and of course my panama which I had had cleaned right after Decoration Day. I've found it's a good idea to consider what kind of place you're going to, and dress accordingly.

Sarah Barstow was expecting me at ten, and I was right on the dot. I parked the roadster in a graveled space the other side of the entrance, and pushed the button at the door on the terrace. It was standing open, but double screen doors kept me from seeing much inside. Soon there were footsteps and one of the screens came out at me and with it a tall skinny guy in a black suit.

He was polite. "If you will excuse me, sir. Mr. Goodwin?"

I nodded. "Miss Barstow expects me."

"I know. If you will come this way. Miss Barstow would like you to join her in the garden."

I followed him across the terrace and along a walk to the other side of the house, then down an arbor and among a lot of shubbery till we came to an acre of flowers. Miss Barstow was on a shady bench over in a corner.

"All right," I said. "I see her."

He stopped, inclined his head, and turned and went back.

She looked bad, worse than she had the day before. She probably hadn't slept much. Forgetting or disregarding Wolfe's instructions on that detail, she had telephoned before six o'clock. I had taken the call, and her voice had sounded as if she was having a hard time of it. She had been short and businesslike, just said she would expect me at ten in the morning and hung up.

She invited me to sit beside her on the bench.

At bedtime the evening before Wolfe had given me no instructions whatever. Saying that he preferred to leave me fancy free, he had merely repeated his favorite saying, any spoke will lead an ant to the hub, and had reminded me that our great advantage lay in the fact that no one was aware how much or how little we knew and that on account of our original coup we were suspected of omniscience. He had finished, after a yawn that would have held a tennis ball: "Return here with that advantage unimpaired."

I said to Miss Barstow, "You may not have any orchids here, but you certainly have a flower or two."

She said, "Yes, I suppose so.—I asked Small to bring you out here because I thought we should not be interrupted. You will not mind."

"No indeed. It's nice out here. I'm sorry to have to pester you, but there's no other way to get the facts. Wolfe says that he feels phenomena and I collect facts. I don't think that means anything, having looked up the word phenomena in the dictionary, but I repeat it for what it's worth." I took out my notebook. "First just tell me things. You know, the family, how old are you, who you're going to marry and so on."

She sat with her hands together in her lap and told me. Some of it I had read in the papers or got out of *Who's Who*, but I didn't interrupt. There was only her mother, her brother and herself. Lawrence, her brother, was twenty-seven, two years older than her; he had graduated from Holland at twenty-one and had then proceeded to waste five years (and, I gathered between the lines, a good portion of his father's time and patience also). A year ago he had suddenly discovered a talent for mechanical design and was now devoted to that, especially as applied to airplanes. Her

mother and father had been mutually devoted for
thirty years. She could not remember the beginning of
her mother's difficulty, for that had been years before
when Sarah was a child; the family had never considered it a thing to be ashamed of or to attempt to
conceal, merely a misfortune of a loved one to sympathize with and as far as possible to ameliorate. Dr.
Bradford and two specialists described it in neurological terms, but they had never meant anything to
Sarah, to her the terms had been dead and cold and
her mother was alive and warm.

The place in Westchester was the old Barstow
family estate, but the family was able to be there less
than three months of the year since it was necessary
to live at the university from September to June. They
came each summer for ten or eleven weeks with the
servants, and closed the place up each fall on leaving.
They knew many people in the surrounding countryside; her father's circle of acquaintance had of course
been wide not only in Westchester, and some of his
best and oldest friends lived within easy driving
distance from the estate. She gave the names of these
and I took them down. I also listed the names of the
servants and details regarding them. I was doing that
when Miss Barstow suddenly got up from the bench
and moved away to the path in the sunshine, from
under the shelter of the trees that shaded us. There
was the sound of an airplane overhead, so close that it
had forced us to raise our voices. I went on writing,
"—Finnish, 6 yrs, NY agcy, sgl," and then looked at
her. Her head was way back showing all her throat,
with her gaze straight above, and one arm was up
waving a handkerchief back and forth. I jumped out
from under the trees and cocked an eye at the airplane. It was right over us, down low, and two arms

could be seen extended, one from one side and one from the other, waving back at her. The plane dipped a little, then swung around and headed back, and soon was out of sight behind the trees. She went back to the bench and I joined her; she was saying:

"That was my brother. This is the first time he has been up since my father—"

"He must be pretty reckless, and he certainly has long arms."

"He doesn't fly; at least, not solo. That was Manuel Kimball with him, it's Mr. Kimball's plane."

"Oh. One of the foursome."

"Yes."

I nodded and went back to facts. I was ready for golf. Peter Oliver Barstow had not been a zealot, she said. He had rarely played at the university, and not oftener than once a week, occasionally twice, during the summer. He had nearly always gone to Green Meadow, where he was a member; he of course had had a locker and kept his paraphernalia there. He had been quite good, considering the infrequency of his play, averaging from ninety-five to a hundred. He had played usually with friends his own age, but sometimes with his son and daughter. His wife had never tried it. The foursome of that fatal Sunday, E. D. Kimball and his son Manuel and Barstow and his son Lawrence, had never before played together, she thought. Probably it had been an accident of propinquity; her brother had not mentioned whether it had been prearranged, but she knew that he did sometimes have a game with Manuel. She especially doubted that the foursome had been arranged beforehand because it had been her father's first appearance at Green Meadow that summer; the Barstows had come to Westchester three weeks earlier than their

custom on account of Mrs. Barstow's condition, and
Barstow had expected to return to the university that
Sunday night.

When she had said that Sarah Barstow stopped. I
glanced up from my notebook. Her fingers were
twisted together and she was staring off at the path,
at nothing. She said, not to me, "Now he will not
return there at all. All the things he wanted to do—all
he would have done—not at all—"

I waited a little and then shook her out of it by
asking, "Did your father leave his golf bag at Green
Meadow all year?"

She turned back to me. "No. Why—of course not,
because he sometimes used them at the university."

"He had only the one bag of clubs?"

"Yes!" She seemed emphatic.

"Then he brought them with him? You only got
here Saturday noon. You drove down from the university and the luggage followed in a truck. Was the bag
in the car or in the truck?"

It was easy to see that I was touching something
raw. Her throat showed muscles and her arms pressed
ever so little against her sides; she was tightening up.
I pretended I didn't notice it, just waited with my
pencil. She said, "I don't know. Really I don't remember."

"Probably in the truck," I said. "Since he wasn't
much of a fan he probably wouldn't bother with it in
the car. Where is it now?"

I expected that would tighten her up some more,
but it didn't. She was calm but a little determined. "I
don't know that either. I supposed you knew it can't be
found."

"Oh," I said. "The golf bag can't be found?"

"No. The men from White Plains and Pleasantville

have searched everywhere, this whole house, the club, even all over the links; they can't find it."

Yes, I thought to myself, and you, young lady, you're damn well pleased they can't! I said, "Do you mean to say that no one remembers anything about it?"

"No. That is, yes." She hesitated. "I understand that the boy who was caddying for Father says that he put the bag in the car, by the driver's seat, when they—when Larry and Dr. Bradford brought Father home. Larry and Dr. Bradford do not remember seeing it."

"Strange. I know I am not here to collect opinions, only facts, Miss Barstow, but if you will permit me, doesn't that strike you as strange?"

"Not at all. They were not likely to notice a golf bag at such a time."

"But after they got here—it must have been removed sometime—some servant, the chauffeur—"

"No one remembers it."

"I may speak with them?"

"Certainly." She was scornful. I didn't know what kind of a career she had mapped out, but I could have warned her not to try the stage.

That was that. It looked to me as if the kernel was gone, leaving practically no nut at all. I switched on her.

"What kind of a driver did your father use? Steel shaft or wooden?"

"Wood. He didn't like steel."

"Face plain or inset?"

"Plain, I think. I think so. I'm not sure I remember. Larry's has an inset, so has mine."

"You seem to remember your brother's all right."

"Yes." Her eyes were level at me. "This is not an inquisition, I believe, Mr. Goodwin."

"Pardon." I grinned at her. "Excuse it please, I'm upset. Maybe I'm even sore. There's nothing in West-chester County I'd rather look at than that golf bag, especially the driver."

"I'm sorry."

"Oh no, you're not. It raises a lot of questions. Who took the bag out of the car? If it was a servant, which one, and how loyal and incorruptible is he? Five days later, when it became known that one of the clubs had performed the murder it had been designed for, who got the bag and hid it or destroyed it? You or your brother or Dr. Bradford? You see the questions I'm up against. And where is it hid or how was it destroyed? It isn't easy to get rid of a thing as big as that."

She had got up while I was talking and stood very composed and dignified. Her voice was composed too. "That will do. It wasn't in the agreement that I was to listen to idiotic insinuations."

"Bravo, Miss Barstow." I stood up too. "You're absolutely right, but I meant no offense, I'm just upset. Now, if I could see your mother for a moment. I'll not get upset any more."

"No. You can't see her."

"That *was* in the agreement."

"You have broken it."

"Rubbish." I grinned. "It's the agreement that makes it safe for you to let me take liberties with it. I'll take no liberties with your mother. While I may be a roughneck, I know when to keep my gloves on."

She looked at me. "Will five minutes be enough?"

"I don't know. I'll make it as short as possible."

She turned and started for the path that led toward the house, and I followed her. On the way I

saw a lot of pebbles I wanted to kick. The missing golf
bag was a hot one. Of course I hadn't expected to
have the satisfaction of taking that driver back to
Wolfe that evening, since Anderson would certainly
have copped it. I gave him credit for being able to put
two and two together after they have been set down
for him ready to add; and I had counted on a request
from Sarah Barstow to persuade him to let me give it
the once over. But now—the whole damn bag was
gone! Whoever had done it, it not only gave me a pain,
it struck me as pretty dumb. If it had been just the
driver it would have made sense, but why the whole
bag?

The house inside was swell. I mean, it was the kind
of a house most people never see except in the movies.
While there were plenty of windows, the light didn't
glare anywhere, it came in soft, and the rugs and
furniture looked very clean and careful and expensive.
There were flowers around and it smelled good and
seemed cool and pleasant, for outdoors the sun was
getting hot. Sarah Barstow took me through a big hall
and a big room through to another hall, and on the
other side of that through a door. Then we were in a
sort of sun-room, with one side all glazed, though most
of the blinds were pulled down nearly to the floor so
there wasn't much sunshine coming in. There were
some plants, and a lot of wicker chairs and lounges. In
one chair a woman sat by a table sorting out the pieces
of a jigsaw puzzle. Miss Barstow went over to her.

"Mother. This is Mr. Goodwin. I told you he was
coming." She turned to me and indicated a chair. I
took it. Mrs. Barstow let the jigsaw pieces drop from
her fingers and turned to look at me.

She was very handsome. She was fifty-six, her
daughter had told me, but she looked over sixty. Her

eyes were gray, deep-set and far apart, her hair was
nearly white, and while her face with its fine features
was quite composed, I got the impression that there
was nothing easy or natural about that, it came from
the force of a strong personal will. She kept looking at
me without saying anything until I was guessing that
I didn't look very composed myself. Sarah Barstow
had taken a chair some distance away. I was about
ready to open up from my end when Mrs. Barstow
suddenly spoke:

"I know your business, Mr. Goodwin."

I nodded. "It really isn't my business, it is that of
my employer, Mr. Nero Wolfe. He asked me to thank
you for permitting me to come."

"He is welcome." The deep-set gray eyes never left
me. "Indeed, I am grateful that someone—even a
stranger whom I shall never see—should acknowledge
my authority over the doors of my house."

"Mother!"

"Yes, Sarah. Don't be offended, dear; I know—and
it is of no importance whether this Mr. Goodwin does
or not—that the authority has not been usurped. It
was not you who forced me to resign, it was not even
your father. According to Than, it was God; probably
His hands were idle and Satan furnished the mischief."

"Mother, please." Sarah Barstow had got up and
approached us. "If you have anything to ask, Mr.
Goodwin—"

I said, "I have two questions. May I ask you two
questions, Mrs. Barstow?"

"Certainly. That is your business."

"Good. The first one is easy to ask, but may be
hard to answer. That is, it may require thought and a
long memory. Of all people, you are the one probably
in the best position to answer. Who wanted, or might

have wanted to kill Peter Oliver Barstow? Who had a
grievance against him, a new one or maybe a very old
one? What enemies did he have? Who hated him?"

"That isn't a question. It is four questions."

"Well—maybe I can hitch them together."

"It isn't necessary." The composure did not escape
from the will. "They can all be answered at once.
Myself."

I stared at her. Her daughter was beside her with
a hand on her shoulder.

"Mother! You promised me—"

"There, Sarah." Mrs. Barstow reached up and
patted her daughter's hand. "You have not permitted
those other men to see me, for which I have been
thankful. But if Mr. Goodwin is to ask me questions he
must have the answers. You remember what your
father used to say? *Never lay an ambush for truth.*"

Miss Barstow was at me. "Mr. Goodwin! Please!"

"Nonsense." The gray eyes were flashing. "I have
my own security, daughter, as good as any you might
provide for me. Mr. Goodwin, I have answered your
first question. The second?"

"Don't rush me, Mrs. Barstow." I saw that if I just
pretended Sarah Barstow wasn't there, Old Gray
Eyes would be right with me. "I'm not done with the
first one. There may have been others, maybe you
weren't the only one."

"Others who might have wanted to kill my husband?" For the first time the will relaxed enough to let
the twitch of a smile show on the lips. "No. That is
impossible. My husband was a good, just, merciful and
well-loved man. I see what you would have me do, Mr.
Goodwin: look back over all the years, the happy ones
and the miserable ones, and pick out of memory for
you a remorseless wrong or a sinister threat. I assure

you it isn't there. There is no man living my husband
wronged, and none his enemy. Nor woman either. He
did not wrong me. My answer to your question was
direct and honest and was a relief to me, but since you
are so young, not much more than a boy, it probably
shocked you as it did my daughter. I would explain the
answer if I could. I do not wish to mislead you. I do not
wish to give pain to my daughter. When God compelled me to resign my authority He did not stop
there. If by any chance you understand Him, you
understand my answer too."

"All right, Mrs. Barstow. Then the second question: why did you offer a reward?"

"No!" Sarah Barstow stood between us. "No! No
more of this—"

"Sarah!" The voice was sharp; then it softened a
little: "Sarah dear. I *will* answer. This is my share.
Will you stand between us? Sarah!"

Sarah Barstow went to her mother's side, placed
her arm across her mother's shoulders, and lowered
her forehead onto the gray hair.

The will re-created the composure. "Yes, Mr.
Goodwin, the reward. I am not insane, I am only
fantastic. I now greatly regret that the reward was
offered, for I see its sordidness. It was in a fantastic
moment that I conceived the idea of a unique vengeance. No one could have murdered my husband
since no one could have wanted to. I am certain that
his death has never seemed desirable to any person
except myself, and to me only during torments which
God should never impose even on the guiltiest. It
came to me that there might be somewhere a man
clever enough to bring God Himself to justice. I doubt
if it is you, Mr. Goodwin; I do not know your em-

ployer. I now regret that I offered the reward, but if it is earned it will be paid."

"Thank you, Mrs. Barstow. Who is Than?"

"Sir?"

"Than. You said that Than told you God forced you to resign your authority."

"Oh. Of course. Dr. Nathaniel Bradford."

"Thank you." I closed my notebook and got up. "Mr. Wolfe asked me to thank you for your forbearance; I guess he knew there would be some if I got started filling up my notebook."

"Tell Mr. Wolfe he is welcome."

I turned and went on out, figuring that Miss Barstow could use my room for a while.

# Chapter 9

Miss Barstow invited me to lunch.

I liked her better than ever. For ten minutes or more I waited for her in the hall which connected the sun-room with other apartments. When she joined me there she wasn't sore, and I could see why: I hadn't pulled Mrs. Barstow's leg for any of that stuff, she had just handed it to me on a platter, and that wasn't my fault. But how many people in Sarah Barstow's place would have stopped to consider that? Not one in a thousand. They would have been sore anyhow, even if they had realized I didn't deserve it and tried not to show it; but she just wasn't sore. She had made a bargain and she was going through with it, no matter how many sleepless nights it brought her and no matter how many kinds of bad luck she had. She certainly had just had some. I could see that ten minutes earlier or ten minutes later Mrs. Barstow might have had different ideas in her head and all I would have got out of it would have been to exchange the time of day with a polite calm. I had no idea what it was that had happened to make her feel like opening up, but if it was my blue shirt and tan tie I hadn't wasted the money I had spent on them.

As Paul Panzer would have said, lovin' babe!

She invited me to lunch. She said her brother would be present, and since I would want to see him anyway that would be convenient. I thanked her. I said, "You're a good sport, Miss Barstow. A real one. Thank the Lord Nero Wolfe is the cleverest man on earth and thought up that agreement with you, because if you're in for trouble that's the only thing that will help you out of it."

"If I'm in trouble," she said.

I nodded. "Sure, I know you've got plenty, but the one that bothers you most is your fear that there's worse ahead. I just wanted to say that you're a good sport."

As it turned out, I not only met her brother at lunch, I met Manuel Kimball too. I was glad of that, for it seemed to me that what I had learned that morning made the members of that foursome more important than they had been before. The preceding afternoon after about two hours of telephoning, I had finally found a hook-up with the professional of the Green Meadow Club and he had accepted Wolfe's invitation to dinner. He had never had any dealings with Barstow, had only known him by sight, but Wolfe had got out of him twenty bushels of facts regarding the general set-up at the club and around the links. By the time the professional left to go home around midnight he had a bottle of Wolfe's best port inside of him, and Wolfe knew as much about a golf club as if he had been a professional himself. Among other things he learned that the members kept their bags in their lockers, that some of them left their lockers unlocked, and that even with the locked ones an ingenious and determined man could have got a duplicate without any great difficulty. With such a key, of course, it would have been simple to await a propitious moment to open the locker, take the driver from the bag and substitute another one. So Barstow's companions in the foursome that Sunday were of no more importance than any of the members or attendants or visitors who had access to the locker rooms.

But now that was out, since Barstow's bag had not been in his locker since the September before. He had brought it down with him from the university. That changed the picture and made the members of the foursome a little more interesting than lots of other people.

Where we ate surely wasn't the dining room because it wasn't big enough, but it had a table and chairs and windows that you couldn't see much through on account of a lot of shrubbery just outside. The tall skinny guy in the black suit—otherwise Small, the butler, as an established guest like myself was aware—waited on us, and while the meal seemed to me a little light it was nothing that Fritz would have been ashamed of. There was some stuff in tambour shells that was first class. The table was small. I sat across from Miss Barstow, with her brother on my right and Manuel Kimball on my left.

Lawrence Barstow didn't resemble his sister any, but I could see traces of his mother. He was well put together and had the assurance that goes with his kind of life; his features were good and regular without anything noticeable about them. I've seen hundreds of him in the lunch restaurants in the Wall Street section and in the Forties. He had a trick of squinting when he decided to look at you, but I thought that was perhaps due to the blowing his eyes had got in the airplane breeze. The eyes were gray, like his mother's, but they didn't have the discipline behind them that hers had.

Manuel Kimball was quite different. He was dark and very neat and compact, with black hair brushed straight back and black restless eyes that kept darting around at us and seemed to find any degree of satisfaction or repose only when they were looking at Sarah Barstow. He made me nervous, and it seemed to me that he set Sarah Barstow a little on edge too, though that may have been only because he didn't know where I came in on the family crisis and wasn't supposed to know. That morning she had informed me that there had been no intimacy between the Kimballs and Barstows; the only points of contact had been propinquity in their summer residences and the fact that Manuel was a skilled amateur pilot and his offers to take Larry Barstow up and teach him to fly had been most convenient since Larry had developed an interest in airplane design. She herself had been up with Manuel Kimball two or three times the summer before, but aside from those occasions she had scarcely ever seen him except as the companion of her brother. The Kimballs were newcomers, having bought their place, two miles south, only three years previously. E. D. Kimball, Manuel's father, was known to the Barstows only slightly, through chance and infrequent meetings at large social or public gatherings. Manuel's mother was dead, long since, she had vaguely gathered. She could not remember that there had ever been more than a few casual words exchanged between her father and Manuel Kimball except one afternoon the preceding summer when Larry had brought Manuel to the Barstow place to settle a wager at tennis, and she and her father had acted as umpire and linesman.

In spite of which, I was interested in Manuel Kimball. He had at any rate been one of the foursome; and he looked like a foreigner and had a funny combination for a name, and he made me nervous.

At lunch the conversation was mostly about airplanes. Sarah Barstow kept it on that, when there was any sign of lagging, and once or twice when her brother started questions on affairs closer to her bosom she abruptly headed him off. I just ate. When Miss Barstow finally pushed her chair back, punching Small in the belly with it, we all stood up. Larry Barstow addressed me directly almost for the first time; I had seen indications of his idea that I might as well have been eating out back somewhere.

"You want to see me?"

I nodded. "If you can spare a quarter of an hour."

He turned to Manuel Kimball. "If you don't mind waiting, Manny. I promised Sis I'd have a talk with this man."

"Of course." The other's eyes darted to rest on Sarah Barstow. "Perhaps Miss Barstow would be kind enough to help me wait."

She said yes, without enthusiasm. But I got a word in: "I'm sorry." To Miss Barstow, "May I remind you that you agreed to be present with your brother?" It hadn't been mentioned, but I had taken it for granted, and I wanted her there.

"Oh." I thought she looked relieved. "Yes. I'm sorry, Mr. Kimball; shall we leave you here with the coffee?"

"No, thanks." He bowed to her and turned to Larry. "I'll trot along and have a look at that gas line. If one of your cars can run me over? Thanks. I'll be expecting you at the hangar any time— Thank you for a pleasant luncheon, Miss Barstow."

One thing that had surprised me about him was his voice. I had expected him, on sight, to sound like a tenor, but the effect he produced was more like that of a murmuring bull. The voice was deep and had a rumble in it, but he kept it low and quite pleasant. Larry Barstow went out with him to tell someone to take him home. His sister and I waited for Larry to come back, and then all three of us went out to the garden, to the bench where I had been taken on my arrival. Larry sat at one side on the grass, and Miss Barstow and I on the bench.

I explained that I wanted Miss Barstow present because she had made the agreement with Nero Wolfe and I wanted her to be satisfied that nothing was said or done that went beyond the agreement. I had certain things I wanted to ask Lawrence Barstow and if there was any question about my being entitled to answers she was the one to question it.

She said, "Very well, I'm here." She looked about played out. In the morning she had sat with her shoulders straight, but now she let them sag down.

Her brother said, "As far as I'm concerned—your name's Goodwin, isn't it?"

"That's it."

"Well, as far as I'm concerned, your agreement, as you call it, is nothing more than a piece of cheap insolence."

"Anything else, Mr. Barstow?"

"Yes. If you want it. Blackmail."

His sister had a flash left. "Larry! What did I tell you?"

"Wait a minute, Miss Barstow." I was flipping back the pages of my notebook. "Maybe your brother ought to hear it. I'll find it in a minute." I found the page. "Here it is." I read it just as Wolfe had said it, not too fast. Then I closed the notebook. "That's the agreement, Mr. Barstow. I might as well say that my employer, Mr. Nero Wolfe, keeps his temper pretty well under control, but every once in a while I blow up. If you call him a blackmailer once more the result will probably be bad all around. If you don't know a favor when you see it handed to you I suppose you'd think a sock on the jaw was a compliment."

He said, "Sis, you'd better go in the house."

"She can go in a minute," I said. "If the agreement is to go overboard she ought to see it sink. If you don't like it, why did you let her come to Wolfe's office alone to make it? He would have been glad to see you. He said to your sister, we shall proceed with the inquiry in any event. That's our business, not such a rotten one either, a few people think who have dealt with us. I say the same to you: agreement or no agreement, we're going to find out who murdered Peter Oliver Barstow. If you ask me, I think your sister made a swell bargain. If you don't think so there must be some reason, and that's one of the things we'll find out on the way."

"Larry," Miss Barstow said. Her voice was full of things. She repeated it. "Larry." She was telling him and asking him and reminding him all at the same time.

"Come on," I said. "You're all worked up and looking at me all through lunch didn't help you any, but if something goes wrong with your airplane you don't just kick and scream, do you? You pull your coat off and help fix it."

He sat looking not at me but his sister, with his

lower lip stuck up and pushed out so that he looked half like a baby about ready to cry and half like a man set to tell the world to go to hell.

"All right, Sis," he said finally. He showed no signs of apologizing to me, but I thought that could wait for a rainy day.

When I began feeding him questions he snapped out of it. He answered prompt and straight and, as far as I could see, without any figuring or hesitation anywhere. Even about the golf bag, where his sister had flopped around like a fish on a bank, it was all clear and ready with him. The bag had been brought down from the university on the truck; there had been no luggage with them in the car except one suitcase, his mother's. When the truck had arrived at the house about three o'clock in the afternoon its load had been removed and distributed at once; presumably the golf bag had been taken straight to his father's room, though he had no knowledge of that. At Sunday breakfast he and his father had arranged to play golf that afternoon . . .

"Who suggested it? You or your father?"

He couldn't remember. When his father had come downstairs after lunch he had had the bag under his arm. They had driven to the Green Meadow Club in the sedan, parked, and his father had gone straight to the first tee, carrying his bag, while Larry had gone around by the hut for caddies. Larry wasn't particular about his caddy, but there had been one the preceding summer that his father had taken a fancy to, and by chance that boy was there and Larry had taken him with another. On his way to the first tee Larry had fallen in with the Kimballs, also ready to tee off, and since he hadn't seen Manuel for some months and was eager to discuss plans for the summer he had asked them to make it a foursome, feeling sure his father wouldn't mind. When they had reached the tee his father had been off to one side, practicing with a mashie. Peter Oliver Barstow had been cordial with the Kimballs and had greeted his caddy with delight and sent him off to chase balls.

They had waited for two or three other matches to get started and had then teed off. Manuel Kimball had driven first, then Larry, then Barstow, and last the elder Kimball. Larry couldn't remember seeing his father take the driver from the bag or from his caddy; while they were waiting he had been busy talking with Manuel, and during the moments immediately preceding his father's drive Larry had been driving himself. But he remembered well his father's actual swing at the ball, on account of an unusual circumstance. At the end of the swing there had been a peculiar jerk of the club, and as the ball sailed away with a bad slice Barstow had made an exclamation, with a startled look on his face, and begun rubbing his belly. Larry had never seen his father so suddenly and completely abandon his accustomed dignity in public. They had asked him what was wrong, and he had said something about a wasp or a hornet and started to open his shirt. Larry had been impressed by his father's agitation and had looked inside his shirt at the skin. There had been a tiny puncture, almost invisible, and his father had regained his composure and insisted that it would be nothing. The elder Kimball had made his drive and they had proceeded down the fairway.

The rest had been detailed in the newspapers many times. Thirty minutes later, on the fairway of the fourth hole, Barstow had suddenly collapsed on the ground, kicking and clutching the grass. He had been still alive when his caddy seized his arm, but by the time the others reached him he was dead. A crowd had collected, among them Dr. Nathaniel Bradford, an old Barstow family friend. Manuel Kimball had gone for the sedan and driven it along the edge of the fairway to the scene. The body had been lifted into the back of the sedan, Dr. Bradford had sat on the seat holding the head of his old friend on his lap, and Larry had taken the wheel.

Larry could remember nothing of the golf bag. Absolutely nothing. He knew the caddy's story, that the bag had been placed in front leaning against the seat, but he could not remember seeing it there while driving or at any other time. He said that he had driven the six miles slowly and carefully, and that later, after getting home, he had found blood all along his lower lip where he had bit it. He was a better liar than his sister. If it had not been for her give-away I might have been fooled by his tale as he told it. I went after him from every angle I could think of, but he didn't leak once.

I passed that up and asked him about the Kimballs. His story was the same as his sister's. There had been no contact to speak of between the families; the only connection had been himself and Manuel, and the basis of that was Manuel's convenience as owner and pilot of an airplane; Larry had intended to get one for himself as soon as he secured a license.

Then I asked the question that had started the fireworks with Mrs. Barstow before lunch. I asked both Larry and his sister, but not only was there no fireworks, there was nothing at all. They declared that they knew of no one who had a serious grievance against their father, or hatred or enmity for him, and that it was unthinkable that there ever should have been such a person. In his remarkable career—he had achieved the presidency of Holland University at forty-eight, ten years before—he had many times faced opposition, but he had always known the trick of melting it instead of crushing it. His private life had been confined to his own home. His son, I gathered, had had deep respect for him and a certain affection; his daughter had loved him. They agreed that no one could have hated him; and as his daughter told me that, knowing what I had heard from her mother's lips only three hours previously, her eyes challenged me and appealed to me at once.

Next Dr. Bradford, I turned to Miss Barstow on that instead of her brother. The way the thing seemed to be shaping up I expected some hesitation and covering, but there certainly was no sign of it. She told me, simply, that Bradford had been a schoolmate at college with her father, that they had always been close friends, and that Bradford, who was a widower, had been almost like one of the family, especially during the summer since he was then also a neighbor. He had been the family physician, and it was on him they had chiefly relied to remove Mrs. Barstow's difficulty, though he had called in specialists to assist.

I asked Sarah Barstow, "Do you like him?"

"Like him?"

"Yes. Do you like Dr. Bradford?"

"Certainly. He is one of the best and finest men I know."

I turned to her brother. "Do you like him, Mr. Barstow?"

Larry frowned. He was tired; he had been pretty patient; I had been after him for two hours. "I like him well enough. He's what my sister says all right, but he likes to preach. Not that he ever bothers me now, but when I was a kid I used to hide from him."

"You arrived here from the university Saturday noon. Was Dr. Bradford here between that hour and Sunday at two?"

"I don't know.—Oh yes, sure. He was here Saturday for dinner."

"Do you think there is any chance that he killed your father?"

Larry stared. "Oh, for God's sake. Is that supposed to shock me into something?"

"Do you, Miss Barstow?"

"Nonsense."

"All right, nonsense. Anyhow, who suggested first that Bradford should certify it as a heart stroke? Which one of you? Him?"

Larry glared at me. His sister said quietly, "You said you wanted me here to see the agreement was observed. Well, Mr. Goodwin. I've been—patient enough."

"Okay. I'll lay off of that." I turned to her brother. "You're sore again, Mr. Barstow. Forget it. People like you aren't used to impertinence, but you'd be surprised how easy it is to let it slide and no harm done. There's only a couple of things left. Where were you between seven o'clock and midnight on Monday evening, June fifth?"

He still glared. "I don't know. How do I know?"

"You can remember. This isn't another impertinence; I seriously request you to tell me. Monday, June fifth. Your father's funeral was on Tuesday. I'm asking about the evening before the funeral."

Miss Barstow said, "I can tell you."

"I'd rather he would, as a favor."

He did. "There's no reason I shouldn't. Or should either. I was here, at home."

"All evening?"

"Yes."

"Who else was here?"

"My mother and sister, the servants, and the Robertsons."

"The Robertsons?"

"I said so."

His sister spoke. "The Robertsons are old friends. Mr. and Mrs. Blair Robertson and two daughters."

"What time did they come?"

"Right after dinner. We hadn't finished. Around seven-thirty."

"Was Dr. Bradford here?"

"No."

"Wasn't that peculiar?"

"Peculiar? Why?—But yes, of course it was. He had to address a meeting in New York, some professional meeting."

"I see. Thank you, Miss Barstow." I turned back to her brother. "I have one more question. A request rather. Does Manuel Kimball have a telephone at his hangar?"

"Yes."

"Will you telephone him that I am coming to see him and that you would like him to give me an interview?"

"No. Why should I?"

Miss Barstow told me, "You have no right to ask it. If you wish to see Mr. Kimball that is your business."

"Correct." I closed my notebook and got up. "Positively correct. But I have no official standing in this affair. If I call on Manuel Kimball on my own he'll just kick me out on my own. He's a friend of the family, anyway he thinks so. I need an introduction."

"Sure you need it." Larry had got up too and was brushing grass from the seat of his trousers. "But you won't get it. Where's your hat, in the house?"

I nodded. "We can get it when you go in to telephone. Look here, it's like this. I've got to ask you to phone Manuel Kimball, and the Robertsons, and the Green Meadow Club. That's all I have on my mind at present but there may be more later. I've got to go around and see people and find out things, and the easier you make it for me the easier it will be for you. Nero Wolfe knew enough, and told the police enough, to make them dig up your father's body. That was a good deal, but he didn't tell them everything. Do you want to force me to go to the District Attorney and spill enough more beans so that he will give me a ticket that will let me in wherever I want to go? He's sore at us now because he knows we're holding out on him. I'd just as soon go and make a friend of him, I don't mind, I like to make friends. You folks certainly don't. If this strikes you as some more blackmail, Mr. Barstow, I'll just get my hat and call it a day as far as you're concerned."

It was a crime, but I had to do it. The trouble with those two, especially the brother, was that they were so used to being safe and independent and dignified all their lives that they kept forgetting how scared they were and had to be reminded. But they were plenty scared when it came to the point, and if I had cared to make them a present of all my ideas that afternoon I would have had to admit that it looked to me as if they had reason to be scared.

They gave in, of course. We went into the house together, and Sarah Barstow telephoned the Robert-

sons and her brother phoned the club and Manuel
Kimball. I had decided that there wasn't a chance in a
million that I would get anything out of any of the
servants, particularly if they had been trained by that
tall skinny butler, so as soon as the telephoning was
over I got my panama from the hall and beat it. Larry
Barstow went with me out to the side terrace, I
suppose to make sure that I didn't sneak back in and
listen at keyholes, and just as we came to the steps a
car rolled along the drive and stopped in front of us. A
man got out, and I had the pleasure of a good grin as
I saw it was H. R. Corbett, the dick from Anderson's
office who had tried to crash the gate at Wolfe's house
the morning I was acting as doorman. I passed him a
cheerful salute and was going on, but he called to me:

"Hey, you!"

I stopped and turned. Larry Barstow stood on the
terrace watching us. I said, "Did you address me, sir?"

Corbett was moving into my neighborhood. He
paid no attention to my fast one. "What the hell are
you doing here?"

I stood and grinned at him a second and then
turned to Larry Barstow on the terrace. "Since this is
your home, Mr. Barstow, maybe it would be better if
you would tell him what the hell I'm doing here."

It was plain from the look on Larry's face that
although he might never send me a Christmas card, I
would get one long before Corbett would. He said to
the dick, "Mr. Goodwin has been here at my sister's
invitation, to consult with us. He will probably be here
again. Would you like to investigate that?"

Corbett grunted and glared at me. "Maybe you'd
like a trip to White Plains."

"Not at all." I shook my head. "I don't like the
town, it's so slow you can't get a bet down." I started

to move off. "So long, Corbett. I don't wish you any bad luck, because even with good luck you won't have much of a tombstone."

Without bothering to think up an answer to the threats and warnings he tossed at my back, I went over to the roadster where it was parked, got in and turned around, and rolled off.

# Chapter 10

I went to the Robertsons' first, because I knew it wouldn't take long and I might as well get it done. Mrs. Robertson and both of the daughters were at home, and expecting me after Sarah Barstow's phone call. They said they had been at the Barstows' the evening of June fifth, the day before the funeral, arriving well before eight o'clock and leaving after midnight. They were certain that Larry and Sarah and Mrs. Barstow had been present the entire evening. I made sure there was no possibility of a mistake about the date, and then tried a few casual questions about the Barstow family but soon gave it up. The Robertsons weren't discussing their old friends that afternoon with a stranger; they wouldn't even let on that Mrs. Barstow was otherwise than completely all right, not award how much I knew.

I got to the Kimball place a little after five o'clock. It wasn't as dressed up as the Barstow estate, but was much larger; I drove over half a mile after I entered their private road. It was mostly on low ground, with some of the old stone fences still running through the meadows and a couple of brooks wandering around. Some woods were at the left. The house was on a knoll in a park of evergreens, with a well-kept lawn not very large and no sign of flowers that I could see as I drove up. Not as big as the Barstows', the house was brand-new, wood with panels and a high steep slate roof, one of the styles that I lumped all together and called Queen William.

Back of the house, over the knoll, was an immense flat meadow. I was sent in that direction, along a narrow graveled drive, by a fat man in a butler's uniform who came out of the house as I drove up. In the large meadow were no stone fences; it was level and clean and recently mowed and was certainly perfect for a private landing field. On the edge about halfway down its length was a low concrete building with a flat roof, and the graveled drive took me there. There was a wide and long concrete runway in front, and two cars were parked on it.

I found Manuel Kimball inside, washing his hands at a sink. The place was mostly full of airplane, a big one with black wings and a red body, sitting on its tail. In it tinkering with something was a man in overalls. Everything was neat and clean, with tools and oil cans and a lot of junk arranged on steel shelves that ran along one side. Beside the sink there was even a rack with three or four clean towels on it.

"My name's Goodwin," I said.

Kimball nodded. "Yes, I was expecting you. I'm through here for the day; we might as well go to the house and be comfortable." He spoke to the man in overalls. "Let that wait till tomorrow if you want to, Skinner, I won't be going up till afternoon." When he had finished wiping his hands he led me out and took his car, and I got in the roadster and drove back to the house.

He was decent and polite, no doubt about that,

even if he did look like a foreigner and had made me nervous at lunch. He took me into a large room in front and steered me to a big comfortable leather chair and told the fat butler to bring us some highballs. When he saw me looking around he said that the house had been furnished by his father and himself after their personal tastes, since there had been no women to consider and they both disliked decorators.

I nodded. "Miss Barstow told me your mother died a long time ago."

I said it casually, without thinking, but I always have my eye on whoever I'm talking to, and I was surprised at what went over his face. It was a spasm, you couldn't call it anything else. It only lasted a fraction of a second, but for that moment something was certainly hurting him inside. I didn't know whether it was just because I had mentioned his mother or he really had a pain; anyhow, I didn't try it again.

He said, "I understand that you are investigating the death of Miss Barstow's father."

"Yes. At her request, in a way. Larry Barstow's father too, and Mrs. Barstow's husband, at the same time."

He smiled and his black eyes swerved to me. "If that is your first question, Mr. Goodwin, it is neatly put. Bravo. The answer is no, I have no right to distinguish the dead man in that fashion. No right, that is, but my own inclination. I admire Miss Barstow—very much."

"Good. So do I. It wasn't a question, just a remark. What I really want to ask you about is what took place on the first tee that Sunday afternoon. I suppose you've told the story before."

"Yes. Twice to a detective whose name is Corbett, I believe, and once to Mr. Anderson."

"Then you ought to have it by heart. Would you mind telling it again?"

I sat back with my highball and listened without interrupting. I didn't use my notebook because I already had Larry's tale to check with and I could record any differences later. Manuel Kimball was precise and thorough. When he got through there was little left to ask, but there were one or two points I wasn't satisfied on, particularly one on which he differed from Larry. Manuel said that after Barstow thought a wasp had stung him he had dropped his driver on the ground and his caddy had picked it up; Larry had said that his father had hung onto the driver with one hand when he was opening his shirt to see what had happened to him. Manuel said he felt sure he was right but didn't insist on it if Larry remembered otherwise. It didn't seem of great importance, since the driver had in any event got back into the bag, and in all other respects Manuel's story tallied with Larry's.

Encouraged by his sending for more highballs, I spread the conversation out a little. He didn't seem to object. I learned that his father was a grain broker and went every day to his office in New York, on Pearl Street, and that he, Manuel, was considering the establishment of an airplane factory. He was, he said, a thoroughly skilled pilot, and he had spent a year at the Fackler works in Buffalo. His father had engaged to furnish the necessary capital, though he doubted the soundness of the venture and was entirely skeptical about airplanes. Manuel thought Larry Barstow showed promise of a real talent in structural design and hoped to be able to persuade him to take a share in the enterprise. He said:

"Naturally Larry is not himself just at present, and I'm not trying to rush him. No wonder, first his father's sudden death, and then the autopsy with its astonishing results.—By the way, Mr. Goodwin, of course everybody around here is wondering how Nero Wolfe—that's it, isn't it?—how he was able to predict those results in such remarkable detail. Anderson, the District Attorney, hints at his own sources of information—he did so to me the other day, sitting in the chair you're in now—but the truth of the matter is pretty generally known. At Green Meadow day before yesterday there were only two topics: who killed Barstow, and how Nero Wolfe found out. What are you going to do, disclose the answers to both riddles at the same dramatic moment?"

"Maybe. I hope so, Mr. Kimball. Anyway we won't answer that last one first.—No, thanks, none for me. With another of your elegant highballs I might answer almost anything. They won't come any better than that even after repeal."

"Then by all means have one. Naturally, like everybody else, I'm curious. Nero Wolfe must be an extraordinary man."

"Well, I'll tell you." I threw my head back to get the end of the highball, and with the slick ice-lumps sliding across my upper lip let the last rare drops tickle in, then suddenly came down with the glass and my chin at the same time. It was just one of my little tricks. All I saw was Manuel Kimball looking curious, and he had just said he was curious, so it couldn't be said that I had made any subtle discovery. I said, "If Nero Wolfe isn't extraordinary Napoleon never got higher than top-sergeant. I'm sorry I can't tell you his secrets, but I've got to earn what he pays me somehow even if it's only by keeping my mouth shut. Which reminds me." I glanced at my wrist. "It must be about your dinner time. You're been very hospitable, Mr. Kimball. I appreciate it, and so will Nero Wolfe."

"You're quite welcome. Don't hurry on my account. My father won't be home and I dislike eating alone. I'll run over to the club for dinner later."

"Oh," I said. "Your father won't be home? That throws me out a little. I had figured on finding a bite to eat in Pleasantville or White Plains and coming back for a little talk with him. In fact, I was just about to ask you for a favor: to tell him I was coming."

"I'm sorry."

"He won't be back tonight?"

"No. He went to Chicago on business last week. Your disappointment isn't the first one. Anderson and that detective have been wiring him every day, I don't exactly see why. After all, he barely knew Barstow. I imagine their telegrams won't start him back till he's through with his business. My father is like that. He finishes things."

"When do you expect him?"

"I hardly know. Around the fifteenth, he thought when he left."

"Well. That's too bad. It's just routine, of course, but any detective would want to complete the foursome, and since you can't do me the favor with your father that I wanted to ask, maybe you will do me another one. More routine. Tell me where you were between seven o'clock and midnight Monday evening, June fifth. That was the evening before the Barstow funeral. Did you go to the funeral? This was the evening before."

Manuel Kimball's black eyes were straight at me,

concentrated, like a man trying to remember. "I went to the funeral," he said. "Yes, that was Tuesday. A week ago today. Oh yes. I think it was; yes, I'm sure. Skinner would know. I was in the clouds."

"In the clouds?"

He nodded. "I've been trying flying and landing at night. A couple of times in May, and again that Monday. Skinner would know; he helped me off and I had him wait till I got back to make sure the lights would be in order. It's quite a trick, very different from the daytime."

"What time did you go up?"

"Around six o'clock. Of course it wasn't dark until nearly nine, but I wanted to be ahead of the twilight."

"You got well ahead of it all right. When did you get back?"

"Ten or a little after. Skinner would know that too; we fooled around with the timer till midnight."

"Did you go up alone?"

"Completely." Manuel Kimball smiled at me with his lips, but it appeared to me that his eyes weren't co-operating. "You must admit, Mr. Goodwin, that I'm being pretty tolerant. What the devil has my flying Monday night or any other night got to do with you? If I wasn't so curious I might have reason to be a little irritated. Don't you think?"

"Sure." I grinned. "I'd be irritated if I was you. But anyway I'm much obliged. Routine, Mr. Kimball, just the damn routine." I got up and shook a leg to get the cuff of my trousers down. "And I am much obliged and I appreciate it. I should think it would be more fun flying at night than in the daytime."

He was on his feet too, polite. "It is. But do not feel obliged. It is going to distinguish me around here to have talked to Nero Wolfe's man."

He called the fat butler to bring my hat.

Half an hour later, headed south around the curves of the Bronx River Parkway, I was still rolling him over on my mind's tongue. Since there was no connection at all between him and Barstow or the driver or anything else, it could have been for no other reason than because he made me nervous. And yet Wolfe said that I had no feeling for phenomena! The next time he threw that at me I would remind him of my mysterious misgivings about Manuel Kimball, I decided. Granted, of course, that it turned out that Manuel had murdered Barstow, which I had to confess didn't seem very likely at that moment.

When I got home, around half-past eight, Wolfe had finished dinner. I had phoned from the drugstore on the Grand Concourse, and Fritz had a dish of flounder with his best cheese sauce hot in the oven, with a platter of lettuce and tomatoes and plenty of good cold milk. Considering my thin lunch at the Barstows' and the hour I was getting my knees under the table, it wasn't any too much. I cleaned it up. Fritz said it seemed good to have me busy and out working again.

I said, "You're darned right it does. This dump would be about ready for the sheriff if it wasn't for me."

Fritz giggled. He's the only man I've ever known who could giggle without giving you doubts about his fundamentals.

Wolfe was in his chair in the office, playing with flies. He hated flies and very few ever got in there, but two had somehow made it and were fooling around on his desk. Much as he hated them, he couldn't kill them; he said that while a live fly irritated him to the point of hatred, a killed one outraged his respect for the dignity of death, which was worse. My opinion was it just made him sick. Anyway, he was in his chair with the swatter in his hand, seeing how close to the fly he could lower it without the fly taking off. When I went in he handed me the swatter and I let them have it and raked them into the wastebasket.

"Thank you," Wolfe said. "Those confounded insects were trying to make me forget that one of the Dendrobiums chlorostele is showing two buds."

"No! Really?"

He nodded. "That one in half sunlight. The others have been moved over."

"One for Horstmann."

"Yes. Who killed Barstow?"

I grinned. "Give me a chance. The name just escapes me—I'll remember it in a minute."

"You should have written it down.—No, just your light. That's better. Did you get enough to eat?—Proceed."

That report was an in-between; I wasn't proud of it or ashamed of it either. Wolfe scarcely interrupted once throughout; he sat as he always did when I had a long story; leaning back, his chin on his chest, his elbows on the arms of the chair with his fingers interlaced on his belly, his eyes half closed but always on my face. Halfway through he stopped me to have Fritz bring some beer, then with two bottles and a glass within reach at the edge of the table he resumed his position. I went on to the end. It was midnight.

He sighed. I went to the kitchen for a glass of milk. When I got back he was pinching the top of his ear and looking sleepy.

"Perhaps you had an impression," he said.

I sat down again. "Vague. Pretty watery. Mrs. Barstow is just some kind of a nut. She might have killed her husband or she might not, but of course she didn't kill Carlo Maffei. For Miss Barstow you can use your own impression. Out. Her brother is out too, I mean on Maffei, his alibi for the fifth is so tight you could use it for a vacuum. Dr. Bradford must be a very interesting person, I would like to meet him some time. As for Manuel Kimball, I suppose there's no chance he killed Barstow, but I'll bet he runs over angels with his airplane."

"Why? Is he cruel? Does he sneer? Do his eyes focus badly?"

"No. But look at his name. He made me nervous. He looks like a Spaniard. What's he doing with the name Kimball?"

"You haven't seen his father."

"I know. Of course the bad news about the golf bag never being in his locker threw me off my stride and I was looking for something to kick."

"Bad news? Why bad?"

"Well, good Lord. We thought we had the membership of the Green Meadow Club to run through the sifter, and now we've got everybody that's been in Barstow's home at the university for the past nine months."

"Oh no. By no means. No known poison, exposed to the air, by being smeared on a needle for instance, will retain an efficacy sufficient to kill a man as Barstow was killed for more than a day or two. Probably only a few hours. It depends on the poison."

I grinned at him. "That's a help. What else did you read?"

"A few interesting things. Many tiresome ones. So the golf bag's itinerary is not bad news at all. Its later disappearance interests us only indirectly, for we never could have expected to come upon the driver. But who caused it to disappear and why?"

"Sure. But as far as that's concerned, who came to ask you to return the reward unopened and why? We already knew there's someone in that family with funny ideas."

Wolfe wiggled a finger at me. "It is easier to recognize a style from a sentence than from a single word. But as for that, the removal of the golf bag from the scene was direct, bold and forthright, while the visit to our office, though direct enough, was merely desperate."

I said, "Doctors know all about poisons."

"Yes. This one—this Dr. Bradford—is satisfactorily forthright. Three times today I was told that he was too busy to come to the telephone, and the indication was that that condition could be expected to continue. You are intending to resume in the morning?"

I nodded. "The club first, I thought, then the coroner, then back to town for Doc Bradford's office. I'm sorry old Kimball's gone; I'd like to clean up that foursome. You don't think Saul Panzer would enjoy a trip to Chicago?"

"It would cost a hundred dollars."

"That's not much of a chunk out of fifty grand."

Wolfe shook his head. "You're a spendthrift, Archie. And unnecessarily thorough. Let us first make sure no murderer can be found within the commuting area."

"Okay." I got up and stretched. "Good night, sir."

"Good night, Archie."

# Chapter 11

There was a point on the public road from which the Green Meadow clubhouse could be seen, but at a considerable distance; to reach it you turned off the highway into a grove, and when you left that you were winding around a hollow. The clubhouse had a grove of its own, on top of a moderate hill; on one side were a bunch of tennis courts and an outdoor pool, everywhere else, in all directions, were smooth rolling fairways dotted with little tee plateaus, sand traps of various shapes and sizes, and the vivid velvet carpets of the putting greens. There were two courses of eighteen holes each; the Barstow foursome had started on the north course, the long one.

The club professional, who had dined with us at Wolfe's place Monday evening, wasn't there yet when I arrived and wasn't expected until eleven o'clock, so the only introduction I had to offer was Larry Barstow's phone call the preceding afternoon which had been received by the chief steward. He was nice enough and went with me out to the caddy master. Two of the caddies I wanted to see didn't come on weekdays, since the schools they attended weren't out yet, and the other two were out on the links somewhere with early morning matches. I monkeyed around for an hour trying to find someone for a page in the notebook, but as far as real information was concerned they were about as helpful as a bunch of Eskimos. I hopped in the roadster and beat it for White Plains.

The coroner's office was in the same building as Anderson's, where I had been six days previously trying to get Wolfe's money covered, and as I passed the door with *District Attorney* painted on the glass panel I stuck out my tongue at it. The coroner wasn't in, but by luck there was a doctor there signing papers and he was the one who had done the Barstow autopsy. Before leaving home in the morning I had telephoned Sarah Barstow, and now this doctor told me that he had had a phone call from Lawrence Barstow and had been told that I would visit the coroner's office as a representative of the Barstow family. I thought to myself, I'll have that Barstow brat fixing my flat tires before I get through with this.

But I came away as good as empty. Everything that the doctor could tell me I had read three days earlier in the newspapers except for a bunch of medical terms which the papers hadn't tried to print for fear of a typesetters' strike. I don't high-hat technical words, because I know there are a lot of things that can't be said any other way, but the doctor's lengthy explanation simply boiled down to this, that nothing conclusive could be said regarding the poison that had killed Barstow, because no one had been able to analyze it. Additional tissues had been sent to a New York laboratory but no report had been received. The needle had been taken by the District Attorney and was presumably being tested elsewhere.

"Anyway," I said, "there's no chance he died of old age or something? He was actually poisoned? He died a violent death?"

The doctor nodded. "Absolutely. Something remarkably virulent. Hæmolysis—"

"Sure. Just between you and me, what is your opinion of a doctor who would go up to a man who had just died like that and would say coronary thrombosis?"

He stiffened as if he had just got rigor mortis himself, only much quicker. "That is not a question for me to decide, Mr. Goodwin."

"I didn't ask you to decide anything, I just asked your opinion."

"I haven't got any."

"You mean you have, only you're going to keep it to remember me by. All right. Much obliged."

On my way out of the building I would have liked to stop in and ask Derwin for Ben Cook's telephone number or some such pleasantry, but I had too much on my mind. By the time I got back to the Green Meadow Club it was nearly noon and I had pretty well decided that life would be nothing but a dreary round until I had had the pleasure of meeting Dr. Bradford.

The two caddies were there. Their boss rounded them up for me, and I made a deal with them: I would get sandwiches, two apiece, bananas, ice cream, and root beer, and we would go over under a tree and eat, drink and be merry, provided they wouldn't expect me to pay for their lost time. They signed up and we collected the provisions from the lunch counter and found the tree.

One of them, a skinny pale kid with brown hair, had been Manuel Kimball's caddy and the other had been Peter Oliver Barstow's. This other was a chunky lad with snappy brown eyes and a lot of freckles; his name was Mike Allen. After we got arranged under the tree, before he took his first bite he said:

"You know, mister, we don't get paid."

"What do you mean, you work for fun?"

"We don't get paid all the time, only when we're out on a round. We're not losing any time. We couldn't get another match till after lunch anyhow."

"Oh. You don't say so. You're too darned honest. If you don't watch out you'll get a job in a bank. Go on and eat your sandwich."

While we chewed I got them onto the Barstow foursome. The way they rattled it off it was easy to see they hadn't gone over it more than a thousand times, with Anderson and Corbett of course, the other caddies, families and friends at home. They were glib and ready with an answer on every little detail, and that made it pretty hopeless to try to get anything fresh out of them, for they had drawn the picture so many times that they were now doing it with their eyes shut. Not that I really expected a damn thing, but I had long since learned from Wolfe that the corner the light doesn't reach is the one the dime rolled to. There was no variation worth mentioning from the versions I had got from Larry Barstow and Manuel Kimball. By the time the sandwiches and stuff were down I saw that the pale skinny kid was milked dry, so I sent him back to his boss. Chunky Mike I kept a while, sitting with him under the tree. He had some sense in him and he might have noticed something: for instance, how Dr. Bradford had acted when he arrived at the scene on the fourth fairway. But I didn't get a bite there. He only remembered that the doctor had been out of breath when he had run up with everyone waiting for him, and when he stood up after examining Barstow he had been white and calm.

I checked up on the golf bag. There was no uncertainty in him about that; he had positively put it in the front of Barstow's car, leaning against the driver's seat.

I said, "Of course, Mike, you were pretty excited. At a time like that everybody is. Isn't there a chance you put it in some other car?"

"No, sir. I couldn't. There was no other car there."

"Maybe it was someone else's bag you put in."

"No, sir. I'm not a dummy. When you're a caddy you get so you glance at the heads to make sure all the clubs are in, and after I leaned the bag against the seat I did that, and I remember seeing all the new heads."

"New heads?"

"Sure, they were all new."

"What made them new? Do you mean Barstow had had new heads put on?"

"No, sir, they were new clubs. The new bag of clubs his wife gave him."

"What!"

"Sure."

I didn't want to startle him; I picked a blade of grass and chewed on it. "How do you know his wife gave them to him?"

"He told me."

"How did he happen to tell you?"

"Well, when I went up to him he shook hands and said he was glad to see me again, of course he was one of my babies last year—"

"For God's sake, Mike, wait a minute. What do you mean he was one of your babies?"

The kid grinned. "That's what us fellows call it.

When a man likes us for a caddy and won't take another one he's our baby."

"I see. Go on."

"He said he was glad to see me again, and when I took his bag I saw they were all new Hendersons, genuine, and he said he was glad to see I admired the new clubs his wife had given him for his birthday."

There were a couple of bananas left and I handed him one and he began peeling it. I watched him. After a minute I said:

"Do you know that Barstow was killed by a poison needle shot out of the handle of a golf driver?"

His mouth was full. He waited till most of it was down before he answered. "I know that's what they say."

"Why, don't you believe it?"

He shook his head. "They've got to show me."

"Why?"

"Well—" He took another bite and swallowed it. "I don't believe you could do it. I've handled a lot of golf clubs. I just don't believe it."

I grinned at him. "You're a skeptic, Mike. You know what my boss says? He says that skepticism is a good watchdog if you know when to take the leash off. I don't suppose you happen to know when Barstow had a birthday?"

He didn't know that. I started to fish around a little more, here and there, but there didn't seem to be any more nibbles in that pool. Besides, the lunch hour was over, afternoon players were beginning to stroll up, and I saw Mike had his eyes on the caddy benches and was beginning to lose interest in me. I was about ready to scramble up and tell him the picnic was over, but he beat me to it. He was on his feet with a sudden spring, the kind young legs can make, and he tossed at me, "Excuse me, mister, that guy's my baby," and was off.

I gathered up the papers and banana skins and went to the clubhouse. There were a good many more people around than when I had arrived in the morning, and finally I had to send an attendant for the chief steward because I couldn't find him. He was busy, but he took time to show me where the library was and tell me to help myself. I looked around the shelves and in a minute had it spotted, the fat red *Who's Who in America*. I turned to the entry I had already read in Wolfe's office: BARSTOW, Peter Oliver, author, educator, physicist; *b*. Chatham, Ill., Apr. 9, 1875 . . .

I put the book back and went out to the lobby where I had seen some telephone booths, and called Sarah Barstow at her home and asked if I could drop in to see her for a minute. It was only a couple of miles out of my way returning to New York, and I thought I might as well clean this detail up. As I was going along the veranda to where I had parked the roadster I met Manuel Kimball. He was with some people, but when he saw me he nodded and I returned it, and I could guess what he was saying to the people with him because after I got past they turned to look at me.

Ten minutes later I was on the Barstow drive.

Small took me to a room in front that I hadn't been in the day before. In a little while Sarah Barstow came in. She looked pale and determined, and I realized that with my phone call I must have scared her some more without wanting to. I should have been a little more explanatory; I don't believe in pulling a dog's tail if there's anything else to do.

I got up. She didn't sit down.

"I'll only keep you a minute," I said. "I wouldn't have bothered you, only I ran across something that made me curious. Please tell me, was your father's birthday April ninth?"

She looked as if she was trying to breathe. She nodded.

"Did your mother give him a bag of golf clubs his last birthday?"

"Oh!" she said, and put her hand on the back of a chair.

"Listen, Miss Barstow. Buck up. I think you know Nero Wolfe wouldn't lie to you, and while he's paying me you can regard me as Nero Wolfe. We might try tricky questions on you, but we wouldn't tell you an honest lie. If you've been nursing the idea that the driver your father killed himself with was in the bag when your mother gave it to him on his birthday, forget it. We have reason to know it couldn't have been. Impossible."

She just looked at me with her lips working but not opening. I don't believe she would have been able to stand without her hand on the chair. She had a good hold on it.

I said, "Maybe I'm telling you something and maybe I'm not. But I've brought this right to you as soon as I found it out, and I'm giving it to you straight. If it's any help to you, you're welcome, and how about making it fifty-fifty? I could use a little help too. Was that what was eating you, that birthday present? Was that the reason for all the fol-de-rol?"

She got her tongue working at last but all she said was, "I don't believe you would lie to me. It would be too cruel."

"I wouldn't. But even if I would, I know about the birthday present anyhow, so you can answer my simple question without running a temperature. Was that what was eating you?"

"Yes," she said. "That—and—yes, it was that."

"What else was it?"

"Nothing. My mother—"

"Sure." I nodded. "Your mother got goofy sometimes and got ideas about your father, and she gave him a golf bag on his birthday. What else?"

"Nothing." She took her hand off the chair, but put it back again. "Mr. Goodwin. I think—I'll sit down."

I went and took her arm and shoved the chair back a little with my foot, and held onto her until she got seated. She shut her eyes and I stood and waited till she opened them again.

"You're right," she said. "I ought to buck up. I'm no good. It has been a strain. Not only this, a long while. I always thought my mother was a wonderful woman, I still think so, I know she is. But it is so ugly! Dr. Bradford says he believes that now, since Father is dead, Mother will be completely cured and will never again have any—difficulties. But much as I love my mother, that is too high a price. I think we would be better off without modern psychology, everything it tells us is so ugly. It was at my father's suggestion that I studied it."

"Anyway, this is one thing off your mind."

"Yes. I can't appreciate it yet, but I will. I ought to thank you, Mr. Goodwin, I'm sorry. You say that my mother had nothing—that she couldn't—"

"I say that the driver that killed your father wasn't anywhere on April ninth. It didn't exist until at least a month later."

"How sure are you?"

"Just damn sure."

"Well. That's a good deal." She tried to smile at me, and I admired her nerve, for it was easy to see that she was so near gone from worry and grief and loss of sleep that you might as well have expected a guffaw from Job. Anyone with an ounce of decency in him would have got up and left her alone with the good news I'd brought her; but business is business, and it wouldn't have been right to pass up the chance that she was unstrung enough to loosen up at a vital point. I said:

"Don't you think you might tell me who took the golf bag from the car and where it is now? Now that we know that the driver is not the one that was in it when your mother gave it to him?"

She said without hesitation, "Small took it from the car."

My heart jumped the way it did when I saw Wolfe's lips push out. She was going to spill it! I went right on without giving her time to consider, "Where did he take it to?"

"Upstairs. To Father's room."

"Who took it away from there?"

"I did. Saturday evening, after Mr. Anderson came. It was Sunday that the men searched the house for it."

"Where did you put it?"

"I drove to Tarrytown and got on the ferry and dropped it in the middle of the river. I filled it full of stones."

"You're lucky they weren't tailing you. Of course you examined the driver. Did you take it apart?"

"I didn't examine it. I—was in a hurry."

"You didn't examine it? You mean you didn't even take it out and look at it?"

"No."

I stared at her. "I've got a better opinion of you. I don't believe you're such an awful fool. You're stringing me."

"No. No, I'm not, Mr. Goodwin."

I still stared. "You mean you actually did all that? Without even looking at the driver? Leave it to a woman! What were your brother and Bradford doing, playing billiards?"

She shook her head. "They had nothing to do with it."

"But Bradford says that your mother will be all right now that your father's dead."

"Well? If that is his opinion—" She stopped; the mention of her mother had been a mistake, it had her down again. After a minute she looked up at me, and for the first time I saw tears in her eyes. Two hung there. "You wanted me to go fifty-fifty, Mr. Goodwin. That's my share."

Something about her, the tears maybe, made her look like nothing but a kid, trying to be brave. I reached down and patted her on the shoulder and said:

"You're a good sport, Miss Barstow. I'll let you alone."

I went to the hall and got my hat and left.

BUT, I thought, in the roadster again headed south down the highway. Plenty of BUT. Part of it was that as much as I respected filial devotion and as much as I liked Sarah Barstow, it would have been a real satisfaction to put her across my knees and pull up her skirts and giver her a swell fanning, for not taking a look at that driver. I had to believe her and I did believe her. She hadn't made that up. Now the driver was gone for good. With a lot of luck and patience it might have been grappled out of the river, but it would have cost more money than Nero Wolfe was apt to let go of. It was just simply good-bye driver. As I went through White Plans it was a temptation to leave the Parkway and run over to the District Attorney's office and say to Anderson, "I'll bet you ten dollars that the golf bag containing the driver that killed Barstow is at the bottom of the Hudson River halfway between Tarrytown and Nyack." It wouldn't have been a bad idea at that, for he might have sent a couple of boats out and found it. But as things turned out it was just as well I didn't.

I had had it in mind to go back to New York by another route, Blueberry Road, and just for curiosity take a look at the spot where Carlo Maffei's body had been found; not that I expected to discover that the murderer had left his scarfpin or automobile license lying around, just thinking that it never hurts a spot to look at it. But dropping in on Sarah Barstow had used up some time, and I wanted to make a call in the city. So I took the quickest way in.

On upper Park Avenue I stopped at a drugstore and phoned Wolfe. He had called Bradford's office once more, around eleven-thirty, but it had been the same story, too busy to come to the phone. He told me to go to it. I thought to myself, if he's busy now he's going to be positively rushed before we get through with him. It took me less than ten minutes to get to Sixty-ninth Street, and I parked around the corner.

Dr. Nathaniel Bradford certainly had an office. The entrance hall was wide enough to have a row of Brazilian ferns along each side, and the anteroom was big and grand. The lights and rugs and pictures and chairs made it plain, but not noisy, that everything done in that place was on a high level, including making out the patients' bills. But the chairs were all empty. The girl in starched white at a desk over in a corner told me that Dr. Bradford was not in. She seemed surprised that I didn't know that, just as I would know that Central Park begins at Fifty-ninth

Street, and asked if I was a former patient. Then she
said that the doctor was never in his office in the
afternoon before four-thirty, and that he never saw
anyone except by appointment. When I said that that
was what I wanted to see him for, to make an
appointment, she raised her eyebrows. I went back to
the street.

At first I thought I would wait around for him, but
it was only a little after three, so I went and sat in the
roadster and let my mind out for a stroll to see if it
would run across an idea for passing the time. In a few
minutes it did, a pretty one. I went to a restaurant on
Park Avenue to look at a telephone book, and then
went back to the car and stepped on the starter and
started along Sixty-ninth Street, and at Fifth Avenue
turned downtown. At Forty-first Street I headed
east.

As usual every car along the curb was laying its
head on the next one's tail, and I had to go nearly to
Third Avenue to find a space where I could edge the
roadster in. I walked back almost two crosstown
blocks, and found that the number I was looking for
was one of the new office buildings a mile high. The
directory said that my meat was on the twentieth
floor. The elevator shot me up and I found it on a door
down the corridor: *Metropolitan Medical Record.*

It was a young man, not a girl, at the desk in the
outside room; that was nice for a change. I said to him:

"I'd like to ask a favor, if you're not too busy to help
me out a little. Would you have any record showing
the meetings of medical associations and so on held in
New York on June fifth?"

He grinned. "The Lord knows I'm not busy. Yes,
sir, we have. Of course. Just a minute. June fifth?"

He went to a stack of magazines on a shelf and took

off the top one. "This is our last issue, it would have it." He began flipping the pages and stopped around the middle and looked at it. I waited. "Nothing on the fifth, I'm afraid—Oh yes, here it is. Most of the big meetings come later. On the fifth the New York Neurological Society was at the Knickerbocker Hotel."

I asked if I could look at it and he handed it to me. I ran through the paragraph. "I see. This is a notice of the meeting. Of course it was printed before the meeting took place. You wouldn't have anything later? A report, a write-up?"

He shook his head. "There'll be one in our next issue I suppose. Was it something particular you wanted? The daily papers may have run it."

"Maybe. I haven't tried them. What I'm looking for is a report of Dr. Bradford's paper. As a matter of fact, all I want is to make sure he was there. You wouldn't know?"

He shook his head. "But if all you want to know is whether he was there or not, why don't you ask him?"

I grinned. "I hate to bother him. But of course it's quite simple, I happened to be in the neighborhood and thought that by dropping in here I could save time."

He said, "Wait a minute," and disappeared through a door to an inner office. He didn't take much more than the minute he mentioned. When he came back he told me, "Mr. Elliot says that Dr. Bradford was at the meeting and delivered his paper."

Elliot, he said, was the editor of the *Record*. I asked if I could speak to him. The young man disappeared through the door again, and after a moment it opened once more and a big red-faced man in his shirt sleeves came through. One of the brusque breezy kind. "What's all this? What's this about?"

I explained. He wiped his forehead with his handkerchief and said that he had attended the meeting and that Dr. Bradford had delivered his most interesting paper to applause. He was writing it up for the August *Record*. I questioned him, and he took it very nicely. Yes, he meant Dr. Nathaniel Bradford whose office was on Sixty-ninth Street. He had known him for years. He couldn't say at what hour Bradford had arrived at the hotel, but it had been a dinner meeting and he had seen Bradford at his table as early as seven and on the speaking platform as late as ten-thirty.

I guess I went out without thanking him. Driving back uptown I was sore as a pup. Of course it was Bradford I was sore at. What the devil did he mean by fooling around at a meeting reading a paper on neurology when I had him all set up in Westchester County sticking a knife into Carlo Maffei?

I supposed it would have taken me about a year to get introduced to Dr. Nathaniel Bradford if I hadn't been so sore when I got back to his office. There were two patients waiting this time. The doctor was in. I asked the girl at the desk for a piece of paper and sat down and held it on a magazine and wrote on it:

> *Dr. Bradford: For the last few days I've been sure you were a murderer but now I know you are just an old fool. The same goes for Mrs. Barstow and her son and daughter. It will take me about three minutes to tell you how I know.*
> *Archie Goodwin*<br>*For Nero Wolfe*

By the time the two patients had been taken care of some more had come in, and I went over to the girl and told her I was next. She got impatient and began explaining to me what an appointment was. I said:

"It wouldn't break any furniture if you just handed him this note. Honest, I'm in a hurry. Be human. I've got a sister at home. Don't read it yourself because there's a swear-word in it."

She looked disgusted, but she took the note and went away with it through the door where the patients had gone. After a while she came back and stood on the threshold and said my name. I took my hat along with me because there had been time enough to call a cop.

One look at Dr. Bradford was enough to show me that I had been wasting a lot of pleasant suspicions which might have been avoided if I had happened to catch sight of him somewhere. He was tall and grave and correct, the distinguished old gentleman type, and he had whiskers! There may have been a historical period when it was possible for a guy with whiskers to pull a knife and plunge it into somebody's back, but that was a long time ago. Nowadays it couldn't be done. Bradford's were gray, so was his hair. To tell the truth, as tight as his alibi for June fifth had been made by my trip to Forty-first Street, I had been prepared to try to find a leak in it until I got a look at him.

I went over to where he sat at his desk, and stood there. He just looked at me until the door had closed behind the girl, then he said:

"Your name is Goodwin. Are you a genius too?"

"Yes, sir." I grinned. "I caught it from Nero Wolfe. Sure, I remember he told Miss Barstow he was a genius, and of course she told you. Maybe you thought it was only a joke."

"No. I kept an open mind. But whether you are a genius or merely an impertinent ass, I can't keep my patients waiting for you. What is this note you sent me, bait? I'll give you three minutes to justify it."

"That's plenty. I'll put it this way: Nero Wolfe discovered certain facts. From those facts he reached a certain conclusion as to the cause and manner of Barstow's death. When the autopsy verified his conclusion it also verified his facts; that is, it made them an inseparable part of the picture, and whoever killed Barstow has got to fit those facts. Well, the Barstows don't fit, none of them. You don't either. You're a washout."

"Go on."

"Go on?"

"That's a good general statement. Specify."

"Oh no." I shook my head. "That's not the way us geniuses work, you can't shake us empty like a bag of peanuts. For one thing, it would take a lot longer than three minutes. For another, what do you expect for nothing? You've got a nerve. Something happens to get you into such a state that you can't tell coronary thrombosis from an epileptic fit, and to keep you on such an edge for days that you're afraid to go to the telephone, and it's all right for Nero Wolfe to spend his time and money chasing the clouds away for you and turning on the sunshine, but he mustn't make a nuisance of himself. I've got to send you in a trick note just to have the honor of looking at your whiskers. You've got a nerve."

"Dear me." Dr. Bradford was swearing. "Your indignation is eloquent and picturesque, but it demonstrates nothing but indignation." He looked at his watch. "I don't need to tell you, Mr. Goodwin, that I'm tremendously interested. And while I shall continue to

regard the vocation of raking scandal out of graveyards as an especially vile method of making a living,
I shall certainly be vastly grateful to you and Nero
Wolfe if the general statement you have made can be
substantiated. Can you return here at half-past six?"

I shook my head. "I'm just a messenger. Nero
Wolfe dines at seven o'clock. He lives on West Thirty-
fifth Street. He invites you to dine with him this
evening. Will you?"

"No. Certainly not."

"All right. That's all." I was fed up with the old
pillar, moss and all. "If you get a rash from your
curiosity itching don't blame us. We don't really need
anything you're likely to have, we just like to clean up
as we go along. My three minutes are up."

I turned to go. I didn't hurry, but I got to the door
with my hand on the knob.

"Mr. Goodwin."

I kept my hand on the knob and looked around at
him.

"I accept Mr. Wolfe's invitation. I shall be there at
seven."

I said, "Okay, I'll give the girl the address," and
went on out.

# Chapter 12

I've sometimes wondered how many people there were in New York from whom Nero Wolfe could have borrowed money. I suppose more than a thousand. I made it a severe test to narrow it down. Of course there were more than that who felt grateful to him, and as many more who had reason to hate him, but there's a special kind of attitude a man has to have toward you before you can bump him for a loan and get something more substantial than a frown and a stammer for your trouble; a mixture of trust and goodwill, and gratitude without any feeling of obligation to make it unpleasant. At least a thousand. Not that Wolfe ever took advantage of it. I remember a couple of years ago we were really hard up for cash for a while, and I made a suggestion regarding a multimillionaire who didn't owe Wolfe much more than his life. Wolfe wouldn't consider it. "No, Archie, nature has arranged that when you overcome a given inertia the resulting momentum is proportionate. If I were to begin borrowing money I would end by devising means of persuading the Secretary of the Treasury to lend me the gold reserve." I told him that as things stood we could use it and more too, but he wasn't listening.

After that Wednesday evening dinner I could have added Dr. Nathaniel Bradford to the thousand. Wolfe got him completely, as he always got everyone when he cared to take the trouble. Between six and seven, before Bradford arrived, I had made a condensed report of the events of the day, and at the dinner table I had seen at once that Wolfe agreed with me in erasing Bradford right off the slate. He was easy and informal, and to my practiced eye he always kept on a formal basis with a man as long as there was a chance in his mind that the man was headed for the frying-pan at Sing Sing or a cell at Auburn, with Wolfe furnishing the ticket.

At dinner they discussed rock gardens and economics and Tammany Hall. Wolfe drank three bottles of beer and Bradford a bottle of wine; I stuck to milk, but I had had a shot of rye upstairs. I had told Wolfe of Bradford's observation about a vile vocation and threw in my opinion of him. Wolfe had said, "Detach yourself, Archie, personal resentment of a general statement is a barbarous remnant of a fetish-superstition." I had said, "That's just another of your flossy remarks that don't mean anything." He had said, "No. I abhor meaningless remarks. If a man constructs a dummy, clothes and paints it in exact outward resemblance of yourself, and proceeds to strike it in the face, does your nose bleed?" I had said, "No, but his will before I get through with him." Wolfe had sighed into my grin, "At least you see that my remark was not meaningless."

In the office after dinner Wolfe said to Bradford that there were things he wanted to ask him but that he would begin by telling him. He gave him the whole story: Maffei, the clipped newspaper, the question about the golf club that stopped Anna Fiore, the game with Anderson, the letter Anna got with a hundred bucks. He told it straight and complete, and then said, "There, Doctor. I asked you for no pledge beforehand, but I now request you to keep everything I have said in confidence. I ask this in my own interest. I wish to earn fifty thousand dollars."

Bradford had got mellow. He was still trying to make Wolfe out, but he was no longer nursing any hurtful notions, and the wine was making him suspect Wolfe of being an old friend. He said, "It's a remarkable story. Remarkable. I shall mention it to no one of course, and I appreciate your confidence. I can't say that I have digested all the implications, but I can see that your disclosure of the truth regarding Barstow was a necessary part of the effort to find the murderer of the man Maffei. And I can see that you have relieved Sarah and Larry Barstow of an intolerable burden of fear, and myself of a responsibility that was becoming more than I had bargained for. I am grateful, believe me."

Wolfe nodded. "There are subtleties, certainly. Naturally some of them escape you. All that we have actually proven is that of you four—Mrs. Barstow, her son and daughter, and yourself—none of you killed Carlo Maffei, and that the fatal driver was not in the golf bag on April ninth. It is still possible that any one of you, or all of you in conspiracy, killed Barstow. That theory would only require a colleague to dispose of Maffei."

Bradford, suddenly a little less mellow, stared. But the stare soon disappeared and he was easy again. "Rot. You don't believe that." Then he stared again. "But as a matter of fact, why don't you?"

"We'll come to that. First let me ask, do you think

my frankness has earned a similar frankness from you?"

"I do."

"Then tell me, for example, when and how Mrs. Barstow previously made an attempt on her husband's life."

It was funny to watch Bradford. He was startled, then he went stiff and quiet, then he realized he was giving it away and tried to dress up his face in natural astonishment. After all that he said, "What do you mean? That's ridiculous!"

Wolfe wiggled a finger at him. "Easy, Doctor. I beg you, do not suspect me of low cunning. I am merely seeking facts to fit my conclusions. I see I had better first tell you why I have dismissed from my mind the possibility of your guilt or that of the Barstows. I cannot feel such a guilt. That is all. Of course I can rationalize my feeling, or lack of it. Consider the requirements: a wife or son or daughter who plans the murder of the father with great deliberation, shrewdness and patience. The lengthy and intricate preparation of the tool. If the wife or daughter, a fellow conspirator who killed Maffei. If the son, the same requirement, since he did not do it himself. Archie Goodwin went there, and he could not spend hours in such a household without smelling the foul odor that it would generate and without bringing the smell to me. You also would have required an accomplice for Maffei. I have spent an evening with you. Though you might murder, you would not murder like that, and you would trust no accomplice whatever. That is the rationalization; it is the feeling that is important."

"Then why—"

"No, let me. You, a qualified and competent observer, certified a heart attack when the contrary evidence must have been unmistakable. That is adventurous conduct for a reputable physician. Of course you were shielding someone. The statement of Miss Barstow indicated whom. Then on finding Barstow dead you must have immediately conjectured that his wife had killed him, and you would not reach so shocking a conclusion without good reason, surely not merely because Mrs. Barstow had in her neurotic moments wished her husband dead. If that constituted murder, what kitchen in this country could shut its door to the hangman? You had better reason, knowledge either of her preparations for this crime or for a previous attempt on her husband's life. Since our facts make the former untenable, I assume the latter, and I ask you simply, when and how did she make the attempt? I ask you only to complete the record, so that we may consign these aspects of the case to the obscurity of history."

Bradford was considering. His mellowness was gone and he was leaning forward in his chair as he followed Wolfe's exposition. He said, "Have you sent someone to the university?"

"No."

"They know about it there. You really guessed it then. Last November Mrs. Barstow shot a revolver at her husband. The bullet went wide. Afterward she had a breakdown."

Wolfe nodded. "In a fit, of course.—Oh, don't object to the word; whatever you may call it, was it not a fit? But I am still surprised, Doctor. From a temporary fit of murderous violence, is it permissible to infer a long-premeditated diabolical plot?"

"I made no such inference." Bradford was exasperated. "Good God, there I was with my best and oldest friend lying dead before me, obviously poisoned. How did I know with what he was poisoned, or when or how? I did know what Ellen—Mrs. Barstow—had said only the evening before. I went by my feelings too, as you say you do, only mine were wrong. I got him safely and quietly buried, and I had no regrets. Then when the autopsy came with its amazing results I was too bewildered, and too far in, to act with any intelligence. When Mrs. Barstow proposed to offer the reward I opposed it unsuccessfully. In one word, I was in a funk."

I hadn't noticed Wolfe pushing the button, but as Bradford finished Fritz was on the threshold. "Some port for Dr. Bradford. A bottle of the Remmers for me. Archie?"

"Nothing, thanks."

Bradford said, "I'm afraid none for me, I should be going. It's nearly eleven and I'm driving to the country."

"But, Doctor," Wolfe protested, "you haven't told me the one thing I want to know. Another fifteen minutes? So far you have merely verified a few unimportant little surmises. Don't you see how shrewdly I have labored to gain your confidence and esteem? To this end only, that I might ask you, and expect a full and candid reply: who killed your friend Barstow?"

Bradford stared, discrediting his ears.

"I'm not drunk, merely dramatic," Wolfe went on. "I am a born actor, I suppose; anyway, I think a good question deserves a good setting. My question is a good one. You see, Doctor, you will have to shake the dust from your mind before you can answer me adequately—the dust remaining from your hasty and unkind inference regarding your friend Mrs. Barstow. From that and your funk. Understand that it really is true, despite the anxieties you have harbored for many months, that Mrs. Barstow did not kill her husband. Then who did? Who, with the patience of a devil and the humor of a fiend, prepared that lethal toy for his hand? I believe you were Barstow's oldest and closest friend?"

Bradford nodded. "Pete Barstow and I were boys together."

"A mutual confidence was sustained? Though superficial interests separated you intermittently, you presented a common front to life?"

"You put it well." Bradford was moved, it showed in his voice. "A confidence undisturbed for fifty years."

"Good. Then who killed him? I'm really expecting something from you, Doctor. What had he ever said or done that he should die? You may never have heard the story whole, but surely you must have caught a chapter of it, a paragraph, a sentence. Let the past whisper to you; it may be the distant past. And you must discard reluctance; I am not asking you for an indictment; the danger here is not that the innocent will be harassed but that the guilty will go free."

Fritz had brought the beer and the port, and the doctor was leaning back in his chair again, glass in hand, with his eyes on the red rich juice. He jerked his head up and nodded at Wolfe and then resumed his contemplation. Wolfe poured himself some beer, waited for the foam to subside, and gulped it down. He always thought he had a handkerchief in the breast pocket of his coat but rarely did, so I went to a drawer where I kept a stack for him and got one and handed it to him.

"I'm not listening to whispers from the past," Bradford finally said. "I'm being astonished, and impressed, that there are none, of the kind you mean. Also I'm seeing another reason why I so readily concluded that Mrs. Barstow—was responsible. Or rather, irresponsible. It was because I knew, or felt, unconsciously, that no one else could have done it. I see now more clearly than I ever did what an extraordinary person Pete Barstow was. As a boy he was scrappy, as a man he fought for every right he believed in, but I'll swear there wasn't a man or woman alive who could have wished him serious harm. Not one."

"Except his wife."

"Not even she. She shot at him from ten feet and missed him."

"Well." Wolfe sighed, and gulped another glass of beer. "I'm afraid I have nothing to thank you for, Doctor."

"I'm afraid not. Believe me, Mr. Wolfe, I'd help you if I could. It is curious, what is happening inside of me at this moment; I would never have suspected it. Now that I know Ellen is out of it, I am not sure I disapprove of the reward she offered. I might even increase it. Am I vindictive, too, then? For Pete, maybe; I think he might have been for me."

It was altogether a bum evening, as far as I was concerned. For the last ten minutes I was half asleep and didn't hear much. It was beginning to look to me as if Wolfe was going to have to develop a feeling for a new kind of phenomenon: murder by eeny-meeny-miny-mo. That was the only way that needle could have got into Barstow, since everybody was agreed that no one had wanted it there.

It was a bum evening, but I got a grin out of it at the end. Bradford had got up to go and walked toward Wolfe's chair to tell him good night. I saw him hesitating. He said, "There's a little thing on my mind, Mr. Wolfe. I—I owe you an apology. In my office this afternoon I made a remark to your man, a quite unnecessary remark, something about raking scandal out of graveyards—"

"But I don't understand. Apology?" Wolfe's quiet bewilderment was grand. "What had your remark to do with me?"

Of course Bradford's only out was the door.

After seeing the distinguished old gentleman to the entrance and sliding the night bolt in, I went to the kitchen for a glass of milk on my way back to the office. Fritz was there and I told him he had wasted enough good port for one evening, he might as well shut up shop. In the office Wolfe was leaning back in his chair with his eyes shut. I sat down and sipped away at the milk. When it was all gone I was pretty well bored and began talking just for practice.

"It's like this, ladies and gentlemen. The problem is to discover what the devil good it does you to use up a million dollars' worth of genius feeling the phenomenon of a poison needle in a man's belly if it turns out that nobody put it there. Put it this way: if a thing gets where no one wants it, what happened? Or this way: since the golf bag was in the Barstow home for the twenty-four hours preceding the killing, how about finding out if one of the servants has got funnier ideas even than Mrs. Barstow? Of course, according to Sarah's information there's no chance of it, and another objection is that it doesn't appeal to me. Lord, how I hate tackling a bunch of servants. So I guess I'll drop in on the Barstows in the morning and go to it. It looks like it's either that or quit and kiss the fifty grand good-bye. This case is a lulu all right. We're right where we started. I wouldn't mind so much if there was anyone to help me out on it, If only I didn't have to do all the thinking and planning for myself, in addition to running around day after day and getting nowhere—"

"Continue, Archie." But Wolfe didn't open his eyes.

"I can't, I'm too disgusted. Do you know something? We're licked. This poison needle person is a better man than we are. Oh, we'll go on for a few days fooling around with servants and trying to find out who put the ad in the paper for the metal-worker and so on, but we're licked as sure as you're full of beer."

His eyes opened. "I'm going to cut down to five quarts a day. Twelve bottles. A bottle doesn't hold a pint. I am now going to bed." He began the accustomed preparations for rising from his chair. He got up. "By the way, Archie, could you get out fairly early in the morning? You might reach the Green Meadow Club before the caddies depart with their babies. That is the only slang epithet you have brought me recently which seems to me entirely apt. Perhaps you could also kidnap the two who are attending school. It would be convenient if all four of them were here at eleven. Tell Fritz there will be guests at lunch. What do boys of that age eat?"

"They eat everything."

"Tell Fritz to have that."

As soon as I had made sure that he could still get into the elevator, I went on upstairs and set my alarm for six o'clock and hit the hay.

In the morning, rolling north along the Parkway again, I wasn't singing at the sunshine. I was always glad to be doing something, but I was not so liable to burst from joy when I suspected that my activity was going to turn out to be nothing but discarding from a bum hand. I didn't need anybody to tell me that Nero

Wolfe was a wonder, but I knew this gathering in the caddies was just a wild stab, and I wasn't hopeful. As a matter of fact, it seemed to me more likely than ever that we were licked, because if this was the best Wolfe could do—

It was a motor cop. With the northbound half of the Parkway empty at that hour of the morning I had been going something above fifty without noticing, and this bicycle Cossack waved me over. I pulled alongside the curb and stopped. He asked for my license and I handed it to him, and he got out his book of tickets.

I said, "Sure I was going too fast. It may not interest you, I don't know, but I'm headed for Anderson's office in White Plains—the District Attorney— with some dope on the Barstow case. He's in a hurry for it."

The cop just had his pencil ready. "Got a badge?"

I handed him one of my cards. "I'm private. It was my boss, Nero Wolfe, that started the party."

He handed the card and the license back. "All right, but don't begin jumping over fences."

I felt better after that. Maybe luck was headed our way after all.

I got the two caddies at the club without any trouble, but it took over an hour to round up the other two. They went to different schools, and while one of them didn't need any persuading to go for a ride to New York, the other one must have been trying to qualify for teacher's pet or a Rhodes scholarship. At first I kidded him, and when that didn't work I switched to the ends of justice and the duties of a good citizen. That got him, and the woman in charge of the school, too. I suspected I wouldn't care an awful lot for his companionship, so I put him and another one in the rumble seat, and with the other two in with me I found the trail back to the Parkway and turned south. I kept the speedometer down to forty thenceforth, for I knew I couldn't expect Anderson to do me nothing but favors.

We arrived at a quarter to eleven, and I took the boys to the kitchen and fed them sandwiches, for the lunch hour was one. I wanted to take them up and show them the orchids, thinking it wouldn't hurt them any to get impressed, but there wasn't time. I got their names and addresses down. One of them, the pale skinny kid who had caddied for Manuel Kimball, had a dirty face and I took him to the bathroom for a wash. By the time Wolfe appeared I was beginning to feel like a boy scout leader.

I had them arranged on chairs in a row for him. He came in with a bunch of Cymbidiums in his hand which he put into a vase on his desk, then he got into his chair and flipped the mail. He had told the boys good morning as he entered; now he turned and settled himself comfortably and looked them over one by one. They were embarrassed and shifted around.

"Excuse me, Archie. Bad staging." He turned to the boy at the end, one with red hair and blue eyes. "Your name, sir?"

"William A. Riley."

"Thank you. If you will move your chair over there, near the wall—much better.—And your name?" When he had got all their names and scattered them around he said, "Which one of you expressed doubt that Peter Oliver Barstow was killed by a needle shot from the handle of a golf driver?—Come, I'm only trying to get acquainted; which one?"

Chunky Mike spoke up. "That was me."

"Ah. Michael Allen. Michael, you are young. You have learned to accept the commonplace, you must yet learn not to exclude the bizarre.—Now, boys, I'm going to tell you a story. Please listen, because I want you to understand it. This happens to be a true story. There was a meeting in a public hall of a hundred psychologists. A psychologist is—by courtesy—a man trained to observe. It had been arranged, without their knowledge, that a man should run into the hall and down the aisle, followed by another man waving a pistol. A third man ran in by another door. The second man shot at the first man. The third man knocked the second man down and took the pistol from him. They all ran out by different doors. One of the psychologists then arose and stilled the clamor, and announced that the events had been prearranged, and asked each of his colleagues to write down immediately a complete detailed report of the whole affair. They did so, and the reports were examined and compared. Not one was entirely correct. No two agreed throughout. One even had the third man shooting at the first man."

Wolfe stopped and looked around at them. "That's all. I'm not a good story-teller, but you may have caught the point. Do you see what I'm getting at?"

They nodded.

"You do. Then I shall not insult your intelligence with an exposition. Let us go on to our own story. We shall sit here and discuss the death of Peter Oliver Barstow, more particularly the events on the first tee which led up to it. At one o'clock we shall have lunch, then we shall return here and resume. We shall discuss all afternoon, many hours. You will get tired, but not hungry. If you get sleepy you may take a nap. I state the program thus in full so that you may know how elaborate and difficult an undertaking confronts us. Mr. Goodwin has heard two of your stereotypes; I fancy the other two are practically identical. A stereo-

type is something fixed, something that harbors no
intention of changing. I don't expect you boys to
change your stories of what happened on that first tee;
what I ask is that you forget all your arguments and
discussions, all your recitals to families and friends, all
the pictures that words have printed on your brains,
and return to the scene itself. That is vitally important. I would have left my house and journeyed to the
scene myself to be with you there, but for the fact that
interruptions would have ruined our efforts. By our
imaginations we must transfer the scene here. Here
we are, boys, at the first tee.

"Here we are. It is Sunday afternoon. Larry
Barstow has engaged two of you; two of you are with
the Kimballs, carrying their bags. You are on familiar
ground, as familiar to you as the rooms of your own
homes. You are occupied with activities so accustomed
as to have become almost automatic. The straps of the
bags are on your shoulders. You, Michael Allen, when
you see Mr. Barstow, your last season's baby, at a
distance from the tee practicing with a mashie, you do
not need to be told what to do; you join him, pick up
his bag, hand him a club perhaps—"

Mike was shaking his head.

"No? What do you do?"

"I begin chasing balls."

"Ah. The balls he was hitting with the mashie."

"Yes, sir."

"Good. What were you doing, William Riley, while
Michael was chasing balls?"

"I was chewing gum."

"Exclusively? I mean, was that the utmost of your
efforts?"

"Well, I was standing holding old Kimball's bag."

Listening to him start, I was thinking that Wolfe's

long words would get the kids so tied up that pretty soon they would just go dead on him, but it worked the other way. Without telling them so he had given them the feeling that he was counting on them to help him show how dumb the hundred psychologists had been, and they weren't going to get licked at it because it took long words to do it.

He went along inch by inch, now with this boy, now with that, sometimes with all of them talking at once. He let them get into a long discussion of the relative merits of various brands of clubs, and sat with his eyes half closed pretending he enjoyed it. He questioned them for half an hour regarding the identities and characteristics of the other caddies and golfers present, those belonging to the matches which immediately preceded the Barstow foursome at the tee. Every time one of the boys bolted ahead to the actual teeing off Wolfe called him back. Among all the irrelevancies I could see one thing, perhaps the main thing, he was doing: he wasn't losing sight for a single instant of each and every club in each and every bag.

For lunch Fritz gave us two enormous chicken pies and four watermelons. I did the serving, as usual when there was company, and by speeding up with my knife and fork I barely managed to get my own meal in by the time the casseroles were empty. The watermelons were simple; I gave a half to each of the boys and the same for Wolfe and myself, and that left one for Fritz. I suspected he wouldn't touch it but thought there might be use for it later on.

After lunch we resumed where we had left off. It was wonderful the way Wolfe had long since opened those boys' minds up and let the air in. They went right ahead. They had forgotten entirely that someone was trying to get something out of them or that they were supposed to be using their memories; they were just like a bunch of kids talking over the ball game they had played the day before, only Wolfe was on top of them every minute not letting them skip a thing and all the time making them go back, and back again. Even so they were making progress. Larry Barstow had made his drive, and Manuel Kimball had made his.

When the break came it was so simple and natural, and went along so easy with all the rest of it, that for a minute I didn't realize what was happening. Wolfe was saying to Chunky Mike:

"Then you handed Barstow his driver. Did you tee up his ball?"

"Yes, sir.—No—I couldn't, because I was over hunting a ball he had put in the rough with his mashie."

"Exactly, Michael, you told us before you were hunting a ball. I wondered then how you could have teed up for Barstow."

William Riley spoke. "He teed up himself. The ball rolled off and I fixed it for him."

"Thank you, William.—So you see, Michael, you did not tee up for him. Wasn't the heavy golf bag a nuisance while you were hunting the lost ball?"

"Naw, we get used to it."

"Did you find the ball?"

"Yes, sir."

"What did you do with it?"

"Put it in the ball pocket."

"Do you state that as a fact or an assumption?"

"I put it in. I remember."

"Right away?"

"Yes, sir."

"Then you must have had the bag with you while you were hunting the ball. In that case, you could not

have handed Barstow his driver when he teed off,
because you weren't there. He could not have removed it from the bag himself, because the bag wasn't
there. Had you perhaps handed him the driver previously?"

"Sure. I must have."

"Michael! We need something much better than
*must have*. You did or you didn't. Remember that you
are supposed to have told us—"

William Riley butted in: "Hey! Mike, that's why he
borrowed old Kimball's driver, because you were off
looking for the ball."

"Ah." Wolfe shut his eyes for a tenth of a second
and then opened them again. "William, it is unnecessary to shout. Who borrowed Mr. Kimball's driver?"

"Barstow did."

"What makes you think so?"

"I don't think so, I know. I had it out ready to hand
to old Kimball, and Barstow's ball rolled off his tee and
I fixed it for him, and when I stood up old Kimball was
saying to Barstow, 'Use mine,' and Barstow reached
out and I handed old Kimball's driver to him."

"And he used it?"

"Sure. He drove right away. Mike didn't come back
with the bag until after old Kimball had drove too."

I was having all I could do to stay in my chair. I
wanted to do a dance like *Spring on the Mountaintop*
that I'd seen in the movies, and pin a bunch of orchids
on William Riley, and throw my arms halfway around
Wolfe which was as far as they would go. I was afraid
to look at Wolfe for fear I would grin so hard and wide
I'd burst my jaw.

He was after the pale skinny kid and the one that
wanted to be a good citizen, but neither of them
remembered anything about Barstow borrowing the

driver. The skinny one said he had his eyes glued far
out on the fairway, spotting the place where Manuel
Kimball had pulled his drive into the bushes, and the
good citizen just didn't remember. Wolfe turned to
Chunky Mike. Mike could not say positively that
Barstow's driver had been in the bag when he had had
it with him hunting the ball, but he could not remember handing it to Barstow, and he could not remember
receiving it back and returning it to the bag. During
all this William Riley was straining his politeness to
keep still. Finally Wolfe got back to him:

"Excuse me, William. Do not think I doubt your
memory or your fidelity to truth. Corroboration is
always helpful. And it might be thought a little curious
that you had forgotten so informing a detail."

The boy protested, "I hadn't forgotten it, I just
didn't happen to think of it."

"You mean that you have not included that incident
in any of your recitals to your friends?"

"Yes, sir."

"Good, William. I put my question badly, but I see
that you have the intelligence to stick to the main
clause. Possibly you mentioned the incident to Mr.
Anderson?"

The boy shook his head. "I haven't seen Mr.
Anderson. The detective came and asked me a few
questions, not much."

"I see." Wolfe sighed, deep and long, and pushed
the button. "It is tea time, messieurs."

Of course for Wolfe that meant beer. I got up and
collected the boys and herded them into the kitchen;
sure enough, the watermelon was intact. I cut it into
four quarters and passed it around. Fritz, having been
to answer Wolfe's bell, was arranging a glass and two
bottles on a tray; but as he went down the hall I

noticed that he turned toward the stairs instead of the office. I glanced at my wrist. It was two minutes to four. The son-of-a-gun had saved his schedule! I left the boys with the melon and hurried out and caught him on his way to the elevator. He said:

"Give the boys my thanks, pay them adequately but not generously, for I am not a generous man, and take them home. Before you leave, telephone the office of E. D. Kimball and learn when he is expected to return from Chicago. He is probably still alive, since he had either the shrewdness or the luck to remove himself a thousand miles from his destiny. If by any chance he has returned get him here at once; on that there must be no delay."

"Yes, sir. And don't you think that if this news got to Mr. Anderson it would only confuse and upset him? Hadn't I better try to persuade the boys to keep it in the family?"

"No, Archie. It is always wiser, where there is a choice, to trust to inertia. It is the greatest force in the world."

When I got back to the kitchen Fritz was cutting an apple pie.

# Chapter 13

After I had finished delivering the caddies here and there all over Westechester, I certainly would have loved to run over to Kimball's place and say to Manuel, "Would you mind telling me whether your father keeps his golf bag in his locker at the club and whether you have a key to it?" I had an idea he would recognize that as a question that couldn't be answered just by lifting his eyebrows. I already had him down for two thousand volts. But I realized that if it was him we had a big advantage in his ignorance of what we had found out, and I also realized that if I expected Manuel Kimball to be arrested and convicted of murder there would have to be a little more evidence than the fact that he made me nervous.

I had another temptation, to stop in at Anderson's office and offer to bet him ten thousand dollars that nobody had murdered Peter Oliver Barstow. Wolfe had certainly started a game of hide-and-seek. For two days he and I had been the only two people alive, except the man that did it, who knew that Barstow had been murdered; now we were the only two, with the same exception and the caddies, who knew that he had been killed by accident.

I did go to the Green Meadow Club, after getting the last caddy delivered; it was close by. I went intending to go into the locker question a little, but after I arrived I got cold feet. It might ruin everything if it became known that we had the faintest interest in lockers, since it was common knowledge that Barstow's bag had never been in his. So I just had a little talk with the caddy master and said hello to the chief steward. Maybe I was hoping to get another eyeful of Manuel Kimball, but I didn't see him anywhere.

E. D. Kimball, as his son had told me, had a grain brokerage office on Pearl Street. When I had telephoned there a little after four o'clock I had been told that Kimball was expected back from Chicago the next day, Friday, on the Century. If it hadn't been for that I think I would have tried to start something there in Westchester that evening, if it had been nothing more than to wait till dark and sneak over to the Kimball place and peek in at the windows; but with Kimball on the way there was nothing to do but wait. I went on home.

After dinner that evening Wolfe had me take my notebook and read to him again about my visit to Manuel Kimball, also everything that Sarah and Larry Barstow had said about him, though that wasn't much. We had a general discussion and got our minds to fit; we even considered the possibility that the lending of the driver had been planned and that old Kimball had murdered Barstow, but of course that was out, that was nothing but drivel. I took a few cracks at Manuel, but when Wolfe put it up to me seriously I had to say that not only was there no evidence against Manuel, there wasn't even any reason to suspect him. As far as I knew, it was no more likely to be him than any other member of the Green Meadow Club who had had opportunity to get at the Kimball locker.

"All the same," I insisted, "if he was my son I'd send him on a trip around the world and build a fence across the Pacific Ocean so he couldn't get through."

Before we went to bed Wolfe outlined again my program for the following day. I didn't care much for the first number on it, but of course he was right; the caddies were sure to talk, and the talk would get to Anderson, and it wouldn't hurt us any to get there first since the information was certain to reach him anyhow. I could perform that errand of mercy and still get to Kimball's office almost as soon as he arrived from Grand Central.

So early the next morning found me in the roadster bound for White Plains again. I was hoping the same motor cop would trip me up, it would have been so neat, since I could have handed him the same yarn as the day before and maybe this time have had the pleasure of an escort to the courthouse. But I made it from Woodlawn to the Main Street bridge without seeing anything more exciting than a squirrel running up a tree.

I was creeping along Main Street behind three lumbering buses like a pony following the elephants in a circus parade, when an idea struck me. I liked it. Wolfe seemed to have the notion that all he needed to do to have anybody call at his office from the Dalai Lama to Al Capone was to tell me to go and get him, but I knew from long experience that you never knew when you were going to run up against someone with as many feet as a centipede and all of them reluctant. And here was I, not only supposed to haul a prominent grain broker out of his office immediately upon his return from a week's absence, but also headed for a

revelation to the District Attorney that would probably result in my having the pleasure of meeting H. R.
Corbett or some other flatfooted myrmidon in the
anteroom of E. D. Kimball's office—and wouldn't that
have been nice? So I parked the roadster in the first
available spot and went to a telephone, and called up
Wolfe and told him we were putting the soup before
the cocktail. He was a little stubborn and gave me an
argument, because he was full of the idea that it would
pay us to hand Anderson something before he inevi-
tably got hold of it himself, but when he saw that I
intended to go on talking right up to a dollar's worth
he said all right, I could return to New York and
proceed to Pearl Street and wait for my victim.

On the way back I reflected that it was just as well
the motor cop hadn't favored me with his attention
after all.

When I got to the number on Pearl Street and left
the elevator at the tenth floor, I discovered that E. D.
Kimball & Company wasn't only selling chicken feed to
backyard poultry kings. It had a suite that took up half
the floor, with its name on doors everywhere and a
double one covered with the names of exchanges all
over the country for an entrance. The clock on the wall
said a quarter to ten; if the Century was on time it was
already at Grand Central, and Kimball might be
expected in fifteen or twenty minutes.

I spoke to a girl at a desk, and after using the
telephone she took me to an inside room and left me with
a square-jawed guy who had his feet on the window sill
looking at the morning paper. He said, "Just a minute,"
and I sat down. After a little he threw the paper on his
desk and turned around.

"Mr. E. D. Kimball will be here pretty soon," I
said. "I know he'll be busy catching up with the week

he's been away. But before he gets started on that I need ten minutes with him on an urgent personal matter. I'm a private detective; here's my card. He never heard of me; I work for Nero Wolfe. Can you fix it for me?"

"What do you want? Tell me what you want."

I shook my head. "It really is personal, and it's damn urgent. You'll just have to trust my honest young face. If you think it's a racket phone the Metropolitan Trust Company at Thirty-fourth Street. They'll tell you that I make a little change in my spare time tending baby carriages."

Square jaws grinned. "I don't know. Mr. Kimball has a dozen appointments, the first one is ten-thirty. I'm his secretary, I know more about his business than he does. You'd better tell me."

"I'm sorry, it has to be him."

"All right, I'll see what I can do. Go on out front—no, wait here. Want to look at the paper?"

He tossed me the paper and got up and gathered some mail and stuff together and left the room with them. At a quick early breakfast I had taken a glance at the front page but hadn't had time for more. Turning through, I saw that the Barstow case was already back to page seven, and not much of it there. Anderson was saying that "progress was being made in the investigation." Dear old progress, I thought, you haven't changed a bit since I saw you last except you're covered with wrinkles and your teeth are falling out. The coroner had nothing definite on the poison, but soon would have. There had never been, in any paper that I had seen, any hint of a suspicion that it was a family job; and now, I thought, there never would be. But this piece took another little crack at Dr. Bradford, and I knew it would be a long time before he would be able to look coronary thrombosis in the face without swallowing hard. I turned to the sports page.

The door opened, and the secretary was there.

"Mr. Goodwin. This way."

In the next room but one, a big room with windows on two sides, a lot of old furniture and a ticker going in a corner, a man sat at a desk. He was smooth-shaven, his hair was turning gray, and while he wasn't fat there was size to him. He looked worried but amused, as if someone had just told him a funny story but he had a toothache. I wondered whether it was the worry or the amusement that came from what the secretary had told him about me, but found out on acquaintance that it was neither one, he always looked that way.

The secretary said, "This is the man, Mr. Kimball."

Kimball grunted and asked me what I wanted. I said that my business was strictly personal. Kimball said, "In that case you'd better take it up with my secretary so I won't have the bother of turning it over to him." He laughed and the secretary smiled and I grinned.

I said, "I only asked for ten minutes, so if you don't mind I'll get started. Nero Wolfe would like to have you call at his office this morning at eleven o'clock."

"Goodness gracious!" The amusement was on top. "Is Nero Wolfe the King of England or something?"

I nodded. "Something. I'll tell you, Mr. Kimball, you'll get this quicker and easier if you let me do it my own way. Just humor me. On Sunday, June fourth, Peter Oliver Barstow died suddenly while he was playing golf with his son and you and your son. On Thursday the eighth you left for Chicago. On Sunday the eleventh the results of an autopsy were announced. I suppose it was in the Chicago papers?"

"Oh, that's it." The worry had ascended. "I knew that would be a nuisance when I got back. I read a lot of poppycock about poison and a needle and whatnot." He turned to his secretary. "Blaine, didn't I write you this would be a nuisance when I returned?"

The secretary nodded. "Yes, sir. You have an appointment at eleven-thirty with a representative of the Westchester District Attorney. I hadn't had time to mention it."

I kept my grin inside. "It's not poppycock, Mr. Kimball. Barstow was killed by a poisoned needle shot out of the handle of a golf driver. That's wrapped up. Now come with me a minute. Here you are at the first tee, ready to shoot. All four of you with your caddies.—No, don't wander off somewhere, stay with me, this is serious. Here you are. Larry Barstow drives. Your son Manuel drives. Peter Oliver Barstow is ready to drive; you are standing near him; remember? His ball rolls off its tee and your caddy fixes it because his caddy is off hunting a ball. Remember? He is ready to drive but hasn't got his driver because his caddy is off with his bag. You say, 'Use mine,' and your caddy straightens up from fixing his ball and hands him your driver. Remember? He drives with your driver, and then jumps and begins rubbing his belly because a wasp stung him. It was that wasp that came out of your driver that killed him. Twenty minutes later he was dead."

Kimball was listening to me with a frown, with the worry and amusement both gone. He went on frowning. When he finally spoke all he said was, "Poppycock."

"No," I said. "You can't make it poppycock just by pronouncing it. Anyway, poppycock or not, it was your driver Barstow used on the first tee. You remember that?"

He nodded. "I do. I hadn't thought of it, but now that you remind me I recall the scene perfectly. It was just as you—"

"Mr. Kimball!" The secretary was secretarying. "It would be better perhaps if you—that is, upon reflection—"

"Better if I what?—Oh. No, Blaine. I knew this would be a nuisance, I knew it very well. Certainly Barstow used my driver. Why shouldn't I say so? I barely knew Barstow. Of course the poisoned needle story is a lot of poppycock, but that won't keep it from being a nuisance."

"It'll be worse than a nuisance, Mr. Kimball." I hitched my chair toward him. "Look here. The police don't know yet that Barstow used your driver. The District Attorney doesn't know it. I'm not suggesting that you hide anything from them, they'll find it out anyway. But whether you think the poisoned needle is poppycock or not, they don't. They know that Barstow was killed by a needle that came out of his driver on the first tee, and when they find out that it was your driver he used, what are they going to do? They won't arrest you for murder just like that, but they'll have you looking in the dictionary for a better word than nuisance. My advice is, see Nero Wolfe. Take your lawyer along if you want to, but see him quick."

Kimball was pulling at his lip. He let his hand fall. At length he said, "Goodness gracious."

"Yes, sir, all of that."

He looked at his secretary. "You know, Blaine, I have no respect for lawyers."

"No, sir."

Kimball got up. "This is a fine to-do. I have told

you before, Blaine, that there is just one thing in the
world I am good at. Trading. I am a good trader, and
that is surprising when you consider how soft I am
really. Soft-hearted. With the more personal aspects
of life I do not know how to deal." He was moving back
and forth behind his desk. "Yes, this appears to be
more than a nuisance. Goodness gracious. What would
you do, Blaine?"

I glared at the secretary. He hesitated. "If you
care to go to see this Nero Wolfe, I could go with you.
If I were you I would take a lawyer."

"What appointments have I?"

"The usual sort of thing, nothing important. At
eleven-thirty the man from the Westchester District
Attorney."

"Oh, I would miss him. Well, tell him anything.
How's the ticker?"

"Firm at the opening. Cotton easing off."

Kimball turned to me. "Where is this Nero Wolfe?
Bring him here."

"Impossible, Mr. Kimball. He is—" But Wolfe had
once found out that I had told a man he was infirm,
and I didn't want that to happen again. "He is an
eccentric genius. It's only up on Thirty-fifth Street.
I've got my car down below and I'd be glad to run you
up."

Kimball said, "I've only met one genius in my life;
he was an Argentine cowboy. A *gaucho*. All right.
Wait for me in the front office."

Back in the front room I had first entered, I sat on
the edge of a chair. Meeting E. D. Kimball and looking
at him and talking with him had somehow cleared my
mind. I saw plainly what I should have realized the
night before, that the minute it came out that it was
Kimball's driver that had been turned into what Wolfe

called a lethal toy, and the minute Kimball himself
arrived on the scene, we were probably turning into
the homestretch. It was the same as if you found a
man murdered and by some kind of hocus-pocus were
able to bring him back to life long enough to ask him
who killed him, and get his answer. That's what E. D.
Kimball was, a man who had been murdered and was
still living. I had to get him up to Wolfe's place and
lock the door, and get him there quick, before Corbett
got a chance at him—or, as far as that was concerned,
anyone else. Anyone at all. How did I know but what
it was the secretary, Square-jaw Blaine, who had had
that driver made and found opportunity to get it into
Kimball's bag? At that moment, as I sat there on the
edge of the chair, Blaine might be sticking a knife into
Kimball as he had into Carlo Maffei. . . .

It was ten-fifty. I got up and began walking up and
down the linoleium. Anderson's man—I was sure it
would be Corbett—was due at half past eleven, and he
might take it into his thick head to come early and
wait. I had just decided to ask the girl at the desk to
phone into Blaine for me, when the inner door opened
and Kimball appeared with his hat on. I was pretty
glad to see him. He nodded at me and I jumped to the
entrance door to open it for him.

As we got into the elevator I observed, "Mr. Blaine
isn't coming."

Kimball shook his head. "He's needed here more
than I need him. I like your face. I find I usually do
like a man's face, and it pays every time. Trust is one
of the finest things in the world, trust in your fellow
man."

Yes, I thought to myself, I'll bet a successful
trader like you can use up lots of trust.

It was only half a block to where I had parked the

Fer-de-Lance    185

roadster. I cut across as far west as I could get to avoid the traffic, and it was still short of eleven-fifteen when I was ushering Kimball in ahead of me at Wolfe's door.

I took Kimball to the front room and asked him to wait there a minute, then returned to the entrance and made sure the latch was caught. Then I went to the kitchen. Fritz was making cherry tarts; a pan was just out of the oven and I nabbed one and stuffed it in and darned near burned my tongue off. I told Fritz, "One guest for lunch and don't put any poison in it. And be careful who you let in; if there's any doubt, call me."

In the office, Wolfe was at his desk. As soon as I saw him I stopped, exasperated, for he was cleaning house. He had only one drawer in his desk, a wide shallow one in the middle, and since he had begun having his beer in bottles instead of brought up from the basement in a pitcher, he had formed the habit, every time he opened a bottle, of pulling the drawer out and dropping the bottle cap in there. Fritz wasn't supposed to open any drawers in the office, and I knew Wolfe had some sort of a nutty notion that he was saving the bottle caps for something so I had let them alone. Now, when I entered, he had the drawer half out and was scattering the caps all over the desk, arranging them in piles.

I said, "Mr. E. D. Kimball is in the front room. Do you want him to come in and help you?"

"The devil." Wolfe looked around at his piles, and at me helplessly. He sighed. "Can't he wait a while?"

"Of course, sure. How would next week do?"

He sighed again. "Confound it. Bring him in."

"With that junk scattered all over the desk?—Oh, all right, I told him you're eccentric." I had kept my voice lowered; now I lowered it some more to let him know how Kimball had shaped up and what I had said to him. He nodded, and I went to get Kimball.

Kimball had his worried-amused look back on again. I introduced him and pulled a chair around for him, and after they had exchanged a few words I said to Wolfe, "If you won't need me, sir, I'll get on to those reports." He nodded, and I got fixed at my desk with papers all around and half underneath a pad which I used for a notebook on such occasions. I had got my signs so abbreviated that I could get down every word of some pretty fast talk and still give the impression to a careless eye that I was just shuffling around looking for last week's delicatessen bill.

Wolfe was saying, "You are perfectly correct, Mr. Kimball. A man's time is his own only by sufferance. There are many ways in which he may be dispossessed: flood, famine, war, marriage—not to speak of death, which is the most satisfactory of all because it closes the question finally."

"Goodness gracious." Kimball was fidgety. "I do not see why that should make it satisfactory."

"You came very near finding out, a week ago last Sunday." Wolfe wiggled a finger at him. "You are a busy man, Mr. Kimball, and you have just returned to your office after a week's absence. Why, under those circumstances, did you take time this morning to come to see me?"

Kimball stared at him. "That's what I want you to tell me."

"Good. You came because you were confused. That is not a desirable condition for a man in the extreme of danger, as you are. I see no indication in your face of alarm or fear, merely confusion. That is astonishing, knowing as I do what Mr. Goodwin has told you. He has informed you that on June fourth, twelve days ago, it was nothing but inadvertence that killed Peter Oliver Barstow, and the same inadvertence saved your life. You met his statement with incredulity, crudely expressed. Why?"

"Because it's nonsense." Kimball was impatient. "Rubbish."

"Before, you said poppycock. Why?"

"Because it is. I didn't come here to argue about that. If the police get into difficulties trying to explain something they don't happen to understand and want to make up any sort of a fancy tale to cover themselves, that's all right, I believe in letting every man handle his own business his own way, but they don't need to expect me to take any stock in it, and they can leave me out of it. I'm a busy man with something better to do. You're wrong, Mr. Wolfe, I didn't come to see you because I was confused, and I certainly didn't come to give you a chance to try to scare me. I came because the police apparently are trying to mix me up in a fancy tale that might give me lot of trouble and publicity I don't want, and your man gave me to understand you could show me how to avoid it. If you can, go ahead and I'll pay you for it. If you can't, say so, and I'll find better advice."

"Well." Wolfe leaned back in his chair and let his half-shut eyes study the broker's face. Finally he shook his head. "I'm afraid I can't show you how to escape trouble, Mr. Kimball. I might with good fortune show you how to escape death. Even that is uncertain."

"I have never expected to escape death."

"Do not quibble. I mean of course unpleasant and imminent death. I shall be frank with you, sir. If I do not at once bid you good day and let you depart on your business, it is not because of my certain knowledge that you are confronting death like a fool. I refrain from contributing to certain Christian enterprises because I think that no man should be saved by coercion. But here I am guided by self-interest. Mrs. Barstow has offered a reward of fifty thousand dollars for the discovery of her husband's murderer. I intend to discover him; and to do so I need only learn who it was that tried to kill you on June fourth and will proceed to do so within a reasonable time if means are not found of preventing him. If you will help me, it will be convenient for both of us; if you will not, it may well be that only through some misstep or mischance in his successful second attempt shall I be able to bring him to account for his abortive first one. Naturally it would be all the same to me."

Kimball shook his head. But he didn't get up; instead, he was settling into his chair. Still he showed no sign of alarm, he merely looked interested. He said, "You're a good talker, Mr. Wolfe. I don't think you're going to be of any use to me, since you seem to like fancy tales as well as the police, but you're a good talker."

"Thank you. You like good talking?"

Kimball nodded. "I like everything good. Good talking, and good trading, and good manners, and good living. I don't mean high living, I mean good. I've tried to live a good life myself, and I like to think everyone else does. I know some can't, but I think they try to. I was thinking of that in the car a little while ago, riding up here with your man. I'm not saying that the tale he told me made no impression on me at all; of course it did. When I told him it was poppycock I meant it, and I still mean it, but nevertheless it got me thinking. What if somebody had tried to kill me? Who would it be?"

He paused, and Wolfe murmured at him, "Well, who would it be?"

"Nobody." Kimball was emphatic.

I thought to myself, if this guy turns out like Barstow, so lovable a mosquito wouldn't bite him, I'm through.

Wolfe said, "I once met a man who had killed two other men because he had been bettered in a horse trade."

Kimball laughed. "I'm glad he wasn't in grain. If his method of averaging down was universal I would have been killed not once, but a million times. I'm a good trader, it's the one thing I'm proud of. What I love is wheat. Of course what you love is a fancy tale and a good murder, and that's all right, that's your business. What I love is wheat. Do you know there are seven hundred million bushels of wheat in the world? And I know where every one of them is this minute. Every one."

"You probably own a hundred or so yourself."

"No, not one. I'm out. Tomorrow I'll be back in, or next week.—But I was saying, I'm a good trader. I've come out on top in a good many deals, but no one has any kick coming, I've stuck to the rules. That's what I was thinking on the way riding up here. I don't know all the details of this Barstow business, just what I've read in the papers. As I understand it, they haven't found the driver. I don't believe it ever existed. But even if they found it, and even if I did lend mine to Barstow on the first tee, I still would have a hard time believing anyone intended it for me. I've stuck to the rules and played fair, in my business and in my private life."

He paused. Wolfe murmured, "There are many kinds of injuries, Mr. Kimball. Real, fancied, material, spiritual, trivial, fatal—"

"I've never injured anyone."

"Really? Come now. The essence of sainthood is expiation. If you will permit it, take me. Whom have I not injured? I don't know why your presence should stimulate me to confession, but it does. Forget the Barstow murder, since to you it is poppycock; forget the police; we shall find means of preventing their becoming a nuisance to you. I enjoy talking with you; unless your affairs are really pressing. I would not keep you from anything urgent."

"You won't." Kimball looked pleased. "When anything's urgent I attend to it. The office has got along without me for a week; an hour more won't hurt them."

Wolfe nodded approvingly. "Will you have a glass of beer?"

"No, thanks. I don't drink."

"Ah." Wolfe pressed the button. "You're an extraordinary man, sir. You have learned to abstain, and you are at the same time a good businessman and a philosopher.—One glass, Fritz.—But we were speaking of injuries, and I was hovering on confession. Whom have I not injured? That of course is rhetorical; I would not pose as a ruffian; and I suffer from a romantic conscience. Even so, making all allowances, it is not easy for me to understand why I am still alive. Less than a year ago a man sitting in the chair you now occupy promised to kill me at his earliest convenience. I had pulled the foundations of his existence from under him from purely mercenary motives. There is a woman living not twenty blocks from here, and a remarkably intelligent one, whose appetite and disposition would be vastly improved by news of my death. I could continue these examples almost to infinity. But there are others more difficult to confess and more impossible to condone.—Thank you, Fritz."

Wolfe removed the opener from the drawer and opened a bottle and dropped the cap into the drawer before he closed it again. Then he filled a glass and gulped it down. Kimball was saying, "Of course every man has to take the risks of his profession."

Wolfe nodded. "That's the philosopher in you again. It is easy to see, Mr. Kimball, that you are a cultured and an educated man. Perhaps you will understand the obscure psychology which prompts— well, me, for instance—to persist in an action which deserves unqualified condemnation. There is a woman under this roof at this moment, living on the top floor of this building, who cannot wish me dead only because her heart is closed to venom by its own sweetness. I torture her daily, hourly. I know I do and that knowledge tortures me; still I persist. You can guess at the obscurity of the psychology and the depth of the torture when I tell you that the woman is my mother."

I got it all down as he said it, and I almost glanced up at him in surprise, he said it so convincingly, with little emotion in his voice but the impression that the feeling underneath was so overwhelming that it was kept down only by a determined will. For a second he darned near had me feeling sorry for his mother though it was I who, balancing the bank account each month, checked off the debit item for his remittance to her at her home in Budapest.

"Goodness gracious," Kimball said.

Wolfe downed another glass of beer and slowly shook his head from side to side. "You will understand why I can recite a category of injuries. I can justly claim familiarity."

It seemed to me that Kimball wasn't going to take the hint. He was looking sympathetic and self-satisfied. In fact, he smirked. "I'm wondering why you think I'm an educated man."

Wolfe's eyebrows went up. "Isn't it obvious?"

"It's a compliment if you think so. I quit school—out in Illinois—when I was twelve, and ran away from home. It wasn't much of a home, with an uncle and aunt. My parents were dead. I haven't been in a school since. If I'm educated it's self-education."

"Not the worst kind." Wolfe's voice was low and quiet, not much more than a murmur; the voice that he used to say "go on" without saying it. "You are another proof of it, sir. And New York is itself an education for a lad of that age if he had spirit and character."

"Probably. It might be, but I didn't come to New York. I went to Texas. After a year on the Panhandle, to Galveston, and from there to Brazil and the Argentine."

"Indeed! You did have spirit; and your education is cosmopolitan."

"Well, I covered a lot of territory. I was in South America twenty years, mostly in the Argentine. When I came back to the States I nearly had to go to school again to learn English. I've lived—well, I've lived a lot of funny ways. I've seen a lot of rough stuff and I've taken part in it, but wherever and whatever it was I always did one thing, I always stuck to the rules. When I came back to the States I was selling beef, but gradually I worked into grain. That was where I found myself; grain takes a man not afraid to guess and ready to ride his guess the way a *gaucho* rides a horse."

"You were a *gaucho?*"

"No, I've always been a trader. It was born in me. Now I wonder if you would believe this. Not that I'm ashamed of it; sitting in my office sometimes, with a dozen markets waiting to see which way I'm going to jump, I remember it and I'm proud of it. For two years I was a rope peddler."

"Not really."

"Yes. Three thousand miles a season in the saddle. I still show it when I walk."

Wolfe was looking at him admiringly. "A real nomad, Mr. Kimball. Of course you weren't married then."

"No. I married later, in Buenos Aires. I had an office then on the Avenida de Mayo—"

He stopped. Wolfe poured another glass of beer. Kimball was looking at him, but his eyes were following the movement without seeing it, for obviously the vision was inside. Something had pulled him up short and transported him to another scene.

Wolfe nodded at him and and murmured, "A memory—I know—"

Kimball nodded back. "Yes—a memory. That's a funny thing. Goodness gracious. It might almost seem as if I had thought of that on account of what you said about injuries. The different kinds, fancied injuries. Fatal injuries. But this wasn't one at all, the only injury was to me. And it wasn't fancied. But I have a conscience too, as you said you have, only I don't think there's anything romantic about it."

"The injury was to you."

"Yes. One of the worst injuries a man can suffer. It was thirty years ago, and it's still painful. I married a girl, a beautiful Argentine girl, and we had a baby boy. The boy was only two years old when I came home from a trip a day too early and found my best friend in my bed. The boy was on the floor with his toys. I stuck to the rules; I've told myself a thousand times that if I had it to do over I'd do it again. I shot twice—"

Wolfe murmured, "You killed them."

"I did. The blood ran onto the floor and got on one of the toys. I left the boy there—I've often wondered why I didn't shoot him too, since I was sure he wasn't mine—and went to a café and got drunk. That was the last time I drank—"

"You came to the States—"

"A little later, a month later. There was no question of escaping, you don't have to run away from that in the Argentine, but I wound things up and left South America for good, and I've only been back once, four years ago."

"You brought the boy with you?"

"No. That's what I went back for. Naturally I didn't want him, my wife's family took him. They lived out on the pampa, that's where I got her from. The boy's name was Manuel, and that had been my friend's name; I had suggested naming him after my friend. I came back alone, and for twenty-six years I lived alone, and I found the market a better wife than the one I had tried. But I suppose there was a doubt in me all the time, or maybe as a man gets older he softens up. Maybe I just got lonely, or maybe I wanted to persuade myself that I really had a son. Four years ago I got things in shape and went to Beunos Aires. I found him right away. The family had gone broke when he was young and they were mostly dead, and he had had a hard time of it, but he had made good. When I found him he was one of the best aviators in the Argentine army. I had to persuade him to break away. For a while he tried my office, but he wasn't cut out for it, and he's going into the airplane business with my money. I bought a place up in Westchester and built a new house on it, and I only hope when he gets married he won't take any trips that end the way mine did."

"Of course he knows—about his mother?"

"I don't think so. I don't know, it's never been mentioned. I hope not. Not that I've got any remorse about it; if I had it to do over I'd do it again. I don't pretend, even to him, that Manuel is exactly the son I would want to get if I could just file a buy order; after all, he's Argentine and I'm Illinois. But his name's Kimball and he's got a head on him. He'll get an American girl, I hope, and that will even it up."

"Indubitably." Wolfe had left his beer untasted so long that the foam was gone, leaving it as still as tea. He reached for the glass and gulped it. "Yes, Mr. Kimball, you proved your point; the injury was to you. But you—let us say—took care of it. If there was an injury to the boy you are repairing it handsomely. Your confession is scarcely as damaging as mine; I perforce admit culpability; as Mr. Goodwin would say, I have no out. But if the boy feels the injury?"

"No."

"But if by chance he does?"

I saw Kimball's eyes fall. It was sometimes not easy to meet Wolfe's eyes, but Kimball the trader should have been impervious to any eye. He wasn't. He didn't try it again. Abruptly he got up and, standing, said:

"He doesn't. I took no such advantage of your confession, Mr. Wolfe."

"You may, sir." Wolfe didn't stir. "You are welcome to all advantages. Why not be frank? There is no danger in me to the innocent." He looked at his watch. "In five minutes there will be lunch. Lunch with me. I do not pretend to be your friend, but certainly for you or yours I have no ill-will. Thirty years ago, Mr. Kimball, you faced a bitter disappointment and acted upon it with energy; have you lost your nerve? Let us see what might be done. Lunch with me."

But Kimball wouldn't. As a matter of fact, it seemed to me that for the first time he looked scared. He wanted to get away from there. I didn't quite get it.

Wolfe tried some more to persuade him to stay, but Kimball wasn't having any. He quit looking scared and got polite. He said goodness gracious, he had no idea it was so late, and that he was sorry Wolfe was able to suggest nothing to prevent the police from making a nuisance of themselves, and that he trusted Wolfe would consider their conversation confidential.

I went to the door with him. I offered to drive him back downtown, but he said no, he could get a taxi at the corner. From the stoop I watched him shoving off, and he was right, you could see he had been in a saddle enough to bend his knees out.

When I got back to the office Wolfe wasn't there, so I went on to the dining-room. He was getting himself set in front of his chair, with Fritz behind ready to push it. After he had got fixed I sat down. I had never known him to discuss business during a meal, but I was thinking that day he might. He didn't. However, he did violate a custom; ordinarily he loved to talk as he ate, leisurely and rambling on any subject that might happen to suggest itself, as much to himself as to me, I suspected, though I think I was always a good audience. That day he didn't say a word. In between his bites I could see his lips pushing out and pulling back again. He didn't even remember to commend Fritz for the dishes; so as Fritz cleared away for the coffee I tossed a wink at him and he nodded back with a solemn smile, as much as to say that he understood and would bear no grudge.

In the office after lunch Wolfe got into his chair, still silent. I straightened up the papers on my desk and removed from the pad the sheets that I had used and clipped them together. Then I sat down and waited for the spirit to move him. After a while he pulled a sigh that would have fed a blacksmith's bellows all afternoon, shoved his chair back so he could get the drawer of his desk open, and began raking the piles of bottle caps into the drawer. I watched him. When it was finished and the drawer shut he said:

"Mr. Kimball is an unhappy man, Archie."

I said, "He's a slicker."

"Perhaps. Nevertheless, unhappy. He is beset from many sides. His son wants to kill him, and intends to. But if Kimball admits that fact, even to himself, he is done for and he knows it. His son, and through his son the future Kimballs, are now all he has to live for. So he cannot admit it and will not. But if he doesn't admit it, and not only admit it but do something about it, again he is done for, for shortly he will die and probably in a thoroughly disagreeable manner. The dilemma is too much for him, and no wonder, for it has additional complications. He wants help, but he dares not ask for it. The reason he dares not ask for it is that like all mortal fools he hopes against all hope. What if—he does not admit this, but no man is so poor that he cannot afford a *what if*—what if his son did attempt to kill him and by mischance killed Barstow instead? Might the son not take that mischance as an omen? Might he not be persuaded—the father could even discuss it with him, man to man—might he not be persuaded to make a sensible trade with destiny and give his father's life for the one he has inadvertently taken? That way Kimball could live to see a grandchild on his knee. In the meantime, until that trade, which would be the most triumphant one of his career, could be consummated, there would be great and constant danger. It would be enough to frighten a younger and an honester man. But he dares not ask for help, for in doing so he would expose his son to a peril as great as the one that confronts himself. It is an admirable dilemma; I have rarely seen one with so many horns and all of them so sharp. It so confused Kimball that he did something which I suspect has been rare with him; he acted like a fool. He exposed his son without gaining any protection for himself. The facts behind the fear he blurted out; the fear itself he denied."

Wolfe stopped. He leaned back in his chair and let his chin fall and laced his fingers on his belly.

"Okay," I said. "Okay for Kimball. Now Manuel. I told you he made me nervous. But aside from that, shall I take the typewriter and make a list of all the swell proof we have that he killed Barstow?"

"Confound it." Wolfe sighed. "I know, the picture must be varnished. The can is empty, Archie. In fact, the can itself is gone. There is nothing."

I nodded. "If I may make a suggestion? There is a flying field at Armonk, which is only a few miles from Pleasantville. If I may drive up there and get curious?"

"You may. But I doubt if he used a public flying field. He would prefer privacy. So before you go, try this. Take this down."

"Long?"

"Very short."

I got a pad and pencil. Wolfe dictated:

*Whoever saw me land in the pasture with my
airplane Monday evening, June fifth, please
communicate. Am winning a bet and will
share.*

I said, "Good. Swell. But it might have been a golf
links."

Wolfe shook his head. "Still too public, and too
much loud objection. Leave it pasture; it will have to
be definite.—No, do not phone it. Stop at the *Times*
office on your way uptown; leave it, and make sure the
answers will reach us. Also—yes, the other papers,
morning and evening, with similar proper arrangements. Manuel Kimball is ingenious enough to be
annoying; should he see the advertisement it might
occur to him to acquire the answers."

I got up. "All right, I'm off."

"Just a moment. Does White Plains come before
Armonk?"

"Yes."

"Then on your way see Anderson. Tell him everything except Carlo Maffei and the Argentine. Present
it to him; a fine gesture. Also tell him that E. D.
Kimball is in imminent and constant danger and
should have protection. Kimball of course will deny it
and the precaution will be futile; nevertheless, when
men undertake to meddle in the affairs of violent
persons as you and I do, certain duties are assumed
and should not be neglected."

I knew it had to be done, but I said, "I'd just as
soon give Anderson a piece of information as tip a
subway guard."

"Soon, now," Wolfe replied, "we may be in a
position to send him a bill."

# Chapter 14

**W**hat with stopping to put the ads in and the Friday afternoon summer traffic, by the time I got to the District Attorney's office in White Plains it was nearly four o'clock. I hadn't bothered to telephone ahead to see if Anderson or Derwin would be in because I had to go through White Plains anyhow to get to Armonk.

They were both there. The girl at the desk threw me a smile when I went up to her, and I liked that; when the time comes that they stop remembering you it means that your pan is losing its shine. Instead of asking my name or who I wanted to see, she nodded and pressed down a key on the switchboard. I said, "Who do you think I am, the prodigal son?" She said, "They'll kill you instead of the calf." After she had talked into the phone a couple of seconds one of the doors snapped open and Derwin came out.

He came up to me. "What do you want?"

I grinned. "This is hot. Can you get Ben Cook here in a hurry?" Because I didn't like fits I went right on, "I want to tell Mr. Anderson something. Or you, or both of you."

I never did find out, I don't know to this day, what

that White Plains bunch thought they had been doing during the six days that had passed since the autopsy. There was a hint or two, of course; that Friday afternoon Anderson told me that Corbett had spent two days at Holland University. Probably they got hold of a rumor that there was a student there whom Barstow had kept in school an extra hour or some such sizzler. I know they hadn't come within a mile of anything warm. Though it was hard to believe, it was a fact that Anderson didn't even know that Barstow had been using a new bag of golf clubs that had been given to him by his wife as a birthday present, until I told him. I only got one piece of news that afternoon; a New York chemist had said definitely that Barstow's blood showed snake venom. It was that report that had got Anderson and Derwin's minds off the golf clubs and dwelling fondly on copperheads; and though I hate like the devil to admit it, it gave me a few bad hours, too. Although it left the needle unexplained, I had seen odder things than a needle in a man's stomach accounted for by coincidence. Copperheads were not unknown in Westchester; what if one had been visiting the Green Meadow Club that Sunday and bit Barstow? On the foot or anywhere. It was about good enough for a headache. The snake venom report hadn't been given to the newspapers, and it wasn't given to me until after Anderson and Derwin had my tale, so it didn't cramp my style.

And of course even if the Green Meadow fairway had been carpeted with copperheads a foot deep, Anderson and Derwin couldn't get around the fact that Nero Wolfe had told them exactly what the autopsy would show them.

Derwin took me into Anderson's room. Anderson was there with another man, not a dick, he looked like a lawyer. I sat down and hooked my panama on my knee.

Anderson said, "What's on your mind?"

I just simply didn't like that man. I couldn't even have any fun with him, to speak of, because whatever it was disagreeable about him, his face and his manner, was so deep and primitive that the only possible way to get any real satisfaction would have been to haul off and plug him in the nose. Derwin was different; he certainly wasn't my favorite uncle, but he would take a lot of kidding.

I said, "Information from Nero Wolfe. Maybe you'd better call a stenographer."

He had to pass a few remarks first, but I went patient and forbearing on him. What was the use of thinking up a lot of snappy comebacks when I couldn't use the one I wanted to? So pretty soon he saw he wasn't getting anywhere, and called a stenographer, and I spieled it off. I told about the birthday present, and the whereabouts of Barstow's golf bag and who had put it there, and the loan of Kimball's driver on the first tee. I suggested that they find out all about Kimball's bag, where he kept it and who had access to it, though I knew that anyone approaching from that direction would never get anywhere, for Manuel must have had any number of opportunities. Then I gave them Wolfe's message about protection for Kimball. I made that strong. I said that Wolfe felt that the responsibility for the safety of a citizen whose life was in jeopardy was a burden for the authorities to assume, and that he would not be answerable, to himself or anyone else, for anything that might happen to E. D. Kimball at any moment.

When I got through Anderson asked questions,

and some I answered and some I didn't. He kept it up quite a while, until finally I had to grin at him.

"Mr. Anderson," I said, "you're trying to lure me on."

He was smooth. "But not succeeding, Goodwin. I'll be frank with you. When the autopsy verified Wolfe's prediction, I thought he knew who did it. When the reward was offered and he didn't grab it, I knew he didn't know. We know everything you do now, and a lot more, except the one detail of how Wolfe came to make the prediction in the first place. I'd like to know that, though I don't believe it can be of much value since Wolfe doesn't get anywhere with it. All the same, you might tell me. I'll tell you anything and everything. For instance, this morning snake venom was identified in Barstow's blood."

"Thanks. That saves me the trouble of reading tonight's papers."

"The papers haven't got it. I can tell you a few other things too."

So he did; he mentioned Corbett's trip to the university and a lot of other junk, and wound it up with a lecture on copperheads. Wanting to get on to Armonk, and to be alone to see if the snake venom news sounds hollow when you dropped it on the sidewalk, I thanked him and got up and put on my hat, and he got sore. I didn't bother anymore; I reminded him about protecting E. D. Kimball, and walked out.

Since it was only a few miles out of the way and I didn't know how long it would take me at Armonk, I decided to drop in at the Barstows first. From a booth on Main Street I telephoned; Sarah Barstow was home. Twenty minutes later I was turning into their drive. The same guard was there, and when I stopped he gave me a look and nodded me on.

Some people were on the front terrace having tea. I went to the side door, and Small took me to the sun-room at the back, only since it was afternoon the blinds were all up and the glass was in shadow. Small told me that Miss Barstow would join me shortly, and asked if I would have some tea.

I said, "You didn't think that up all alone."

Of course not a flicker. "Miss Barstow told me to offer you tea, sir."

"Sure. She would. A glass of milk would be nice."

In a minute he was back with the milk, and when it was about half gone Sarah Barstow came in. I had told her on the phone it was just a social call, nothing to worry about, and as I got up and looked at her coming toward me, natural and young and human, I thought to myself that if she ever started a clinic for broken hearts I'd be the first in line if I wasn't too busy. I said to her:

"You've had a nap since I saw you last."

She smiled. "I've slept forever. Sit down."

I took my chair and picked up my glass. "Thank you for the milk, Miss Barstow. It's swell milk, too. I'm sorry to call you away from your friends, but it won't take long. I've just been over at Mr. Anderson's office having a chat. I told him about the birthday present and about your night trip to the Tarrytown ferry.—Now wait a minute, you certainly are quick on the trigger. It don't mean a thing, it was just strategy, you know, what generals lose battles with. That junk is all out. There never was any phony driver in your father's bag, when your mother gave it to him or any other time. Nobody ever tried to kill him. He died by an accident."

She was staring at me. I waited to let her digest it.

She said, "Then it wasn't murder at all— Nero Wolfe was wrong—but how—"

"I didn't say it wasn't murder. Wolfe wasn't wrong. The accident happened on the first tee. Your father's caddy was off with his bag, and your father borrowed E. D. Kimball's driver. It was that borrowed driver that did it. It was a rotten break, that's all. Nobody wanted to kill him."

She said, "My father—I knew my father—"

I nodded. "Yes, I guess you knew your father all right. That's all I wanted to tell you, Miss Barstow. I didn't like to phone it, because I don't know when Anderson will want to release it. So it's confidential. I didn't want you to find out from him what I had told him and maybe think I had double-crossed you. If he should be so curious that he begins asking you why you go around throwing golf bags in the river, in spite of the fact that that's all washed up, tell him to go to hell. That's why I told you that. The reason I told you about Kimball lending his driver was because I know it can't be any fun lying in bed wondering who murdered your father when you ought to be asleep. Nobody murdered him. But it would be okay to keep that in the family for a while." I got up. "That's all."

She sat still. She looked up at me. "Are you going? I think I'll sit here a little. Thank you, Mr. Goodwin.— You didn't finish your milk."

I picked up the glass and emptied it and went on out. I was thinking that even on a busy day I might find time to drop in at that clinic.

By the time I got to Armonk it was after six o'clock, but the sun was still high and a couple of planes were perched on the field and another one was just landing. There was signs all around, FLY $5, and TRY THE SKY, and other come-ons, painted on the fence and the walls of the wooden hangars. It wasn't much of a field as far as equipment was concerned, that is, it wasn't very elaborate, but the field itself was good-sized and well-kept and flat as a pancake. I parked the roadster off the highway and went through the gate alongside one of the hangars. There was no one around outside except the pilot and two passengers getting out of the plane that had just landed. I went along looking in the doors and in the third hangar found a couple of guys throwing pennies at a crack.

They straightened up and looked at me and I nodded.

"Hello." I grinned. "I hate to interrupt your game, but I'm looking for a map, a bound book of flying maps. Maybe that isn't the technical term for it, but I'm not a flyer."

One of them was just a kid. The other one, a little older, in a mechanic's uniform, shook his head.

"We don't sell maps."

"I don't mean I want to buy one. I'm looking for one, bound in red leather, that my brother left here a week ago Monday. June fifth, it was. You probably remember. He knew I was coming past here today on my way to the Berkshires and asked me to stop and get it. He landed here at your field, in his private plane, around six o'clock that evening, and took off again around ten. He's pretty sure he must have left the map here somewhere."

The mechanic was shaking his head. "He didn't land at this field."

I was surprised. "What? Of course he did. He ought to know what field he landed at."

"Maybe he ought to, but he don't, not if he says he landed here. There's been no machine here except ours for over a month, except a biplane that came down one morning last week."

"That's funny." I couldn't understand it. "Are you sure? Maybe you weren't here."

"I'm always here, mister. I sleep here. If you ask me, I think your brother had better find his map. I think he needs it."

"It sure looks that way. Are there any other fields around here?"

"Not very close. There's one at Danbury, and one up toward Poughkeepsie."

"Well. This is one on him. Sorry I interrupted your game. I'm much obliged."

"Don't mention it."

I went out and sat in the roadster to decide what to do. The mechanic hadn't talked like a man earning the five-spot that someone had given him to keep his mouth shut; he had just been telling what had happened, or rather what hadn't happened. Armonk was out. Poughkeepsie too; for although Manuel might have made it there in twenty minutes in his plane, he had to have time to get to wherever he had left his car and drive to where he was going to meet Carlo Maffei. He had almost certainly met Maffei near some subway station uptown in New York, and the date had been for seven-thirty. He could never have made it from Poughkeepsie. Danbury, I thought, was barely possible, and I headed the roaster north.

I didn't like to do that at all, for it was June 16, the anniversary of the day little Tommie Williamson had been restored to his parents in Wolfe's office, and Mr. and Mrs. Burke Williamson and Tommie—four years older now—were going to celebrate as usual by dining with Wolfe. Each year they tried to get him to go to their place, but they never succeeded. They were all

right, and I liked Tommie, but the point I had in mind
was the importance that Fritz attached to that occasion. Of course he knew that Williamson owned a chain
of hotels, and I suppose he wanted to show him what
a pity it was that hotels never had anything fit to eat.
As Saul Panzer would say, lovin' babe, what a feed!
One-fifth of that cargo was labeled for my hold, and
instead of being there to stow it away where it
belonged, at eight o'clock that evening I was unenjoy-
ing myself at a fern and palm joint in Danbury with a
plate of liver and bacon that had absolutely been fried
in differential grease.

Nothing went right in Danbury. After the lubri-
cated liver I went out to the flying field. Nobody knew
anything. I waited around, and finally long after dark
a man showed up who gave me complete dissatisfac-
tion. He kept records but didn't need to, for he
remembered what minute the sun had set every day
since Easter. When I left I was certain that Manuel
Kimball had never been near the place; and though it
was a grand summer night I didn't particularly enjoy
the drive back to New York. It was after midnight
when I reached Thirty-fifth Street; the Williamsons
had departed and Wolfe had gone to bed.

In the top drawer of my desk was a note in his fine
slender writing: *Archie, if you learned nothing, in the
morning try the metal-worker advertisement; and if
your grace and charm can again entice Miss Fiore,
have her here at eleven. N.W.*

I never like to eat late at night unless it seems
unavoidable, but I went to the kitchen anyhow for a
glass of milk and to look sadly over the remains like a
man visiting the graveyard where his sweetheart's
bones are resting. Then I went on upstairs and turned
in.

I slept late. While I was eating breakfast Fritz told me about the dinner I had missed, but I was only politely interested; yesterday's meals never concern me much. Looking through the newspaper, I turned to the classified ads to see the one I had put in the day before; it was there and I thought it read good. Before I went out I went to the office and cleaned around a little, for it wasn't going to be much of a morning.

One of the various little things that were keeping me doubtful about Manuel Kimball was the fact that the metal-worker ad was keyed at the downtown office. Wouldn't he have been more apt—since even a man plotting murder will not ignore convenience—to use Times Square or 125th Street? But of course that wasn't a real objection, just one of the little things you think about when you're looking around for something to hang a chance on. In any event, I was counting on getting nowhere with that ad.

That's where I got to. To walk into the *Times* downtown classified ad office and try to find out what girl took a particular ad two months before, and what kind of a person handed it in and who called for the replies, was about like asking a Coney Island lifeguard if he remembers the fellow with a bald head who went in bathing on the Fourth of July. I had stopped at the D. A.'s office on the way down and got Purley Stebbins to go with me with his badge, but the only one that did any good was him since I had to buy him a drink. By going over the files I did learn that the ad had appeared in the issue of April 16, and while that spoiled nothing since it fitted in all right, I couldn't even figure that it paid for the drink.

I took Purley back to his temple of justice and went on to Sullivan Street.

Mrs. Ricci wasn't going to let me in. She came to

the door herself and put on a scowl as soon as she saw me. I grinned at her and told her I had come to take Anna Fiore for a ride, and I behaved like a gentleman in the face of all her observations until she began shoving the door on me so hard that my foot nearly slipped. Then I got businesslike.

"See here, Mrs. Ricci, wait a minute, you might as well listen while you've still got some breath. Now listen! Anna is in bad, not with us but with the police. Cops. She told us something that could get her in a lot of trouble if the police knew it. They don't know it and we don't want them to know it, but they suspect something. My boss wants to put Anna wise. He's got to. Do you want her to go to jail? Come on now, and cut out the injured womanhood."

She glared at me. "You just lie."

"No. Never. Ask Anna. Trot her out."

"You stay here."

"Right."

She shut the door and I sat down on the top step and lit a cigarette. Since it was Saturday the street was a madhouse again. I got hit on the shin with a ball and my eardrums began to stretch out, but otherwise it was a good show. I had just flipped the butt away when I heard the door open behind me and got up.

Anna came out with her hat and jacket on. Mrs. Ricci, standing behind her on the threshold, said:

"I phoned Miss Maffei. She says you're all right, anyway I don't believe it. If you get Anna into trouble my husband will kill you, her father and mother are dead and she is a good girl, no matter if her head is full of flies."

"Don't you worry, Mrs. Ricci." I grinned at Anna. "Don't you want to go for a ride?"

She nodded, and I led her out to the roadster.

If I ever kill anybody I'm pretty sure it will be a woman. I've seen a lot of stubborn men, a lot of men who knew something I wanted to know and didn't intend to tell me, and in quite a few cases I couldn't make him tell no matter what I tried; but in spite of how stubborn they were they always stayed human. They always gave me a feeling that if only I hit on the right lever I could pry it out of them. But I've seen women that not only wouldn't turn loose; you knew damn well they wouldn't. They can get a look on their faces that would drive you crazy, and I think some of them do it on purpose. The look on a man's face says that he'll die before he'll tell you, and you think you may bust that up; a woman's look says that she would just about as soon tell you as not, only she isn't going to.

I sat and watched Anna Fiore for an hour that morning while Wolfe tried every trick he knew, and if she got away whole it was only because I remembered that you mustn't kill the goose that has the golden egg inside of her even if she won't lay it. Of course I didn't know whether she really had the golden egg and Wolfe didn't either, but there was no other goose we could think of that had any eggs at all.

Anna and I got to 35th Street before eleven and were waiting for Wolfe when he came down. He started on her easy, as if all he wanted to do was tell her a story, not to get anything out of her, just to keep her informed. He told her that the man who had sent her the hundred dollars was the one who killed Carlo Maffei; that he was wicked and dangerous; that the man knew that she knew something he didn't want known and that he might therefore kill her; that Miss Maffei was a nice woman; that Carlo Maffei had been a nice man and should not have been killed and that the man who had killed him should be caught and punished.

Looking at Anna's face, I saw we were up against it.

Wolfe went into the subtleties of contract. He explained several times, using different kinds of words, that a contract between two parties was valid only when they both voluntarily agreed to it. She was under no contract of silence with the murderer because no contract had been made; he had merely sent her money and told her what to do. He had even given her an alternative; she could have burned the money if she had wanted to. She could burn it now. Wolfe opened the drawer of his desk and took out five new twenty-dollar bills and spread them out in front of her.

"You can burn them now, Miss Fiore. It would be sacrilege, and I would have to leave the room, but Mr. Archie will help you. Burn them, and you may have these to take their place. You understand, I will give you these—here, I lay them on the desk. You still have the money?"

She nodded.

"In your stocking?"

She pulled up her skirt and twisted her leg around and the bump was there.

Wolfe said, "Take it out." She unfastened the top of her stocking and reached inside and pulled out the twenties and unfolded them. Then she looked at me and smiled.

"Here," Wolfe said, "here are matches. Here is a tray. I shall leave the room and Mr. Archie will help you and give you this new money. Mr. Archie would be very pleased."

Wolfe glanced at me, and I said, "Come on, Anna, I know you've got a good heart. You know Mr. Maffei

was good to you, and you ought to be good to him.
We'll burn it together, huh?"

I made the mistake of reaching out with my hand,
just starting to reach out, and the twenties went back
into her sock like a streak of lightning. I said, "Don't
get scared, and don't be foolish. Nobody will touch
your money as long as I'm around. You can burn it
yourself; I won't even help you."

She said to me, "I never will."

I nodded. "You said that before, but you see it's
different now. Now you have to burn it to get this
other money."

She shook her head, and what a look she had on her
face! She may not have had much of a mind, but what
there was of it was all made up. She said, "I don't have
to. I never will. I know, Mr. Archie, you think I'm not
very bright. I think that too because everybody says
I'm not. But I'm not dumb, I mean I'm not all dumb.
This is my money and I never will burn it. I won't
spend it until I can get married. That's not very
dumb."

"You'll never get married if the man kills you the
way he killed Mr. Maffei."

"He won't kill me."

I thought, by heaven, if he doesn't I will.

Wolfe took a new tack. He began trying to trick
her. He asked her questions about her parents, her
early life, her duties and habits at the Riccis', her
opinions of this and that. She seemed relieved and
answered pretty well, but she took her time, especially when he got on to the rooming-house. And the
first time he started to edge up on her, by asking
something about cleaning Carlo Maffei's room, she
closed up like a clam. He started somewhere else and
came around by another way, but the same stone wall

shut him off. It was really beautiful of her; I would have admired it if I had had time. Dumb or not, she had it fixed up inside so that something went click when Carlo Maffei's name or anything associated with him was approached and it worked just as well as Wolfe's sagacity worked. He didn't give up. He had take a quiet casual tone, and knowing his incredible patience and endurance I was thinking that after all there was a chance he might wear her down in a couple of weeks.

The door of the office opened. Fritz was there. He closed the door behind him, and when Wolfe nodded, came over and presented a card on the tray. Wolfe took it and looked at it and I saw his nostrils open a little.

He said, "A pleasant surprise, Archie," and handed the card across the desk and I reached and took it. The card said:

MANUEL KIMBALL

# Chapter 15

I stood up.

Wolfe sat a moment silent, his lips pushing out and in, then he said, "Show the gentleman into the front room, Fritz. The hall is so dark I would scarcely recognize his face if I saw him there.—Just a moment. Be sure the blinds are up in the front room; and leave the door to the hall open so there will be plenty of air."

Fritz went out. Wolfe said, his voice a little quieter even than usual, "Thank you, Miss Fiore. You have been very patient and have kept within your rights. Would you mind if Mr. Archie does not take you home? He has work to do. Mr. Fritz is an excellent driver. Archie, will you take Miss Fiore to the kitchen and arrange with Fritz? You might then accompany her to the entrance."

I nodded. "I get you. Come on, Anna."

She started, too loud, "Can't Mr. Archie—"

"Don't talk. I'll take you home some other day. Come on."

I got her into the kitchen, and explained to Fritz the pleasure that awaited him. I don't think I had ever really felt sorry for Anna until I saw that Fritz didn't blush when I told him to take her home. That was

terrible. But I left the feeling sorry for later; while
Fritz was getting off his apron and his coat and hat on,
I was figuring how to handle it.

I said, "Look here, Anna, let's have some fun. You
said something about getting married, and that made
me wonder what kind of a man you'd like to marry.
There's a man sitting in the front room now, I'll bet
he's just the kind. Very good-looking. As we go out
we'll stop and look through the door at him, and then
I'll go outside with you and you will tell me if he's the
kind. Will you do that?"

Anna said, "I know the kind—"

"All right. Don't talk. I don't want him to hear your
voice, so he won't know we're looking at him. Ready,
Fritz?"

We went out. Fritz had followed instructions and
left the door open between the hall and the front room,
and I steered Anna to the left of the hall so she
wouldn't be too close to the door. Manuel Kimball was
in there, a good view, in an armchair, with one knee
hanging over the other. Having heard our steps he
was looking in our direction, but it was so dark in the
hall he couldn't see much. I had a hand on Anna's
elbow and my eyes on her face as she looked in at
Kimball. I let her look a couple of seconds and then
eased her toward the entrance where Fritz was holding the door open for us. Outside, I closed the door
behind me.

"Is that the kind you like, Anna?"

"No. Mr. Archie, if I tell you—"

"Some other day. That's the girl. So long.—It won't
matter if lunch is late, Fritz, I've an idea we may be
late too, and there'll be no guest."

I ducked back in, and went past the open front
room door to the office. Wolfe hadn't moved. I said,

"She never saw him before. Or if she did, she could give Lynn Fontanne a furlong start and lope in ahead of her." He inclined his head. I asked, "Shall I bring him in?" He inclined his head again.

I went directly through to the front room, by the connecting door. Manuel Kimball got up from his chair and faced around and bowed. I said, "Sorry to keep your waiting. We had a young lady client who thinks we can bring back her husband just by whistling to him, and it's not that easy. Come this way."

Wolfe didn't feel formal enough to get up, but he kept his hands laced on his belly. As I led Manuel toward him he said, "How do you do, Mr. Kimball. You will forgive me for not rising; I am not rude, merely unwieldy. Be seated."

I couldn't see any signs that Manuel Kimball was suffering with agitation, but he did look concentrated. His black eyes seemed smaller than when I had seen him before, and concerned with something too important to permit of darting around everywhere to see what they could see. He was wiry and neat in a lightweight, finely tailored suit, with a yellow bow tie and yellow gloves in his pocket. He wasn't bothering with me. After he got into the chair which was still warm from Anna Fiore, his eyes went to Wolfe and stayed there.

Wolfe asked, "Will you have some beer?"

He nodded his head. "Thank you."

I took the hint. In the kitchen I got a couple of bottles from the ice-box and a glass from the shelf and fixed up a tray. I made it snappy because I didn't want to miss anything. I went back with the tray and put it on Wolfe's desk, and then sat down at my desk and pulled some papers out of a drawer and got things fixed up. Manuel Kimball was talking.

". . . told me of his visit to your office yesterday. My father and I are on a completely confidential basis. He told me everything you said to him. Why did you say what you did?"

"Well." Wolfe pulled out his drawer to get the opener, removed the cap from a bottle and dropped it into the drawer, and filled a glass. He watched the foam a moment, then turned back to Manuel. "In the first place, Mr. Kimball, you say that your father repeated everything to you that I told him. You can hardly know that. So let us be properly selective. Your tone is minatory. What specifically do you wish to berate me for? What did I say to your father that you would rather I had left unsaid?"

Manuel smiled, and got colder. "Don't try to twist my words, Mr. Wolfe. I am not expressing my preferences, I am asking you to account for statements that seem to me unwarranted. I have that right, as the son of a man who is getting old. I have never before seen my father frightened, but you have frightened him. You told him that Barstow was killed as a result of borrowing my father's golf driver."

"I did, indeed."

"You admit it. I trust that your man there taking this down will include your confession. What you told my father is criminal nonsense. I have never believed the tale of the poisoned needle as regarded Barstow; I believe it less now. What right have you to invent such absurdities and distress, first the whole Barstow family, now my father, with them? Probably it is actionable, my lawyer will know about that. Certainly it is unjustifiable and it must be stopped."

"I don't know." Wolfe appeared to be considering; as for me, I was handing it to Manuel for being cute enough to get what I was doing in the first five minutes; not many had done that. Wolfe downed a glass of beer and wiped his lips. "I really don't know. If it is actionable at all, I suppose it could only be through a complaint of libel from the murdered. I don't suppose you had that in mind?"

"I have only one thing in mind." Manuel's eyes were even smaller. "That it has got to stop."

"But, Mr. Kimball," Wolfe protested. "Give me a chance. You accused me of inventing absurdities. I have invented nothing. The invention, and a most remarkable and original one, even brilliant—and I am careful of words—was another's; only the discovery was mine. If the inventor were to say to me what you have said, I would put him down for a commendably modest man. No, sir, I did not invent that golf driver."

"And no one else did. Where is it?"

"Alas." Wolfe turned a hand palm up. "I have yet to see it."

"What proof is there that it ever existed?"

"The needle that it propelled into Barstow's belly."

"Bah. Why from a golf driver? Why on the first tee?"

"The wasp came from nowhere, and synchronized."

"No good, Mr. Wolfe." Manuel's intent little black eyes were scornful. "It's what I said, criminal nonsense. If you have no better proof than that, I repeat, I have a right to demand that you retract. I do so. I have this morning called on Mr. Anderson, the District Attorney at White Plains. He agrees with me. I demand that you see my father and retract and apologize; likewise the Barstows if you have told them. I have reason to suspect that you have."

Wolfe shook his head slowly from side to side. After a moment he said regretfully, "It's too bad, Mr. Kimball."

"It is. But you caught the crow, now you can eat it."

"No. You misunderstand me. I mean it's too bad that you are dealing with me. I am perhaps the only man on this hemisphere whom your courage and wit cannot defeat, and by incredibly bad luck you find yourself confronted by me. I am sorry; but just as you have assumed a task suitable for your abilities, I have found one congenial for mine. You will forgive me for wheeling onto your flank, since you have made it impossible for me to meet you frontally. I hardly suppose that you expected your direct attack to gain its feigned objective; you could hardly have had so poor an opinion of me as that. Your true objective must have been concealed, and probably it was the discovery of the nature and extent of the evidence I have so far acquired. But surely you know that, for how else could I have foretold the result of the autopsy?—I beg you, let me finish. Yes, I know when and where and by whom the golf driver was made, I know where the man who made it is now, and I know what results to expect from the advertisement which I inserted in this morning's newspapers and which you have perhaps seen."

Not a muscle on Manuel's face had stirred, and no change was perceptible in his tone. His eyes kept straight on Wolfe as he said, "If you know all that—I doubt if you do—is that not information for the District Attorney?"

"Yes. Do you want me to give it to him?"

"I? I want? Of course, if you have it."

"Good." Wolfe wiggled a finger at him. "I'll tell you what you do, Mr. Kimball. Do me a favor. On your way home this afternoon stop at Mr. Anderson's office; tell him what information I have and suggest that he

send for it. Now—I am sorry—it is past my lunch
hour. May I offer you a compliment? If almost anyone
else I have known were in your position I would try to
detain him longer on the chance of learning something.
With you, I feel that eating my lunch will be more
profitable."

Manuel was on his feet. "I should tell you, I am
going from here to my lawyer. You will hear from
him."

Wolfe nodded. "Certainly your best move. Obvious, but still the best. Your father would wonder if
you did not."

Manuel Kimball turned and went. I got up and
started after him for the courtesy of the house, but he
was out of the front door before I made it.

I went back to Wolfe. He was leaning back with his
eyes closed. I asked loud enough to wake him up, "Did
that guy come here to find out if he'd have to go ahead
and kill his father during the weekend?"

He sighed. "His eyes opened and he shook his
head. "Lunch, Archie."

"It won't be ready for ten minutes. Fritz only got
back at one."

"The anchovies and celery will divert us."

So we went to the dining-room.

Right there, at that point, the Barstow-Kimball
case went dead. At least Wolfe went dead, and that
was the case as far as I was concerned. It wasn't a
relapse, he just closed up. While plenty went into him
during lunch, of course nothing came out; and when
the meal was finished he went to the office and sat. I
sat at my desk and caught up with a few things, but
there wasn't much to do, and I kept glancing at Wolfe
wondering when he would open up. Although his eyes

were closed he must have felt my glances, for all of a sudden he looked at me and said:

"Confound it, Archie, cannot paper be made not to rattle?"

I got up. "All right, I'll beat it. But damn it, where? Have you lost your tongue?"

"Anywhere. Go for a walk."

"And return?"

"Any time. It doesn't matter. Dinner."

"Are you waiting for Manuel to bump off his old man?"

"Go, Archie."

It seemed to me that he was rubbing it in, since it was already three-thirty and in another half hour he would himself have left to go up to the plant-rooms. But seeing the mood he was in, I got my hat from the hall and went out.

I went to a movie to think, and the more I thought the more uncomfortable I got. Manuel Kimball's visit and his challenge, for that was what it amounted to, darned near succeeded as far as I was concerned. I had been aware that we weren't quite ready to tell Mrs. Barstow what address to mail the check to, but I hadn't fully realized how awfully empty our bag was. We had found out some things to our own satisfaction, but we had no more proof that there had been a murder than we had had when we started. Let alone who had done it. But that wasn't all; the worst was that there was no place to go from there. Granted that it was Manuel Kimball, how could we tie him up? Find the golf driver. Fat chance. I could see him in his plane flying low over the river or a reservoir, dropping the club out with a chunk of lead wired to the shaft. Trace the poison to him. About the same chance. He had been planning this for years maybe, certainly months;

he may even have had the poison with him when he came up with his father from the Argentine; anyway, he could have got it from there at any time—and try and find out. Get him to talk on the telephone with Mrs. Ricci and have her recognize his voice. Sure, that was it; any jury would convict on that without leaving the courtroom.

I sat in a movie three hours without seeing anything that happened on the screen, and all I got was a headache.

I never did know what Wolfe was up to that Saturday afternoon and Sunday. Was he just bumping his head against the wall, as I was? Maybe; he wasn't very sociable. Or was he possibly waiting for Manuel to make a move? But the only move Manuel could have made would have been to kill his father, and then where would we have been? Anderson would have left us out in the cold, and while neither Wolfe nor I would have worn any back for E. D. Kimball we certainly would have done so for the fifty grand. As far as E. D. Kimball was concerned, I figured that by rights he had been killed on June fourth anyway and he might be grateful for two weeks of grace. But Wolfe wasn't waiting for that; I was sure he didn't expect it from what he said about Manuel Sunday afternoon. It was then that he opened up and talked a little, but not to much point. He was being philosophic.

It was raining; it rained all that Sunday. I wrote some letters and went through two Sunday papers and spent a couple of hours on the roof chinning with Horstmann and looking over the plants, but no matter what I did I was in a bad humor. The damn rain never let up once. Not that it would have bothered me if I had had anything to do; I don't notice rain or shine if I'm out in it busy; but monkeying around that dry dark quiet house all day long with that constant patter outside and never a let up didn't help my disposition a bit. I was thankful when something happened around five-thirty that I could get good and sore about.

I was in the office yawning over a magazine when the telephone rang. It took me a few seconds to unwind myself out of the armchair I was in and get across to my desk, and when I got the receiver to my ear I was surprised to hear Wolfe's voice. He was answering from the plant-room phone. He always took calls in the plant-room when I was out, but usually when he knew I was in the house he left them to me. But it was his voice:

"This is Wolfe."

Another voice: "This is Durkin, Mr. Wolfe. Everything is okay. She went to church this morning, and a while ago she came out and went to a candy store and bought an ice-cream cone. She's back in now, I expect for the night."

"Thank you, Fred. You'd better stay there until ten o'clock. Saul will be there in the morning at seven, and you resume at two."

"Yes, sir. Anything else?"

"That's all."

I banged the receiver onto the hook, thinking there was a chance it might crack Wolfe's eardrum.

When he came into the office half an hour afterward I didn't look up, and I was careful to be buried in my magazine enough to make sure it wasn't upside down. I held onto that pose another half hour, turning a page when I thought of it. I was boiling.

Wolfe's voice, finally: "It's raining, Archie."

I didn't look up. "Go to hell. I'm reading."

"Oh no. Surely not, in those fitful gusts. I wish to inquire, would it be a good plan in the morning for you to collect the replies to our advertisement and follow their suggestions?"

I shook my head. "No, sir. The excitement would be too much for me."

Wolfe's cheeks folded up. "I begin to believe, Archie, that a persistent rain distresses you even more acutely than it does me. You are not merely imitating me?"

"No, sir. It's not the rain, you know damn well it isn't." I dropped the magazine on the floor and glared at him. "If the very best way you can think of to catch the cleverest murderer that ever gave me a highball is to start a game of tiddlywinks in Sullivan Street, you might at least have told me so I could remember Durkin in my prayers. Praying is all I'm good for maybe. What's Durkin trying to do, catch Anna hocking the golf stick?"

Wolfe wiggled a finger at me. "Compose yourself, Archie. Why taunt me? Why upbraid me? I am merely a genius, not a god. A genius may discover the hidden secrets and display them; only a god could create new ones. I apologize to you for failing to tell you of Durkin; my mind was occupied; I telephoned him yesterday after you went for a walk. He is not trying to catch Miss Fiore but to protect her. In the house she is probably safe; outside probably not. I do not think Manuel Kimball will proceed to devise means of completing his enterprise until he is satisfied that there is no danger of his being called to account for his first attempt, which failed through no fault of his. It was perfectly conceived and perfectly executed. As for us, I see no possibility but Miss Fiore; *clever* is too weak a word for Manuel Kimball; he has his own genius. I would not ask for a better means of defeating a rainy Sunday than contemplation of the beauty of his arrangements. He has left us nothing but Miss Fiore, and Durkin's function is to preserve her."

"*Preserve* is good. Since she might as well be sealed up in a can."

"I think the can may be opened. We shall try. But that must wait until we are completely satisfied as to June fifth. By the way, is Maria Maffei's telephone number in the book?—Good. Of course, we do not know what Miss Fiore is guarding so jealously. If it turns out to be trivial and insufficient, then we must abandon the skirmish and plan a siege. No man can commit so complicated a deed as a murder and leave no vulnerable points; the best he can do is render them inaccessible save to a patience longer than his own and an ingenuity more inspired. In Manuel Kimball's case those specifications are—well, considerable. If in fact Miss Fiore is guarding the jewel that we seek, I earnestly hope that he is not aware of it; if he is, she is as good as dead."

"With Durkin protecting her?"

"We cannot protect from lightning, we can only observe it strike. I have explained that to Fred. If Manuel Kimball kills that girl we shall have him. But I think he will not. Remember the circumstances under which he sent her the hundred dollars. At that time he could not have supposed that she knew anything that could connect him with Barstow, or he would not have made so inadequate a gesture. He knew only her first name. Probably Carlo Maffei had mentioned it, and had said enough of her character and of some small discovery she had made to suggest to Manuel Kimball, after he had killed Maffei, to risk a hundred dollars on the chance of additional safety without the possibility of added danger. If that surmise is correct, and if Miss Fiore knows nothing beyond what Kimball was aware that she knew, we are in for a siege. Saul Panzer will go to South America; I warned him yesterday on the telephone to be in readiness. Your program, already in my mind, will be elaborate and tiresome. It would be a pity, but we would have no just grievance against Manuel Kimball. It was only by his ill fortune, and my unwarranted pertinacity in asking Miss Fiore a trivial question a second time, that the first piece of his puzzle was discovered."

Wolfe stopped. I got up and stretched. "All I have to say is, he's a dirty spiggoty."

"No, Archie. Mr. Manuel Kimball is an Argentinian."

"Spiggoty to me. I want a glass of milk. Can I bring you some beer?"

He said no, and I went to the kitchen.

I felt better. There were times when Wolfe's awful self-assurance gave me a touch of a dash of a suggestion of a pain in the neck, but there were other times when it was as good as a flock of pure and beautiful maidens smoothing my brow. This was one of the latter. After I had finished with a sufficient quantity of milk and cookies I went out to a movie and didn't miss a scene. When I went home it was still raining.

But Monday morning was beautiful. I got out early. Even in New York the washed air was so fresh and sweet in the sunlight that it somehow dissolved all the motor exhausts and the other million smells sneaking out of windows and doors and alleys and elevator lids, and made it a pleasure to breathe. I stepped on it. By half past eight I was out of Bronx Park and turning into the Parkway.

I had collected more than twenty answers to the ad and had gone through them. About half of them were phony; chiselers trying to horn in or poor fish trying to be funny. Some others were honest enough but off of my beat; apparently June fifth had been a good day for landing in pastures with airplanes. Three of them not only looked good but fitted together; it seemed that they had all seen the same plane land in a meadow somewhere a couple of miles east of Hawthorne. That was too good to be true.

But it wasn't. A mile out of Hawthorne, following the directions in the letter, I left the highway and turned into an uphill dirt road with the ruts left washed out and stony by the rain. After a while the road got so narrow and doubtful that it looked as if it might play out any minute, and I stopped at a house and asked where the Carters lived. On up. I went on.

The Carter residence, on top of the hill, was about ready to fall down. It hadn't been painted since the war, and the grass was weeds. But the dog that got up to meet me was friendly and happy, and the wash on the line looked clean in the sunshine. I found Mrs. Carter around back, getting the rest of the wash through. She was skinny and active, with a tooth gone in front.

"Mrs. T. A. Carter?"

"Yes, sir."

"I've come to see you about your reply to an ad I put in Saturday's paper. About my landing with my airplane. Your letter is quite complete. You saw me land?"

She nodded. "I sure did. I didn't see the ad though, Minnie Vawter saw it and I had told her about the airplane and she remembered it and brought the ad up Saturday afternoon. It was lucky I had told her about it. Sure I saw you land."

"I wouldn't have supposed you could see me from here."

"Sure, look. This is a pretty high hill." She led me across the yard and through a clump of sumacs. "See that view? My husband says that view's worth a million dollars. See the reservoir, like a lake?" She pointed. "That field down there's where you landed. I wondered what was up, I thought you'd broke something. I've seen plenty of airplanes in the air, but I never saw one land before."

I nodded. "That's it all right. Thanks to the completeness of your letter, there's not much I need to ask you. You saw me land at ten minutes past six, and saw me get out and walk south across the meadow, toward the road. You came into the house then to look at the dinner on the stove, and saw me no more. At twilight my plane was still there; you went to bed at half past nine, and in the morning it was gone."

"That's right. I thought it would be better to put it all in the letter, because—"

"Correct. I imagine you are usually correct, Mrs. Carter. Your description of my plane is better than I could do myself. And from such a distance; you have good eyes. By the way, could you tell me who lives in that house down there, the white one?"

"Sure. Miss Wellman. She's an artist from New York. It was Art Barrett, the man that works for her that drove you to Hawthorne."

"Oh. Of course. Yes, that's the place. I'm much obliged to you, Mrs. Carter, you're going to help me win my bet. It was a question of how many people saw me."

I decided to give her a five-spot. The Lord knows she needed it, judging from appearances; and she had sewed Manuel Kimball up tighter than a bag of bran.

I don't know how sure Wolfe had been of Manuel up to
that point, but I do know that he postponed the works
for Anna Fiore until after June fifth was settled. I
hadn't been sure at all. I never did like my feelings as
well as Wolfe liked his; they often got me talking big,
but they always left me uneasy until I got satisfactory
facts to tuck them in with. So I figured that Mrs.
Carter's handout was cheap at five bucks. Manuel
Kimball was settled with us. To get enough to settle
him with a jury was another matter, but as far as we
were concerned he was all set. Mrs. Carter got her
hand all around the five dollar bill and started toward
the house, remarking that the wash wouldn't finish
itself.

I stood a minute looking down at the meadow far
below. That was where Manuel Kimball had landed
and left his plane; across that field he had walked to
the white house and asked a man there to drive him to
Hawthorne; at Hawthorne, which was only a few
miles from his home, he had either had his own car
waiting or had rented one at a garage; he had driven to
New York, stopping probably at White Plains to
telephone Carlo Maffei and arrange a meeting. He was
already screwed up, and alarmed, because Maffei had
abandoned the trip to Europe; and when he met him
that evening at seven-thirty and Maffei produced the
clipping he had cut from the *Times* that morning and
began to talk about how hard it was to keep his mouth
shut about golf drivers, that was plenty for Manuel.
With Maffei in the car with him, he drove to some
secluded nook and found an opportunity to sink a knife
five inches into Carlo's back at the point where the
heart was waiting for it. Leaving the knife there to
hold the blood in, he drove around the countryside
until he found the sort of spot he needed, dragged

Maffei's body out of the car and carried it into a thicket, returned to the car and drove to Hawthorne, where he got a taxi to take him back to the white house that was there in the valley below me. If he needed help taking off in the plane, Art Barrett and the taxi driver were both handy. Around ten o'clock he landed on his own private lighted field, and told Skinner that it was really more fun flying at night than in the daytime.

There was nothing wrong with that, except possibly one thing: it was giving Carlo Maffei credit for a lot of activity between his ears to suppose that reading that piece about Barstow's death was enough to put him wise. But I laid that away; there was no knowing what might have happened before to make Maffei suspicious, and the mere oddity of the outlandish contraption he had been paid so well to construct had certainly made him wonder.

I decided not to tackle Art Barrett. I couldn't very well present myself as the aviator as I had with Mrs. Carter, since he had driven Manuel to Hawthorne, and there was nothing he could tell me that would be worth the trouble of doping out an approach. For the present I had enough. There would be time for that later, if we needed him for a case. The other two replies to the ad could wait too. I was itching to get back to Thirty-fifth Street, remembering that Wolfe had promised to use a can opener on Anna Fiore if I succeeded in pulling Manuel Kimball down out of the clouds for the evening of June fifth.

I stopped at the clothesline for a good-bye to Mrs. Carter, got the roadster turned around by inching back and forth between the boulders that lined the narrow road, and floated off downhill toward the highway.

I discovered I was singing, and I asked myself, why all the elation? All I had found was the proof that we were on a spoke and not on the rim; we still had to get to the hub, and we were just as far away from that as we had been before. I went on singing anyhow, rolling along the Parkway; and at Fordham Road I stopped and telephoned Wolfe what I had got. He was already down from the plant-rooms, and when I halted at Thirty-sixth Street for a red light Tiffany's whistle was blowing noon.

I left the roadster in front. Wolfe was in the office. He was seated at his desk, and Fritz was bringing in a tray with a glass and two bottles of beer.

Wolfe said, "Good morning, Friend Goodwin."

"What?" I stared. "Oh, I get you." I had left my hat on. I went to the hall and tossed it on a hook and came back. I sat down and grinned. "I wouldn't go sour now even for Emily Post. Didn't I tell you Manuel Kimball was just a dirty spiggoty? Of course it was your ad that did it."

Wolfe didn't look as if he was on my boat; he didn't seem interested. But he nodded and said, "You found the pasture."

"I found everything. A woman that saw him land and know just which parts of his plane are red and which blue, and a man that drove him to Hawthorne— everything we could ask for."

"Well." He wasn't looking at me.

"Well! What are you trying to do, get me sore again? What's the matter—"

The palm of his hand coming up from the chair arm stopped me. "Easy, Archie. Your discovery is worthy of celebration, but you must humor me by postponing it. Your explosive return chanced unfortunately to interrupt an interesting telephone call I was about to make. I was reaching for the book when you entered; possibly you can save me that effort. Do you happen to know the Barstow number?"

"Sure. Something's up, huh? Do you want it?"

"Get it, please, and listen in. Miss Sarah Barstow."

I went to my desk, glanced at the book to make sure of the number, and called. In a moment Small's voice was in my ear. I asked to speak to Miss Barstow, and after a little wait she was on the wire and I nodded to Wolfe. He took off his receiver. I kept mine at my ear.

He said, "Miss Barstow?—This is Nero Wolfe— Good morning. I am taking the liberty of calling to inquire if the orchids reached you safely.—No, orchids.—I beg your pardon?—Oh. It is a mistake apparently. Did you not do me the honor of sending me a note this morning requesting me to send you some orchids?—You sent no note?—No, no, it is quite all right.—A mistake of some sort, I am sorry.—Good-bye."

We hung up. Wolfe leaned back in his chair. I put on a grin.

"You're getting old, sir. In the younger set we don't send the girls orchids until they ask for them."

Wolfe's cheeks stayed put. His lips were pushing out and in, and I watched him. His hand started for the drawer to get the opener for a bottle, but he pulled his hand back again without touching the drawer.

He said, "Archie, you have heard me say that I am an actor. I am afraid I have a weakness for dramatic statement. It would be foolish not to indulge it when a good opportunity is offered. There is death in this room."

I suppose I must have involuntarily glanced

around, for he went on, "Not a corpse; I mean not death accomplished but death waiting. Waiting only for me perhaps, or for all of us; I don't know. It is here. While I was upstairs this morning with the plants Fritz came up with a note—this note."

He reached in his pocket and took out a piece of paper and handed it to me. I read it:

*Dear Mr. Wolfe,—*

*Last week, at your house, Mr. Goodwin kindly presented me with two orchids, remarkably beautiful. I am daring to be cheeky enough to ask if you can send me six or eight more of them? They were so lovely. The messenger will wait for them, if you do decide to be generous. I shall be so grateful!*

*Sarah Barstow*

I said, "It don't sound like her."

"Perhaps not. You know her better than I do. I of course remembered the Brassocattlaelias Truffautianas in her hand when she came downstairs with you. Theodore and I cut a dozen and boxed them, and Fritz took them down. When I came to the office at eleven o'clock and sat at my desk there was a smell of a stranger in the air. I am too sensitive to strangers, that is why I keep these layers over my nerves. I knew of course of the stranger who had called, but I was uncomfortable. I sent for Fritz. He told me that the young man who had brought the note and waited for the orchids had had with him a fiber box, an oblong box with a handle. On departing he had taken the box with him; Fritz saw it in his hand as he left the house. But for at least ten minutes the young man was alone in the front room; the door between that room and the office was unlocked; the door from the hall to the office was closed."

Wolfe sighed. "Alas, Miss Barstow did not write the note."

I was on my feet and going toward him, saying, "You get out of here." He shook his head. "Come on," I demanded, "I can jump and you can't. Damn it, come on, quick! I'm used to playing with bombs. Fritz! Fritz!" Fritz came running. "Fill up the sink with water. To the top. Mr. Wolfe, for God's sake get out of here, it may go off any second. I'll find it."

I heard Fritz back in the kitchen starting the water. Wolfe wouldn't budge, and the Lord knows I couldn't budge him. He shook his head and wiggled a finger at me.

"Archie, please.—Stop that! Don't touch anything. There is no bomb. They tick or they sizzle, and I have good ears and have listened. Besides, Mr. Kimball has not had time since his call to construct a good one, and he would use no other. It is not a bomb.—I beg you, no trepidation; drama, but not trepidation. I have reflected, and I have felt. Consider: when Mr. Kimball was in this room he saw me make no movement worthy the name but one. He saw me open the drawer of my desk and put my hand in it. If that suggests nothing to you, I am sure it did to him. We shall see."

I jumped at him, for I thought he was going to open the drawer, but he waved me back; he was merely getting ready to leave his chair. He said, "Get my red thorn walking stick.—Confound it, will you do as I say?"

I ran to the hall and got the stick from the stand and ran back. Wolfe was moving around the desk. He came clear around to the side opposite his chair, and reached over for the tray and pulled it across to him, with the glass and bottles still on it.

"Now," he said, "please do it this way.—No, first close the door to the hall." I went and closed the door and returned. "Thank you. Grasp the stick by its other end. Reach across the desk and catch the tip of the handle on the lower edge of the drawer-front. Push, and the drawer will open.—Wait. Open it, if you can, quite slowly; and be ready to free the stick quickly should it occur to you to use it for any other purpose. Proceed."

I proceeded. The tip of the handle's curve caught nicely under the edge of the drawer, but on account of the angle I had to keep the drawer wouldn't start. I tried to push so as to open the drawer gradually, but I had to push harder, and suddenly the drawer popped out half a foot and I nearly dropped the stick. I lifted up to get the stick loose, and yelled:

"Look out!"

Wolfe had a beer bottle in each hand, by the neck, and he brought one of them crashing onto the desk but missed the thing that had come out of the drawer. It was coming fast and its head was nearly to the edge of the desk where we were while its tail was still in the drawer. I had got the stick loose and was pounding at its head but it kept slashing around and I couldn't hit it, and the desk was covered with beer and the pieces of the broken bottle. I was ready to jump back and was grabbing Wolfe to pull him back with me when he came down with the second bottle right square on the ugly head and smashed it flat as a piece of tripe. The long brown body writhed all over the desk, but it was done for.

The second bottle had busted too, and we were splattered all over. Wolfe stepped back and pulled out his handkerchief and began to wipe his face. I held on to the stick.

*"Nom de Dieu!"*

It was Fritz, horrified.

Wolfe nodded. "Yes. Fritz, here's a mess for you. I'm sorry. Get things."

# Chapter 16

I tried it again. *"Fair-duh-lahnss?"*

Wolfe nodded. "Somewhat better. Still too much *n* and not enough nose. You are not a born linguist, Archie. Your defect is probably not mechanical. To pronounce French properly you must have within you a deep antipathy, not to say scorn, for some of the most sacred of the Anglo-Saxon prejudices. In some manner you manage without that scorn, I do not quite know how. Yes, fer-de-lance. *Bothrops atrox.* Except for the bushmaster, it is the most dreaded of all the vipers."

Fritz had cleaned up the mess, with my help, and served lunch, and we had eaten. When the snake had finished writhing I had stretched it out on the kitchen floor and measured it: six feet, three inches. At the middle it was almost as thick as my wrist. It was a dirty yellowish brown, and even dead it looked damn mean. After measuring it I stood up and, poking at it with the yardstick, wondered what to do with it— observing to Wolfe, standing near, that I couldn't just stuff it in the garbage pail. Should I take it and throw it in the river?

Wolfe's cheeks folded. "No, Archie, that would be a

pity. Get a carton and excelsior from the basement, pack it nicely, and address it to Mr. Manuel Kimball. Fritz can take it to the post office. It will relieve Mr. Kimball's mind."

That had been done, and it hadn't spoiled my lunch. Now we were back in the office, waiting for Maria Maffei, whom Wolfe had telephoned after receiving my call from Fordham Road.

I said, "It comes from South America."

Wolfe was leaning back in his chair content, with half-shut eyes. He was not at all displeased that it had been his blow that had killed it, though he had expressed regret for the beer. He murmured, "It does. It is a crotalid, and one of the few snakes that will strike without challenge or warning. Only last week I was looking at a picture of it, in one of the books you procured for me. It is abundant throughout South America."

"They found snake venom in Barstow."

"Yes. That could have been suspected when the analysis was found difficult. The needle must have been well smeared. These considerations, Archie, will become of moment if Anna Fiore fails us and we must have recourse to a siege. Many things will be discoverable with sufficient patience and—well, abandonment of reserve. Is there somewhere on the Kimball estate a pit where Manuel has carried rats to his fer-de-lance? Did he extract the venom himself by teasing its bite into the pulp of a banana? Unlikely. Has he an Argentine friend who sent the poison to him? More likely. The young man—dark and handsome, Fritz says—who brought the note not from Miss Barstow, and who is admirably deft with vipers, will he be found to be on duller days an usher in a 116th Street movie theater? Or a seaman on a South American boat, providentially arrived at the port of New York only yesterday? Difficult questions, but each has its answer, if it comes to a siege. It is likely that Manuel Kimball arranged some time ago for the journey of the fer-de-lance, as a second string to his bow; thinking that if the contrivance designed by man should for any reason fail it would be well to give nature's own mechanism a chance. Then, when it arrived, there was a more urgent need for it; vengeance stepped back for safety. And now, to this moment at least, he has neither."

"Maybe. But he just barely missed getting one, and he may get the other any minute."

Wolfe wiggled a finger at me. "Faulty, Archie, inexcusably faulty. Vengeance will continue to wait. Mr. Manuel Kimball is not a creature of impulse. Should circumstances render him suddenly desperate he would act with desperation, but even then not impulsively.—But Miss Maffei is due in half an hour, and you should know the arrangements before she arrives. Your notebook."

I got at my desk, and he dictated twenty minutes without stopping. After the first two minutes I put on a grin, and kept it on till the end. It was beautiful, it was without a flaw, and it covered every detail. He had even allowed for Maria Maffei's refusal or her inability to persuade Anna; in that case the action was approximately the same, but the characters were shifted around; I was to take it with Anna. He had telephoned Burke Williamson and arranged for a clear stage for us, and Saul Panzer was to call at the office at six o'clock for the sedan and his instructions. When he had finished dictating it was all so clear that there were few questions for me to ask. I asked those few, and ran back over the pages. He was leaning back in his chair, full of beer, pretending he wasn't pleased with himself.

I said, "All right, I admit it, you're a genius. This will get it if she's got it."

He nodded without concern.

Maria Maffei arrived on the dot. I was waiting for her on my toes and got to the door before Fritz was out of the kitchen. She was dressed in black, and if I had met her on the street I doubt if I would have known her, she looked so worn out. I was so full of Wolfe's program that I had a grin ready for her, but I killed it in time. She wasn't having any grins. After I saw her I didn't feel like grinning anyway; it sobered me up to see what the death of a brother might do to a woman. She was ten years older and the bright life in her eyes was gone.

I took her to the office and moved a chair in front of Wolfe for her and went to my desk.

She exchanged greetings with Wolfe and said, "I suppose you want money."

"Money for what?" Wolfe asked.

"For finding my brother Carlo. You didn't find him. Neither did the police. Some boys found him. I won't pay you any money."

"You might." Wolfe sighed. "I hadn't thought of that, Miss Maffei. I'm sorry you suggested it. It arouses me to sordid considerations. But for the moment let us forget it; you owe me nothing. Forget it. But let me ask you—I am sorry if it is painful, but it is necessary—you saw your brother's body?"

Her eyes were dull on him, but I saw that I had been wrong: the life in them was not gone, it had merely sunk within, waiting back there as if in ambush. She said quietly, "I saw him."

"You saw perhaps the hole in his back. The hole made by the knife of the man who killed him."

"I saw it."

"Good. And if there was a chance of my discovering the man who used that knife and bringing him to punishment, and needed your help, would you help me?"

In the dull eyes a gleam came and went. Maria Maffei said, "I would pay you money for that, Mr. Wolfe."

"I suspect you would. But we shall forget that for the present. It is another kind of assistance I require. Since you are intelligent enough to make reasonable assumptions, and therefore to be made uncomfortable when only reasonable ones are available, I had better explain to you. The man who murdered your brother is sought by me, and by others, for another act he committed. An act more sensational and not less deplorable. I know who he is, but your help is needed—"

"You know? Tell me!" Maria Maffei had jerked forward in her chair, and this time the gleam in her eyes stayed.

Wolfe wiggled a finger at her. "Easy, Miss Maffei. I am afraid you must delegate your vengeance. Remember that those of us who are both civilized and prudent commit our murders only under the complicated rules which permit us to avoid personal responsibility. Let us get on. You can help. You must trust me. Your friend Fanny's husband, Mr. Durkin, will tell you that I am to be trusted; besides, he will also help. I wish to speak of Miss Anna Fiore, the girl who works at the rooming house where your brother lived. You know her?"

"Of course I know her."

"Does she like you and trust you?"

"I don't know. She is a girl who hides her flowers."

"If any? A tender way of putting it; thank you. Could you go in my automobile this evening, with a driver, and persuade Miss Fiore to take a long ride with you; give her a good excuse, so she would go willingly?"

Maria Maffei looked at him; after a moment she nodded. "She would go. It would be a strange thing, I would have to think—"

"You will have time for that. I prefer to leave it to your wit to invent the excuse; you will use it better if it is your own. But that is all that will be left to you; one of my men will drive the car; in all the rest you must carefully and precisely follow my instructions. Or rather, Mr. Goodwin's instructions. Archie, if you please." Wolfe put his hands on the edge of the desk and shoved his chair back, and got himself up. "You will forgive me for leaving you, Miss Maffei, it is the hour for my plants. Perhaps when you and Mr. Goodwin have finished you would like him to bring you up to see them."

He left us.

I didn't take Maria Maffei upstairs to see the orchids that day; it was nearly five o'clock when I had finished with her, and I had something else to do. She didn't balk at all, but it took a lot of explaining, and then I went over the details three times to make sure she wouldn't get excited and ball it up. We decided it would be better for her to make a preliminary call on Anna and get it arranged, so I took her out and put her in a taxi and saw her headed for Sullivan Street.

Then I started on my own details. I had to get the knife and the masks and the guns ready, and arrange with the garage for hiring a car, since we couldn't take a chance on Anna recognizing the roadster, and get hold of Bill Gore and Orrie Cather. I had suggested them, and Wolfe said okay. He had already told Durkin to report at seven o'clock.

I got it all done, but without any time to spare. At six-thirty I ate a hurry-up dinner in the kitchen, while Wolfe was in the office with Saul Panzer. On his way out Saul looked in at the kitchen to make a face at me, as if his ugly mug wasn't good enough without any embroidery. He called in to me, "Enjoy it, Arch, it may be your last meal, you're not dealing with a quitter this night!"

I had my mouth full, so I only said, "Shrivel, shrimp."

Bill Gore and Durkin were there on time, and Orrie wasn't late enough to matter. I gave them the story, and rehearsed Orrie several times because a lot depended on him. We hadn't been together on anything for over two years, and it seemed like old times to see him again twisting his thin lips and looking around for a place to squirt his tobacco juice.

Wolfe was still in at his dinner when we got away a little before eight o'clock. The garage had given me a black Buick sedan, and it had four wheels and an engine but it wasn't the roadster. Orrie got in front with me and Bill Gore and Durkin in the back. I thought to myself that it was too bad it was only a set-up, because with those three birds I would have contracted to stop anything from a Jersey bus to a truck of hooch. Orrie said I should have hung a sign on the radiator, *Highwaymen's Special*. I grinned, but only with my mouth. I knew everything had to go exactly right and it was up to me, and what Wolfe had said about Anna Fiore was true: her mental vision was limited, but within its limits she might see things that a broader vision would miss entirely.

I went up the west side and got onto the Sawmill River Road. The Williamson place was in the back country east of Tarrytown, on a secondary road; I knew the way as well as I knew 35th Street on account of my trips there four years before. I had expected to make it by nine-thirty but traffic up to Yonkers had held me up a little, and it was a few minutes later than that and I had the lights on when I turned into the drive where I had once picked Mrs. Williamson up in a faint and carried her to the pond to throw water on her.

I drove on up to the house, about a third of a mile, and left the three in the car and went and rang the doorbell. Tanzer, the butler, remembered me and we shook hands. I told him I wouldn't go in, I just wanted to speak to his boss a minute. Burke Williamson came right away; he shook hands too and said he was sorry they had missed me Friday night. I said I was sorry too.

"I'm a little late, Mr. Williamson, I came on up just to make sure that everything's set. No loose servants out hunting lightning bugs? Can we go ahead?"

"Everything's arranged." He laughed. "No one will disturb your sinister plot. Of course we're all itching with curiosity. I don't suppose we could get behind a bush and watch?"

I shook my head. "You'd better stay in the house, if you don't mind. I won't see you again, I've got to make a quick getaway. Wolfe will phone you tomorrow, I expect, to thank you."

"He needn't bother. I'll never do enough to make Nero Wolfe owe me any thanks."

I went back to the car and turned it around and

started back down the drive. I had the spot picked out, about halfway down, a full three hundred yards from the public road, where high shrubbery was on both sides with trees just beyond and it would be good and dark. There the drive was narrow enough so that I could block it with the sedan without bothering to swing it crosswise.

I got the sedan into position and turned off the lights and we all got out. It was nearly ten o'clock and our prey was due at a quarter past. I passed around the guns and gave Orrie the knife, and then handed out the masks and we put them on. We were a hard-looking bunch and I couldn't help grinning at Orrie's wisecracks, though to tell the truth I was pretty much keyed up. The thing had to go absolutely right. I went over it again with them. They had it pat, and we scattered into the bushes. It was plenty dark. They began calling back and forth to one another, and pretty soon I told them to shut up so I could listen.

After a couple of minutes the sound came up from below of Wolfe's sedan going into second on the grade. I couldn't see the lights on account of the bushes, but soon I did. They got brighter, and then I saw the car. It buzzed along, getting close, and when the driver saw my sedan right ahead it slowed down. I left the bushes on a run, jumped to the running board of Wolfe's sedan just as it came to a stop, and shoved my gun into the face of Saul Panzer in the driver's seat.

The others were with me. Bill Gore was on my side, on the running board, sticking his gun through the open window; Orrie, with Durkin behind him, was opening the other tonneau door. Maria Maffei was screaming. There was no sound from Anna.

Orrie said, "Get out of there quick. Come on, do you want me to put a hole in you?"

Anna came out and stood on the ground by the running board. Bill Gore went in and got Maria Maffei and hauled her out. Orrie growled, "Shut your trap, you." He called to me, "If that driver grunts let him have it. Turn out the lights."

Bill Gore said, "I've got her purse, it's fat."

"Which one?"

"This one."

"All right, keep it, and keep her trap shut. If she yells rap her one." Orrie turned to Durkin. "Here, hold this one while I put a light on her."

Durkin moved behind Anna and gripped her arms, and Orrie put a flashlight on her face. She looked pale and her lips were clamped tight; she hadn't let out a chirp. Orrie held his light right against her and his masked face was just behind it. He said, "It's you all right. By God, I've got you. So you will tell people about Carlo Maffei cutting out newspaper clippings and talking on the phone and everything you ought to forget. Will you? You won't any more. The knife that was good enough for Carlo Maffei is good enough for you. Tell him hello for me."

He pulled out the long sticker and waved it and it gleamed in the light of the flash. He was too damn good. Maria Maffei yelled and jumped for him and nearly got away from Bill Gore. Bill, who weighed two hundred and no fat, got all around her. Durkin was pulling Anna Fiore back away from the knife and saying to Orrie, "None of that! Cut it! You said you wouldn't. None of that!" Orrie stopped waving the knife and put the light on Anna again.

"All right." He made it sound bloodthirsty. "Where's your purse? I'll get you later. Come on, don't stand there shaking your head. Where's your purse?

Where's that hundred dollars I sent you? No?—Hold her, I'll frisk her for it."

He started for her stocking, and Anna was a wildcat. She busted loose from Durkin and let out a squawk that must have reached to White Plains. Orrie grabbed for her and tore her sleeve half off; Durkin was on her again, and when she saw she couldn't get away she put on a kicking and biting exhibition that made me glad I was leaving that to the help. Durkin finally got her snug, with an arm wrapped around her pinning her arms and his other hand holding her head back, but Orrie never did get his hand inside her stocking, he had to tear it right off. I saw the getaway would have to be quick or we'd have to tie her up, so I had Saul back his car along the edge of the drive so I could get by with mine. Durkin came carrying Anna Fiore, still kicking and trying to bite him, and shoved her into the tonneau; Orrie was with him, growling at her, "You kept my money, did you? You wouldn't burn it, huh? Next time you'll keep your mouth shut."

I ran to the Buick and started the engine and rolled alongside. The others piled in. As we started off Maria Maffei was yelling at us, but I didn't hear Anna's voice. I twisted around the curves of the drive as fast as was practicable, and as soon as I had turned into the public road I stepped on it.

Bill Gore in the back seat was laughing about ready to choke. I got to the Sawmill River Road and turned south, and eased down to forty. Orrie, beside me, wasn't saying anything. I asked him:

"You got the money?"

"Yeah, I got it." He didn't sound very sweet. "I think I'll keep it until I find out if Nero Wolfe carries workmen's compensation insurance."

"Why, did she get you?"

"She bit me twice. That lassie didn't think any more of that hundred bucks than I do of my right eye. If you'd told me I had to subdue a tiger with my bare hands I'd have remembered I had a date."

Bill Gore started laughing again.

I thought it had been pretty well staged. Wolfe couldn't ask better than that. The only thing I had been afraid of was that Anna would get such a scare thrown into her that she would fold up for good, but now that didn't seem likely. I was glad Wolfe had thought of using Maria Maffei and she had been ready for the job, for I wouldn't have cared a bit about driving Anna Fiore back to town with her empty sock. The only question now was, what did she have and how soon would we get it? Would Wolfe's program carry through to the end as he had outlined it, and if it did what kind of a climax would she hand us?

Anyhow, my next move was to get back to the office without delay, so I didn't take time to distribute my passengers where they belonged. I dropped Bill Gore off at 19th Street and took Durkin and Orrie on uptown and left them at the Times Square subway station. Since it wouldn't do to leave the Buick out in front, I drove to the garage and delivered it, and walked home.

I hadn't cared much for the notion Manuel Kimball had got about the sort of present that would be appropriate for Nero Wolfe, and on leaving I had told Fritz to put the bolt on as soon as we got out, so now I had to ring him up to let me in. It was nearly midnight, but he came to the first ring.

Wolfe was in the office, eating cookies and marking items in Hoehn's catalog. I went in and stood, waiting for him to look up. He did so at length, and said, "On time."

I nodded. "And not on my shield, but Orrie Cather is, nearly. She bit him. She bit Durkin too. She was a holy terror. Your play went off swell. They ought to be here soon; I'm going up and dress for the next act. Can I have a glass of milk?"

Wolfe said, "Good," and turned back to his catalog.

I took the milk upstairs with me to my room, and sipped it in between while I was getting undressed and putting on my pajamas. This part of the stunt seemed to me pretty fussy, but I didn't mind because it gave me a chance to doll up in the dressing gown Wolfe had given me a couple of years before which I hadn't had on more than about once. I lit a cigarette and finished the milk, then put on the dressing gown and gave it the once over in the mirror. While I was doing that I heard a car drive up and stop outside, and I moved closer to the open window and heard Saul Panzer's voice, and then Maria Maffei's. I sat down and lit another cigarette.

I sat there nearly half an hour. I heard Fritz letting them in, and their voices in the hall as they passed on their way to the office, and then all I got was silence. I waited so long that I was beginning to wonder whether it wasn't working right, or Wolfe was finishing his charade without me. Then there were footsteps in the hall, and in a minute on the stairs, and Fritz was at my door saying that Wolfe wanted me in the office. I waited a little, long enough to get awake and into my dressing gown, as if I had been asleep, and ruffled up my hair, and went down.

Wolfe was seated at his desk. Maria Maffei was in a chair in front of him and Anna in one against the wall. Anna was a sight, with one sleeve nearly off, a leg bare, her face dirty and her hair all over.

I stared. "Miss Maffei! Anna! Did they set the dogs on you?"

Wolfe wiggled a finger at me. "Archie. I'm sorry to have to disturb you. Miss Maffei and Miss Fiore have been subjected to violence. They were driving into the country, to visit Miss Maffei's sister, when they were set upon by brigands. Their car was stopped; they were treated with discourtesy, and robbed. Miss Maffei's purse was taken, and her rings. Miss Fiore was despoiled of the money which she has shown to us and which she so hardly earned."

"No!" I said. "Anna! They didn't take that money!"

Anna's eyes were on me. I met them all right, but after a second I thought it would do to turn back to Wolfe.

Anna said, "*He* took it."

Wolfe nodded. "Miss Fiore got the impression that the man who took her money was the one who had sent it to her. I have advised her and Miss Maffei to go to the police at once, but they do not fancy that suggestion. Miss Maffei mistrusts the police on principle. Miss Fiore seems to have conceived the idea that we, more especially you, are more likely to be of help. Of course you are not at the moment properly dressed to go out in search of robbers, and the scene is thirty miles off, but Miss Fiore asked for you. Does anything occur to you?"

"Well," I said. "This is awful. It's terrible. And me upstairs sound asleep. I wish you had got me to drive you to the country, Anna; if you had this wouldn't have happened, I don't care who it was that tried to get your money. I don't believe it could have been the man who sent it to you; that man kills people; he would have killed you."

Anna's eyes were going back and forth between

Wolfe and me, but I no longer thought there might be
suspicion in them; she was only stunned, overwhelmed
by her unimaginable loss. She said, "He wanted to kill
me. I bit him."

"Good for you. You see, Anna, what happens when
you try to act decent with a bad man. If you had
burned that money the other day when I wanted you
to, and told us what you know about things, now you
would have Mr. Wolfe's money. Now you can't burn
the money because you haven't got it, and the only
way you could get it back would be if I could catch
him. Remember, he's the man who killed Carlo Maffei.
And look what he did to you! Tore your dress and
pulled off your stockings—did he hurt you?"

Anna shook her head. "He didn't hurt me. Could
you catch him?"

"I could try. I could if I knew where to look."

"Would you give it back to me?"

"Your money? I sure would."

Anna looked down at her bare leg, and her hand
slid slowly under the hem of her skirt and rested on
the spot where the twenties had been. Maria Maffei
started to speak, but Wolfe wiggled her into silence.
Anna was still looking at her leg when she said, "I've
got to undress."

I was slow; Wolfe got it at once. He spoke: "Ah.
Certainly, Archie: the lights in the front room. Miss
Maffei, if you will accompany Miss Fiore?"

I went to the front room and turned the lights on,
and closed the windows and the curtains. Anna and
Miss Maffei had followed me in and stood there
waiting for me to leave; as I went out I gave Anna a
friendly grin; she looked pale but her eyes were
brighter than I had ever seen them. In the office I
closed the door behind me. Wolfe was sitting up in his

chair, not leaning back; there was nothing to remark on the drowsy patient hemisphere of his face, but his forearms extended along the arms of the chair and the forefinger of his right hand was moving so that its tip described a little circle over and over on the polished wood. For Wolfe that was going pretty far in the way of agitation.

I sat down. Faint sounds of movements and voices came from the front room. They were taking long enough. I said, "This is a swell toga you gave me."

Wolfe looked at me, sighed, and let his eyes go half shut again.

When the door opened I sprang up. Anna came through in front, clutching a piece of paper in her hand; her torn sleeve had been pinned together and her hair fingered back. She came up to me and stuck the paper at me and mumbled, "Mr. Archie." I wanted to pat her on the shoulder but I saw she was sure to cry if I did, so I just nodded and she went back to her chair and Maria Maffei to hers. The paper was a fat little manila envelope. I turned to Wolfe's desk to hand it to him, but he nodded to me to open it. It wasn't sealed. I pulled out the contents and spread them on the desk.

There was quite a collection. Wolfe and I took our time inspecting it. Item, the Barstow death clipping that Carlo Maffei had cut from the *Times* on June fifth. Item, a series of drawings on separate little sheets, exact and fine, with two springs and a trigger and a lot of complications; the shape of one was the head of a golf driver. Item, a clipping from a Sunday Rotogravure, a photograph of Manuel Kimball standing by his airplane, and a caption with his name commenting on the popularity of aviation among the Westchester younger set. At the bottom was written in pencil, *The*

*man I made the golf club for. See drawings. May 26,*
*1933. Carlo Maffei.* Item, a ten-dollar bill. It was a
gold note, and there was pencil-writing on it too, the
signatures of four people: Sarah Barstow, Peter Oliver
Barstow, Lawrence Barstow, and Manuel Kimball.
The signatures had been written with a broad-pointed
soft pencil and covered half of one side of the bill.

I looked it all over a second time and then murmured at Wolfe, "Lovin' babe."

He said, "I tolerate that from Saul Panzer, Archie,
I will not from you. Not even as a tribute to this
extraordinary display. Poor Carlo Maffei! To combine
the foresight that assembled this with the foolhardiness that took him to his fatal rendezvous! We alone
profit by the foresight, he pays for the foolhardiness
himself—a contemptible bargain.—Miss Maffei, you
have lost your purse but gained the means of stilling
the ferment of your blood; the murderer of your
brother is known and the weapon for his punishment is
at hand.—Miss Fiore, you will get your money back.
Mr. Archie will get it and return it, I promise you. He
will do it soon, for I can guess how little promises
mean to you; the fierce flame of reality is your only
warmth and light; the reality of twenty-dollar bills.
Soon, Miss Fiore. Please tell me: when did Mr. Maffei
give you all this?"

Anna talked. Not what you could call voluble, but
willingly enough to Wolfe's questions. He got every
detail and had me take it down. She had actually seen
the driver. For many days Carlo Maffei had forbidden
her to enter his room when he was there working, and
had kept his closet locked; but one day during his
absence the closet door had opened to her trial only to
disclose nothing to her curiosity more uncommon than
a golf club evidently in process of construction. On

Maffei's return, finding that the driver was not placed as he had left it, he had been sufficiently disturbed to inform her that if she ever mentioned the golf club he would cut her tongue out. That was all she knew about it. The envelope had been given to her on June fifth, the day Maffei disappeared. Around seven o'clock, just after he had answered the telephone call, she had gone upstairs for something and he had called her into his room and given her the envelope. He had told her that he would ask her to return it in the morning, but that if he did not come back that night and nothing was heard from him Anna was to deliver the envelope to his sister.

When Anna told that Maria Maffei got active. She jumped up and started toward the girl. I went after her, but Wolfe's voice like a whip beat me to it:

"Miss Maffei!" He wiggled his finger. "To your chair.—Be seated, I say!—Thank you. Your brother was already dead. Save your fury. After pulling Miss Fiore's hair you would, I suppose, inquire why she did not give you the envelope. That appears to me obvious; perhaps I can save her the embarrassment of replying. I do not know whether your brother told her not to look into the envelope; in any any event, she looked. She saw the ten dollar bill; it was in her possession.—Miss Fiore, before Carlo Maffei gave you that envelope, what was the largest sum you ever had?"

Anna said, "I don't know."

I asked her, "Did you ever have ten dollars before?"

"No, Mr. Archie."

"Five dollars?"

She shook her head. "Mrs. Ricci gives me a dollar every week."

"Swell. And you buy your shoes and clothes?"

"Of course I do."

I threw up my hands. Wolfe said, "Miss Maffei, you or I might likewise be tempted by a kingdom, only its boundaries would not be so modest. She probably struggled, and by another sunrise might have won and delivered the envelope to you intact; but that morning's mail brought her another envelope, and this time it was not merely a kingdom, it was a glorious world. She lost; or perhaps it is somewhere down as a victory; we cannot know. At any rate her struggle is over.—And now, Miss Maffei, do this and make no mistake: take Miss Fiore home with you and keep her there. Your driver is waiting outside for you. You can explain to your employer that your niece has come for a visit. Explain as you please, but keep Miss Fiore safe until I tell you that the danger is past. Under no circumstances is she to go to the street.—Miss Fiore, you hear?"

"I will do what Mr. Archie says."

"Good. Archie, you will accompany them and explain the requirements. It will be only a day or so."

I nodded and went upstairs to put the dressing gown away for another year and get some clothes on.

# Chapter 17

When I got back after escorting Anna and Maria Maffei to the apartment on Park Avenue where Maria Maffei was housekeeper, the office was dark and Wolfe had gone upstairs. There was a note for me: *Archie, learn from Miss Barstow her excuse for mutilating United States currency. N. W.* I knew that would be it. I went on up to the hay, but out of respect to Manuel Kimball I stepped to the rear of the upper hall to look for a line of light under Wolfe's door. There wasn't any. I called out:

"Are you all in one bed?"

Wolfe's voice came, "Confound it, don't badger me!"

"Yes, sir. Is the switch on?"

"It is."

I went to my own room and the bed I was ready for; it was after two o'clock.

In the morning there was a drizzle, but I didn't mind. I took my time at breakfast, and told Fritz to keep the bolt on while I was gone, and then with a light raincoat and a rubber hat went whistling along on my way to the garage. One thing that gave me joy was an item in the morning paper which said that the White Plains authorities were on the verge of being satisfied that the death of Peter Oliver Barstow had resulted from an accidental snake bite and that various other details of the tragedy not connected with that theory could all be explained by coincidence. It would have been fun to call up Harry Foster at the *Gazette* and let him know how safe it would be to stick pins in Anderson's chair for him to sit on, but I couldn't risk it because I didn't know what Wolfe's plans were in that direction. Another source of joy was the completeness of the briefcase which Anna Fiore had been carrying around all the time pinned to whatever she wore underneath. When I considered that it must have been there that first day I had called at Sullivan Street with Maria Maffei and I hadn't been keen enough to smell it, I felt like kicking myself. But maybe it was just as well. If the envelope had been delivered to Maria Maffei there was no telling what might have happened.

I telephoned the Barstow place from uptown, and when I got there around nine-thirty Sarah Barstow was expecting me. In the four days since I had last seen her she had made some changes in her color scheme; her cheeks would have made good pinching; her shoulders sat straight with all the sag gone. I got up from my seat in the sun-room, a drizzle-room that day, when she came in, and she came over and shook hands. She told me her mother was well again, and this time Dr. Bradford said more likely than not she was well for good. Then she asked if I wanted a glass of milk!

I grinned. "I guess not, thanks. As I told you on the phone, Miss Barstow, this time it's a business call. Remember, the last time I said it was social? Today, business." I pulled an envelope from my pocket and got out the ten dollar bill and handed it to her. "Nero Wolfe put it this way: what excuse did you have for mutilating United States currency?"

She looked at it puzzled for a second, then smiled, and then a shadow went over her face, the shadow of her dead father. "Where did you ever—where did you get it?"

"Oh, a hoarder turned it in. But how did those names get on there? Did you write yours?"

She nodded. "Yes, we all did. I think I told you—didn't I?—That one day last summer Larry and Manuel Kimball played a match of tennis and my father and I acted as umpire and linesman. They had a bet on it, and Larry paid Mr. Kimball with a ten dollar bill and Mr. Kimball wanted us to write our names on it as a souvenir. We were sitting—on the side terrace—"

"And Manuel Kimball took the bill?"

"Of course. He won it."

"And this is it?"

"Certainly, there are our signatures.—Mr. Goodwin, I suppose it's just vulgar curiosity, but where did you ever get it?"

I took the bill and replaced it carefully in the envelope—not Carlo Maffei's envelope, a patent one with a clip on it so the signatures wouldn't rub any more than they had already—and put it in my pocket.

"I'm sorry, Miss Barstow. Since it's just vulgar curiosity you can wait. Not long, I hope. And may I say without offense, you're looking swell. I was thinking when you came in, I'd like to pinch your cheeks."

"What!" She stared, then she laughed. "*That's* a compliment."

"It sure is. If you know how many cheeks there are I wouldn't bother to pinch. Good day, Miss Barstow."

We shook hands while she still laughed.

Headed south again through the drizzle, I considered that the ten-dollar bill clinched it. The other three items in Carlo Maffei's envelope were good evidence, but this was something that no one but Manual Kimball could have had, and it had got to Carlo Maffei. How, I wondered. Well: Manuel Kimball had kept it in his wallet as a souvenir. His payments of money, one or more, to Maffei for making the driver, had been made not in a well-lighted room but in places dark enough to defeat the idle curiosity of observers; and in the darkness the souvenir had been included in a payment. Probably Manuel had later discovered his carelessness and demanded the souvenir back, and Maffei had claimed it had been spent unnoticed. That might have aroused Manuel's early suspicions of Maffei, and certainly it accounted for Maffei's recognition of the significance of the death, and its manner, of Peter Oliver Barstow; for that name, and two other Barstow names, had been signed on the ten-dollar bill he was preserving.

Yes, Manuel Kimball would live long enough to be sorry he had won that tennis match.

At White Plains, on a last-minute decision, I slowed down and turned off the Parkway. It looked to me as if it was all over and the only thing left was a brief call at the District Attorney's office to explain the facts of life to him; and in that case there was no point in my driving through the rain all the way down to Thirty-fifth Street and clear back again. So I found a telephone booth and called Wolfe and told him what I had learned from Sarah Barstow, and asked him what next. He told me to come on home. I mentioned that I was right there in White Plains with plenty of time and inclination to do any errands he might have in mind. He said, "Come home. Your errand will be here waiting for you."

I got back onto the Parkway.

It was a little after eleven when I arrived. I couldn't park right in front of the house as usual, because another car was there, a big black limousine. After turning off my engine I sat for a minute staring at the limousine, particularly at the official plate hanging alongside the license plate. I allowed myself the pleasure of a beautiful grin, and I got out and just for fun went to the front of the limousine and spoke to the chauffeur.

"Mr. Anderson is in the house?"

He looked at me a couple of seconds before he could make up his mind to nod. I turned and ran up the steps with the grin still on.

Anderson was with Wolfe in the office. When I went in I pretended not to see him; I went across to Wolfe's desk and took the envelope out of my pocket and handed it to him. "Okay," I said, "I've written the date of the match on the envelope." He nodded and told me to put it in the safe. I opened the heavy door and took my time about finding the drawer where the rest of Anna's briefcase was stowed away. Then I turned, and let my eyes fall on the visitor and looked surprised.

"Oh," I said, "it's you! Good morning, Mr. Anderson."

He mumbled back at me.

"If you ever get your notebook, Archie, we shall proceed." Wolfe was using his drawly voice, and when I heard it I knew that one lawyer was in for a lot of irritation. "No, not at your desk, pull a chair around and be one of us.—Good. I have just been explaining to Mr. Anderson that the ingenious theory of the

Barstow case which he is trying to embrace is an offense to truth and an outrage on justice, and since I cherish the one and am on speaking terms with the other, it is my duty to demonstrate to him its inadequacy. I shall be glad of your support. Mr. Anderson is a little put out at the urgency of my invitation to him to call, but as I was just remarking to him, I think we should be grateful that the telephone permits the arrangement on short notice of these little informal conferences.—On reflection, Mr. Anderson, I'm sure you will agree."

Anderson's neck was swelling. There was never anything very lovely about him, but now he was trying to keep his meanness down because he knew he had to, and it kept choking him trying to come up. His face was red and his neck bulged. He said to Wolfe, "You can tell your man to put his notebook away. You're a bigger ass than I thought you were, Wolfe, if you imagine you can put over this sort of thing."

"Take it down, Archie." Wolfe's drawl was swell. "It is irrelevant, being merely an opinion, but get it down.—Mr. Anderson, I see that you misapprehend the situation; I had not supposed you were so obtuse. I gave you a free choice of alternatives on the telephone, and you chose to come here. Being here, in my house, you will permit me to direct the activity of its inmates; should you become annoyed beyond endurance, you may depart without ceremony or restraint. Should you depart, the procedure will be as I have indicated: within twenty-four hours Mr. Goodwin will drive in my car to your office in White Plains. Behind him, in another car, will be an assortment of newspaper reporters; beside him will be the murderer of Peter Oliver Barstow and Carlo Maffei; in his pocket

will be the indubitable proof of the murderer's guilt. I
was minded to proceed—"

Anderson broke in, "Carlo Maffei? Who the devil is
that?"

"Was, Mr. Anderson. Not is. Carlo Maffei was an
Italian craftsman who was murdered in your county
on Monday evening, June fifth—stabbed in the back.
Surely the case is in your office."

"What if it is? What has that got to do with
Barstow?"

"They were murdered by the same man."

Anderson stared. "By God, Wolfe, I think you're
crazy."

"I'm afraid not." Wolfe sighed. "There are times
when I would welcome such a conclusion as an escape
from life's meaner responsibilities—what Mr. Goodwin would call an out—but the contrary evidence is
overwhelming.—But to our business. Have you your
checkbook with you?"

"Ah." Anderson's lips twisted. "What if I have?"

"It will make it more convenient for you to draw a
check to my order for ten thousand dollars."

Anderson said nothing. He put his eyes straight
into Wolfe's and kept them there, and Wolfe met him.
Wolfe sighed. Finally Anderson said, smooth:

"It might make it convenient, but not very reasonable. You are not a hijacker, are you?"

"Oh, no." Wolfe's cheeks folded up. "I assure you,
no. I have the romantic temperament, but physically
I'm not built for it. You do not grasp the situation? Let
me explain. In a way, it goes four years back, to the
forgetfulness you displayed in the Goldsmith case. I
regretted that at the time, and resolved that on some
proper occasion you should be reminded of it. I now
remind you. Two weeks ago I came in possession of

information which presented an opportunity to extend you a favor. I wished to extend it; but with the Goldsmith case in my memory and doubtless, so I thought, in yours also, it seemed likely that delicacy of feeling would prevent you from accepting a favor from me. So I offered to sell you the information for a proper sum; that of course was what the proffer of a wager amounted to; the proof that you understood it so was furnished by your counter-offer to Mr. Goodwin of a sum so paltry that I shall not mention it."

Anderson said, "I offered a substantial fee."

"Mr. Anderson! Please. Don't drag us into absurdities." Wolfe leaned back and laced his fingers on his belly. "Mr. Goodwin and I have discovered the murderer and have acquired proof of his guilt; not plausible proof, jury proof. That brings us to the present. The murderer, of course, is not my property, he belongs to the sovereign State of New York. Even the information I possess is not my property; if I do not communicate it to the State I am liable to penalties. But I can choose my method. First: you will now give me your personal check for ten thousand dollars, this afternoon Mr. Goodwin will go to your bank and have it certified, and tomorrow morning he will conduct you to the murderer, point him to you, and deliver the proof of his guilt—all in a properly diffident and unostentatious manner. Or, second: we shall proceed to organize the parade to your office as I have described it: the prisoner, the press, and the proof, with a complete absence of diffidence. Take your choice, sir. Though you may find it hard to believe, it is of little concern to me, for while it would give me pleasure to receive your check, I have a great fondness for parades."

Wolfe stopped. Anderson looked at him, silent and

smooth, calculating. Wolfe pressed the button on his desk and, when Fritz appeared, ordered beer. Every chance I got to look up from my notebook, I stared at Anderson; I cold see it made him sore, and I stared all I could.

Anderson asked, "How do I know your proof is any good?"

"My word, sir. It is as good as my judgment. I pledge both."

"There is no possible doubt?"

"Anything is possible. There is no room for doubt in the minds of a jury."

Anderson twisted his lips around. Fritz brought the beer, and Wolfe opened a bottle and filled a glass.

Anderson said, "Ten thousand dollars is out of the question. Five thousand."

"Pfui! You would dicker? Contemptible. Let it be the parade." Wolfe picked up his glass of beer and gulped it.

"Give me the proof and tell me the murderer and you can have the check the minute I've got him."

Wolfe wiped his lips, and sighed. "Mr. Anderson, one of us has to trust the other. Do not compel me to advance reasons for the preference I have indicated."

Anderson began to put up an argument. He was tough, no doubt about that, he was no softy. Of course he didn't have any real reasons or persuasions, but he had plenty of words. When he stopped Wolfe just shook his head. Anderson went on, and then again, but all he got was the same reply. I took it all down, and I had to admit there wasn't any whine in it. He was fighting with damn poor ammunition, but he wasn't whining.

He wrote the check in a fold he took from his pocket, holding it on his knee, with his fountain pen.

He wrote it like a good bookkeeper, precisely and carefully, without haste, and then with the same preciseness filled in the spaces on the stub before he tore the check off and laid it on Wolfe's desk. Wolfe gave me a nod and I reached over and picked up the check and looked it over. I was relieved to see it was on a New York bank; that would save me a trip to White Plains before three o'clock.

Anderson got up. "I hope you never regret this, Wolfe. Now, when and where?"

Wolfe said, "I shall telephone."

"When?"

"Within twenty-four hours. Probably within twelve. I can get you at any time, at your office or your home?"

Anderson said, "Yes," turned on the word, and left. I got up and went to the hall and watched him out. Then I went back to the office and leaned the check up against a paperweight and blew a kiss at it.

Wolfe was whistling; that is, his lips were rounded into the proper position and air was going in and out, but there was no sound. I loved seeing him do that; it never happened when anybody was there but me, not even Fritz. He told me once that it meant he was surrendering to his emotions.

I put my notebook away and stuck the check in my pocket and pulled the chairs back where they belonged. After a little Wolfe said, "Archie, four years is a long time."

"Yes, sir. And ten grand is a lot of money. It's nearly an hour till lunch; I'll run down to the bank now and get their scrawl on it."

"It is raining. I thought of you this morning, adventuring beyond the city. Call for a messenger."

"Good Lord, no. I wouldn't miss the fun of having this certified for a gallon of milk."

Wolfe leaned back, murmured, "Intrepid," and closed his eyes.

I got back in time to bust the tape at lunch.

I figured, naturally, that the hour had stuck, but to my surprise Wolfe seemed to have notions of leisure. He was in no hurry about anything. He took his time at the table, with two long cups of coffee at the end, and after lunch he went to the office and reposed in his chair without appearing to have anything of importance on his mind. I fussed around. After a while he roused himself enough to give me some directions: first, type out Anna Fiore's statement completely and chronologically; second, have photostatic copies made, rush, of the contents of Carlo Maffei's envelope; third, go to the Park Avenue apartment and return Maria Maffei's purse to her and have Anna Fiore sign the statement in duplicate before witnesses; and fourth, check with Horstmann the shipment of pseudo-bulbs which had arrived the preceding day on the *Cortez*.

I asked him, "Maybe you're forgetting something?" He shook his head, faintly so as not to disturb his comfort, and I let it slide. I was curious but not worried, for I could tell by the look on his face that he was adding something up to the right answer.

For the rest of the afternoon I was busy. I went out first, to a studio down on Sixth Avenue, to get them started on the photostats, and I made sure that they understood that if the originals were lost or injured they had better use the fire escape when they heard me coming. Then back to the office, to type Anna's statement. I fixed it up in swell shape and it took quite a while. When I went out to the roadster again the rain had stopped and it was brightening up, but the pavements were still wet. I had telephoned the apartment where Maria Maffei worked, and when

I got there she was expecting me. I would hardly have known her. In a neat well-cut housekeeper's dress, black, with a little black thing across the top of her hair, she looked elegant, and her manner was as Park Avenue as the doorman at the Pierre. Well, I thought, they're all different in the bathtub from what they're like at Schrafft's. I was almost afraid to hand her her purse, it seemed vulgar. But she took it. Then she led me to a room away off, and there was Anna Fiore sitting looking out of a window. I read the statement to her, and she signed it, and Maria Maffei and I signed as witnesses.

Anna said next to nothing with her tongue, but her eyes kept asking me one question all the time, from the minute I entered the room. When I got up to go I answered it. I patted her on the shoulder and said, "Soon, Anna. I'll get your money real soon, and bring it right to you. Don't you worry."

She just nodded and said, "Mr. Archie."

After I got the photostats from the studio I saw no point in leaving the roadster out ready for action if there wasn't going to be any, so I garaged it and walked home. Until dinner time I was busy checking up the *Cortez* shipment and writing letters to the shippers about the casualties. Wolfe was pottering around most of the time while I was upstairs with Horstmann, but at six o'clock he left us and Horstmann and I went on checking.

It was after eight o'clock by the time dinner was over. I was getting the fidgets. Seven years with Nero Wolfe had taught me not to bite my nails waiting for the world to come to an end, but there were times when I was convinced that an eccentric was a man who ought to have his nose pulled. That evening he kept the radio going all through dinner. As soon as it was over and he nodded to Fritz to pull his chair back, I got up and said:

"I guess I won't sit in the office and watch you yawn. I'll try a movie."

Wolfe said, "Good. No man should neglect his cultural side."

"What!" I exploded. "You mean—damn it all, you would let me go and sit in a movie while maybe Manuel Kimball is finishing his packing for a nice little trip to his native land? Then I can go to the Argentine and buy a horse and ride all over the damn pampa, whatever that is, looking for him? Do you think all it takes to catch a murderer is to sit in your damn office and let your genius work? That maybe most of it, but it also takes a pair of eyes and a pair of legs and sometimes a gun or two. And the best thing you can think of is to tell me to go to a movie, while you—"

He showed me the palm of his hand to stop me. Fritz had pulled his chair back and he was up, a mountain on its feet. "Archie," he said. "Spare me. A typical man of violence; the placidity of a humming-bird. I did not suggest the movie, you did. Even were Manuel Kimball a man to tremble at shadows, there has been no shadow to disturb him. Why should Manuel Kimball take a trip, to his native land or anywhere else? There is nothing he is likely to take at this moment, I should say. If it will set your mind at rest, I can tell you that he is at his home, but not packing for a trip. I was speaking to him on the telephone only two hours ago.—Fritz, the buzzer, attend the front door, please.—He will receive another telephone call from me in the morning at eight o'clock, and I assure you he will wait for it."

"I hope he does." I wasn't satisfied. "I tell you, monkeying around at this stage is dangerous. You've

done your part, a part no other living man could do,
and now it's simple but it's damn important. I just go
there and wrap myself around him, and stay wrapped
until you tell Anderson to go and get him. Why not?"

Wolfe shook his head. "No, Archie. I understand
your contention: that a point arrives when finesse
must retire and leave the coup de grâce for naked
force. I understand it, and I deny it vehemently.—But
come; guests are arriving; will you stop in the office a
moment before you proceed to your entertainment?"

He turned and went to the office, and I followed
him, wondering what the devil kind of a charade he
was getting up. Whatever it was, I didn't like it.

Fritz had gone to the door, and the guests had been
shown into the office ahead of us. I had no definite
ideas as to who it might be, but certainly I didn't
expect that bunch. I stared around at them. It was
Fred Durkin and Bill Gore and Orrie Cather. My first
thought was that Wolfe had got the funny notion that
I needed all that army to subdue the fer-de-lance, as I
had decided to call Manuel Kimball instead of the
spiggoty, but of course Wolfe knew me too well for
that. I tossed a nod around to them, and grinned when
I saw a gauze bandage on Orrie's left wrist. Anna
Fiore had got under his skin all right.

After Wolfe got into his chair he asked me to get a
pencil and a large piece of paper and make a rough
map of the Kimball estate. With the guests there I
asked no questions; I did as he said. I told him that I
was acquainted with the ground only immediately
around the house and the landing field, and he said
that would do. While I made the map, sitting at my
desk, Wolfe was telling Orrie how to get the sedan
from the garage at six-thirty in the morning, and

instructing the other two to meet him there at that hour.

I took the map to Wolfe at his desk. He looked it over a minute and said, "Good. Now tell me, if you were sending three men to that place to make sure that Manuel Kimball did not leave without being seen, and to follow him if seen, how would you dispose of them?"

I asked, "Under cover?"

"No. Exposed would do."

"How long?"

"Three hours."

I considered a minute. "Easy. Durkin on the highway, across from the entrance to the drive, with the sedan backed into a gate so it could start quick either way. Bill Gore in the bushes—about here—where he could cover all approaches to the house except the back. Orrie on top of a hill back here, about a third of a mile off, with field glasses, and a motorcycle down on the road. But they might as well stay home and play pinochle, since they can't fly."

Wolfe's cheeks folded. "Saul Panzer can. The clouds will have eyes. Thank you, Archie. That is all. We will not keep you longer from your entertainment."

I knew from his tone that I was to go, but I didn't want to. If there had to be a charade I wanted to help make it up. I said, "The movies have all been closed. Raided by the Society for the Suppression of Vice."

Wolfe said, "Then try a harlot's den. When gathering eggs you must look in every nest."

Bill Gore snickered. I gave Wolfe as dirty a look as I cold manage, and went to the hall for my hat.

# Chapter 18

I was awake Wednesday morning before seven o'clock, but I didn't get up. I watched the sun slanting against the windows, and listened to the noises from the street and the boats and ferries on the river, and figured that since Bill and Fred and Orrie had been instructed to meet at the garage at six-thirty they must already be as far as the Grand Concourse. My part hadn't been handed to me. When I had got home the night before Wolfe had gone up to bed, and there had been no note for me.

I finally tumbled out and shaved and dressed, taking my time, and went downstairs. Fritz was in the kitchen, buzzing around contented. I passed him some kind of a cutting remark, but realizing that it wasn't fair to take it out on him I made up for it by eating an extra egg and reading aloud to him a piece from the morning paper about a vampire bat that had had a baby in the zoo. Fritz came from the part of Switzerland where they talk French. He had a paper of his own every morning, but it was in French and it never seemed very likely to me that there was much in it. I was always surprised when I saw a word in it that meant anything up-to-date; for instance, the word

Barstow which had been prominent in the headlines for a week.

I was starting the second cup of coffee when the phone rang. I went to the office and got the receiver to my ear, but Wolfe had answered from his room. I listened. It was Orrie Cather reporting that they had arrived and that everything was set. That was all. I went back to my coffee in the kitchen.

After a third cup and a cigarette I moseyed into the office. Sooner or later, I thought, genius will impart its secrets; sooner or later, compose yourself; just straighten things around and dust off the desk and fill the fountain pen and make everything nice for teacher. Sooner or later, honey—you damn fool. I wasn't getting the fidgets, I had them. A couple of times I took off the receiver and listened, but I didn't catch Wolfe making any calls. I got the mail and put it on his desk, and opened the safe. I pulled out the drawer where the Maffei stuff was just to make sure it hadn't walked off. The envelope into which I had put the photostats felt thin, and I took them out. One set was gone. I had had two sets made, and only one was there. That gave me my first hint about Wolfe's charade, but I didn't follow it up very far, because as I was sticking the envelope back into the drawer Fritz came in and said that Wolfe wanted to see me in his room.

I went up. His door was open. He was up and dressed all but his coat; the sleeves of his yellow shirt—he used two fresh shirts every day, always canary yellow—looked like enormous floating sheeps' bladders as he stood at his mirror brushing his hair. I caught his eyes in the mirror, and he winked at me! I was so astonished that I suppose my mouth fell open.

He put the brush down and turned to me. "Good

morning, Archie. You have breakfast?—Good. It is pleasant to see the sun again, after yesterday's gray unceasing trickle. Get the Maffei documents from the safe. By all means take a gun. Proceed to White Plains and get Mr. Anderson at his office—he will be awaiting you—and drive him to the Kimball estate. Show him Manuel Kimball; point, if necessary. When Manuel Kimball has been apprehended deliver the documents to Mr. Anderson. Return here, and you will find that Fritz will have prepared one of your favorite dishes for lunch."

I said, "Okay. But why all the mystery—"

"Comments later, Archie. Save them, please. I am due upstairs in ten minutes and I have yet to enjoy my chocolate."

I said, "I hope you choke on it," and turned and left him.

With the Carlo Maffei stuff and Anna's statement on my breast and a thirty-eight, loaded this time, on my hip, I walked to the garage. It was warm and sunny, June twenty-first, the day for the sun to start back south. It was a good day for the finale of the fer-de-lance, I thought, the longest one of the year. I filled up with gas and oil and water, made it crosstown to Park Avenue, and turned north. As I passed the marble front of the Manhattan Trust Company I saluted; that was where I had had Anderson's check certified. Going north on the Parkway at that hour of the morning there was plenty of room, but I kept my speedometer at forty or under; Wolfe had told Anderson this would be unostentatious, and besides, I wasn't in the mood for repartee with a motor cop. I was pretty well on edge. I always am like that when I'm really on my way for a man; there never seems to be quite enough air for me; I breathe quicker and everything I touch—the steering wheel, for instance—seems to be alive with blood going in it. I don't like the feeling much but I always have it.

Anderson was waiting for me. In his office the girl at the desk tossed me a nod and got busy on the phone. In a minute Anderson came out. There were two men with him, carrying their hats and looking powerful. One of them was H. R. Corbett; the other was new to me. Anderson stopped to say something to the girl at the desk, then came over to me.

"Well?" he said.

I grinned. "I'm ready if you are. Hello, Corbett. You going along?"

Anderson said, "I'm taking two men. You know what the job is. Is that enough?"

I nodded. "All we'll need 'em for is to hold my hat anyway. Let's go." The third guy opened the door and we filed out.

Anderson came with me in the roadster; the other two followed us in a closed car, official, but I noticed it wasn't Anderson's limousine. Going down Main Street all the traffic cops saluted my passenger, and I grinned considering how surprised they would have been if they had known how much the District Attorney was paying for that little taxi ride. I opened her up as soon as I got onto the highway, and rolled over the hills, up and down, so fast that Anderson looked at me. He didn't know but what the speed was part of the program, so I kept going, slowing down only at the points where I had to make a turn and needed to make sure that Corbett, trailing along behind, had caught it. It took just twenty-five minutes from the White Plains courthouse to the entrance to the Kimball drive; the clock on my dash said ten-forty as I slowed up to turn in.

Durkin was there, across the road, sitting on the running board of the sedan which had been backed in as I had suggested. I waved at him but didn't stop. Anderson asked, "That Wolfe's man?" I nodded and swept into the drive. I had gone about a hundred feet when Anderson said, "Stop!" I pushed the pedals down, shifted into neutral, and pulled the hand brake.

Anderson said, "This is E. D. Kimball's place. You've got to show me right here."

I shook my head. "Nothing doing. You know Nero Wolfe, and that'll do for you. I'm obeying orders. Do I go on?"

Corbett's car had stopped right behind us. Anderson was looking at me, his mouth twisted with uncertainty. I had my ears open, straining, not for Anderson's reply, but for what I was taking for the sound of an airplane. Even if I had been willing to get out and look up I couldn't, on account of trees. But it was an airplane, sure. I shifted and started forward on the jump.

Anderson said, "By God, Goodwin, I hope you know what you're risking. If I had known—"

I stopped him, "Shut up!"

I pulled up at the house and ran over and rang the bell. In a minute the door was opened by the fat butler.

"I'd like to speak to Mr. Manuel Kimball."

"Yes, sir, Mr. Goodwin? He is expecting you. He told me to ask you to go to the hangar and wait for him there."

"Isn't he there?"

The butler hesitated, and he certainly looked worried. "I believe he intended to go aloft in his plane."

I nodded and ran back to the car. Corbett had got out and walked to the roadster and was talking with

Anderson. As I got in Anderson turned to me and started, "Look here, Goodwin—"

"Did you hear me say shut up? I'm busy. Look out, Corbett."

I shot forward onto the back drive and headed for the graveled road that led to the hangar. On that, out from under the trees, the sound of the airplane was louder. I made the gravel fly, and whirled to a stop on the concrete platform in front of the hangar. The mechanic, Skinner, was standing there in the wide open door. I jumped out and went over to him.

"Mr. Manuel Kimball?"

Skinner pointed up, and I looked. It was Manuel Kimball's plane, high, but not too high for me to see the red and blue. It seemed to make a lot of noise, and the next second I saw why, when I caught sight of another plane circling in from the west, higher than Manuel's and going faster. It was helping with the noise. Both planes were circling, dark and beautiful in the sun. I brought my head down to sneeze.

Skinner said, "He's got company this morning."

"So I see. Who is it?"

"I don't know. I saw it first a little after eight o'clock and it's been fooling around up there ever since. It's a Burton twin-motor, it's got a swell dip."

I remember Wolfe saying the clouds would have eyes. There weren't any clouds, but no doubt about the eyes.

I asked, "What time did Mr. Kimball go up?"

"A little after ten. They came out around nine-thirty, but the second seat wasn't ready and I had to fix the straps."

I knew what it meant as soon as he said it, but I asked him anyhow. I said, "Oh, is there someone with him?"

"Yes, sir, his father. The old gentleman's having a ride. It's only his third time up. He nearly backed out when the seat wasn't ready, but we got him in."

I looked up at the airplanes again. Manuel Kimball and his father having a ride together, up there in the sun, the wind and the roar. No conversation probably, just a morning ride.

I started toward the roadster, to speak to Anderson. Corbett had left his car and came to meet me. I stopped to listen to him: "Well, we've come to your party, where's your guest of honor?"

I brushed past him and went on to the roadster. Seeing no point in giving the mechanic an earful, I lowered my voice. "You'll have to wait, Mr. Anderson. Barstow's murderer is taking an airplane ride. I'm sorry you won't get him on time, but you'll get him."

Anderson said, "Get in here. I want a showdown."

I shook my head. Maybe it was just contrariness, but I was set on carrying it out exactly as Wolfe had ordered. "That's not next on the program." Corbett had come up, around on the other side of the roadster, and now he stuck his face in at the window and said to Anderson, "If he's got anything you want I'd be glad to get it for you."

I had my mouth open to invite him formally when I heard my name called. I turned. Skinner had left the hangar and was approaching me; in one hand he had a golf driver and in the other an envelope. I stared at him. He was saying, "I forgot. You're Mr. Goodwin? Mr. Kimball left these for you."

I got to him and grabbed. The driver! I looked at it, but there was nothing to see; in outward appearance it was just a golf club. But of course it was it. Lovin' babe! I tucked it under my arm and looked at the envelope; on the outside was written, *Mr. Nero*

*Wolfe*. It was unsealed, and I pulled out the contents, and had in my hand the set of photostats I had missed from the safe. They were fastened with a paper clip, and slipped under the clip was a piece of paper on which I read: *Thank you, Nero Wolfe. In appreciation of your courtesy I am leaving a small gift for you. Manuel Kimball.* I looked up at the sky. The red and blue airplane of the leading character in Wolfe's charade was still there, higher I thought, circling, with the other plane above. I put the photostats back into the envelope.

Corbett was in front of me. "Here, I'll take that."

"Oh no. Thanks, I can manage."

He sprang like a cat and I wasn't expecting it. It was neat. He got the envelope with one hand and the driver with the other. He started for the roadster. Two jumps put me in front of him, and he stopped. I wasn't monkeying. I said, "Look out, here it comes," and plugged him on the jaw with plenty behind it. He wobbled and dropped his loot, and I let him get his hands up, and then feinted with my left and plugged him again. That time he went down. His boy friend came running up, and Skinner from his side. I turned to meet the boy friend, but Anderson's voice, with more snap in it than I knew he had, came from the roadster:

"Curry! Lay off! Cut it!"

Curry stopped. I stepped back. Corbett got up, glaring wild. Anderson again: "Corbett, you too! Lay off!"

I said, "Not on my account, Mr. Anderson. If they want to play snatch and run I'll take them both on. They need to be taught a little respect for private property."

I stooped to pick up the driver and the envelope. It

was while I was bent over, reaching down, that I heard Skinner's yell.

"Good God! He's lost it!"

For an instant I imagined he meant I had lost the driver, and I thought he was crazy. Then as I straightened up and glanced at him and saw where he was looking, I jerked my eyes and my head up. It was Manuel Kimball's plane directly overhead, a thousand feet up. It was twisting and whirling as if it had lost its senses, and coming down. It seemed to be jerking and coiling back and forth, it didn't look as if it was falling straight, but I suppose it was. It was right above us—faster—I stared with my mouth open—

"Look out!" Skinner was shouting. "For God's sake!"

We ran for the hangar door. Anderson was out of the roadster and with us. We got inside the door and turned in time to see the crash. Black lightning split the air. A giant report, not thunderous like a big gun, an instantaneous ear-splitting snap. Pieces flew; splinters lay at our feet. It had landed at the edge of the concrete platform, not ten yards from Corbett's car. We jumped out and ran for the wreckage, Skinner calling, "Look out for an explosion!"

What I saw first wasn't pretty. The only way I knew it had been E. D. Kimball was that it was mixed up with a strap in the position of the back seat and Skinner had said that the old gentleman had gone up for a ride. Apparently it had landed in such a way that the front seat had got a different kind of a blow, for Manuel Kimball could have been recognized by anybody. His face was still together and even pretty well in shape. Skinner and I got him loose while the others worked at the old gentleman. We carried them away from there and inside the hangar and put them on some canvas on the floor.

Skinner said, "You'd better move your cars. An explosion might come yet." I said, "When I move my car I'll keep on moving it. Now's a good time. Mr. Anderson. You may remember that Nero Wolfe promised I would be diffident. That's me." I pulled the documents from my pocket and handed them to him. "Here's your proof. And there's your man on the floor, the one with the face."

I picked up Manuel Kimball's envelope and the golf driver from the floor where I had dropped them, and beat it. It took me maybe four seconds to get the roadster started and out of there and sooting down the road.

At the entrance, turning onto the highway, I stopped long enough to call to Durkin, "Call your playmates and come on home. The show's over."

I got to White Plains in twenty-two minutes. The roadster never did run nicer. I telephoned Wolfe at the same drugstore where two weeks before I had phoned him that Anderson had gone to the Adirondacks and I had only Derwin to bet with. He answered right off, and I gave him the story, brief but complete.

He said, "Good. I hope I haven't offended you, Archie. I thought it best that your mind should not be cluttered with the lesser details. Fritz is preparing to please your palate.—By the way, where is White Plains? Would it be convenient for you to stop on your way at Scarsdale? Gluekner has telephoned me that he has succeeded in hybridizing a Dendrobium Melpomene with a Findlayanum and offers me a seedling."

# Chapter 19

It certainly didn't look like much. It was a sick-looking pale blue, and was so small you could get it in an ordinary envelope without folding it. It looked even smaller than it was because the writing in the blank spaces was tall and scrawly; but it was writing with character in it. That, I guessed, was Sarah Barstow. The signature below, Ellen Barstow, was quite different—fine and precise. It was Saturday morning, and the check had come in the first mail; I was giving it a last fond look as I handed it in at the teller's window. I had phoned Wolfe upstairs that a Barstow envelope was there and he had told me to go ahead and open it and deposit the check.

At eleven o'clock Wolfe entered the office and went to his desk and rang for Fritz and beer. I had the Barstow case expense list all typed out for his inspection, and as soon as he had finished glancing through the scanty mail I handed it to him. He took a pencil and went over it slowly, checking each item. I waited. When I saw him hit the third item from the bottom and stop at it, I swallowed.

Wolfe raised his head. "Archie. We must get a new typewriter."

I just cleared my throat. He went on, "This one is too impulsive. Perhaps you didn't notice: it has inserted an extra cipher before the decimal point in the amount opposite Anna Fiore's name. I observe that you carelessly included the error in summing up."

I managed a grin. "Oh! Now I get you. I forgot to mention it before. Anna's nest-egg has hatched babies, it's a thousand dollars now. I'm taking it down to her this afternoon."

Wolfe sighed. The beer came, and he opened a bottle and gulped a glass. He put the expense list under the paperweight with the mail and leaned back in his chair. "Tomorrow I shall cut down to five quarts."

My grin felt better. I said, "You don't have to change the subject. I wouldn't make the mistake of calling you generous even if you said to double it; you'd still be getting a bargain. Do you know what Anna will do with it? Buy herself a husband. Look at all the good you're doing."

"Confound it. Don't give her anything. Tell her the money cannot be found."

"No, sir. I'll give her the money and let her dig her own grave. I'm not violent, the way you are, and I don't put myself up as a substitute for fate."

Wolfe opened his eyes. He had been drowsy for three days, and I thought it was about time something woke him up. He murmured, "Do you think you're saying something, Archie?"

"Yes, sir. I'm asking where you got the breezy notion of killing E. D. Kimball."

"Where his son got the notion, you mean?"

"No, you. Don't quibble. You killed him."

Wolfe shook his head. "Wrong, Archie. I quibble? E. D. Kimball was killed by the infant son whom he deserted sitting on the floor among his toys in a pool of his mother's blood.—If you please. Properly speaking, E. D. Kimball was not killed last Wednesday morning, but on Sunday June fourth. Through one of the unfortunate accidents by which blind chance interferes with the natural processes of life and death, Barstow died instead. It is true that I helped to remedy that error. I had Durkin deliver to Manuel Kimball copies of our evidence against him, and I telephoned Manuel Kimball that he was surrounded, on the earth and above the earth. I left it to nature to proceed, having ascertained that E. D. Kimball was at home and would not leave that morning."

I said, "You told me once that I couldn't conceal truth by building a glass house around it. What are you trying it for? You killed him."

Wolfe's cheeks folded. He poured another glass of beer and leaned back again and watched the foam. When nothing was left of it but a thin white rim he looked at me and sighed.

"The trouble is," he murmured, "that as usual you are so engrossed in the fact that you are oblivious to its environment. You stick to it, Archie, like a leech on an udder. Consider the situation that faced me. Manuel had tried to kill his father. By an accident beyond his control the innocent Barstow had been killed instead. Evidence that would convict Manuel of murder was in my possession. How should I use it? Had I been able to afford the luxury of a philosophic attitude, I should of course not have used it at all, but that attitude was beyond my means, it was an affair of business. Put myself up as a substitute for fate? Certainly; we do it constantly; we could avoid it only by complete inaction. I was forced to act. If I had permitted you to get Manuel Kimball, without warn-

ing, and deliver him alive to the vengeance of the
people of the State of New York, he would have gone
to the chair of judicial murder a bitter and defeated
man, his heart empty of one deep satisfaction life had
offered to it; and his father equally bitter and no less
defeated, would have tottered through some few last
years with nothing left to trade. If I had brought that
about I would have been responsible for it, to myself,
and the prospect was not pleasing. Still I had to act. I
did so, and incurred a responsibility which is vastly
less displeasing. You would encompass the entire
complex phenomenon by stating bluntly that I killed
E. D. Kimball. Well, Archie. I will take the responsibility for my own actions; I will not also assume the
burden of your simplicity. Somehow you must bear it."

I grinned. "Maybe. I don't mean maybe I can bear
it, I mean maybe all you've just said. Also, maybe I'm
simple. I'm so simple that a simple thought occurred
to me as I was walking back from the bank this
morning."

"Indeed." Wolfe gulped his glass of beer.

"Yes, sir. It occurred to me that if Manuel Kimball
had been arrested and brought to trial you would have
had to put on your hat and gloves, leave the house,
walk to an automobile, ride clear to White Plains, and
sit around a courtroom waiting for your turn to testify.
Whereas now, natural processes being what they are,
and you having such a good feeling for phenomena,
you can just sit and hold your responsibilities on your
lap."

"Indeed," Wolfe murmured.

Not for publication
Confidential Memo
From Rex Stout
September 15 1949

## DESCRIPTION OF NERO WOLFE

Height 5 ft. 11 in.  Weight 272 lbs.  Age 56.
Mass of dark brown hair, very little greying, is not
parted but sweeps off to the right because he brushes
with his right hand.  Dark brown eyes are average in
size, but look smaller because they are mostly half
closed.  They always are aimed straight at the person
he is talking to.  Forehead is high.  Head and face
are big but do not seem so in proportion to the whole.
Ears rather small.  Nose long and narrow, slightly
aquiline.  Mouth mobile and extremely variable; lips
when pursed are full and thick, but in tense moments
they are thin and their line is long.  Cheeks full but
not pudgy; the high point of the cheekbone can be seen
from straight front.  Complexion varies from some
floridity after meals to an ivory pallor late at night
when he has spent six hard hours working on someone.
He breathes smoothly and without sound except when he
is eating; then he takes in and lets out great gusts of
air.  His massive shoulders never slump; when he stands
up at all he stands straight.  He shaves every day.  He
has a small brown mole just above his right jawbone,
halfway between the chin and the ear.

## DESCRIPTION OF ARCHIE GOODWIN

Height 6 feet.  Weight 180 lbs.  Age 32.  Hair is
light rather than dark, but just barely decided not to
be red; he gets it cut every two weeks, rather short,
and brushes it straight back, but it keeps standing up.
He shaves four times a week and grasps at every excuse
to make it only three times.  His features are all regular, well-modeled and well-proportioned, except the
nose.  He escapes the curse of being the movie actor
type only through the nose.  It is not a true pug and
is by no means a deformity, but it is a little short
and the ridge is broad, and the tip has continued on
its own, beyond the cartilage, giving the impression
of startling and quite independent initiative.  The eyes
are grey, and are inquisitive and quick to move.  He is
muscular both in appearance and in movement, and upright
in posture, but his shoulders stoop a little in unconscious
reaction to Wolfe's repeated criticism that he is too
self-assertive.

## DESCRIPTION OF WOLFE'S OFFICE

The old brownstone on West 35th Street is a double-
width house.  Entering at the front door, which is seven
steps up from the sidewalk, you are facing the length of

a wide carpeted hall. At the right is an enormous coat
rack, eight feet wide, then the stairs, and beyond the
stairs the door to the dining room. There were originally two rooms on that side of the hall, but Wolfe had
the partition removed and turned it into a dining room
forty feet long, with a table large enough for six (but
extensible) square in the middle. It (and all other
rooms) are carpeted; Wolfe hates bare floors. At the
far end of the big hall is the kitchen. At the left of the
big hall are two doors; the first one is to what Archie calls
the front room, and the second is to the office. The front
room is used chiefly as an anteroom; Nero and Archie do
no living there. It is rather small, and the furniture
is a random mixture without any special character.

The office is large and nearly square. In the far
corner to the left (as you enter from the hall) a small
rectangle has been walled off to make a place for a
john and a washbowl — to save steps for Wolfe. The door
leading to it faces you, and around the corner, along its
other wall, is a wide and well-cushioned couch.

## SKETCH OF OFFICE

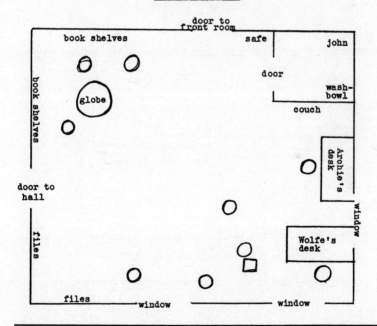

In furnishings the room has no apparent unity but it has plenty of character. Wolfe permits nothing to be in it that he doesn't enjoy looking at, and that has been the only criterion for admission. The globe is three feet in diameter. Wolfe's chair was made by Meyer of cardato. His desk is of cherry, which of course clashes with the cardato, but Wolfe likes it. The couch is upholstered in bright yellow material which has to go to the cleaners every three months. The carpet was woven in Montenegro in the early nineteenth century and has been extensively patched. The only wall decorations are three pictures: a Manet, a copy of a Corregio, and a genuine Leonardo sketch. The chairs are all shapes, colors, materials, and sizes. The total effect makes you blink with bewilderment at the first visit, but if you had Archie's job and lived there you would probably learn to like it.

# The League
## of Frightened Men

# Introduction

The *League of Frightened Men*, published both by the *Saturday Evening Post* (in serialization) and by Farrar & Rinehart in 1935, was Rex Stout's second Nero Wolfe novel, appearing the year after *Fer-de-Lance*. It ranks as a personal favorite, for several reasons.

First, the story's pivotal figure, the quirky, brilliant, and depraved Paul Chapin, supplies Wolfe with his most complex adversary, a far more intriguing character, for instance, than the megalomaniacal underworld kingpin Arnold Zeck, who makes his appearance several books deeper into the series.

Chapin, author of "obscene" novels probing the dark side of the human spirit, was badly crippled as the result of a college hazing incident at Harvard. Chagrined classmates formed a "League of Atonement," which paid his hospital bills and through the years tried in other, less tangible ways to make amends. Although accepting the group's money and sympathy, Chapin remained bitter, sardonically reacting to their efforts.

Now, at a class reunion, one member of the league falls to his death from a seaside cliff, and the others

receive copies of a poem apparently authored by
Chapin in which he claims credit for the act. Then
another of the group dies violently, followed by an-
other poem suggesting that more deaths will occur.
And when a third member of the league disappears,
Nero Wolfe is hired by remaining members to "stop
Chapin."

Although famed clinician Karl Menninger praised
the Wolfe stories because the detective "never dives
into the realm of psychiatry" or "pretends to believe
that murderers are mostly sick," John McAleer wrote
in his biography of Stout that in the early Wolfe
stories, the author "still was close to his own interlude
as a psychological novelist." McAleer went on to
suggest that "possibly such characterizations [as Paul
Chapin] were intended to counterpoint Rex's unan-
nounced probing of his own psyche." Whatever Stout's
motivation, Chapin remains the most interesting psychological study in the series, and one whom Wolfe
comes to know primarily through reading his novels.

In addition to the compelling characterization of
Chapin, the book is a treasure trove for lovers of the
corpus. In no other volume, for instance, do we find
such a rich variety of Wolfean aphorisms:

—"It takes a fillip on the flank for my mare to
   dance."
—"To assert dignity is to lose it."
—"All genius is distorted. Including my own."
—"To be broke is not a disgrace, it is only a
   catastrophe."
—"If you eat the apple before it's ripe, your only
   reward is a bellyache."
—"I love to make a mistake, it is the only assur-

ance that I cannot reasonably be expected to assume the burden of omniscience."

—"I have all the simplicities, including that of brusqueness."

The Archie Goodwin in this book, as in other early Stout works, is markedly more rough edged and unsophisticated than the smoother version who evolved in the postwar years. His grammar is deficient (". . . the obscenity don't matter" and "Where's the other club members?"), but that is as integral to his street-smart persona as his colorful phrasing. For example, he complains of inactivity to Wolfe: "If you keep a keg of dynamite around the house you've got to expect some noise sooner or later. That's what I am, a keg of dynamite." Or his threat to a would-be tough guy: "Don't try to scare me with your bad manners. I might decide to remove your right ear and put it where the left one is, and hang the left one on your belt for a spare."

Inspector Cramer shows an uncharacteristically self-effacing side in *League*, when he tells Archie that "I arrested a man once and he turned out to be guilty, that's why I was made an inspector." And in what other Wolfe book does the cigar-chomping Cramer actually *light* one of his stogies? And smoke a pipe, too? You can look it up.

Cramer's match-lighting moments are only two of several singular occurrences in *League*. A sampling of others:

—The "client" is actually a committee, the members of which Wolfe assesses varying rates, depending on their financial condition.

—Wolfe is "kidnapped" from the brownstone in a car driven by a *woman*.
—Archie gets drugged and Wolfe is forced to rescue him.
—Wolfe claims he once was married.
—Name brands, which Rex Stout normally avoided in his writing, are extolled by Archie, specifically Underwood typewriters and the Cadillac in which Cramer is chauffeured.

Back to the psychopathic genius Paul Chapin, who makes Archie nervous ("for once Wolfe might be underrating a guy") and Wolfe cautious ("He is possessed of a demon, but he is also, within certain limits, an extraordinarily astute man"). Chapin refers to one of Wolfe's ploys as "vulgar and obvious cunning," and later he tells the detective that he, Wolfe, will be a character in an upcoming Chapin novel. "You will die, sir, in the most abhorrent manner conceivable to an appalling infantile imagination. I promise you."

We are never to learn whether Paul Chapin indeed dispatched the detective in print, but the suggestion was enough for Archie to "permit myself a grin at the thought of the awful fate in store for Nero Wolfe."

**—Robert Goldsborough**

# Chapter 1

Wolfe and I sat in the office Friday afternoon. As it turned out, the name of Paul Chapin, and his slick and thrifty notions about getting vengeance at wholesale without paying for it, would have come to our notice pretty soon in any event; but that Friday afternoon the combination of an early November rain and a lack of profitable business that had lasted so long it was beginning to be painful, brought us an opening scene—a prologue, not a part of the main action—of the show that was about ready to begin.

Wolfe was drinking beer and looking at pictures of snowflakes in a book someone had sent him from Czechoslovakia. I was reading the morning paper, off and on. I had read it at breakfast, and glanced through it again for half an hour after checking accounts with Hortsmann at eleven o'clock, and here I was with it once more in the middle of the rainy afternoon, thinking halfheartedly to find an item or two that would tickle the brain which seemed about ready to dry up on me. I do read books, but I never yet got any real satisfaction out of one; I always have a feeling there's nothing alive about it, it's all dead and gone, what's the use, you might as well try to enjoy yourself on a picnic in a graveyard. Wolfe asked me once why the devil I ever pretended to read a book, and I told him for cultural reasons, and he said I might as well forgo the pains, that culture was like money, it comes easiest to those who need it least. Anyway, since it was a morning paper and this was the middle of the afternoon, and I had already gone through it twice, it wasn't much better than a book and I was only hanging onto it as an excuse to keep my eyes open.

Wolfe seemed absorbed in the pictures. Looking at him, I said to myself, "He's in a battle with the elements. He's fighting his way through a raging blizzard, just sitting there comfortably looking at pictures of snowflakes. That's the advantage of being an artist, of having imagination." I said aloud, "You mustn't go to sleep, sir, it's fatal. You freeze to death."

Wolfe turned a page, paying no attention to me. I said, "The shipment from Caracas, from Richardt, was twelve bulbs short. I never knew him to make good a shortage."

Still no result. I said, "Fritz tells me that the turkey they sent is too old to broil and will be tough unless it is roasted two hours, which according to you will attenuate the flavor. So the turkey at forty-one cents a pound will be a mess."

Wolfe turned another page. I stared at him a while and then said, "Did you see the piece in the paper about the woman who has a pet monkey which sleeps at the head of her bed and wraps its tail around her wrist? And keeps it there all night? Did you see the one about the man who found a necklace on the street and returned it to its owner and she claimed he stole two pearls from it and had him arrested? Did you see the one about the man on the witness-stand in a case about an obscene book, and the lawyer asked him what was his purpose in writing the book, and he said because he had committed a murder and all murderers had to talk about their crimes and that was his way of talking about it? Not that I get the idea, about the author's purpose. If a book's dirty it's dirty, and what's the difference how it got that way? The lawyer says if the author's purpose was a worthy literary purpose the obscenity don't matter. You might as well say that if my purpose is to throw a rock at a tin can it don't matter if I hit you in the eye with it. You might as well say that if my purpose is to buy my poor old grandmother a silk dress it don't matter if I grabbed the jack from a Salvation Army kettle. You might as well say—"

I stopped. I had him. He did not lift his eyes from the page, his head did not move, there was no stirring of his massive frame in the specially constructed enormous chair behind his desk; but I saw his right forefinger wiggle faintly—his minatory wand, as he once called it—and I knew I had him. He said:

"Archie. Shut up."

I grinned. "Not a chance, sir. Great God, am I just going to sit here until I die? Shall I phone Pinkertons and ask if they want a hotel room watched or something? If you keep a keg of dynamite around the house you've got to expect some noise sooner or later. That's what I am, a keg of dynamite. Shall I go to a movie?"

Wolfe's huge head tipped forward a sixteenth of an inch, for him an emphatic nod. "By all means: At once."

I got up from my chair, tossed the newspaper halfway across the room to my desk, turned around, and sat down again. "What was wrong with my analogies?" I demanded.

Wolfe turned another page. "Let us say," he murmured patiently, "that as an analogist you are supreme. Let us say that."

"All right. Say we do. I'm not trying to pick a quarrel, sir. Hell no. I'm just breaking under the strain of trying to figure out a third way of crossing my legs. I've been at it over a week now." It flashed into my mind that Wolfe could never be annoyed by that problem, since his legs were so fat that there was no possibility of them ever getting crossed by any tactics whatever, but I decided not to mention that. I swerved. "I stick to it, if a book's dirty it's dirty, no matter if the author had a string of purposes as long as a rainy day. That guy on the witness-stand yesterday was a nut. Wasn't he? You tell me. Or else he wanted some big headlines no matter what it cost him. It cost him fifty berries for contempt of court. At that it was cheap advertising for his book; for half a century he could buy about four inches on the literary page of the *Times*, and that's not even a chirp. But I guess the guy was a nut. He said he had done a murder, and all murderers have to confess, so he wrote the book, changing the characters and circumstances, as a means of confessing without putting himself in jeopardy. The judge was witty and sarcastic. He said that even if the guy was an inventor of stories and was in a court, he needn't try for the job of court jester. I'll bet the lawyers had a good hearty laugh at that one. Huh? But the author said it was no joke, that was why he wrote the book and any obscenity in it was only incidental, he really had croaked a guy. So the judge soaked him fifty bucks for contempt of court and chased him off the stand. I guess he's a nut? You tell me."

Wolfe's great chest went up and out in a sigh; he

put a marker in the book and closed it and laid it on the desk, and leaned himself back, gently ponderous, in his chair.

He blinked twice. "Well?"

I went across to my desk and got the paper and opened it out to the page. "Nothing maybe. I guess he's a nut. His name is Paul Chapin and he's written several books. The title of this one is *Devil Take the Hindmost*. He graduated from Harvard in 1912. He's a lop; it mentions here about his getting up to the stand with his crippled leg but it doesn't say which one."

Wolfe compressed his lips. "Is it possible," he demanded, "that lop is an abbreviation of lopsided, and that you use it as a metaphor for cripple?"

"I wouldn't know about the metaphor, but lop means cripple in my circle."

Wolfe sighed again, and set about the process of rising from his chair. "Thank God," he said, "the hour saves me from further analogies and colloquialisms." The clock on the wall said one minute till four—time for him to go up to the plant-rooms. He made it to his feet, pulled the points of his vest down but failed as usual to cover with it the fold of bright yellow shirt that had puffed out, and moved across to the door.

At the threshold he paused. "Archie."

"Yes, sir."

"Phone Murger's to send over at once a copy of *Devil Take the Hindmost*, by Paul Chapin."

"Maybe they won't. It's suppressed pending the court decision."

"Nonsense. Speak to Murger or Ballard. What good is an obscenity trial except to popularize literature?"

He went on towards the elevator, and I sat down at my desk and reached for the telephone.

# Chapter 2

After breakfast the next morning, Saturday, I fooled with the plant records a while and then went to the kitchen to annoy Fritz.

Wolfe, of course, wouldn't be down until eleven o'clock. The roof of the old brownstone house on West Thirty-fifth Street where he had lived for twenty years, and me with him for the last seven of them, was glassed in and partitioned into rooms where varying conditions of temperature and humidity were maintained—by the vigilance of Theodore Horstmann—for the ten thousand orchids that lined the benches and shelves. Wolfe had once remarked to me that the orchids were his concubines; insipid, expensive, parasitic and temperamental. He brought them, in their diverse forms and colors, to the limits of their perfection, and then gave them away; he had never sold one. His patience and ingenuity, supported by Horstmann's fidelity, had produced remarkable results and gained for the roof a reputation in quite different circles from those whose interest centered in the downstairs office. In all weathers and under any circumstances whatever, his four hours a day on the roof with Horstmann—from nine to eleven in the morning and from four to six in the afternoon—were inviolable.

This Saturday morning I finally had to admit that Fritz's good humor was too much for me. By eleven o'clock I was back in the office trying to pretend there might be something to do if I looked for it, but I'm not much good at pretending. I was thinking, ladies and gentlemen, my friends and customers, I won't hold out for a real case with worry and action and profit in it, just give us any old kind of a break. I'll even tail a chorus-girl for you, or hide in the bathroom for the guy that's stealing the toothpaste, anything this side of industrial espionage. Anything . . .

Wolfe came in and said good morning. The mail didn't take long. He signed a couple of checks I had made out for bills he had gone over the day before, and asked me with a sigh what the bank balance was, and gave me a few short letters. I tapped them off and went out with them to the mailbox. When I got back Wolfe was starting on a second bottle of beer, leaning back in his chair, and I thought I saw a look in his half-closed eyes. At least, I thought, he's not back on the pretty snowflakes again. I sat at my desk and let the typewriter down.

Wolfe said, "Archie. One would know everything in the world there is to know, if one waited long enough. The one fault in the passivity of Buddha as a technique for the acquisition of knowledge and wisdom is the miserably brief span of human life. He sat through the first stanza of the first canto of the *preamble*, and then left for an appointment with . . . let us say, with a certain chemist."

"Yes, sir. You mean, we just go on sitting here and we learn a lot."

"Not a lot. But more, a little more each century."

"You maybe. Not me. If I sit here about two more days I'll be so damn goofy I won't know anything."

Wolfe's eyes flickered faintly. "I would not care to seem mystic, but might not that, in your case, mean an increase?"

"Sure." I grunted. "If you had not once instructed me never again to tell you to go to hell, I would tell you to go to hell."

"Good." Wolfe gulped beer and wiped his lips. "You are offended. So, probably, awake. My opening remark was in the nature of a comment on a recent fact. You will remember that last month you were away for ten days on a mission that proved to be highly unremunerative, and that during your absence two young men were here to perform your duties."

I nodded. I grinned. One of the men had been from the Metropolitan Agency as Wolfe's bodyguard, and the other had been a stenographer from Miller's. "Sure. Two could handle it on a sprint."

"Just so. On one of those days a man came here and asked me to intercept his destiny. He didn't put it that way, but that was the substance of it. It proved not feasible to accept his commission . . . "

I had opened a drawer of my desk and taken out a loose-leaf binder, and I flipped through the sheets in it to the page I wanted. "Yes, sir. I've got it. I've read it twice. It's a bit spotty, the stenographer from Miller's wasn't so hot. He couldn't spell—"

"The name was Hibbard."

I nodded, glancing over the typewritten pages. "Andrew Hibbard. Instructor in psychology at Columbia. It was on October twentieth, a Saturday, that's two weeks ago today."

"Suppose you read it."

"*Viva voce?*"

"Archie." Wolfe looked at me. "Where did you pick

that up, where did you learn to pronounce it, and what do you think it means?"

"Do you want me to read this stuff out loud, sir?"

"It doesn't mean out loud. Confound you." Wolfe emptied his glass, leaned back in his chair, got his fingers to meet in front of his belly and laced them. "Proceed."

"Okay. First there's a description of Mr. Hibbard. *Small gentleman, around fifty, pointed nose, dark eyes—*"

"Enough. For that I can plunder my memory."

"Yes, sir. Mr. Hibbard seems to have started out by saying, *How do you do, sir, my name is—*"

"Pass the amenities."

I glanced down the page. "How will this do? Mr. Hibbard said, *I was advised to come to you by a friend whose name need not be mentioned, but the motivating force was plain funk. I was driven here by fear.*"

Wolfe nodded. I read from the typewritten sheets:

Mr. Wolfe: *Yes. Tell me about it.*

Mr. Hibbard: *My card has told you, I am in the psychology department at Columbia. Since you are an expert, you probably observe on my face and in my bearing the stigmata of fright bordering on panic.*

Mr. Wolfe: *I observe that you are upset. I have no means of knowing whether it is chronic or acute.*

Mr. Hibbard: *It is chronic. At least it is becoming so. That is why I have resorted to . . . to you. I am under an intolerable strain. My life is in danger . . . no, not that, worse than that, my life has been forfeited. I admit it.*

Mr. Wolfe: *Of course. Mine too, sir. All of us.*

Mr. Hibbard: *Rubbish. Excuse me. I am not discussing original sin. Mr. Wolfe, I am going to be killed. A man is going to kill me.*

Mr. Wolfe: *Indeed. When? How?*

Wolfe put in, "Archie. You may delete the Misters."

"Okay. This Miller boy was brought up right, he didn't miss one. Somebody told him, always regard your employer with respect forty-four hours a week, more or less, as the case may be. Well. Next we have:

Hibbard: *That I can't tell you, since I don't know. There are things about this I do know, also, which I must keep to myself. I can tell you . . . well . . . many years ago I inflicted an injury, a lasting injury, on a man. I was not alone, there were others in it, but chance made me chiefly responsible. At least I have so regarded it. It was a boyish prank . . . with a tragic outcome. I have never forgiven myself. Neither have the others who were concerned in it, at least most of them haven't. Not that I have ever been morbid about it—it was twenty-five years ago—I am a psychologist and therefore too involved in the morbidities of others to have room for any of my own. Well, we injured that boy. We ruined him. In effect. Certainly we felt the responsibility, and all through these twenty-five years some of us have had the idea of making up for it. We have acted on the idea—sometimes. You know how it is; we are busy men, most of us. But we have never denied the burden, and now and then some of us have tried to carry it. That was difficult, for pawn—that is, as the boy advanced into manhood he became increasingly peculiar. I learned that in the lower schools he had given evidence of talent, and certainly in college— that is to say, of my own knowledge, after the injury, he possessed brilliance. Later the brilliance perhaps remained, but became distorted. At a certain point—*

Wolfe interrupted me. "A moment. Go back a few

sentences. Beginning *that was difficult, for pawn—did you saw pawn?"*

I found it. "That's it. *Pawn.* I don't get it."

"Neither did the stenographer. Proceed."

*At a certain point, some five years ago, I decided definitely he was psychopathic.*

Wolfe: *You continued to know him then?*

Hibbard: *Oh yes. Many of us did. Some of us saw him frequently; one or two associated with him closely. Around that time his latent brilliance seemed to find itself in maturity. He . . . well . . . he did things which aroused admiration and interest. Convinced as I was that he was psychopathic, I nevertheless felt less concern for him than I had for a long time, for he appeared to be genuinely involved in satisfactory—at least compensatory—achievement. The awakening came in a startling manner. There was a reunion—a gathering—of a group of us, and one of us was killed—died—obviously, we unanimously thought, by an accident. But he—that is, the man we had injured—was there; and a few days later each of us received through the mail a communication from him saying that he had killed one of us and that the rest would follow; that he had embarked on a ship of vengeance.*

Wolfe: *Indeed. Psychopathic must have begun to seem almost an euphemism.*

Hibbard: *Yes. But there was nothing we could do.*

Wolfe: *Since you were equipped with evidence, it might not have proven hazardous to inform the police.*

Hibbard: *We had no evidence.*

Wolfe: *The communication?*

Hibbard: *They were typewritten, unsigned, and were expressed in ambiguous terms which rendered them worthless for practical purposes such as evi-*

*dence. He had even disguised his style, very cleverly;
it was not his style at all. But it was plain enough to
us. Each of us got one; not only those who had been
present at the gathering, but all of us, all members of
the league. Of* course—

Wolfe: *The league?*

Hibbard: *That was a slip. It doesn't matter. Many
years ago, when a few of us were together discussing
this, one—maudlin, of course—suggested that we
should call ourselves the League of Atonement. The
phrase hung on, in a way. Latterly it was never heard
except in jest. Now I fancy the jokes are ended. I was
going to say, of course all of us do not live in New
York, only about half. One got his warning, just the
same, in San Francisco. In New York a few of us got
together and discussed it. We made a sort of an
investigation, and we saw—him, and had a talk with
him. He denied sending the warnings. He seemed
amused, in his dark soul, and unconcerned.*

Wolfe: *Dark soul is an odd phrase for a psychologist?*

Hibbard: *I read poetry week-ends.*

Wolfe: *Just so. And?*

Hibbard: *Nothing happened for some time. Three
months. Then another of us was killed. Found dead.
The police said suicide, and it seemed that all indications pointed in that direction. But two days later a
second warning was mailed to each of us, with the
same purport and obviously from the same source. It
was worded with great cleverness, with brilliance.*

Wolfe: *This time, naturally, you went to the police.*

Hibbard: *Why naturally? We were still without
evidence.*

Wolfe: *Only that you would. One or some of you
would.*

Hibbard: *They did. I was against it, but they did go—*

Wolfe: *Why were you against it?*

Hibbard: *I felt it was useless. Also . . . well . . . I could not bring myself to join in a demand for retribution, his life perhaps, from the man we had injured . . . you understand . . .*

Wolfe: *Quite. First, the police could find no proof. Second, they might.*

Hibbard: *Very well. I was not engaged in an essay on logic. A man may debar nonsense from his library of reason, but not from the arena of his impulses.*

Wolfe: *Good. Neat. And the police?*

Hibbard: *They got nowhere. He made total asses of them. He described to me their questioning and his replies—*

Wolfe: *You still saw him?*

Hibbard: *Of course. We were friends. Oh yes. The police went into it, questioned him, questioned all of us, investigated all they could, and came out empty-handed. Some of them, some of the group, got private detectives. That was two weeks, twelve days ago. The detectives are having the same success as the police. I'm sure of it.*

Wolfe: *Indeed. What agency?*

Hibbard: *That is irrelevant. The point is that something happened. I could speak of apprehensions and precautions and so forth, I know plenty of words of that nature, I could even frame the situation in technical psychological terms, but the plain fact is that I'm too scared to go on. I want you to save me from death. I want to hire you to protect my life.*

Wolfe: *Yes. What happened?*

Hibbard: *Nothing. Nothing of any significance except to me. He came to me and said something, that's all. It would be of no advantage to repeat it. My shameful admission is that I am at length completely frightened. I'm afraid to go to bed and I'm afraid to get up. I'm afraid to eat. I want whatever measure of security you can sell me. I am accustomed to the arrangement of words, and the necessity of talking intelligently to you has enforced a semblance of order and urbanity in a section of my brain, but around and beneath that order there is a veritable panic. After all my exploration, scientific and pseudo-scientific, of that extraordinary phenomenon, the human psyche, devil-possessed and heaven-soaring, I am all reduced to this single simple primitive concern: I am terribly afraid of being killed. The friend who suggested my coming here said that you possess a remarkable combination of talents and that you have only one weakness. She did not call it cupidity; I forget her phrasing. I am not a millionaire, but I have ample private means besides my salary, and I am in no state of mind for haggling.*

Wolfe: *I always need money. That is of course my affair. I will undertake to disembark this gentleman from his ship of vengeance, in advance of any injury to you, for the sum of ten thousand dollars.*

Hibbard: *Disembark him? You can't. You don't know him.*

Wolfe: *Nor does he know me. A meeting can be arranged.*

Hibbard: *I didn't mean—hah. It would take more than a meeting. It would take more, I think, than all your talents. But that is beside the point. I have failed to make myself clear. I would not pay ten thousand dollars, or any other sum, for you to bring this man to—justice? Ha! Call it justice. A word that reeks with maggots. Anyhow, I would not be a party to that, even in the face of death. I have not told you his name. I shall not. Already perhaps I have disclosed too much. I wish your services as a safeguard for myself, not as an agency for his destruction.*

Wolfe: *If the one demands the other?*

Hibbard: *I hope not. I pray not . . . could I pray? No. Prayer has been washed from my strain of blood. Certainly I would not expect you to give me a warrant of security. But your experience and ingenuity—I am sure they would be worth whatever you might ask—*

Wolfe: *Nonsense. My ingenuity would be worth less than nothing, Mr. Hibbard. Do I understand that you wish to engage me to protect your life against the unfriendly designs of this man without taking any steps whatever to expose and restrain him?*

Hibbard: *Yes, sir. Precisely. And I have been told that once your talents are committed to an enterprise, any attempt to circumvent you will be futile.*

Wolfe: *I have no talents. I have genius or nothing. In this case, nothing. No, Mr. Hibbard; and I do need money. What you need, should you persist in your quixotism, is first, if you have dependents, generous life insurance; and second, a patient acceptance of the fact that your death is only a matter of time. That of course is true of all of us; we all share that disease with you, only yours seems to have reached a rather acute stage. My advice would be, waste neither time nor money on efforts at precaution. If he has decided to kill you, and if he possesses ordinary intelligence— let alone the brilliance you grant him—you will die. There are so many methods available for killing a fellow-being! Many more than there are for most of our usual activities, like pruning a tree or threshing wheat or making a bed or swimming. I have been often impressed, in my experience, by the ease and lack of bother with which the average murder is executed. Consider: with the quarry within reach, the purpose fixed, and the weapon in hand, it will often require up to eight or ten minutes to kill a fly, whereas the average murder, I would guess, consumes ten or fifteen seconds at the outside. In cases of slow poison and similar ingenuities death of course is lingering, but the act of murder itself is commonly quite brief. Consider again: there are certainly not more than two or three methods of killing a pig, but there are hundreds of ways to kill a man. If your friend is half as brilliant as you think him, and doesn't get in a rut as the ordinary criminal does, he may be expected to evolve a varied and interesting repertory before your league is half disposed of. He may even invent something new. One more point: it seems to me there is a fair chance for you. You may not, after all, be the next, or even the next or the next; and it is quite possible that somewhere along the line he may miscalculate or run into bad luck; or one of your league members, less quixotic than you, may engage my services. That would save you.*

I took my eyes from the sheet to look at Wolfe. "Pretty good, sir. Pretty nice. I'm surprised it didn't get him, he must have been tough. Maybe you didn't go far enough. You only mentioned poison really, you could have brought in strangling and bleeding and crushed skulls and convulsions—"

"Proceed."

Hibbard: *I will pay you five hundred dollars a week.*

Wolfe: *I am sorry. To now my casuistry has managed a satisfactory persuasion that the money I have put in my bank has been earned. I dare not put this strain upon it.*

Hibbard: *But . . . you wouldn't refuse. You can't refuse a thing like this. My God. You are my only hope. I didn't realize it, but you are.*

Wolfe: *I do refuse. I can undertake to render this man harmless, to remove the threat—*

Hibbard: *No. No!*

Wolfe: *Very well. One little suggestion: if you take out substantial life insurance, which would be innocent of fraud from the legal standpoint, you should if possible manage so that when the event comes it cannot plausibly be given the appearance of suicide; and since you will not be aware of the event much beforehand you will have to keep your wit sharpened. That is merely a practical suggestion, that the insurance may not be voided, to the loss of your beneficiary.*

Hibbard: *But . . . Mr. Wolfe . . . look here . . . you can't do this. I came here . . . I tell you it isn't reasonable—*

Wolfe stopped me. "That will do, Archie."

I looked up. "There's only a little more."

"I know. I find it painful. I refused that five hundred dollars—thousands perhaps—once; I maintained my position; your reading it causes me useless discomfort. Do not finish it. There is nothing further except Mr. Hibbard's confused protestations and my admirable steadfastness."

"Yes, sir. I've read it." I glanced over the remaining lines. "I'm surprised you let him go. After all—"

Wolfe reached to the desk to ring for Fritz, shifted a little in his chair, and settled back again. "To tell you the truth, Archie, I entertained a notion."

"Yeah. I thought so."

"But nothing came of it. As you know, it takes a

fillip on the flank for my mare to dance, and the fillip was not forthcoming. You were away at the time, and since your return the incident has not been discussed. It is odd that you should have innocently been the cause, by mere chance, of its revival."

"I don't get you."

Fritz came with beer. Wolfe took the opener from the drawer, poured a glass, gulped, and leaned back again. He resumed, "By annoying me about the man on the witness-stand. I resigned myself to your tantrum because it was nearly four o'clock. As you know, the book came. I read it last night."

"Why did you read it?"

"Don't badger me. I read it because it was a book. I had finished *The Native's Return*, by Louis Adamic, and *Outline of Human Nature*, by Alfred Rossiter, and I read books."

"Yeah. And?"

"This will amuse you. Paul Chapin, the man on the witness-stand, the author of *Devil Take the Hindmost*, is the villain of Andrew Hibbard's tale. He is the psychopathic avenger of an old and tragic injury."

"The hell he is." I gave Wolfe a look; I had known him to invent for practice. "Why is he?"

Wolfe's eyelids went up a shade. "Do you expect me to explain the universe?"

"No, sir. Retake. How do you know he is?"

"By no flight. Pedestrian mental processes. Must you have them?"

"I'd greatly appreciate it."

"I suppose so. A few details will do. Mr. Hibbard employed the unusual phrase, *embark on a ship of vengeance*, and that phrase occurs twice in *Devil Take the Hindmost*. Mr. Hibbard did not say, as the stenographer has it, *that was difficult, for pawn*, which is of course meaningless; he said, *that was difficult, for Paul,* and caught himself up pronouncing the name, which he did not intend to disclose. Mr. Hibbard said things indicating that the man was a writer, for instance speaking of his disguising his style in the warnings. Mr. Hibbard said that five years ago the man began to be involved in compensatory achievement. I telephoned two or three people this morning. In 1929 Paul Chapin's first successful book was published, and in 1930 his second. Also, Chapin is a cripple through an injury which he suffered twenty-five years ago in a hazing accident at Harvard. If more is needed . . . "

"No. Thank you very much. I see. All right. Now that you know who the guy is, everything is cozy. Why is it? Who are you going to send a bill to?"

Two of the folds in Wolfe's cheeks opened out a little, so I knew he thought he was smiling. I said, "But you may just be pleased because you know it's corn fritters with anchovy sauce for lunch and it's only ten minutes to the bell."

"No, Archie." The folds were gently closing. "I mentioned that I entertained a notion. It may or may not be fertile. As usual, you have furnished the fillip. Luckily our stake will be negligible. There are several possible channels of approach, but I believe . . . yes. Get Mr. Andrew Hibbard on the phone. At Columbia, or at his home."

"Yes, sir. Will you speak?"

"Yes. Keep your wire and take it down as usual."

I got the number from the book and called it. First the university. I didn't get Hibbard. I monkeyed around with two or three extensions and four or five people, and it finally leaked out that he wasn't any-

where around, but no one seemed to know where he
was. I tried his home, an Academy number, up in the
same neighborhood. There a dumb female nearly riled
me. She insisted on knowing who I was and she
sounded doubtful about everything. She finally
seemed to decide Mr. Hibbard probably wasn't home.
Through the last of it Wolfe was listening in on his
wire.

I turned to him. "I can try again and maybe with
luck get a human being."

He shook his head. "After lunch. It is two minutes
to one."

I got up and stretched, thinking I would be able to
do a lot of destructive criticism on a corn fritter
myself, especially with Fritz's sauce. It was at that
moment that Wolfe's notion decided to come to him
instead of waiting longer for him to go to it. It was a
coincidence, too, though that was of no importance;
she must have been trying to get our number while I
was talking.

The telephone rang. I sat down again and got it. It
was a woman's voice, and she asked to speak to Nero
Wolfe. I asked if I might have her name, and when she
said "Evelyn Hibbard" I told her to hold the line and
put my hand over the transmitter.

I grinned at Wolfe. "It's a Hibbard."

His brows lifted.

"A female Hibbard named Evelyn. Voice young,
maybe a daughter. Take it."

He took his receiver off and I put mine back to my
ear and got my pad and pencil ready. As Wolfe asked
her what she wanted I was deciding again that he was
the only man I had ever met who used absolutely the
same tone to a woman as to a man. He had plenty of
changes in his voice, but they weren't based on sex. I

scribbled on the pad my quick symbols, mostly private, for the sounds in the receiver:

"I have a note of introduction to you from a friend, Miss Sarah Barstow. You will remember her, Mr. Wolfe, you . . . you investigated the death of her father.* Could I see you at once? If possible. I'm talking from the Bidwell, Fifty-second Street. I could be there in fifteen minutes."

"I'm sorry, Miss Hibbard, I am engaged. Could you come at a quarter past two?"

"Oh." A little gasp floated after that. "I had hopes . . . I just decided ten minutes ago. Mr. Wolfe, it is very urgent. If you could possibly . . . "

"If you would describe the urgency."

"I'd rather not, on the telephone—but that's silly. It's my uncle, Andrew Hibbard, he went to see you two weeks ago, you may remember. He has disappeared."

"Indeed. When?"

"Tuesday evening. Four days ago."

"You have had no word of him?"

"Nothing." The female Hibbard's voice caught. "Nothing at all."

"Indeed." I saw Wolfe's eyes shift to take in the clock—it was four minutes past one—and shift again towards the door to the hall, where Fritz stood on the threshold, straight for announcing. "Since ninety hours have passed, another one may be risked. At a quarter past two? Will that be convenient?"

"If you can't . . . all right. I'll be there."

Two receivers were returned simultaneously to their racks. Fritz spoke as usual:

"Luncheon, sir."

---

*See *Fer-de-Lance*, by Rex Stout.

# Chapter 3

I'm funny about women. I've seen dozens of them I wouldn't mind marrying, but I've never been pulled so hard I lost my balance. I don't know whether any of them would have married me or not, that's the truth, since I never gave one a chance to collect enough data to form an intelligent opinion. When I meet a new one there's no doubt that I'm interested and I'm fully alive to all the possibilities, and I've never dodged the issue as far as I can tell, but I never seem to get infatuated. For instance, take the women I meet in my line of business—that is, Nero Wolfe's business. I never run into one, provided she's not just an item for the cleaners, without letting my eyes do the best they can for my judgment, and more than that, it puts a tickle in my blood. I can feel the nudge on the accelerator. But then of course the business gets started, whatever it may happen to be, and I guess the trouble is I'm too conscientious. I love to do a good job more than anything else I can think of, and I suppose that's what shorts the line.

This Evelyn Hibbard was little and dark and smart. Her nose was too pointed and she took too much advantage of her eyelashes, but nobody that knew merchandise would have put her on a bargain counter. She had on a slick gray twill suit, with a fur piece, and a little red hat with a narrow brim on the side of her head. She sat straight without crossing her legs, and her ankles and halfway to her knees was well trimmed but without promise of any plumpness.

I was at my desk of course with my pad, and after the first couple of minutes got only glances at her in between. If worry about her uncle was eating her, and I suppose it was, she was following what Wolfe called the Anglo-Saxon theory of the treatment of emotions and desserts: freeze them and hide them in your belly. She sat straight in the chair I had shoved up for her, keeping her handsome dark eyes level on Wolfe but once in a while flapping her lashes in my direction. She had brought with her a package wrapped in brown paper and held it on her lap. Wolfe leaned back in his seat with his chin down and his forearms laid out on the arms of the chair; it was his custom to make no effort to join his fingers at the high point of his middle mound sooner than a full hour after a meal.

She said that she and her younger sister lived with their uncle in an apartment on One Hundred Thirteenth Street. Their mother had died when they were young. Their father was remarried and lived in California. Their uncle was single. He, Uncle Andrew, had gone out Tuesday evening around nine o'clock, and had not returned. There had been no word from him. He had gone out alone, remarking casually to Ruth, the younger sister, that he would get some air.

Wolfe asked, "This has no precedent?"

"Precedent?"

"He has never done this before? You have no idea where he may be?"

"No. But I have an idea . . . I think . . . he has been killed."

"I suppose so." Wolfe opened his eyes a little. "That would naturally occur to you. On the telephone you mentioned his visit to me. Do you know what its purpose was?"

"I know all about it. It was through my friend Sarah Barstow that I heard of you. I persuaded my uncle to come to see you. I know what he told you and what you said to him. I told my uncle he was a sentimental romantic. He was." She stopped, and kept her lips closed a moment to get them firm again; I looked up to see it. "I'm not. I'm hard-boiled. I think my uncle has been murdered, and the man who killed him is Paul Chapin, the writer. I came here to tell you that."

So here was the notion Wolfe had entertained, coming right to his office and sitting on a chair. But too late? The five hundred a week had gone out to get some air.

Wolfe said, "Quite likely. Thank you for coming. But it might be possible, and more to the point, to engage the attention of the police and the District Attorney."

She nodded. "You are like Sarah Barstow described you. The police have been engaged since Wednesday noon. They have been willing so far, at the request of the president of the university, to keep the matter quiet. There has been no publicity. But the police—you might as well match me at chess against Capablanca. Mr. Wolfe . . ." The fingers of her clasped hands, resting on the package on her lap, twisted a closer knot, and her voice tightened. "You don't know. Paul Chapin has the cunning and subtlety of all the things he mentioned in his first warning, the one he sent after he killed Judge Harrison. He is genuinely evil . . . all evil, all dangerous . . . you know he is not a man . . ."

"There, Miss Hibbard. There now." Wolfe sighed. "Surely he is a man, by definition. Did he indeed kill a judge? In that instance the presumption is of course in his favor. But you mentioned the first warning. Do you by any chance have a copy of it?"

She nodded. "I have." She indicated the package. "I have all the warnings, including . . ." She swallowed. ". . . the last one. Dr. Burton gave me his."

"The one after the apparent suicide."

"No. The one . . . another one came this morning to them. I suppose to all of them; after Dr. Burton told me I telephoned two or three. You see, my uncle has disappeared . . . you see . . ."

"I see. Indeed. Dangerous. For Mr. Chapin, I mean. Any kind of a rut is dangerous in his sort of enterprise. So you have all the warnings. With you? In that package?"

"Yes. Also I have bundles of letters which Paul Chapin has at various times written to my uncle, and a sort of diary which my uncle kept, and a book of records showing sums advanced to Paul Chapin from 1919 to 1928 by my uncle and others, and a list of the names and addresses of the members—that is, of the men who were present in 1909 when it happened. A few other things."

"Preposterous. You have all that? Why not the police?"

Evelyn Hibbard shook her head. "I decided not. These things were in a very private file of my uncle's. They were precious to him, and they are now precious to me . . . in a different way. The police would get no help from them, but you might. And you would not abuse them. Would you?"

At the pause I glanced up, and saw Wolfe's lips pushing out a little . . . then in, then out again . . . That excited me. It always did, even when I had no idea what it was all about. I watched him. He said, "Miss Hibbard. You mean you removed this file from the notice of the police, and kept it, and have now brought it to me? Containing the names and addresses of the members of the League of Atonement? Remarkable."

She stared at him. "Why not? It has no information that they cannot easily obtain elsewhere—from Mr. Farrell or Dr. Burton or Mr. Drummond—any of them—"

"All the same, remarkable." Wolfe reached to his desk and pushed a button. "Will you have a glass of beer? I drink beer, but would not impose my preferences. There is available a fair port, Solera, Dublin stout, Maderia, and more especially a Hungarian *vin du pays* which comes to me from the cellar of the vineyard. Your choice . . ."

She shook her head. "Thank you."

"I may have beer?"

"Please do."

Wolfe did not lean back again. He said, "If the package could perhaps be opened? I am especially interested in that first warning."

She began to untie the string. I got up to help. She handed me the package and I put it on Wolfe's desk and got the paper off. It was a large cardboard letter-file, old and faded but intact. I passed it to Wolfe, and he opened it with the deliberate and friendly exactness which his hands displayed towards all inanimate things.

Evelyn Hibbard said, "Under *I*. My uncle did not call them warnings. He called them intimations."

Wolfe nodded. "Of destiny, I suppose." He removed papers from the file. "Your uncle is indeed a romantic. Oh yes, I say *is*. It is wise to reject all suppositions, even painful ones, until surmise can stand on the legs of fact. Here it is. Ah! *Ye should have killed me, watched the last mean sigh.* Is Mr. Chapin in malevolence a poet? May I read it?"

She nodded. He read:

*Ye should have killed me, watched the last mean sigh*
   *sigh*
*Sneak through my nostril like a fugitive slave*
*Slinking from bondage.*
*Ye should have killed me.*
*Ye killed the man,*
*Ye should have killed me!*

*Ye killed the man, but not*
*The snake, the fox, the mouse that nibbles his hole,*
*The patient cat, the hawk, the ape that grins,*
*The wolf, the crocodile, the worm that works his*
   *way*
*Up through the slime and down again to hide.*
*Ah! All these ye left in me,*
*And killed the man.*
*Ye should have killed me!*

*Long ago I said, trust time.*
*Banal I said, time will take its toll.*
*I said to the snake, the ape, the cat, the worm:*
*Trust time, for all your aptitudes together*
*Are not as sure and deadly. But now they said:*
*Time is too slow; let us, Master.*

*Master, count for us!*
*I said no.*
*Master, let us. Master, count for us!*
*I felt them in me. I saw the night, the sea,*
*The rocks, the neutral stars, the ready cliff.*
*I heard ye all about, and I heard them:*
*Master, let us. Master, count for us!*
*I saw one there, secure at the edge of death;*
*I counted: One!*
*I shall count two I know, and three and four . . .*
*Not waiting for time's toll.*
*Ye should have killed me.*

Wolfe sat with the paper in his hand, glancing from it to Miss Hibbard. "It would seem likely that Mr. Chapin pushed the judge over the edge of a cliff. Presumably impromptu. I presume also, totally unobserved, since no suspicions were aroused. There was a cliff around handy?"

"Yes. It was in Massachusetts, up near Marblehead. Last June. A crowd was there at Fillmore Collard's place. Judge Harrison had come east, from Indiana, for commencement, for his son's graduation. They missed him that night, and the next morning they found his body at the foot of the cliff, beaten among the rocks by the surf."

"Mr. Chapin was among them?"

She nodded. "He was there."

"But don't tell me the gathering was for purposes of atonement. It was not a meeting of this incredible league?"

"Oh no. Anyway, Mr. Wolfe, no one ever quite seriously called it a league. Even Uncle Andrew was not—" she stopped short, shut her lips, stuck her chin up, and then went on, "as romantic as that. The crowd was just a crowd, mostly from the class of 1912, that Fillmore Collard had taken up from Cambridge. Seven or eight of the—well, league—were there."

Wolfe nodded and regarded her for a moment, then got at the file again and began pulling things out of its compartments. He flipped through the sheets of a loose-leaf binder, glanced inside a record book, and shuffled through a lot of papers. Finally he looked at Miss Hibbard again:

"And this quasi-poetic warning came to each of them after they had returned to their homes, and astonished them?"

"Yes, a few days later."

"I see. You know, of course, that Mr. Chapin's little effort was sound traditionally. Many of the most effective warnings in history, particularly the ancient ones, were in verse. As for the merits of Mr. Chapin's execution, granted the soundness of the tradition, it seems to me verbose, bombastic, and decidedly spotty. I cannot qualify as an expert in prosody, but I am not without an ear."

It wasn't like Wolfe to babble when business was on hand, and I glanced up wondering where he thought he was headed for. She was just looking at him. I had to cut my glance short, for he was going on:

"Further, I suspect him specifically, in his second stanza—I suppose he would call it stanza—of plagiarism. It has been many years since I have read Spenser, but in a crack of my memory not quite closed up there is a catalogue of beasts—Archie. If you wouldn't mind, bring me that Spenser? The third shelf, at the right of the door. No, farther over—more yet—dark blue, tooled. That's it."

I took the book over and handed it to him, and he opened it and began skimming.

"*The Shepheardes Calender*, I am certain, and I think *September*. Not that it matters; even if I find it, a petty triumph scarcely worth the minutes I waste. You will forgive me, Miss Hibbard? *Bulls that bene bate . . . Cocke on his dunghill. . . . This wolvish sheepe would catchen his pray* . . . no, certainly not that. Beasts here and there, but not the catalogue in my memory. I shall forgo the triumph; it isn't here. Anyway, it was pleasant to meet Spenser again, even for so brief a nod." He slid forward in his chair, to a perilous extreme, to hand the book to Miss Hibbard. "A fine example of bookmaking, worth a glance of friendship from you. Printed of course in London, but bound in this city by a Swedish boy who will probably starve to death during the coming winter."

She summoned enough politeness to look at it, turn it over in her hand, glance inside, and look at the backbone again. Wolfe was back at the papers he had taken from the file. She was obviously through with the book, so I got up and took it and returned it to the shelf.

Wolfe was saying, "Miss Hibbard. I know that what you want is action, and doubtless I have tried your patience. I am sorry. If I might ask you a few questions?"

"Certainly. It seems to me—"

"Of course. Pardon me. Only two questions, I think. First, do you know whether your uncle recently took out any life insurance?"

She nodded impatiently. "But, Mr. Wolfe, that has nothing to do with—"

He broke in to finish for her, "With the totalitarian evil of Paul Chapin. I know. Possibly not. Was it a large amount of insurance?"

"I think so. Yes. Very large."

"Were you the beneficiary?"

"I don't know. I suppose so. He told me you spoke to him of insurance. Then, about a week ago, he told me he had rushed it through and they had distributed it among four companies. I didn't pay much attention because my mind was on something else. I was angry with him and was trying to persuade him . . . I suppose my sister Ruth and I were the beneficiaries."

"Not Paul Chapin?"

She looked at him, and opened her mouth and closed it again. She said, "That hadn't occurred to me. Perhaps he would. I don't know."

Wolfe nodded. "Yes, a sentimental romantic might do that. Now, the second question. Why did you come to see me? What do you want me to do?"

She gave him her eyes straight. "I want you to find proof of Paul Chapin's guilt, and see that he pays the penalty. I can pay you for it. You told my uncle ten thousand dollars. I can pay that."

"Do you have a personal hostility for Mr. Chapin?"

"Personal?" She frowned. "Is there any other kind of hostility except personal? I don't know. I hate Paul Chapin, and have hated him for years, because I loved my uncle and my sister Ruth loved him and he was a fine sensitive generous man, and Paul Chapin was ruining his life. Ruined his life . . . oh . . . now . . ."

"There, Miss Hibbard. Please. You did not intend to engage me to find your uncle? You had no hope of that?"

"I think not. Oh, if you do! If you do that . . . I think I have no hope, I think I dare not. But then— even if you find him, there will still be Paul Chapin."

"Just so." Wolfe sighed, and turned his eyes to me. "Archie. Please wrap up Miss Hibbard's file for her. If I have not placed the contents in their proper compartments, she will forgive me. The paper and string are intact? Good."

She was protesting, "But you will need that—I'll leave it—"

"No, Miss Hibbard. I'm sorry. I can't undertake your commission."

She stared at him. He said, "The affair is in the hands of the police and the District Attorney. I would be hopelessly handicapped. I shall have to bid you good day."

She found her tongue. "Nonsense. You don't mean it." She exploded, forward in her chair. "Mr. Wolfe, it's outrageous! I've told you all about it . . . you've asked me and I've told you . . . the reason you give is no reason at all . . . why—"

He stopped her, with his finger wiggling and the quality in his voice, without raising it, that always got me a little sore because I never understood how he did it. "Please, Miss Hibbard. I have said no, and I have given you my reason. That is sufficient. If you will just take the package from Mr. Goodwin. Of course I am being rude to you, and on such occasions I always regret that I do not know the art of being rude elegantly. I have all the simplicities, including that of brusqueness."

But he got up from his chair, which, though she didn't know it, was an extraordinary concession. She, on her feet too, had taken the package from me and was mad as hell. Before turning to go, though, she realized that she was more helpless than she was mad. She appealed to him:

"But don't you see, this leaves me . . . what can I do?"

"I can make only one suggestion. If you have made no other arrangements and still wish my services, and the police have made no progress, come to see me next Wednesday."

"But that's four whole days—"

"I'm sorry. Good day, Miss Hibbard."

I went to open the door for her, and she certainly had completely forgotten about her eyelashes.

When I got back to the office Wolfe was seated again, with what I supposed Andrew Hibbard would have called the stigmata of pleasure. His chin was up, and he was making little circles with the tip of his finger on the arm of his chair. I came to a stop by his desk, across from him, and said:

"That girl's mad. I would say, on a guess, she's about one-fifth as mad as I am."

He murmured, "Archie. For a moment, don't disturb me."

"No, sir. I wouldn't for anything. A trick is okay, and a deep trick is the staff of life for some people, but where you've got us to at present is wallowing in the unplumbed depths of—wait a minute, I'll look it up, I think it's in Spenser."

"Archie, I warn you, some day your are going to become dispensable." He stirred a little. "If you were a woman and I were married to you, which God forbid, no amount of space available on this globe, to separate us, would put me at ease. I regret the necessity for my rudeness to Miss Hibbard. It was desirable to get rid of her without delay, for there is a great deal to be done."

"Good. If I can help any—"

"You can. Your notebook, please. Take a telegram."

I sat down. I wasn't within a hundred miles of it, and that always irritated me. Wolfe dictated:

"Regarding recent developments and third Chapin warning you are requested to attend meeting this address nine o'clock Monday evening November fifth without fail. Sign it Nero Wolfe and address."

"Sure." I had it down. "Just send it to anybody I happen to think of?"

Wolfe had lifted up the edge of his desk blotter and taken a sheet of paper from underneath and was pushing it at me. He said, "Here are the names. Include those in Boston, Philadelphia, and Washington; those farther away can be informed later by letter. Also, make a copy of the list; two—one for the safe. Also—"

I had taken the paper from him and a glance showed what it was. I stared at him, and I suppose something in my face stopped him. He interrupted himself, "Reserve your disapproval, Archie. Save your fake moralities for your solitude."

I said, "So that's why you had me get the Spenser, so she would have something to look at. Why did you steal it?"

"I borrowed it."

"You say. I've looked in the dictionary. That's what I mean, why didn't you borrow it? She would have let you have it."

"Probably not." Wolfe sighed. "I didn't care to risk it. In view of your familiarity with the finer ethical points, you must realize that I couldn't very well accept her as a client and then propose to others, especially to a group—"

"Sure, I see that all right. Now that the notion you entertained has drifted in on me, I'd have my hat off if I had one on. But she'd have let you have it. Or you could have got the dope—"

"That will do, Archie." He got a faint tone on. "We shall at any rate be acting in her interest. It appears likely that this will be a complicated and expensive business, and there is no reason why Miss Hibbard should bear the burden alone. In a few minutes I shall be going upstairs, and you will be fairly busy. First, send the telegrams and copy the list. Then—take this, a letter to Miss Hibbard, sign my name and mail it this evening by special delivery: *I find that the enclosed paper did not get back into your file this afternoon, but remained on my desk. I trust that its absence has not caused you any inconvenience. If you are still of a mind to see me next Wednesday, do not hesitate to call upon me.*"

"Yes, sir. Send her the list."

"Naturally. Be sure your copies are correct. Make three copies. I believe you know the home address of Mr. Higgam of the Metropolitan Trust Company?"

I nodded. "Up at Sutton—"

"Find him tomorrow and give him a copy of the list. Ask him to procure first thing Monday morning a financial report on the men listed. No history is required; their present standing is the point. For those in other cities, telegraph. We want the information by six o'clock Monday."

"Hibbard's name is here. Maybe the other dead ones."

"The bank's ingenuity may discover them, and not disturb their souls. Get in touch with Saul Panzer and tell him to report here Monday evening at eight-thirty. Durkin likewise. Find out if Gore and Cather and two others—your selection—will be available for Tuesday morning."

I grinned. "How about the Sixty-first Regiment?"

"They will be our reserve. As soon as you have sent the telegrams, phone Miss Hibbard at her home. Try until you get her. Employ your charm. Make an appointment to call on her this evening. If you get to see her, tell her that you regret that I refused her commission, and that you have my leave to offer her your assistance if she wishes it. It will save time. It will afford you an opportunity to amass a collection of facts from her, and possibly even a glance through the papers and effects of Mr. Hibbard. Chiefly for any indication of an awareness on his part that he would not soon return. We are of course in agreement with some of the tendencies of the law; for instance, its reluctance to believe a man dead merely because he is not visible on the spot he is accustomed to occupy."

"Yes, sir. Take my own line with her?"

"Any that suggests itself."

"If I go up there I could take the list along."

"No, mail it." Wolfe was getting up from his chair. I watched him; it was always something to see. Before he got started for the door, I asked:

"Maybe I should know this, I didn't get it. What was the idea asking her about the life insurance?"

"That? Merely the possibility that we were encountering a degree of vindictive finesse never before reached in our experience. Chapin's hatred, diluted of course, extended from the uncle to the niece. He learned of the large sum she would receive in insurance, and in planning Hibbard's murder planned also that the body would not be discovered; and the insurance money would not be paid her."

"It would some day."

"But even a delay in an enemy's good fortune is at least a minor pleasure. Worth such a finesse if you have it in you. That was the possibility. And another one: let us say Chapin himself was the beneficiary. Miss Hibbard was sure he would kill her uncle, would evade discovery, and would collect a huge fortune for his pains. The thought was intolerable. So she killed her uncle herself—he was about to die in any event—and disposed of the body so that it could not be found. You might go into that with her this evening."

I said, "You think I won't? I'll get her alibi."

# Chapter 4

There was plenty doing Saturday evening and Sunday. I saw Evelyn Hibbard and had three hours with her, and got Saul and Fred and the other boys lined up, and had a lot of fun on the telephone, and finally got hold of Higgam the bank guy late Sunday evening after he returned from a Long Island week-end. The phone calls were from members of the league who had got the telegrams. There were five or six that phoned, various kinds; some scared, some sore, and one that was apparently just curious. I had made several copies of the list, and as the phone calls came I checked them off on one and made notes. The original, Hibbard's, had a date at the top, February 16, 1931, and was typewritten. Some of the addresses had been changed later with a pen, so evidently it had been kept up-to-date. Four of the names had no addresses at all, and of course I didn't know which ones were dead. The list was like this, leaving out the addresses and putting in the business or profession as we got it Monday from the bank:

Andrew Hibbard, psychologist
Ferdinand Bowen, stockbroker

Loring A. Burton, doctor
Eugene Dreyer, art dealer
Alexander Drummond, florist
George R. Pratt, politician
Nicholas Cabot, lawyer
Augustus Farrell, architect
Wm. R. Harrison, judge
Fillmore Collard, textile-mill owner
Edwin Robert Byron, magazine editor
L. M. Irving, social worker
Lewis Palmer, Federal Housing Administration
Julius Adler, lawyer
Theodore Gaines, banker
Pitney Scott, taxi-driver
Michael Ayers, newspaperman
Arthur Kommers, sales manager
Wallace McKenna, congressman from Illinois
Sidney Lang, real estate
Roland Erskine, actor
Leopold Elkus, surgeon
F. L. Ingalls, travel bureau
Archibald Mollison, professor
Richard M. Tuttle, boys' school
T. R. Donovan
Phillip Leonard
Allan W. Gardner
Hans Weber

For the last four there were no addresses, and I couldn't find them in the New York or suburban phone books, so I couldn't ask the bank for a report. Offhand, I thought, reading the names and considering that they were all Harvard men, which meant starting better than scratch on the average, offhand it looked pretty juicy; but the bank reports would settle that. It was fun stalling them on the phone.

But the real fun Sunday came in the middle of the afternoon. Someone had leaked on Hibbard's disappearance and the Sunday papers had it, though they didn't give it a heavy play. When the doorbell rang around three o'clock and I answered it because I happened to be handy and Fritz was busy out back, and I saw two huskies standing there shoulder to shoulder, I surmised at first glance it was a couple of bureau dicks and someone had got curious about me up at Hibbard's the night before. Then I recognized one of them and threw the door wide with a grin.

"Hello, hello. You late from church?"

The one on the right spoke, the one with a scar on his cheek I had recognized. "Nero Wolfe in?"

I nodded. "You want to see him? Leap the doorsill, gentlemen."

While I was closing the door and putting the chain on they were taking off their hats and coats and hanging them on the rack. Then they were running their hands over their hair and pulling their vests down and clearing their throats. They were as nervous as greenhorns on their first tail. I was impressed. I was so used to Wolfe myself and so familiar with his prowess that I was apt to forget the dents some of his strokes had made on some tough professional skulls. I asked them to wait in the hall and went to the office and told Wolfe that Del Bascom of the Bascom Detective Agency was there with one of his men and wanted to see him.

"Did you ask them what they wanted?"

"No."

Wolfe nodded, and I went out and brought them in. Bascom went across to the desk to shake hands; the other gentleman got his big rumpus onto a chair I shoved up, but nearly missed it on the way down on account of staring at Wolfe. I suspected he wasn't overwhelmed by prestige as much as he was by avoirdupois, having never seen Wolfe before.

Bascom was saying, "It's been nearly two years since I've seen you, Mr. Wolfe. Remember? The hay fever case. That's what I called it. Remember the clerk that didn't see the guy lifting the emeralds because he was sneezing?"

"I do indeed, Mr. Bascom. That young man had invention, to employ so common an affliction for so unusual a purpose."

"Yeah. Lots of 'em are smart, but very few of them is quite smart enough. That was quite a case. I'd have been left scratching my ear for a bite if it hadn't been for you. I'll never forget that. Is business pretty good with you, Mr. Wolfe?"

"No. Abominable."

"I suppose so. We've got to expect it. Some of the agencies are doing pretty well on industrial work, but I never got into that. I used to be a workingman myself. Hell, I still am." Bascom crossed his legs and cleared his throat. "You taken on anything new lately?"

"No."

"You haven't?"

"No."

I nearly jumped at the squeak, it was so unexpected. It came from the other dick, his chair between Bascom and me. He squeaked all of a sudden:

"I heard different."

"Well, who opened your valve?" Bascom glared at him, disgusted. "Did I request you to clamp your trap when we came in here?" He turned to Wolfe. "Do you

know what's eating him? You'll enjoy this, Mr. Wolfe.
He's heard a lot of talk about the great Nero Wolfe,
and he wanted to show you haven't got him buffaloed."
He shifted and turned on the glare again. "You sap."

Wolfe nodded. "Yes, I enjoy that. I like bravado.
You were saying, Mr. Bascom?"

"Yeah. I might as well come to the point. It's like
this. I'm on a case. I've got five men on it. I'm pulling
down close to a thousand dollars a week, four weeks
now. When I wind it up I'll get a fee that will keep me
off of relief all winter. I'm getting it sewed up. About
all I need now is some wrapping paper and a piece of
string."

"That's fine."

"All of that. And what I'm here for is to ask you to
lay off."

Wolfe's brows went up a shade. "To ask me?"

"To lay off." Bascom slid forward in his chair and
got earnest. "Look here, Mr. Wolfe. It's the Chapin
case. I've been on it for four weeks. Pratt and Cabot
and Dr. Burton are paying me—that's no secret, or if
it was, it wouldn't be for you after Monday. Pratt's a
sort of a friend of mine, I've done him a good turn or
two. He phoned me last night and said if I wanted to
hang my own price tag on Paul Chapin I'd better get
a move on because Nero Wolfe was about to begin.
That was how I found out about the telegrams you
sent. I dusted around and saw Burton and Cabot and
one or two others. Burton had never heard of you
before and asked me to get a report on you, but he
phoned me this morning and told me not to bother. I
suppose he had inquired and got an earful."

Wolfe murmured, "I am gratified at the interest
they displayed."

"I don't doubt it." Bascom laid a fist on the desk for

emphasis and got more earnest still. "Mr. Wolfe. I want to speak to you as one professional man to another. You would be the first to agree that ours is a dignified profession."

"Not explicitly. To assert dignity is to lose it."

"Huh? Maybe. Anyway, it's a profession, like the law. As you know, it is improper for a lawyer to solicit a client away from another lawyer. He would be disbarred. No lawyer with any decency would ever try it. And don't you think our profession is as dignified as the law? That's the only question. See?"

Bascom waited for an answer, his eyes on Wolfe's face, and probably supposed that the slow unfolding on Wolfe's cheeks was merely a natural phenomenon, like the ground swell on an ocean. Wolfe finally said, "Mr. Bascom. If you would abandon the subtleties of innuendo? If you have a request to make, state it plainly."

"Hell, didn't I? I asked you to lay off."

"You mean, keep out of what you call the Chapin case? I am sorry to have to refuse your request."

"You won't?"

"Certainly not."

"And you think it is absolutely okay to solicit another man's clients away from him?"

"I have no idea. I shall not enter into a defense of my conduct with you; what if it turned out to be indefensible? I merely say, I refuse your request."

"Yeah. I thought you would." Bascom took his fist off the desk and relaxed a little. "My brother claimed you regarded yourself as a gentleman and you'd fall for it. I said you might be a gentleman but you wasn't a sap."

"Neither, I fear."

"Well and good. Now that that's out of the way,

maybe we can talk business. If you're going to take on the Chapin case, that lets us out."

"Probably. Not necessarily."

"Oh yes, it does. You'll soak them until they'll have to begin buying the cheaper cuts. I know when I'm done, I can take it. I couldn't hang onto it much longer anyhow. God help you. I'd love to drop in here once a week and ask you how's tricks. I'm telling you, this cripple Chapin is the deepest and slickest that's ever run around loose. I said I had it about sewed up. Listen. There's not the faintest chance. Not the faintest. I had really given that up, and had three men tailing him to catch him on the next one—and by God there goes Hibbard and we can't even find what's left of him, and do you know what? My three men don't know where Chapin was Tuesday night! Can you beat it? It sounds dumb, but they're not dumb, they're damn good men. So as I say, I'd love to drop in here—"

Wolfe put in, "You spoke of talking business."

"So I did. I'm ready to offer you a bargain. Of course you've got your own methods, we all have, but in these four weeks we've dug up a lot of dope, and it's cost us a lot of money to get it. It's confidential naturally, but if your clients are the same as mine that don't matter. It would save you a lot of time and expense and circling around. You can have all the dope and I'll confer with you on it any time, as often as you want." Bascom hesitated a moment, wet his lips, and concluded, "For one thousand dollars."

Wolfe shook his head gently. "But, Mr. Bascom. All of your reports will be available to me."

"Sure, but you know what reports are. You know, they're all right, but oh hell. You would really get some dope if I let you question any of my men you wanted to. I'd throw that in."

"I question its value."

"Oh, be reasonable."

"I often try. I will pay one hundred dollars for what you offer.—Please! I will not haggle. And do not think me discourteous if I say that I am busy and need all the time the clock affords me. I thank you for your visit, but I am busy." Wolfe's fingers moved to indicate the books before him on the desk, one of them with a marker in it. "There are the five novels written by Paul Chapin; I managed to procure the four earlier ones yesterday evening. I am reading them. I agree with you that this is a difficult case. It is possible, though extremely unlikely, that I shall have it solved by midnight."

I swallowed a grin. Wolfe liked bravado all right; for his reputation it was one of his best tricks.

Bascom stared at him. After a moment he pushed his chair back and got up, and the dick next to me lifted himself with a grunt. Bascom said, "Don't let me keep you. I believe I mentioned we all have our own methods, and all I've got to say is thank God for that."

"Yes. Do you wish the hundred dollars?"

Bascom, turning, nodded. "I'll take it. It looks to me like you're throwing the money away, since you've already bought the novels, but hell I'll take it."

I went across to open the door, and they followed.

# Chapter 5

By dinner time Monday we were all set, so we enjoyed the meal in leisure. Fritz was always happy and put on a little extra effort when he knew things were moving in the office. That night I passed him a wink when I saw how full the soup was of mushrooms, and when I tasted the tarragon in the salad dressing I threw him a kiss. He blushed. Wolfe frequently had compliments for his dishes and expressed them appropriately, and Fritz always blushed; and whenever I found occasion to toss him a tribute he blushed likewise, I'd swear to heaven, just to please me, not to let me down. I often wondered if Wolfe noticed it. His attention to food was so alert and comprehensive that I would have said off hand he didn't, but in making any kind of a guess about Wolfe off hand wasn't good enough.

As soon as dinner was over Wolfe went up to his room, as he had explained he would do; he was staging it. I conferred with Fritz in the kitchen a few minutes and then went upstairs and changed my clothes. I put on the gray suit with pin checks, one of the best fits I ever had, and a light blue shirt and a dark blue tie. On my way back down I stopped in at Wolfe's room, on the same floor, to ask him a question. He was in the tapestry chair by the reading lamp with one of Paul Chapin's novels, and I stood waiting while he marked a paragraph in it with a lead pencil.

I said, "What if one of them brings along some foreign object, like a lawyer for instance? Shall I let it in?"

Without looking up, he nodded. I went down to the office.

The first one was early. I hadn't looked for the line to start forming until around nine, but it lacked twenty minutes of that when I heard Fritz going down the hall and the front door opening. Then the knob of the office door turned, and Fritz ushered in the first victim. He almost needed a shave, his pants were baggy, and his hair wasn't combed. His pale blue eyes darted around and landed on me.

"Hell," he said, "you ain't Nero Wolfe."

I admitted it. I exposed my identity. He didn't offer to shake hands. He said:

"I know I'm early for the party. I'm Mike Ayers, I'm in the city room at the *Tribune.* I told Oggie Reid I had to have the evening off to get my life saved. I stopped off somewhere to get a pair of drinks, and after a while it occurred to me I was a damn fool, there was no reason why there shouldn't be a drink here. I am not referring to beer."

I said, "Gin or gin?"

He grinned. "Good for you. Scotch. Don't bother to dilute it."

I went over to the table Fritz and I had fixed up in the alcove, and poured it. I was thinking, hurrah for Harvard and bright college days and so on. I was also thinking, if he gets too loud he'll be a nuisance but if I refuse to pander to his vile habit he'll beat it. And having learned the bank reports practically by heart,

I knew he had been on the *Post* four years and the *Tribune* three, and was pulling down ninety bucks a week. Newspapermen are one of my weak spots anyhow; I've never been able to get rid of a feeling that they know things I don't know.

I poured him another drink and he sat down and held onto it and crossed his legs. "Tell me," he said, "is it true that Nero Wolfe was a eunuch in a Cairo harem and got his start in life by collecting testimonials from the girls for Pyramid Dental Cream?"

Like an ass, for half a second I was sore. "Listen," I said, "Nero Wolfe is exactly—" Then I stopped and laughed. "Sure," I said. "Except that he wasn't a eunuch, he was a camel."

Mike Ayers nodded. "That explains it. I mean it explains why it's hard for a camel to go through a needle's eye. I've never seen Nero Wolfe, but I've heard about him, and I've seen a needle. You got any other facts?"

I had to pour him another drink before the next customer arrived. This time it was a pair, Ferdinand Bowen, the stockbroker, and Dr. Loring A. Burton. I went to the hall for them to get away from Mike Ayers. Burton was a big fine-looking guy, straight but not stiff, well-dressed and not needing any favors, with dark hair and black eyes and a tired mouth. Bowen was medium-sized, and he was tired all over. He was trim in black and white, and if I'd wanted to see him any evening, which I felt I wouldn't, I'd have gone to the theater where there was a first night and waited in the lobby. He had little feet in neat pumps, and neat little lady-hands in neat little gray gloves. When he was taking his coat off I had to stand back so as not to get socked in the eye with his arms swinging around, and I don't cotton to a guy with that sort of an attitude towards his fellowmen in confined spaces.

Particularly I think they ought to be kept out of elevators, but I'm not fond of them anywhere.

I took Burton and Bowen to the office and explained that Wolfe would be down soon and showed them Mike Ayers. He called Bowen Ferdie and offered him a drink, and he called Burton Lorelei. Fritz brought in another one, Alexander Drummond the florist, a neat little duck with a thin mustache. He was the only one on the list who had ever been to Wolfe's house before, he having come a couple of years back with a bunch from an association meeting to look at the plants. I remembered him. After that they came more or less all together: Pratt the Tammany assemblyman, Adler and Cabot, lawyers, Kommers, sales manager from Philadelphia, Edwin Robert Byron, all of that, magazine editor, Augustus Farrell, architect, and a bird named Lee Mitchell, from Boston, who said he represented both Collard and Gaines the banker. He had a letter from Gaines.

That made twelve accounted for, figuring both Collard and Gaines in, at ten minutes past nine. Of course they all knew each other, but it couldn't be said they were getting much gaiety out of it, not even Mike Ayers, who was going around with an empty glass in his hand, scowling. The others were mostly sitting with their funeral manners on. I went to Wolfe's desk and gave Fritz's button three short pokes. In a couple of minutes I heard the faint hum of the elevator.

The door of the office opened and everybody turned their heads. Wolfe came in; Fritz pulled the door to behind him. He waddled halfway to his desk, stopped, turned, and said, "Good evening, gentlemen." He went to his chair, got the edge of the seat up against the back of his knees and his grip on the arms, and lowered himself.

Mike Ayers demanded my attention by waving his glass at me and calling, "Hey! A eunuch *and* a camel!"

Wolfe raised his head a little and said in one of his best tones, "Are you suggesting those additions to Mr. Chapin's catalogue of his internal menagerie?"

"Huh? Oh. I'm suggesting—"

George Pratt said, "Shut up, Mike," and Farrell the architect grabbed him and pulled him into a chair.

I had handed Wolfe a list showing those who were present, and he had glanced over it. He looked up and spoke. "I am glad to see that Mr. Cabot and Mr. Adler are here. Both, I believe, attorneys. Their knowledge and their trained minds will restrain us from vulgar errors. I note also the presence of Mr. Michael Ayers, a journalist. He is one of your number, so I merely remark that the risk of publicity, should you wish to avoid it—"

Mike Ayers growled, "I'm not a journalist, I'm a newshound. I interviewed Einstein—"

"How drunk are you?"

"Hell, how do I know?"

Wolfe's brow lifted. "Gentlemen?"

Farrell said, "Mike's all right. Forget him. He's all right."

Julius Adler the lawyer, about the build of a lead-pencil stub, looking like a necktie clerk except for his eyes and the way he was dressed, put in, "I would say yes. We realize that this is your house, Mr. Wolfe, and that Mr. Ayers is lit, but after all we don't suppose that you invited us here to censor our private habits. You have something to say to us?"

"Oh, yes . . ."

"My name is Adler."

"Yes, Mr. Adler. Your remark illustrates what I knew would be the chief hindrance in my conversation with you gentlemen. I was aware that you would be antagonistic at the outset. You are all badly frightened, and a frightened man is hostile almost by reflex, as a defense. He suspects everything and everyone. I knew that you would regard me with suspicion."

"Nonsense." It was Cabot, the other lawyer. "We are not frightened, and there is nothing to suspect you of. If you have anything to say to us, say it."

I said, "Mr. Nicholas Cabot."

Wolfe nodded. "If you aren't frightened, Mr. Cabot, there is nothing to discuss. I mean that. You might as well go home." Wolfe opened his eyes and let them move slowly across the eleven faces. "You see, gentlemen, I invited you here this evening only after making a number of assumptions. If any one of them is wrong, this meeting is a waste of time, yours and mine. The first assumption is that you are convinced that Mr. Paul Chapin has murdered two, possibly three, of your friends. The second, that you are apprehensive that unless something is done about it he will murder you. The third, that my abilities are equal to the task of removing your apprehension; and the fourth, that you will be willing to pay well for that service. Well?"

They glanced at one another. Mike Ayers started to get up from his chair and Farrell pulled him back. Pratt muttered loud enough to reach Wolfe, "Good here." Cabot said:

"We are convinced that Paul Chapin is a dangerous enemy of society. That naturally concerns us. As to your abilities . . ."

Wolfe wiggled a finger at him. "Mr. Cabot. If it amuses you to maintain the fiction that you came here this evening to protect society, I would not dampen the diversion. The question is, how much is it worth to you?"

Mike Ayers startled all of us with a sudden shout, "Slick old Nick!" and followed it immediately with a falsetto whine, "Nicky darling . . ." Farrell poked him in the ribs. Someone grumbled, "Gag him." But the glances of two or three others in the direction of Cabot showed that Wolfe was right; the only way to handle that bird was to rub it in.

A new voice broke in, smooth and easy. "What's the difference whether we're scared or not?" It was Edwin Robert Byron, the magazine editor. "I'd just as soon say I'm scared, what's the difference? It seems to me the point is, what does Mr. Wolfe propose to do about it? Grant him his premise—"

"Grant hell." Mike Ayers got up, flinging his arm free of Farrell's grasp, and started for the table in the alcove. Halfway there he turned and blurted at them, "You're damned tootin' we're scared. We jump at noises and we look behind us and we drop things, you know damn well we do. All of you that didn't lay awake last night wondering how he got Andy and what he did with him, raise your hands. You've heard of our little organization, Wolfe you old faker? The League of Atonement? We're changing it to the Craven Club, or maybe the League of the White Feather." He filled his glass and lifted it; I didn't bother to call to him that he had got hold of the sherry decanter by mistake. "Fellow members! To the League of the White Feather!" He negotiated the drink with one heroic swallow. "You can make mine an ostrich plume." He scowled, and made a terrific grimace of disgust and indignation. "Who the hell put horse manure in that whiskey?"

Farrell let out a big handsome guffaw, and Pratt seconded him. Drummond the florist was giggling. Bowen the stockbroker, either bored or looking successfully like it, took out a cigar and cut off the end and lit it. I was over finding the right bottle for Mike Ayers, for I knew he'd have to wash the taste out of his mouth. Lee Mitchell of Boston got to his feet:

"If I may remark, gentlemen." He coughed. "Of

course I am not one of you, but I am authorized to say that both Mr. Collard and Mr. Gaines are in fact apprehensive, they have satisfied themselves of the standing of Mr. Wolfe, and they are ready to entertain his suggestions."

"Good." Wolfe's tone cut short the buzz of comment. He turned his eyes to me. "Archie. If you will just pass out those slips."

I had them in the top drawer of my desk, twenty copies just in case, and I took them and handed them around. Wolfe had rung for beer and was filling his glass. After he had half emptied it he said:

"That, as you see, is merely a list of your names with a sum of money noted after each. I can explain it most easily by reading to you a memorandum which I have here . . . or have I? Archie?"

"Here it is, sir."

"Thank you.—I have dictated it thus; it may be put into formal legal phrasing or not, as you prefer. I would be content to have it an initialed memorandum. For the sake of brevity I have referred to you, those whose names are on the list you have—those absent as well as those present—as *the league*. The memorandum provides:

1. *I undertake to remove from the league all apprehension and expectation of injury from*
   *(a) Paul Chapin.*
   *(b) The person or persons who sent the metrical typewritten warnings.*
   *(c) The person or persons responsible for the deaths of Wm. R. Harrison and Eugene Dreyer, and for the disappearance of Andrew Hibbard.*
2. *Decision as to the satisfactory performance of*

*the undertaking shall be made by a majority
vote of the members of the league.*

3. *The expenses of the undertaking shall be borne
by me, and in the event of my failure to perform it satisfactorily the league shall be under
no obligation to pay them, nor any other obligation.*

4. *Upon decision that the undertaking has been
satisfactorily performed, the members of the
league will pay me, each the amount set after
his name on the attached list; provided, that the
members will be severally and jointly responsible for the payment of the total amount.*

"I believe that covers it. Of course, should you
wish to make it terminable after a stated period—"

Nicholas Cabot cut in, "It's preposterous. I won't
even discuss it." Julius Adler said with a smile, "I
think we should thank Mr. Wolfe's secretary for
adding it up and saving us the shock. Fifty-six thousand, nine hundred and fifteen dollars. Well!" His
brows went up and stayed up. Kommers, who had
spent at least ten bucks coming from Philadelphia,
made his maiden speech, "I don't know much about
your abilities, Mr. Wolfe, but I've learned something
new about nerve." Others began to join in the chorus;
they were just going to crowd us right in the ditch.

Wolfe waited, and in about a minute put up his
hand, palm out, which was a pretty violent gesture for
him. "Please, gentlemen. There is really no ground for
controversy. It is a simple matter: I offer to sell you
something for a stated price on delivery. If you think
the price exorbitant you are under no compulsion to
buy. However, I may observe in that connection that
on Saturday Miss Evelyn Hibbard offered to pay me

ten thousand dollars for the service proposed. There is no single item on that list as high as ten thousand dollars; and Miss Hibbard is not herself in jeopardy."

George Pratt said, "Yeah, and you turned her down so you could soak us. You're just out to do all the good you can, huh?"

"Anyhow, the memorandum is preposterous throughout." Nicholas Cabot had gone to Wolfe's desk and reached for the memorandum, and was standing there looking at it. "What we want is Paul Chapin put where he belongs. This attempt at evasion—"

"I'm surprised at you, Mr. Cabot." Wolfe sighed. "I phrased it that way chiefly because I knew two shrewd lawyers would be here and I wished to forestall their objections. Circumstances have got the idea of Paul Chapin's guilt so firmly fixed in your mind that you are a little off balance. I could not undertake specifically to remove your apprehension by getting Mr. Chapin convicted of murder, because if I did so and investigation proved him innocent two difficulties would present themselves. First, I would have to frame him in order to collect my money, which would be not only unfair to him but also a great bother to me, and second, the real perpetrator of these indiscretions would remain free to continue his career, and you gentlemen would still be scared—or dead. I wished to cover—"

"Rubbish." Cabot pushed the memorandum impatiently away. "We are convinced it is Chapin. We know it is."

"So am I." Wolfe nodded, down, and up, and at rest again. "Yes, I am convinced that it is Chapin you should fear. But in preparing this memorandum I thought it well to cover all contingencies, and you as a lawyer must agree with me. After all, what is really known? Very little. For instance, what if Andrew Hibbard, tormented by remorse, was driven to undertake vengeance on behalf of the man you all had injured? *Ye should have killed me.* What if, after killing two of you, he found he couldn't stomach it, and went off somewhere and ended his own life? That would contradict nothing we now know. Or what if another of you, or even an outsider, proceeded to balance some personal accounts, and took advantage of the exudations of the Chapin stew to lay a false scent? That might be you, Mr. Cabot, or Dr. Burton, or Mr. Michael Ayers . . . anyone. You say rubbish, and really I do too, but why not cover the contingencies?"

Cabot pulled the memorandum back beneath his eyes. Julius Adler got up and went to the desk and joined in the inspection. There was some murmuring among the others. Mike Ayers was sprawled in his chair with his hands deep in his pockets and his eyes shut tight. Julius Adler said:

"This last provision is out of the question. This joint responsibility for the total amount. We wouldn't consider it."

Wolfe's cheeks unfolded a little. "I agree with you, Mr. Adler. I shall not insist upon it. As a matter of fact, I inserted it purposely, so there would be something for you to take out."

Adler grunted. Drummond the florist, who had gone to join them, as had Pratt and Arthur Kommers, giggled again. Cabot looked at Wolfe with a frown and said, "You aren't at all nimble, are you?"

"Moderately. I'm really not much good at negotiation, I am too blunt. It is a shortcoming of temperament not to be overcome. For instance, my proposal to you. I can only present it and say, take it or leave it. I compensate for the handicap by making the proposal so attractive that it cannot very well be refused."

I was surprised, all of a sudden, to see the shadow of a smile on Cabot's face, and for a second I damn near liked him. He said, "Of course. I sympathize with your disability."

"Thank you." Wolfe moved his eyes to take in the others. "Well, gentlemen? I will mention two little points. First, I did not include in the memorandum a stipulation that you should co-operate with me, but I shall of course expect it. I can do little without your help. I would like to feel free to have Mr. Goodwin and another of my men call upon you at any reasonable time, and I would like to talk with a few of you myself. I may?"

Three or four heads nodded. George Pratt, with the group at the desk, said, "Good here." Cabot smiled openly and murmured, "Don't forget your disability."

"Good. The second point, about the money. In my opinion, the sums I have listed are adequate but not extortionate. If I fail to satisfy you I get nothing, so it comes to this: would Mr. Gaines be willing at this moment to pay me eight thousand dollars, and Dr. Burton seven thousand, and Mr. Michael Ayers one hundred and eighty, in return for a guarantee of freedom from the fear which has fastened itself upon them? I take it that you agree that it is proper to have the amounts graded in accordance with ability to pay."

Again heads nodded. He was easing them into it; he was sewing them up. I grinned to myself, "Boss, you're cute, that's all, you're just cute." Lee Mitchell from Boston spoke again:

"Of course I can't speak definitely for Mr. Collard and Mr. Gaines. I think I may say—you can probably count them in. I'll go back to Boston tonight and they'll wire you tomorrow."

Cabot said, "You can cross Elkus out. He wouldn't pay you a cent."

"No?"

"No. He's as sentimental as Andy Hibbard was. He'd sooner see us all killed than help catch Paul Chapin."

"Indeed. It is disastrous to permit the vagaries of the heart to infect the mind. We shall see—Gentlemen. I would like to satisfy myself now on one point. Frankly, I do not wish it to be possible for any of you to say, at any time in the future, that I have acted with a ruthlessness or vindictiveness which you did not contemplate or desire. My understanding is that you are all convinced that Paul Chapin is a murderer, that he has threatened you with murder, and that he should be caught, discovered, convicted and executed. I am going to ask Mr. Goodwin to call off your names. If my understanding is correct, you will please respond with *yes*."

He nodded at me. I took up the list on which I had checked those present. Before I could call one, Lee Mitchell said, "On that I can answer for Mr. Collard and Mr. Gaines. Unqualifiedly. Their response if *yes*."

There was a stir, but no one spoke. I said, "Ferdinand Bowen." ·

The broker said, husky but firm, "Yes."

"Dr. Loring A. Burton."

For a moment there was no reply, then Burton murmured in a tone so low it was barely heard, "No." Everyone looked at him. He looked around, swallowed, and said suddenly and explosively, "Nonsense! Yes, of course! Romantic nonsense. Yes!"

Farrell said to him, "I should hope so. The wonder is you weren't first."

I went on, "Augustus Farrell."

"Yes."

I called the others, Drummond, Cabot, Pratt, Byron, Adler, Kommers; they all said *yes*. I called, "Michael Ayers." He was still sprawled in his chair. I said his name again. Farrell, next to him, dug him in the ribs: "Mike! Hey! Say yes." Mike Ayers stirred a little, opened his eyes into slits, bawled out, "Yes!" and shut his eyes again.

I turned to Wolfe, "That's all, sir."

I usually heard Fritz when he went down the front hall to answer the doorbell, but that time I didn't; I suppose because I was too interested in the roll I was calling. So I was surprised when I saw the door of the office opening. The others saw me look and they looked too. Fritz came in three steps and waited until Wolfe nodded at him. "A gentleman to see you, sir. He had no card. He told me to say, Mr. Paul Chapin."

"Indeed." Wolfe didn't move. "Indeed. Show him in."

# Chapter 6

ritz went back to the hall to get the visitor. I missed a bet, but Wolfe probably didn't—I don't know; I should have been taking notice of the expressions on the faces of our guests, but I wasn't; my eyes were glued on the door. I imagine all the others' were too, except Wolfe's. I heard the thud of Paul Chapin's walking-stick on the rubber tile of the hall.

He limped in and stopped a few paces from the door. From where he was he couldn't see Wolfe, on account of the group gathered at the desk. He looked at the group, and at those around on chairs, and tossed his head up twice, his chin out, like a nervous horse trying to shake the rein. He said, "Hello, fellows," and limped forward again, far enough into the room so he could see Wolfe, first sending a quick sharp glance at me. He was standing less than eight feet from me. He was dressed for evening, a dinner coat. He wasn't a big guy at all, rather under medium size than over; you couldn't call him skinny, but you could see the bone structure of his face—flat cheeks, an ordinary nose, and light-colored eyes. When he turned his back to me so as to face Wolfe I saw that his coat didn't hang straight down over his right hip pocket, and I un-crossed my legs and brought my feet back to position, just in case.

There had been no audible replies to his salutation. He looked around again, back again at Wolfe, and smiled at him. "You are Mr. Wolfe?"

"Yes." Wolfe had his fingers intertwined on his belly. "You are Mr. Chapin."

Paul Chapin nodded. "I was at the theater. They've done a book of mine into a play. Then I thought I'd drop in here."

"Which book? I've read all of them."

"You have? Really. I wouldn't suppose . . . *The Iron Heel.*"

"Oh yes. That one. Accept my congratulations."

"Thank you. I hope you don't mind my dropping in. I knew of this gathering, of course. I learned of it from three of my friends, Leo Elkus and Lorry Burton and Alex Drummond. You mustn't hold it against them, except possibly Leo. He meant well, I think, but the others were trying to frighten me. They were trying it with a bogy, but for a bogy to be effective its terrors must be known to the victim. Unfortunately you were unknown to me. You have terrors, I suppose?"

Since Chapin's first word he had kept his eyes on Wolfe, ignoring the others. They were regarding him with varying reactions on their faces: Mitchell of Boston with curiosity, Bowen with a sour poker face, Cabot with uncomfortable indignation, Mike Ayers with scowling disgust . . . I was looking them over. Of a sudden Dr. Burton left his chair, strode to the desk, and grabbed Chapin by the arm. He said to him:

"Paul, for God's sake. Get out of here! This is terrible. Get out!"

Drummond the florist put in, his cultured tenor

transformed by intensity into a ferocious squeal, "This is the limit, Paul! After what we—after what I—you dirty murdering rat!"

Others, breaking their tension, found their tongues. Wolfe stopped them. He said sharply, "Gentlemen! Mr. Chapin is my guest!" He looked at Chapin, leaning on his stick. "You should sit down. Take a chair.—Archie."

"No, thanks. I'll be going in a moment." Chapin sent a smile around; it would have been merely a pleasant smile but for his light-colored eyes where there was no smile at all. "I've been standing on one foot for twenty-five years. Of course all of you know that; I don't need to tell you. I'm sorry if I've annoyed you by coming here; really, I wouldn't disconcert you fellows for anything. You've all been too kind to me, you know very well you have. If I may get a little literary and sentimental about it—you have lightened life's burden for me. I'll never forget it, I've told you that a thousand times. Of course, now that I seem to have found my métier, now that I am standing on my own feet—that is, my own foot—" he smiled around again—"I shall be able to find my way the rest of the journey without you. But I shall always be grateful." He turned to Wolfe. "That's how it is, you see. But I didn't come here to say that, I came to see you. I was thinking that possibly you are a reasonable and intelligent man. Are you?"

Wolfe was looking at him. I was saying to myself, look out, Paul Chapin, look out for those half-closed eyes, and if you take my advice you'll shut up and beat it quick. Wolfe said:

"I reach that pinnacle occasionally, Mr. Chapin."

"I'll try to believe you. There are few who do. I just wanted to say this to you: my friends have wasted a lot of time and money pursuing a mirage which someone has cleverly projected for them. I tell you straight, Mr. Wolfe, it's been a shock to me. That they should suspect *me*, knowing as they do how grateful I am for all their kindness! Really, incredible. I wanted to put this before you and save you from the loss of your time and money too. You would not be so fatuous as to chase a mirage?"

"I assure you, sir, I am far too immobile to chase anything whatever. But perhaps—since you are by your own admission definitely out of it—perhaps you have a theory regarding the incidents that have disturbed your friends? It might help us."

"I'm afraid not." Chapin shook his head regretfully. "Of course, it appears more than likely that it's a practical joke, but I have no idea—"

"Murder isn't a joke, Mr. Chapin. Death is not a joke."

"Oh, no? Really, no? Are you so sure? Take a good case. Take me, Paul Chapin. Would you dare to assert that my death would not be a joke?"

"Why, would it?"

"Of course. A howling anticlimax. Death's pretensions to horror, considering what in my case has preceded it, would be indescribably ludicrous. That is why I have so greatly appreciated my friends, their thoughtfulness, their solicitude—"

A cry from behind interrupted him; a cry, deeply anguished, in the voice of Dr. Burton: "Paul! Paul, for God's sake!"

Chapin wheeled about on his good leg. "Yes?" Without raising his voice a particle he got into it a concentrated scorn that would have withered the love of God. "Yes, Lorry?"

Burton looked at him, said nothing, shook his head,

and turned his eyes away. Chapin turned back to Wolfe. Wolfe said:

"So you adhere to the joke theory."

"Not adhere precisely. It seems likely. So far as I am concerned, Mr. Wolfe, the only point is this: I suffer from the delusion of my friends that I am a source of peril to them. Actually, they are afraid of me. Of *me*! I suffer considerably, I really do. The fact is that it would be difficult to conceive of a more harmless creature than I am. I am myself afraid! Constitutionally afraid of all sorts of things. For instance, on account of my pathetic physical inadequacy, I go in constant fear of this or that sort of violent attack, and I habitually am armed. See—"

Paul Chapin had us going all right. As his right hand came around behind him and his fingers started under the edge of his dinner coat, there were two or three cries of warning from the group, and I took it on the jump. With my momentum and him balanced against his walking-stick, I damn near toppled him over, but I had my grip on his right wrist and saved him from a tumble. With my left hand I jerked the gat from his hip pocket.

"Archie!" Wolfe snapped at me. "Release Mr. Chapin."

I let go his wrist. Wolfe was still snapping: "Give him back his—article."

I looked at the gat. It was a thirty-two, an old veteran, and a glance showed me it wasn't loaded. Paul Chapin, his light-colored eyes having no look in them at all, held out his hand. I put the gun in it and he let it sit there on his palm as if it was a dish of applesauce.

Wolfe said, "Confound you, Archie. You have deprived Mr. Chapin of the opportunity for a dramatic

and effective gesture. I know, Mr. Chapin. I am sorry.
May I see the gun?"

Chapin handed it to him and he looked it over. He
threw the cylinder out and back, cocked it, snapped
the trigger, and looked it over again. He said, "An
ugly weapon. It terrifies me. Guns always do. May I
show it to Mr. Goodwin?"

Chapin shrugged his shoulders, and Wolfe handed
the gat to me. I took it under my light and gave it a
few warm glances; cocked it, saw what Wolfe had
seen, and grinned. Then I looked up and saw Paul
Chapin's eyes on me and stopped grinning. You could
still have said there was no look in them, but behind
them was something I wouldn't have cared to bring
into plain sight. I handed him the gun, and he stuck it
back into his hip pocket. He said, half to me and half to
Wolfe, in an easy tone:

"That's it, you see. The effect is psychological. I
learned a good deal about psychology from my friend
Andy Hibbard."

There were ejaculations. George Pratt stepped to
Chapin and glared at him. Pratt's hands were working
at his sides as he stammered, "You—you snake! If you
weren't a goddam cripple I'd knock you so far I'll say
you'd be harmless—"

Chapin showed no alarm. "Yes, George. And what
made me a goddam cripple?"

Pratt didn't retreat. "I helped to, once. Sure I did.
That was an accident, we all have 'em, maybe not as
bad as yours. Christ, can't you ever forget it? Is there
no man in you at all? Has your brain got twisted—"

"No. Man? No." Chapin cut him off, and smiled at
him with his mouth. He looked around at the others.
"You fellows are all men though. Aren't you? Every
one. God bless you. That's an idea, depend on God's

blessing. Try it. I tried it once. Now I must ask you to excuse me." He turned to Wolfe. "Good evening, sir. I'll go. Thank you for your courtesy. I trust I haven't put too great a strain on your intelligence."

He inclined his head to Wolfe and to me, turned and made off. His stick had thumped three times on the rug when he was halted by Wolfe's voice:

"Mr. Chapin. I almost forgot. May I ask you for a very few minutes more? Just a small—"

Nicholas Cabot's voice broke in, "For God's sake, Wolfe, let him go—"

"Please, Mr. Cabot. May I, gentlemen? Just a small favor, Mr. Chapin. Since you are innocent of any ill intent, and as anxious as we are to see your friends' difficulties removed, I trust you will help me in a little test. I know it will seem nonsensical to you, quite meaningless, but I should like to try it. Would you help me out?"

Chapin had turned. I thought he looked careful. He said, "Perhaps. What is it?"

"Quite simple. You use a typewriter, I suppose?"

"Of course. I type all my manuscripts myself."

"We have a typewriter here. Would you be good enough to sit at Mr. Goodwin's desk and type something at my dictation?"

"Why should I?" He hesitated, and was certainly being careful now. He looked around and saw twelve pairs of eyes at him; then he smiled and said easily, "But for that matter, why shouldn't I?" He limped back towards me.

I pulled the machine up into position, inserted a sheet of paper, got up, and held my chair for him. He shook his head and I moved away, and he leaned his stick up against the desk and got himself into the chair, shoving his bum leg under with his hand.

Nobody was saying a word. He looked around at Wolfe and said, "I'm not very fast. Shall I double-space it?"

"I would say, single-space. In that way it will most nearly resemble the original. Are you ready?" Wolfe suddenly and unexpectedly put volume and depth into his voice: *"Ye should have killed me*—comma— *watched the last mean sigh*—"

There was complete silence. It lasted ten seconds. Then Chapin's fingers moved and the typewriter clicked, firm and fast. I followed the words on it. It got through the first three, but at the fourth it faltered. It stopped at the second *l* in *killed,* stopped completely. There was silence again. You could have heard a feather falling. The sounds that broke it came from Paul Chapin. He moved with no haste but with a good deal of finality. He pushed back, got himself onto his feet, took his stick, and thumped off. He brushed past me, and Arthur Kommers had to move out of his way. Before he got to the door he stopped and turned. He did not seem especially perturbed, and his light-colored eyes had nothing new in them as far as I could see from where I was.

He said, "I would have been glad to help in any authentic test, Mr. Wolfe, but I wouldn't care to be the victim of a trick. I was referring, by the way, to intelligence, not to a vulgar and obvious cunning."

He turned. Wolfe murmured, "Archie," and I went out to help him on with his coat and open the door for him.

# Chapter 7

When I got back to the office everybody was talking. Mike Ayers had gone to the table to get a drink, and three or four others had joined him. Dr. Burton stood with his hands dug into his pockets, frowning, listening to Farrell and Pratt. Wolfe had untwined his fingers and was showing his inner tumult by rubbing his nose with one of them. When I got to his desk Cabot the lawyer was saying to him:

"I have an idea you'll collect your fees, Mr. Wolfe. I begin to understand your repute."

"I shall make no discount for flummery, sir." Wolfe sighed. "For my part, I have an idea that if I collect my fees I shall have earned them. Your friend Mr. Chapin is a man of quality."

Cabot nodded. "Paul Chapin is a distorted genius."

"All genius is distorted. Including my own. But so for that matter is all life; a mad and futile ferment of substances meant originally to occupy space without disturbing it. But alas, here we are in the thick of the disturbance, and the only way that has occurred to us to make it tolerable is to join in and raise all the hell our ingenuity may suggest.—How did Paul Chapin acquire his special distortion? I mean the famous accident. Tell me about it. I understand it was at college, a hazing affair."

"Yes. It was pretty terrible." Cabot sat on the edge of the desk. "No doubt of that, but good God, other men, the war, for instance . . . oh well. I suppose Paul was distorted from the beginning. He was a freshman, the rest of us were sophomores and on up. Do you know the Yard?"

"The Yard?"

"At Harvard."

"I have never been there."

"Well. There were dormitories—Thayer Hall. This was at Thayer Middle Entry—Hell Bend. We were having a beer night downstairs, and there were some there from outside—that's how fellows like Gaines and Collard happened to be present. We were having a good time around ten o'clock when a fellow came in and said he couldn't get in his room; he had left his key inside and the doors had snap locks. Of course we all began to clap."

"That was a masterpiece, to forget one's key?"

"Oh no. We were clapping the opportunity. By getting out a hall window, or another room, you could make your way along a narrow ledge to the window of any locked room and get in that way. It was quite a trick—I wouldn't try it now for my hope of the Supreme Court—but I had done it in my freshman year and so had many others. Whenever an upperclassman forgot his key it was the native custom to conscript a freshman for that service. There was nothing extraordinary about it, for the agility of youth. Well, when this fellow—it was Andy Hibbard—when he announced he had locked himself out, of course we welcomed the opportunity for a little discipline. We looked around for a victim. Somebody heard a noise in the hall and looked out and saw one

going by, and called to him to come in. He came in. It
was Chapin."

"He was a freshman."

Cabot nodded. "Paul had a personality, a force in
him, already at that age. Maybe he was already
distorted. I'm not a psychiatrist. Andy Hibbard has
told me . . . but that wouldn't help you any. Anyway, we had been inclined to let him alone. Now, here
he was delivered to us by chance. Somebody told him
what was expected of him. He was quite cool about it.
He asked what floor Andy's room was on, and we told
him the fourth, three flights up. He said he was sorry,
in that case he couldn't do it. Ferd Bowen said to him,
'What's the matter, you're not a cripple, are you?' He
said he was perfectly sound. Bill Harrison, who was
serious-minded in his cradle, asked him if he had
vertigo. He said no. We marched him upstairs. Ordinarily not more than a dozen or so would probably
have gone up to see the fun, but on account of the way
he was taking it thirty-five of us herded him up. We
didn't touch him. He went, because he knew what
would happen if he didn't."

"What would happen?"

"Oh, things. Whatever might occur to us. You
know college kids."

"As few as possible."

"Yes. Well, he went. I'll never forget his face as he
was getting out of the hall window, backwards. It was
white as a sheet, but it was something else too, I don't
know what. It got me. It got Andy Hibbard too, for he
jumped forward and called to Chapin to come back in,
he would do it himself. Others grabbed Andy and told
him not to be a damn fool. All who could crowded up
and looked out of the window. It was moonlight.
Others ran to one of the rooms and looked out of the

windows there. Chapin got onto the ledge all right, and got straightened up and moved along a little, his hand stretched out as far as he could, trying to reach the next window. I didn't see it, I wasn't looking, but they said that all of a sudden he began to tremble, and down he went."

Cabot stopped. He reached in his pocket for his case and lit a cigarette. He didn't hold the match to it as steady as he might have. He took a couple of puffs and said, "That's all. That's what happened."

Wolfe grunted. "You say there were thirty-five of you?"

"Yes. So it turned out." Cabot pulled at his cigarette. "We chipped in, of course, and did all we could. He was in the hospital two months and had three operations. I don't know where he got a list of our names; I suppose from Andy. Andy took it hard. Anyway, the day he left the hospital he sent all of us copies of a poem he had written. Thanking us. It was clever. There was only one of us smart enough to see what kind of thanks it was. Pitney Scott."

"Pitney Scott is a taxi-driver."

Cabot raised his brows. "You should write our class history, Mr. Wolfe. Pit took to drink in 1930, one of the depression casualties. Not, like Mike Ayers, for the annoyance of other people. For his own destruction. I see you have him down for five dollars. I'll pay it."

"Indeed. That would indicate that you are prepared to accept my proposal."

"Of course I am. We all are. But you know that. What else can we do? We are menaced with death, there's no question about it. I have no idea why, if Paul had this in him, he waited so long to get it out— possibly his recent success gave him a touch of confidence that he needed, or money to finance his plans—I don't know. Of course we accept your proposal. Did you know that a month ago Adler and Pratt and Bowen seriously discussed the notion of hiring a gangster to kill him? They invited me in, but I wouldn't—everyone's squeamishness begins somewhere, and I suppose that was the starting point for mine—and they abandoned the idea. What else can we do? The police are helpless, which is understandable and nothing against them; they are equipped to frustrate many kinds of men, but not Paul Chapin—I grant him his quality. Three of us hired detectives a month ago, and we might as well have engaged a troop of Boy Scouts. They spent days looking for the typewriter on which the warnings were written, and never even found it; and if they had found it they would not have been able to fasten it on Paul Chapin."

"Yes." Wolfe reached out and pressed the button for Fritz. "Your detectives called on me and offered to place their findings at my disposal—with your consent." Fritz appeared, and Wolfe nodded for beer. "Mr. Cabot. What does Mr. Chapin mean when he says that you killed the man in him?"

"Well . . . that's poetry, isn't it?"

"It might be called that. Is it merely poetry, or is it also technical information?"

"I don't know." Cabot's eyes fell. I watched him and thought to myself, he's actually embarrassed; so there's kinks in your love-life too, huh, smoothie? He went on, "I couldn't say; I doubt if any of us could. You'd have to ask his doctor."

A new voice cut in. Julius Adler and Alex Drummond had come over a few minutes before and stood listening; Adler, I suppose, because he was a lawyer and therefore didn't trust lawyers, and Drummond since he was a tenor. I never saw a tenor that wasn't inquisitive. At this point Drummond horned in with a giggle:

"Or his wife."

Wolfe snapped at him, "Whose wife?"

"Why, Paul's."

If I had seen Wolfe astonished only three times in seven years, which is what I would guess, this was the fourth. He even moved in his chair. He looked at Cabot, not at Drummond, and demanded, "What is this nonsense?"

Cabot nodded. "Sure, Paul has a wife."

Wolfe poured a glass of beer, gulped half of it, let it settle a second, and swallowed the rest. He looked around for his handkerchief, but it had dropped to the floor. I got him one out of the drawer where I kept them, and he wiped his lips.

He said, "Tell me about her."

"Well . . ." Cabot looked for words. "Paul Chapin is full of distortions, let us say, and his wife is one of them. Her name was Dora Ritter. He married her three years ago, and they live in an apartment on Perry Street."

"What is she like and who was she?"

Cabot hesitated again, differently. This time he didn't seem to be looking for words, he was looking for a way out. He finally said, "I don't see—I really don't see that this is going to help you any, but I suppose you'll want to know it. But I'd rather not—you'd better get it from Burton himself." He turned and called, "Lorry! Come over here a minute."

Dr. Burton was with the group at the table, talking and working on a highball. He looked around, made some remark to Farrell the architect, and crossed to Wolfe's desk. Cabot said to him:

"Mr. Wolfe has just asked me who Paul's wife was. Maybe I'm being more delicate than the circumstances require, but I'd rather you'd tell him."

Burton looked at Wolfe and frowned. He looked at Cabot, and his voice sounded irritated: "Why not you, or anybody? Everybody knows it."

Cabot smiled. "I said maybe I was overdelicate."

"I think you were." Burton turned to Wolfe. "Dora Ritter was a maid in my employ. She is around fifty, extremely homely, disconcertingly competent, and stubborn as a wet boot. Paul Chapin married her in 1931."

"What did he marry her for?"

"I am as likely to tell you as he is. Chapin is a psychopath."

"So Mr. Hibbard informed me. What sort of maid was she?"

"What sort?"

"Was she in your office, for instance?"

Burton was frowning. "No. She was my wife's maid."

"How long have you known her and how long has Chapin known her?—Wait." Wolfe wiggled a finger. "I must ask you to bear with me, Dr. Burton. I have just received a shock and am floundering in confusion. I have read all of Paul Chapin's novels, and so naturally supposed myself to be in possession of a fairly complete understanding of his character, his temperament, his processes of thought and his modes of action. I thought him incapable of following any of the traditional channels leading to matrimony, either emotional or practical. Learning that he has a wife, I am greatly shocked; I am even desperate. I need to have disclosed everything about her that is discoverable."

"Oh. You do." Burton looked at him, sizing him up, with sour steadiness. "Then I might as well disclose it myself. It was common gossip." He glanced at the others. "I knew that, though naturally it didn't reach my ears. If I show reluctance, it is only because it was . . . unpleasant."

"Yes."

"Yes, it was. I presume you don't know that of all of us, this group, I was the only one who knew Paul Chapin before the college days. We came from the same town—I more or less grew up with him. He was in love with a girl. I knew her—one of the girls I knew, that was all. He was infatuated with her, and he finally, through persistence, reached an understanding with her before he went away to college. Then the accident occurred, and he was crippled, and it was all off. In my opinion it would have been off anyway, sooner or later, without the intervention of an accident. I didn't go home for my vacations; I spent my summers working. It wasn't until after I was through with medical school that I went back for a visit, and discovered that this girl had become . . . that is . . . I married her."

He glanced aside at Cabot's cigarette case thrust at him by the lawyer, shook his head, turned back to Wolfe and went on, "We came to New York. I was lucky in my profession; I have a good bedside manner and a knack with people's insides, especially women. I made a lot of money. I think it was in 1923 that my wife engaged Dora Ritter—yes, she was with us eight years. Her competence was a jewel in a nigger's ear—"

"Ethiope."

"Well, that's a nigger. One day Paul came to me and said he was going to marry my wife's maid. That was what was unpleasant. He made a nasty scene out of it."

Wolfe inclined his head. "I can imagine him explaining that the action contemplated was by way of a paraphrase on the old institution of whipping-boy."

Dr. Burton jerked his head up, startled, and stared at him. "How the devil did you know that?"

"He said that?"

"Those words. He said paraphrase."

"I suspected he would have lit on that." Wolfe scratched his ear, and I knew he was pleased. "Having read his novels, I am not unacquainted with his style of thought and his taste in allusion.—So he married her. She, of course, having but one jewel and the rest all slag, would not be finicky. Do they make a happy pair? Do you ever see her?"

"Not frequently." Burton hesitated, then went on, "I see her very seldom. She comes once or twice a week to dress my wife's hair, and occasionally to sew. I am usually not at home."

Wolfe murmured, "It is a temptation to cling to competence when we find it."

Burton nodded. "I suppose so. My wife finds it impossible to forgo the indulgence. Dora is an expert hag."

"Well." Wolfe took some beer. "Thank you, doctor. It has often been said, you will find romance in the most unlikely spots. Mr. Chapin's no longer upsets me, since it fits my presumptions. By the way, this probably clears up another little point. Permit me.— Archie, would you ask Mr. Farrell to join us?"

I went and got Farrell and brought him over. He was brisk; the Scotch was putting some spring into him. He gave Wolfe an amiable look.

"Mr. Farrell. Earlier this evening you remarked to Dr. Burton that it was a wonder he was not the first. I suppose that you meant, the first victim of Mr.

Chapin's campaign. Did that remark mean anything in particular?"

Farrell looked uncomfortable. "Did I say that?"

"You did."

"I don't remember it. I suppose I thought I was cracking a joke, I don't know."

Wolfe said patiently, "Dr. Burton has just been telling me the exegesis of Chapin's marriage and the former occupation of his wife. I thought perhaps—"

"Oh, he has." Farrell shot a glance at Burton. "Then what are you asking me for?"

"Don't be testy, Mr. Farrell; let me save your life in amity. That was the basis of your remark?"

"Of course. But what the devil have Lorrie Burton's private affairs got to do with it? Or mine or anybody's? I thought what we are going to pay you for is to stop—"

He broke off. He looked around at the others and his face got red. He finished to Wolfe in a completely different tone, "Forgive me. I forgot for a moment."

"Forgot what?"

"Nothing of any importance. Only that I'm out of it. In your total of fifty-odd thousand, you've got me down for ten dollars. Your sources of information are up-to-date. Have you any idea what architects have been up against the past four years? Even good ones. I did the new city hall at Baltimore in 1928. Now I couldn't get—you're not thinking of doing any building, Mr. Wolfe? A telephone stand or a dog kennel or anything? I'd be glad to submit designs—Oh, the devil. Anyway, I forgot I'm just here ex-officio, I'm not paying my way.—Come on, Lorrie, come and finish your drink. You ought to be home in bed, you're sagging worse than I am." He took Burton's arm.

Moving off, they halted for Wolfe: "Mr. Farrell. I

am under the same necessity of earning your ten dollars as Mr. Collard's nine thousand. If you have comments—"

"Hell no. I haven't even got a comment. Nor am I even contributing ten bucks to the pot of retribution, I'm taking it out in Scotch."

George Pratt said to Cabot, "Come on, Nick, have a little refreshment," and they followed the other two. Alex Drummond was left alone at the corner of Wolfe's desk; he jerked to join the procession, then jerked back. He looked at Wolfe with his bright little eyes, stepped closer to him, and made his voice low:

"Uh—Mr. Wolfe. I imagine your sources of information are pretty good."

Wolfe said without looking at him, "They are superlative."

"I imagine so. Gus Farrell hasn't really been up against it for more than a couple of months, but I notice you are aware of it. Uh—I wonder if you would be willing to enlighten me regarding another item on your list. Just curiosity."

"I haven't engaged to satisfy your curiosity."

"No. But I was wondering. Why have you got Gaines down for eight thousand and Burton for seven thousand and so on, and Ferd Bowen for only twelve hundred? He's something in Wall Street—I mean really something. Isn't he? The firm of Galbraith and Bowen . . ." Drummond made his voice a little lower. "Frankly, it's more than curiosity . . . he handles a few little investments for me . . ."

Wolfe looked at him and looked away again. I thought for a minute he wasn't going to reply at all, but he did, with his eyes shut. "Don't bother to disparage your investments. It can have no effect on the amount of your payment to me, for that has

already been calculated and recorded. As for your
question, my sources of information may be superlative, but they are not infallible. If Mr. Bowen ventures
to object that I have belittled him, I shall consider his
protest with an open mind."

"Of course," Drummond agreed. "But if you could
just tell me in confidence—"

"If you will excuse me." Wolfe opened his eyes, got
his chin up, and raised his voice a little. "Gentlemen.
Gentlemen? Could I have a word with you?"

They approached his desk, three or four from the
corner the bookshelves made, and the wet contingent
from the alcove table. Two or three still in chairs
stayed there. Drummond, his hide too thick to show
any red from Wolfe's sandpapering, trotted around to
the far side. Mike Ayers flopped into a chair again,
stretching out his legs; his mouth gaped wide in a
free-for-all yawn, then suddenly he clamped his lips
tight with a look of indignant and wary surprise. I had
a notion to go and move him off the rug, but decided he
was going to hold it. Wolfe was handing it to them in
his handsome manner:

"The hour is getting late, and I would not wish to
detain you beyond necessity. I take it that we are in
agreement—"

Arthur Kommers interrupted, "I ought to leave in
a minute to catch the midnight back to Philadelphia.
Do you want my initials on that thing?"

"Thank you, sir. Not at present. There is a phrase
to be deleted. I shall ask Mr. Cabot to prepare copies
in his office tomorrow morning and send them to me
for distribution." He sent a glance at the lawyer, and
Cabot nodded. "Thank you.—In that connection, Mr.
Farrell, I wish to make a proposal to you. You are
broke, but you have a fairly intelligent face. To be

broke is not a disgrace, it is only a catastrophe. You can help me. For instance, you can take, or send, copies of the memorandum to those members of the league not present this evening, and arrange for their co-operation. I will pay you twenty dollars a day. There will be other little jobs for you."

The architect was staring at him. "You're quite a guy, Mr. Wolfe. By God if you're not. But I'm not a detective."

"I shall keep my demands modest, and expect no intrepidity."

"All right." Farrell laughed. "I can use twenty dollars."

"Good. Report here tomorrow at eleven.—Now, Dr. Burton. Your lifelong acquaintance with Paul Chapin places you in a special position, for my purpose. Could you dine with me tomorrow evening?"

Without hesitation, Burton shook his head. "I'm sorry, I shall be engaged."

"Could you call on me after dinner? Forgive me for not asking permission to call on you instead. My disinclination to leave my home has a ponderable basis."

But Burton shook his head again. "I'm sorry, Mr. Wolfe, I can't come." He hesitated, and went on, "More frankly, I won't. It's softness in me. I'm not as soft about it as Andy Hibbard and Leo Elkus. I answered yes to the question you put this evening, though you made it as raw as possible. Of course you did that purposely. I answered yes, and I'll pay my share, but that's as far as I'll go. I will not confer on ways and means of exposing Paul Chapin's guilt and getting him convicted and electrocuted.—Oh, don't misunderstand me. I don't pretend to be standing on a principle, I'm perfectly aware it's only a temperamental prejudice. I wouldn't move a finger to protect Paul or save him from the consequences of his crimes. In fact, in so far as the thing may be considered a personal issue between him and myself, I am ready to defeat him by a violence equal to his own."

"You are ready?" Wolfe had opened his eyes on him. "You mean you are prepared?"

"Not specially." Burton looked irritated. "It is of no importance whatever. I always seem to talk too much when Paul Chapin is concerned; I wish to the Lord I'd never heard of him. As far as that goes, of course we all do. I only meant . . . well, for years I've kept an automatic pistol in the drawer of my study-table. One evening last week Paul came to see me. For years, of course, he was welcome at my house, though he seldom came. On this occasion, on account of recent events, I told the butler to keep him in the reception hall; and before I went to the reception hall I took the pistol from the drawer and stuck it in my pocket.— That was all I meant; I would be perfectly willing to use personal violence if the circumstances required it."

Wolfe sighed. "I regret your soft spot, Dr. Burton. But for that you might, for instance, tell us which evening Mr. Chapin went to see you and what it was he wanted."

"That wouldn't help you." Burton was brusque. "It was personal—that is, it was only neurotic nonsense."

"So, they say, was Napoleon's dream of empire. Very well, sir. By all means cling to the tattered shreds of humanity that are left you; there are enough of us in that respect quite unclothed. I must somehow manage my enterprise without stripping you. I would like as ask, gentlemen: which of you were most intimate with Mr. Hibbard?"

They looked at each other. George Pratt said, "We all saw Andy off and on." Julius Adler put in, "I would say that among us Roland Erskine was his closest friend. I would boast that I was next."

"Erskine the actor?" Wolfe glanced at the clock. "I was thinking he might join us after the theater, but scarcely at this hour. He is working, I believe."

Drummond said, "He's in *The Iron Heel*, he has the lead."

"Then he couldn't dine. Not at a civilized hour." Wolfe looked at Julius Adler. "Could you come here at two o'clock tomorrow afternoon and bring Erskine with you?"

"Perhaps." The lawyer looked annoyed. "I suppose I could manage it. Couldn't you come to my office?"

"I'm sorry, sir. Believe me, I am; but knowing my habits as I do, it seems extravagantly improbable. If you could arrange to bring Mr. Erskine—"

"All right. I'll see what I can do."

"Thank you.—You had better run, Mr. Kommers, or you'll miss your train. Another reason, and one of the best, for staying at home.—Gentlemen, so far as our business is concerned I need not further detain you. But in connection with my remark to Mr. Kommers it occurs to me that no publication either before or since the invention of printing, no theological treatise and no political or scientific creed, has ever been as narrowly dogmatic or as offensively arbitrary in its prejudices as a railway timetable. If any of you should care to remain half an hour or so to help me enlarge upon that . . ."

Byron the magazine editor, who had stuck in his shell all evening, suddenly woke up. He got up from his chair and slipped his head in between a couple of shoulders to see Wolfe. "You know, that idea could be developed into a first-rate little article. Six hundred to seven hundred words, about. The Tyranny of the Wheel, you could call it, with a colored margin of trains and airplanes and ocean liners at top speed—of course liners don't have wheels, but you could do something about that—if I could persuade you, Mr. Wolfe—"

"I'm afraid you could only bewilder me, Mr. Byron."

Cabot the lawyer smiled. "I never saw a man less likely to be bewildered, even by Eddie Byron. Good night, Mr. Wolfe." He picked up the memorandum and folded it and put it in his pocket. "I'll send you these in the morning."

They got moving. Pratt and Farrell went and got Mike Ayers to his feet and slapped him around a little. Byron started trying to persuade Wolfe again and was pulled off by Adler. Kommers had gone. The others drifted to the hall, and I went out and stood around while they got their hats and coats on. Bowen and Burton went off together, as they had come. I held the door for Pratt and Farrell to get Mike Ayers through; they were the last out.

After I had shut the door and bolted it I went to the kitchen for a pitcher of milk. Fritz was sitting there reading that newspaper printed in French, with his butler shoes still on, in spite of how he loved to put on his slippers after dinner on account of things left on his toes and feet by the war to remember it by. We said what we always said under those circumstances. He said, "I could bring your milk, Archie, if you would just tell me," and I said, "If I can drink it I can carry it."

In the office, Wolfe sat back with his eyes closed. I took the milk to my desk and poured a glass and sat down and sipped at it. The room was full of smoke and the smell of different drinks and chairs were scattered around and cigar and cigarette ashes were all over the rugs. It annoyed me, and I got up and opened a window. Wolfe said, "Close it," and I got up and closed it again. I poured another glass of milk.

I said, "This bird Chapin is a lunatic, and it's long past midnight. I'm damn good and sleepy."

Wolfe kept his eyes shut, and also ignored me in other ways. I said, "Do you realize we could earn all that jack and save a lot of trouble just by having a simple little accident happen to Paul Chapin? Depression prices on accidents like that run from fifty bucks up. It's smart to be thrifty."

Wolfe murmured, "Thank you, Archie. When I exhaust my own expedients I shall know where to turn.—A page in your notebook."

I opened a drawer and took out a book and pencil.

"Phone Mr. Cabot's office at nine o'clock and make sure that the memorandums will be here by eleven, ready for Mr. Farrell. Ask where the reports from the Bascom Agency are and arrange to get them. The men will be here at eight?"

"Yes, sir."

"Send one of them to get the reports. Put three of them on Paul Chapin, first thing. We want a complete record of his movements, and phone anything of significance."

"Durkin and Keems and Gore?"

"That is your affair. But Saul Panzer is to get his nose onto Andrew Hibbard's last discoverable footstep. Tell him to phone me at eleven-thirty."

"Yes, sir."

"Put Cather onto Chapin's past, outside the circle of our clients, especially the past two years. As complete as possible. He might succeed in striking an harmonious chord with Dora Chapin."

"Maybe I could do that myself. She's probably a lulu."

"I suspect that of being a vulgarization of the word *allure*. If she is alluring, resist the temptation for the moment. Your special province will be the deaths of

Harrison and Dreyer. First read the Bascom reports, then proceed. Wherever original investigation is indicated and seems still feasible after the lapse of time, undertake it. Use men as necessary, but avoid extravagance. Do not call upon any of our clients until Mr. Farrell has seen them.—That's all. It's late."

Wolfe opened his eyes, blinked, and closed them again. But I noticed that the tip of his finger was doing a little circle on the arm of the chair. I grinned:

"Maybe we've got this and that for tomorrow and next day, but maybe right now you're troubled by the same thing I am. Why is this Mr. Chapin giving hip room to a Civil War gat with the hammer nose filed off so that it's about as murderous as a beanshooter?"

"I'm not troubled, Archie." But his finger didn't stop. "I'm wondering whether another bottle of beer before going to bed would be judicious."

"You've had six since dinner."

"Seven. One upstairs."

"Then for God's sake call it a day. Speaking of Chapin's cannon, do you remember the lady dope-fiend who carried a box of pellets made out of flour in her sock, the usual cache, and when they took that and thought she was frisked, she still had the real thing in the hem of her skirt? Of course I don't mean that Chapin had another gun necessarily, I just mean, psychologically . . ."

"Good heavens." Wolfe pushed back his chair, not of course with violence, but with determination. "Archie. Understand this. As a man of action you are tolerable, you are even competent. But I will not for one moment put up with you as a psychologist. I am going to bed."

# Chapter 8

I had heard Wolfe, at various times, make quite a few cracks about murder. He had said once that no man could commit so complicated a deed as a premeditated murder and leave no opening. He had also said that the only way to commit a murder and remain safe from detection, despite any ingenuity in pursuit and trusting to no luck, was to do it impromptu; await your opportunity, keep your wits about you, and strike when the instant offered; and he added that the luxury of the impromptu murder could be afforded only by those who happened to be in no great hurry about it.

By Tuesday evening I was convinced of one thing about the death of Wm. R. Harrison, Federal judge from Indianapolis: that if it had been murder at all it had been impromptu. I would like to say another thing right here, that I know when I'm out of my class. I've got my limitations, and I never yet have tried to give them the ritz. Paul Chapin hadn't been in Nero Wolfe's office more than three minutes Monday night when I saw he was all Greek to me; if it was left to me to take him apart he was sitting pretty. When people begin to get deep and complicated they mix me up. But pictures never do. With pictures, no matter how many pieces they've got that don't seem to fit at first, I'm there forty ways from Sunday. I spent six hours Tuesday with the picture of Judge Harrison's death—reading the Bascom reports, talking with six people including thirty minutes on long distance with Fillmore Collard, and chewing it along with two meals—and I decided three things about it: first, that if it was murder it was impromptu; second, that if anybody killed him it was Paul Chapin; and third, that there was as much chance of proving it as there was of proving that honesty was the best policy.

It had happened nearly five months back, but the things that had happened since, starting with the typewritten poems they had got in the mail, had kept their memories active. Paul Chapin had driven up to Harvard with Leopold Elkus, the surgeon, who had gone because he had a son graduating. Judge Harrison had come on from Indianapolis for the same reason. Drummond had been there, Elkus told me, because each year the doubt whether he had really graduated from a big university became overwhelming and he went back every June to make sure. Elkus was very fond of Drummond, the way a taxi-driver is of a cop. Cabot and Sidney Lang had been in Boston on business, and Bowen had been a house-guest at the home of Theodore Gaines; presumably they were hatching some sort of a financial deal. Anyway, Fillmore Collard had got in touch with his old classmates and invited them for the week-end to his place near Marblehead. There had been quite a party, more than a dozen altogether.

Saturday evening after dinner they had strolled through the grounds, as darkness fell, to the edge of a hundred-foot cliff at the base of which the surf roared among jagged rocks. Four, among them Cabot and

Elkus, had stayed in the house playing bridge. Paul Chapin had hobbled along with the strollers. They had separated, some going to the stables with Collard to see a sick horse, some back to the house, one or two staying behind. It was an hour or so later that they missed Harrison, and not until midnight did they become really concerned. Daylight came before the tide was out enough for them to find his cut and bruised body at the foot of the cliff, wedged among the rocks.

A tragic accident and a ruined party. It had had no significance beyond that until the Wednesday following, when the typewritten poem came to each of them. It said a good deal for Paul Chapin's character and quality, the fact that none of them for a moment doubted the poem's implications. Cabot said that what closed their minds to any doubt was the similarity in the manner of Harrison's death to the accident Chapin had suffered from many years before. He had fallen from a height. They got together, and considered, and tried to remember. After the interval of four days there was a good deal of disagreement. A man named Meyer, who lived in Boston, had stated Saturday night that he had gone off leaving Harrison seated on the edge of the cliff and had jokingly warned him to be ready to pull his parachute cord, and that no one else had been around. Now they tried to remember about Chapin. Two were positive that he had limped along after the group strolling to the house, that he had come up to them on the veranda, and had entered with them. Bowen thought he remembered seeing him at the stables. Sidney Lang had seen him reading a book soon after the group returned, and was of the opinion that he had not stirred from his seat for an hour or more.

All the league was in on it now, for they had all got warnings. They got nowhere. Two or three were

inclined to laugh it off. Leopold Elkus thought Chapin
guiltless, even of the warnings, and advised looking
elsewhere for the culprit. Some, quite a few at first,
were in favor of turning it over to the police, but they
were talked down, chiefly by Hibbard and Burton and
Elkus. Collard and Gaines came down from Boston, and
they tried to reconstruct the evening and definitely
outline Chapin's movements, but failed through dis-
agreements. In the end they delegated Burton, Cabot
and Lang to call on Chapin.

Chapin had smiled at them. At their insistence he
described his Saturday evening movements, recollect-
ing them clearly and in detail; he had caught up with
them at the cliff and sat there on a bench, and had left
with the group that returned to the house; he had not
noticed Harrison sitting on the cliff's edge. At the
house, not being a card-player, he had got into a chair
with a book and had stayed there with it until aroused
by the hubbub over Harrison's absence—approaching
midnight. That was his smiling story. He had been not
angry, but delicately hurt, that his best friends could
think him capable of wishing injury to one of them,
knowing as they did that the only struggle in his
breast was between affection and gratitude, for the
lead. Smiling, but hurt. As for the warnings they had
received, that was another matter. Regarding that, he
said, his sorrow that they should suspect him not only
of violence but threats of additional violence, was lost
in his indignation that he should be accused of so
miserable a piece of versifying. He criticized it in
detail and with force. As a threat it might be thought
effective, he couldn't say as to that, but as poetry it
was rotten, and he had certainly never supposed that
his best friends could accuse him of such an offense.
But then, he had ended, he realized that he would

have to forgive them and he did so, fully and without reservation, since it was obvious that they were having quite a scare and so should not be held to account.

Who had sent the warnings, if he hadn't? He had no idea. Of course it could have been done by anyone knowing of that ancient accident who had also learned of this recent one. One guess was as good as another, unless they could uncover something to point their suspicion. The postmark might furnish a hint, or the envelopes and paper, or the typewriting itself. Maybe they had better see if they couldn't find the typewriter.

The committee of three had called on him at his apartment in Perry Street, and were sitting with him in the little room that he used for a study. As he had offered his helpful suggestion he had got up and limped over to his typewriter, patted it, and smiled at them:

"I'm sure that discreditable stuff wasn't written on this, unless one of you fellows sneaked in here and used it when I wasn't looking."

Nicholas Cabot had been tough enough to go over and stick in a sheet of paper and type a few lines on it, and put the sheet in his pocket and take it away with him, but a later examination had shown that Chapin was quite correct. The committee had made its report, and subsequent discussions had taken place, but weeks had gone by and the thing petered out. Most of them, becoming a little ashamed of themselves and convinced that someone had tried a practical joke, made a point of continuing their friendly relations with Chapin. So far as was known by the six men I talked to, it hadn't been mentioned to him again.

I reported all this, in brief outline, to Wolfe Tuesday evening. His comment was, "Then the death of this Judge Harrison, this man who in his conceit permitted himself the awful pretensions of a reader of chaos—whether designed by Providence or by Paul Chapin, his death was extempore. Let us forget it; it might clutter up our minds, but it cannot crowd oblivion. If Mr. Chapin had been content with that man's death and had restrained his impulse to rodomontade, he might have considered himself safely avenged—in that instance. But his vanity undid him; he wrote that threat and sent it broadcast. That was dangerous."

"How sure are you?"

"Sure—"

"That he sent the threat."

"Did I not say he did?"

"Yeah. Excuse me for living."

"I would not take that responsibility; I have all I can do to excuse myself.—But so much for Judge Harrison; whatever chaos he inhabits now, let us hope he contemplates it with a wiser modesty. I would tell you about Mr. Hibbard. That is, I would tell you nothing, for there is nothing to tell. His niece, Miss Evelyn Hibbard, called on me this morning."

"Oh, she did. I thought she was coming Wednesday."

"She anticipated it, having received a report of last evening's gathering."

"Did she spill anything new?"

"She could add nothing to what she told you Saturday evening. She has made another thorough search of the apartment, helped by her sister, and can find nothing whatever missing. Either Mr. Hibbard's absence was unforeseen by him, or he was a remarkably intelligent and strong-willed man. He was devoted to two pipes, which he smoked alternately. One of them is there in its usual place. He made no uncommon withdrawal from his bank, but he always carried a good deal of cash."

"Didn't I tell you about the pipe?"

"You may have. Saul Panzer, after a full day, had to offer one little morsel. A news vendor at One Hundred Sixteenth Street and Broadway, who has known Mr. Hibbard by sight for several years, saw him enter the subway between nine and ten o'clock last Tuesday evening."

"That was the only bite Saul got?"

Wolfe nodded, on his way slanting forward to reach the button on his desk. "The police had got that too, and no more, though it has been a full week since Mr. Hibbard disappeared. I telephoned Inspector Cramer this morning, and Mr. Morley at the District Attorney's office. As you know, they lend information only at usurious rates, but I gathered that they have exhausted even conjecture."

"Morley would deal you an extra card any time."

"Perhaps, but not when he has none to deal. Saul Panzer is following a suggestion I offered him, but its promise is negligible. There is no point in his attempting a solitary fishing expedition; if Mr. Chapin went for a walk with Mr. Hibbard and pushed him off a bridge into the East River, we cannot expect Saul to dive for the corpse. The routine facilities of the police and Bascom's men have covered, and are covering, possibilities of that nature. As for Mr. Chapin, it would be useless to question him. He has told both Bascom and the police that he spent last Tuesday evening in his apartment, and his wife sustains him. No one in the neighborhood remembers seeing him venture forth."

"You suggested something to Saul?"

"Merely to occupy him." Wolfe poured a glass of beer. "But on the most critical front, at the moment, we have met success. Mr. Farrell has gained the adherence of twenty individuals to the memorandum—all but Dr. Elkus in the city, and all but one without, over the telephone. Mr. Pitney Scott, the taxi-driver, is excluded from these statistics; there would be no profit in hounding him, but you might find occasion to give him a glance; he arouses my curiosity, faintly, in another direction. Copies of the memorandum have been distributed, for return. Mr. Farrell is also collecting the warnings, all copies except those in the possession of the police. It will be well to have—"

The telephone rang. I nearly knocked my glass of milk over getting it. I'm always like that when we're on a case, and I suppose I'll never get over it; if I had just landed ten famous murderers and had them salted down, and was at the moment engaged in trying to run down a guy who had put a slug in a subway turnstile, Fritz going to answer the doorbell would put a quiver in me.

I heard a few words, and nodded at Wolfe. "Here's Farrell now." Wolfe pulled his phone over, and I kept my receiver to my ear. They talked only a minute or two.

After we had hung up, I said, "What what? Farrell taking Mr. Somebody to lunch at the Harvard Club? You're spending money like a drunken sailor."

Wolfe rubbed his nose. "I am not spending it. Mr. Farrell is. Decency will of course require me to furnish it. I requested Mr. Farrell to arrange for an interview with Mr. Oglethorpe; I did not contemplate feeding him. It is now beyond remedy. Mr. Oglethorpe is a member of the firm which publishes Mr. Chapin's books, and Mr. Farrell is slightly acquainted with him."

I grinned. "Well, you're stuck. I suppose you want him to publish your essay on The Tyranny of the Wheel. How's it coming on?"

Wolfe ignored my wit. He said, "Upstairs this morning I spent twenty minutes considering where Paul Chapin might elect to type something which he would not wish to be traced to him. The suggestion in one of Bascom's reports, that Chapin has a duplicate set of type-bars for his machine which he substitutes on occasion, I regard as infantile. Not only would the changing of the bars be a difficult, laborious and uninspired proceeding; there is also the fact that the duplicate set would have to be concealed in some available spot, and that would be hazardous. No. Not that. Then there is the old trick of going to a typewriter agency and using one of their machines exposed for sale. But a visit from Paul Chapin, with his infirmity, would be remembered; also, that is excluded by the fact that all three of the warnings were executed on the same typewriter. I considered other possibilities, including some of those explored by Bascom, and one seemed to offer at least a faint promise. Mr. Chapin might call at the office of his publisher and, wishing to alter a manuscript, or even merely to write a letter, request the use of a typewriter. I am counting on Mr. Farrell to discover that; having discovered it, he may be able to get Mr. Oglethorpe's permission to take a sample of the work of the machine that Chapin used—or if that is not known, of each machine in their office."

I nodded. "That's not very dumb. I'm surprised that Farrell can still pay his dues at the Harvard Club."

"When a man of a certain type is forced into drastic financial retrenchment, he first deserts his family, then goes naked, and then gives up his club. Which reminds me, I gave Mr. Farrell twenty dollars this afternoon. Please record it. You may also note on your list those who have initialed the memorandum, and file the various copies. Also, note that we have an additional contributor, Miss Evelyn Hibbard. I arranged it with her this morning. The amount is three thousand dollars." He sighed. "I made a large reduction from the ten thousand she offered Saturday on account of the altered circumstances."

I had been waiting for that, or something like it. I made the Farrell entry in the cashbook, but didn't get out the list. I felt like clearing my throat, but I knew that wouldn't do, so I swallowed instead. I put the cashbook back and turned to Wolfe:

"You understand, sir, I wouldn't accuse you of trying to put anything over. I know you just forgot about it."

His eyes opened at me. "Archie. You are trying the cryptic approach again. To what this time?"

"No, sir. This is on the level. You just forgot that Miss Evelyn Hibbard is *my* client. I went to see her Saturday at your suggestion; you couldn't take her on because you had other plans in mind. Remember, sir? So of course any arrangement she might make in this connection could only be with my advice and consent."

Wolfe was keeping his eyes open. He murmured, "Preposterous. Puerile trickery. You would not attempt to maintain that position."

I sighed, as much like one of his sighs as I could make it. "I hate to, sir. I really do. But it's the only honest thing I can do, protect my client. Of course you understand the ethics of it, I don't have to explain—"

He cut me off. "No. I would suggest that you refrain from explaining. How much would you advise your client to pay?"

"One thousand bucks."

"Absurd. In view of her original offer—"

"All right. I won't haggle. I'll split the difference with you. Two thousand. I stick there. I'm glued."

Wolfe shut his eyes. "Done, confound you. Enter it.—Now take your notebook. Tomorrow morning . . ."

# Chapter 9

**W**ednesday morning pretty early I was sitting in the kitchen, with the *Times* propped up in front of me but not really seeing it because I was busy in my mind mapping out the day, getting on towards the bottom of my second cup of coffee, when Fritz returned from a trip to the front door to say that Fred Durkin wanted to see me. One thing I hate to be disturbed at is my last two healthy swallows of morning coffee, so I nodded and took my time. When I got to the office Fred was sitting there scowling at his hat on the floor, where it had landed when he had tried to toss it so it would hook on the back of my chair. He always missed. I picked it up and handed it to him and said:

"A dollar even you can't do it once out of ten tries."

He shook his big Irish bean. "No time. I'm a workingman. I was just waiting for you to pick your teeth. Can I see Wolfe?"

"You know damn well you can't. Up to eleven o'clock Mr. Nero Wolfe is a horticulturist."

"Uh-huh. This is special."

"Not special enough for that. Spill it to the Chief of Staff. Has the lop put dust in your eyes? Why aren't you on his tail?"

"I don't relieve Johnny until nine. I'll be there."
Durkin grabbed his hat by the brim, squinted for an
aim, tossed it at the back of my chair again, and
missed it by a mile. He grunted with disgust. "Listen
here, Archie. It's a washout."

"What's the matter with it?"

"Well, you put three of us on this to cover him
twenty-four hours a day. When Wolfe spends money
like that, that shows it's important. He really wants
this bird's program. Also, you told us to use taxis all
we needed to, and so on. Well, it's a washout. Chapin
lives in an apartment house at 203 Perry Street with
six floors and an elevator. He's on the fifth. The house
has a big court in the back, with a couple of trees and
some shrubs, and in the spring it's full of tulips. The
elevator boy told me three thousand tulips. But the
idea is that there's another house on the court, facing
on Eleventh Street, built by the same landlord, and so
what? Anybody that wants to can go out of the Perry
Street house the back way instead of the front. They
can cross the court and go through a passage and come
out on Eleventh Street. Of course they could get back
in the same way if they felt like it. So parked in a cigar
store the other side of Perry Street with my eye
fastened on 203, I feel about as useful as if I was
watching one of the tunnel exits at the Yankee Sta-
dium for a woman in a dark hat. Not that I've got any
kick coming, my only trouble is my honest streak. I
just wanted to see Wolfe and tell him what he's paying
me money for."

"You could have phoned him last night."

"I could not. I got lit last night. This is the first job
I've had in a month."

"Got any expense money left?"

"Enough for a couple of days. I've learned self-control."

"Okay." I picked his hat up and put it on my desk. "That's a nice picture you've got down there. It's no good. It looks to me like there's no way out of it but three more men for Eleventh Street. That would be buying it, six tails for one cripple and—"

"Wait a minute." Fred waved a hand at me. "That's not all of it. The other trouble is that the traffic cop at the corner is going to run us in. For blocking the street. There's too many of us, all after that cripple. There's a city feller there, I guess from the Homicide Squad, I don't recognize him, and a little guy with a brown cap and a pink necktie that must be one of Bascom's men. I don't recognize him either. But get this, for example. Yesterday afternoon a taxi drives up and stops in front of 203, and in a minute Chapin hobbles out of the building on his stick, and gets in the taxi. You should have seen the hustle around there. It was like Fifth Avenue in front of St. Patrick's at one o'clock Sunday, only Perry Street is narrow. There was another taxi coming along and I beat the town dick to it by a jump and he had to run half a block to find one. Bascom's pet got into one that apparently he had waiting. I had a notion to yell to Chapin to wait a minute till we got lined up, but it wasn't necessary. It was all right, his driver went slow and none of us lost him. He went to the Harvard Club and stayed there a couple of hours and then stopped off at 248 Madison Avenue and then went back home and we all followed him. Honest to God, Archie. Three of us, but I was in front."

"Yeah. It sounds swell."

"Sure it was. I kept looking around to see if they was all right. My idea was this, it came to me while I was riding along. Why couldn't we pal up? You get one more man and him and Bascom and the town dick could cover Eleventh Street and let us on Perry Street have a little peace. I suppose they're on twelve hours now, maybe they've got reliefs, I don't know. How's that for an idea?"

"Rotten." I got up and handed him his hat. "No good at all, Fred. Out. Wolfe's not using any second-hand tailing. I'll get three men from the Metropolitan and we'll cover Eleventh Street. It's a damn shame, because as I told you, Wolfe wants Chapin covered as tight as a drum. Get back on the job and don't lose him. It sounds sad, the way you describe that traffic jam, but do the best you can. I'll get in touch with Bascom and maybe he'll call his dog off, I didn't know he had any more money to spend. Run along now, I've got some errands you wouldn't understand."

"I'm not due till nine o'clock."

"Run along anyway.—Oh, all right. One shot, just one. A quarter to a dime."

He nodded, shifted in his seat to get good position, and let her go. It was a close call; the hat hung there on its edge for a tenth of a second, then toppled off. Durkin fished a dime out of his pocket and handed it to me, and beat it.

I thought at first I'd run up to Wolfe's room and get his okay on covering Eleventh Street, but it was only eight-twenty and it always made me half-sick to see him in bed with that black silk cover drinking chocolate, not to mention that he would be sure to raise hell, so I got the Metropolitan Agency on the telephone and gave them the dope. I only ordered six-dollar men because it was nothing but a check anyway; I couldn't see why Chapin should be trying to pull anything foxy like rear exits. Then I sat for a minute and wondered who was keeping Bascom on the job, and I thought I'd phone him on the chance of his spilling it, but nobody answered. All this had made me a little late on my own schedule, so I grabbed my hat and coat and went to the garage for the roadster.

I had collected a few facts about the Dreyer business in my wanderings the day before. Eugene Dreyer, art dealer, had been found dead, on the morning of Thursday, September 20, in the office of his gallery on Madison Avenue near Fifty-sixth Street. His body had been found by three cops, one a lieutenant, who had broken in the door on orders. He had been dead about twelve hours, and the cause had been nitroglycerin poisoning. After an investigation the police had pronounced it suicide, and the inquest had verified it. But on the Monday following, the second warnings arrived; everybody got one. We had several copies in Wolfe's office, and they read like this:

*Two.*
*Ye should have killed me.*
*Two;*
*And with no ready cliff, rocks waiting below*
*To rub the soul out; no ready waves*
*To lick it off and clean it of old crimes,*
*I let the snake and fox collaborate.*
*They found the deadly oil, sweet-burning, cunningly*
*Devised in tablets easily dissolved.*
*And I, their Master, I,*
*I found the time, the safe way to his throat,*
*And counted: two.*
*One, and two, and eighty long days between.*
*But wait in patience; I am unhurried but sure.*
*Three and four and five and six and seven. . . .*
*Ye should have killed me.*

Wolfe said it was better than the first one, because it was shorter and there were two good lines in it. I took his word for it.

Hell had popped right off. They forgot all about practical jokes and yelled to the cops and the D.A.'s office to come on back and nab him; suicide was out. When I got a description of the run-around that little poem had started, I was inclined to agree with Mike Ayers and cross out League of Atonement and make it the League of the White Feather. The only ones that hadn't seemed to develop an acute case of knee-tremor were Dr. Burton and Leopold Elkus the surgeon. Hibbard had been as much scared as anyone, more if anything, but had still been against the police. Apparently he had been ready to go to bed with the willies, but also ready for the sacrifice. Elkus, of course, had been in on it, but I'm coming to that.

My date with Elkus that Wednesday morning was for nine-thirty, but I made an early start because I wanted to stop off at Fifty-sixth Street for a look at the Dreyer gallery where it had happened. I got there before nine. It wasn't a gallery any more, but a bookstore. A middle-aged woman with a wart in front of her ear was nice to me and said of course I could look around, but there wasn't much to be made of it because everything had been changed. The little room on the right, where the conference had taken place on a Wednesday evening and the body had been found the following morning, was still an office, with a desk and a typewriter and so on, but a lot of shelves had been put in that were obviously new. I called the woman over and she came in the office. I pointed at a door in the back wall and said:

"I wonder if you could tell me. Is that the closet

where Mr. Eugene Dreyer kept the materials for mixing his drinks?"

She looked hazy. "Mr. Dreyer . . . oh . . . that's the man . . ."

"The man that committed suicide in this room, yes, ma'am. I suppose you wouldn't know."

"Well, really . . ." She seemed startled. "I hadn't realized it was right in this little room . . . of course I've heard about it . . ."

I said, "Thank you, ma'am," and went back to the street and got in the roadster. People who quit living a year ago Christmas and haven't found out about it yet give me a pain, and all I've got for them is politeness and damn little of that.

Leopold Elkus hadn't quit living, I discovered when I got to him in his private room, but he was a sad guy. He was medium-sized, with a big head and big hands, and strong black eyes that kept floating away from you, not sideways or up or down but back into his head. He invited me to sit down and said in a friendly soft voice:

"Understand, Mr. Goodwin, I am seeing you only as a courtesy to my friends who have requested it. I have explained to Mr. Farrell that I will not support the enterprise of your employer. Nor will I lend any assistance."

"Okay." I grinned at him. "I didn't come to pick a scrap, Dr. Elkus. I just want to ask some questions about September nineteenth, when Eugene Dreyer died. Questions of fact."

"I have already answered any question you could possibly put. To the police several times, and to that incredibly ignorant detective . . ."

"Right. So far we agree. Just as a matter of courtesy to your friends, there's no reason why you shouldn't answer them once more, is there? To converse with the cops and Del Bascom and then draw the line at Nero Wolfe and me . . . well, that would be like . . ."

He smiled a sad smile. "Swallow a camel and strain at a gnat?" God that guy was sad.

"Yeah, I guess so. Only if you saw Nero Wolfe you wouldn't call him a gnat.—It's like this, Dr. Elkus. I know you won't lend a hand to get the goods on Paul Chapin. But in this Dreyer business you're my only source of firsthand information and so I had to get at you. I understand the other man, the art expert, has gone back to Italy."

He nodded. "Mr. Santini sailed some time ago."

"Then there's only you. There's no sense in my trying to ask you a lot of trick questions. Why don't you just tell me about it?"

He smiled sad again. "I presume you know that two or three of my friends suspect me of lying to shield Paul Chapin?"

"Yeah. Are you?"

"No. I would neither shield him nor injure him, beyond the truth.—Here is the story, Mr. Goodwin. You know, of course, that Eugene Dreyer was an old friend of mine, a classmate in college. He was pretty successful with his art gallery before the depression. I bought things from him occasionally. I have never been under the necessity of pursuing success, since I inherited wealth. My reputation as a surgeon is a by-product of my conviction that there is something wrong with all human beings, beneath the surface. By chance I have a sure and skillful hand."

I looked at his big hands folded on his lap, and nodded at his black eyes floating back into his head. He went on:

"Six years ago I gave Eugene Dreyer a tentative order for three Mantegnas—two small ones and a larger one. The price was one hundred and sixty thousand dollars. The paintings were in France. Paul Chapin happened to be in Europe at that time, and I wrote to ask him to look at them. After I received his report I ordered them. You know, I suppose, that for ten years Paul Chapin tried to be a painter. His work showed great sensitiveness, but his line was erratic and he had no feeling for form. It was interesting, but not good. I am told that he is finding himself in literature—I do not read novels.

"The paintings arrived at a time when I was overworked and had no leisure for a proper examination. I accepted them and paid for them. I was never happy with them; the friendly overtures which I made to those pictures from time to time, and there were many, were always repelled by them with an indelicacy, a faint harshness, which embarrassed and irritated me. I did not at first suspect them of imposture, I simply could not get along with them. But a few remarks made by expert persons finally aroused my suspicion. In September, nearly two months ago now, Enrico Santini, who knows Mantegna as I know the human viscera, visited this country. I asked him to look at my Mantegnas, and he pronounced them frauds. He further said that he knew their source, a certain talented swindler in Paris, and that it was not possible that any reputable dealer had handled them in good faith.

"I imagine it was the uncomfortable five years those pictures had given me, more than anything else, that caused me to act as I did with Dreyer. Ordinarily I am far too weak in my convictions to display any sort of ruthlessness, but on this occasion there was no hesitation in me at all. I told Eugene that I wished to return the pictures and receive my money back without delay. He said he had not the money, and I knew he hadn't, since I had within a year lent him considerable sums to tide him over. Nevertheless, I insisted that he must find it or suffer the consequences. I suspect that in the end I would have weakened as usual, and agreed to any sort of compromise, but unfortunately it is a trick of my temperament now and then to show the greatest determination of purpose when the resolution is most likely to falter. Unfortunately also, Mr. Santini was about to return to Italy. Eugene demanded an interview with him; that, of course, was a bluff.

"It was arranged that I should call at five o'clock Wednesday afternoon with Mr. Santini and Paul Chapin. Paul was included on account of the inspection he had given the pictures in France. I surmised that Eugene had arranged for his support, but as it turned out that was probably incorrect. We arrived. Eugene's suavity—"

I interrupted, "Just a minute, doctor. Did Paul Chapin get to the gallery before you did?"

"No. We arrived together. I was in my car, and called for him at the Harvard Club."

"Had he been there earlier that afternoon?"

"My dear sir." Elkus looked sad at me.

"Okay. You wouldn't know that. Anyway, the girl there says he hadn't."

"So I understand. I was saying, Eugene's suavity was painful, because of the nervousness it failed to hide. He mixed highballs for us, jerkily, not himself. I was embarrassed and therefore brusque. I asked Mr. Santini to make a statement and he did so; he had written it down. Eugene contradicted him. They argued; Eugene was somewhat excited but Mr. Santini remained cool. Finally Eugene called on Paul for his views, in obvious expectation of support. Paul smiled around at us, the smile that comes from his Malpighian capsules, and made a calm brief statement. He said that three months after his inspection of the pictures—a month after they had been shipped to New York—he had learned definitely that they had been painted by Vasseult, the greatest forger of the century, in 1924. That was the man Mr. Santini had named. Paul also said that he had kept silent about it because his affection for both Eugene and myself was so great that he could take no step that would injure either of us.

"I feared Eugene would collapse. He was plainly as astonished as he was hurt. I was of course embarrassed into silence. I do not know whether Eugene had in desperation swindled me, or whether he had himself been imposed upon. Mr. Santini rose. I did likewise, and we left. Paul Chapin came with us. It was noon the following day when I learned that Eugene had committed suicide by drinking nitroglycerin—apparently within a few minutes, at the most an hour, after we left. I learned it when the police arrived at my office to question me."

I nodded, and sat and looked at him a while. Then all of a sudden I straightened up in my chair and shot at him, "What made *you* think it was suicide?"

"Now, Mr. Goodwin." He smiled at me, sadder than ever. "Are all detectives alike? You know perfectly well why I thought it was suicide. The police thought so, and the circumstances indicated it."

"My mistake." I grinned. "I said no trick questions, didn't I? If you're willing to grant that a detective can have an idea in his mind, you know what mine is. Did Paul Chapin have any opportunity to put the nitroglycerin tablets in Dreyer's highball? That ignorant detective, and all the bright cops, seem to have the impression that you think he didn't."

Dr. Elkus nodded. "I labored to produce that impression. You know of course that Mr. Santini agreed with me. We are perfectly certain that Paul had no such opportunity. He went to the gallery with us, and we all entered the office together. Paul sat at my left, near the door, at least six feet away from Eugene. He touched no glass but his own. Eugene prepared the drinks and handed them around; we had only one. Departing, Paul preceded me through the door. Mr. Santini was ahead."

"Yeah. That's on the record. But in a fracas like that, so much excitement, there must have been some moving around, getting up and sitting down, walking back and forth . . ."

"Not at all. We were not excited, except possibly Eugene. He was the only one who left his chair."

"Did he change his coat, or put it on or anything, after you got there?"

"No. He wore a morning coat. He did not remove it."

"The bottle with what was left of the nitroglycerin was found in the pocket of his coat."

"So I understand."

I sat back and looked at him again. I would have given the roadster and a couple of extra tires to know if he was lying. He was as much out of my class as Paul Chapin was. There was no way for me to get at him that I could see. I said:

"Will you have lunch with Mr. Nero Wolfe tomorrow at one o'clock?"

"I'm sorry. I shall be engaged."

"Friday?"

He shook his head. "No. Not any day. You are in error regarding me, Mr. Goodwin. I am not a knot to be untangled or a nut to be cracked. Give up your hope that I am deceptive, as most men are; I am really as simple as I seem. Give up your hope, too, to demonstrate the guilt of Paul Chapin in the death of Eugene Dreyer. It is not feasible. I know it isn't; I was there."

"Could you make it Saturday?"

He shook his head and smiled, still sad. I got up from my chair and picked up my hat, and thanked him. But before I started for the door I said:

"By the way, you know that second warning Paul Chapin wrote—anyhow, somebody else wrote it. Is nitroglycerin oily and sweet-burning?"

"I am a surgeon, not a pharmacologist."

"Well, try one guess."

He smiled. "Nitroglycerin is unquestionably oily. It is said to have a sweet, burning taste. I have never tried it."

I thanked him again and went out, and down to the street, and got in the roadster and stepped on the starter. As I rolled off downtown I was thinking that Dr. Leopold Elkus was exactly the kind of man that so often makes life a damn nuisance. I never yet have had any serious trouble with an out-and-out liar, but a man that might be telling the truth is an unqualified pain in the rumpus. And what with the Harrison line-up, and now this, I suspected that I began to perceive dimly that the memorandum Wolfe had concocted was going to turn out to be just a sheet of paper to be used for any purpose that might occur to you, unless we managed somehow to bust Elkus's story wide open.

I had intended to stop off again at Fifty-sixth Street for another look at the Dreyer gallery, but after listening to Elkus I decided it would be a waste of time, considering how the place had been done over. I kept on downtown, headed for home. The best bet I could think of at the moment was a try at Santini. The police had only questioned him once on account of his sailing for Italy that Thursday night, and of course the warnings hadn't been received yet and they had no particular suspicions. Wolfe had connections in several cities in Europe, and there was a smart guy in Rome who had turned in a good one on the Whittemore bonds. We could cable him and set him on Santini and maybe get a wedge started. I'd have to persuade Wolfe it was worth about ninety-nine dollars in transatlantic words.

It was a quarter to eleven when I got there. In the office the phone was ringing, so I went on in with my hat and coat on. I knew Wolfe would eventually answer it from upstairs, but I thought I might as well get it. It was Saul Panzer. I asked him what he wanted and he said he wanted to report. I asked him what, and he said, nothing, just report. I was sore at everything anyway, so I got sarcastic. I said if he couldn't find Hibbard alive or dead, maybe he could rig up a dummy that would do. I said I had just got a smack in the eye on another angle of the case, and if he was no better than I was he'd better come on down to the office with a pinochle deck, and I hung up on him, which alone is enough to aggravate a nun.

It took me five minutes to dig the address of the Roman snoop out of the file. Wolfe came down on time, right at eleven. He said good morning, sniffed at the air, and got seated at his desk. I was impatient, but I knew I'd have to wait until he had glanced through the mail, fixed the orchids in the vase, tried his pen to see if it was working, and rung for beer. After that was all over he murmured at me:

"Had you thought of venturing forth?"

"I tiptoed out at eight-thirty and just got back. Saul just telephoned. Another nickel wasted. If you want to get puckered up, here's a nice pickle to chew on."

Fritz brought his beer and he poured a glass. I told him all about Elkus, every word of it, even that nitroglycerin was oily and sweet-burning. I thought if I gave him all of Elkus I could, he might get a notion. Then I handed him my own notion about the Roman. Right away, as I expected, he got restive. He blinked, and drank some more beer. He said:

"You can cable four thousand miles for a fact or an object, but not for a subtlety like this. As a last resort you or Saul Panzer might go to call on Mr. Santini in Florence; it might in the end be worth that chance."

I tried an argument on him, for I couldn't see any other move. I didn't seem to be making much impression, but I kept on anyway, getting stubborn, because my main point was that it was only a matter of a hundred bucks. I was forgetting that I still had to tell him about the three Metropolitan men I had ordered for Eleventh Street. I got good and stubborn.

I was stopped in the middle of my stride by the sound of Fritz going down the hall to answer the doorbell. I didn't try to pick it up again, but waited to see who it was.

Fritz stepped in and closed the door behind him. He said there was a lady there to see Wolfe. No card.

"Her name?"

Fritz shook his head; usually he was more correct. He looked uncertain.

"Show her in, Fritz."

I felt uncertain too, when I saw her. They don't come any uglier. She came in and stood looking straight at Wolfe, as if she was deciding how to do him over. At that she wasn't really ugly, I mean she wasn't hideous. Wolfe said it right the next day: it was more subtle than plain ugliness, to look at her made you despair of ever seeing a pretty woman again. Her eyes were rather small, gray, and looked as if they'd never move again when they got fixed. She had on a dark gray woolen coat with a hat to match, and an enormous gray furpiece was fastened around her neck. She sat down on the chair I pulled up for her and said in a strong voice:

"I had a hard time getting here. I think I'm going to faint."

Wolfe said, "I hope not. A little brandy."

"No." She gave a little gasp. "No, thank you." She put her hand up to the furpiece and seemed to be trying to reach under it, behind. "I've been wounded. Back there. I think you'd better look at it."

Wolfe shot me a glance, and I went. She got the thing unfastened in front, and I pulled it around and lifted it off. I gave a gasp then myself. Not that I haven't seen a little blood here and there, but not often that much, and it was so unexpected. The back of the furpiece, inside, was soaked. The collar of her coat was soaked too. She was a sight. It was still oozing out, plenty, from gashes across the back of her neck; I couldn't tell how deep they were. She moved and it came out in a little spurt. I dropped the furpiece on the floor and said to her:

"For God's sake keep still. Don't move your head." I looked at Wolfe and said, "Somebody's tried to cut her head off. I can't tell how far they got."

She spoke to Wolfe: "My husband wanted to kill me."

Wolfe's eyes on her were half closed. "Then you're Dora Ritter."

She shook her head, and the blood started, and I told her to quit. She said, "I am Dora Chapin. I have been married three years."

# Chapter 10

Wolfe didn't say anything. I stood behind her and waited, ready to catch her if she started to faint and fall forward, because I didn't know how much it might open up. Wolfe hadn't moved. He sat looking at her with his eyes nearly shut and his lips pushing out, and in, and out and in again.

She said, "He got into a fit. One of his cold fits."

Wolfe said politely, "I didn't know Mr. Chapin had fits. Feel her pulse."

I reached out and got her wrist and placed my fingers. While I was counting she began to talk:

"He doesn't have fits exactly. It's a look that comes into his eyes. I am always afraid of him, but when I see that look I am terrified. He has never done anything to me before. This morning when I saw him look like that I said something I shouldn't have said . . . look here."

She jerked her hand away from me to use it for getting into her handbag, a big leather one. Out of it she pulled something wrapped in newspaper. She unrolled the newspaper and held up a kitchen knife that had blood on it still wet and red.

"He had this and I didn't know it. He must have

been getting ready for me when he was out in the kitchen."

I took the knife from her and laid it on the desk, on top of the newspaper, and said to Wolfe:

"Her pulse is on a little sprint, but it's okay."

Wolfe put his hands on the arms of the chair, braced himself, and got to his feet. He said, "Please do not move, Mrs. Chapin," and walked around behind her and took a look at her neck. He bent down with his eyes close to her; I hadn't seen him so active for a month or more. Peering at the gashes, he said, "Please tilt your head forward, just a little, and back again." She did so, and the blood came out again; in one spot it nearly spurted at him.

Wolfe straightened up. "Indeed. Get a doctor, Archie."

She started to turn around at him, and I stopped her. She protested, "I don't need a doctor. I got here, I can get home again. I just wanted to show you, and ask you—"

"Yes, madam. For the moment my judgment must prevail . . . if you please . . ."

I was at the phone, giving a number. Someone answered, and I asked for Dr. Vollmer. She said he wasn't there, he was just leaving, if it was urgent she might be able to catch him out in front. I started to ask her to do that, then it occurred to me that I might be quicker at it myself, and I hung up and took it on the trot. Fritz was in the hall dusting and I told him to stick around. As I hopped down the stoop I noticed a taxi there at the curb: our visitor's of course. A couple of hundred feet east Dr. Vollmer's blue coupé was standing, and he was just getting in. I sprinted for him and let out a yell. He heard me and by the time I got there he was out on the sidewalk again. I told him about the casualty that had dropped in on us, and he got his bag out of the coupé and came along.

In my business I've seen it proved a hundred times that one thing you never want to leave in the bureau drawer is your curiosity. As we turned in at our stoop I took another look at the taxi standing there. I nearly lost my aplomb for a second when the driver looked straight at me and tipped me a wink.

I went on in with the doc. Fritz was in the hall and told me that Wolfe had gone to the kitchen and would return when the doctor had finished. I told Fritz for God's sake not to let him get started eating, and took Vollmer into the office. Dora Chapin was still in her chair. I introduced them, and he put his bag on the desk and went to take a look at her. He poked around a little and said she might have to be sewed up and he could tell better if he could wash her off. I showed him where the bathroom was and said there were bandages and iodine and so on, and then said:

"I'll call Fritz in to help you. I've got an errand out front. If you need me I'll be there."

He said all right, and I went to the hall and explained Fritz's new duties to him. Then I went out to the sidewalk.

The taxi was still there. The driver wasn't winking any more; he just looked at me. I said, Greetings."

He said, "I very seldom talk that much."

"How much?"

"Enough to say greetings. Any form of salutation."

"I don't blame you. May I glance inside?"

I pulled the door open and stuck my head in far enough to get a good look at the framed card fastened to the panel, showing the driver's picture and name. That was only a wild guess, but I thought if it happened to hit it would save time. I backed out again and put a foot up on the running-board and grinned at him:

"I understand you're a good engineer."

He looked funny for a second, then he laughed. "That was when I was in burlesque. Now I'm just doing straight parts. Damn it, quit grinning at me. I've got a headache."

I rubbed the grin off. "Why did you wink at me as I went by?"

"Why shouldn't I?"

"I don't know. Hell, don't try to be quaint. I just asked you a friendly question. What was the idea of the wink?"

He shook his head. "I'm a character. Didn't I say I had a headache? Let's see if we can't think of some place for you to go to. Is your name Nero Wolfe?"

"No. But yours is Pitney Scott. I've got you down on a list I made up for a contribution of five dollars."

"I heard about that list."

"Yes? Who from?"

"Oh . . . people. You can cross me off. Last week I made eighteen dollars and twenty cents."

"You know what it's for."

He nodded. "I know that too. You want to save my life. Listen, my dear fellow. To charge five dollars for saving my life would be outrageous. Believe me, exorbitant. Rank profiteering." He laughed. "These things have a bottom, I suppose. There is no such thing as a minus quantity except in mathematics. You have no idea what a feeling of solidity and assurance that reflection can gave a man. Have you got a drink in your house?"

"How about two dollars? Make it two."

"You're still way high."

"One even buck."

"Still you flatter me. Listen." Though it was cold for November, with a raw wind, he had no gloves and his hands were red and rough. He got his stiff fingers into a pocket, came out with some chicken feed, picked a nickel and pushed it at me. "I'll pay up now and get it off my mind. Now that I don't owe you anything, have you got a drink?"

"What flavor do you want?"

"I . . . if it were good rye . . ." He leaned toward me and a look came into his eyes. Then he jerked back. His voice got harsh and not friendly at all. "Can't you take a joke? I don't drink when I'm driving. Is that woman hurt much?"

"I don't think so, her head's still on. The doctor'll fix her up. Do you take her places often? Or her husband?"

He was still harsh. "I take her when she calls me, her husband too. I'm a taxi-driver. Mr. Paul Chapin. They give me their trade when they can, for old time's sake. Once or twice they've let me get drunk at their place, Paul likes to see me drunk and he furnishes the liquor." He laughed, and the harshness went. "You know, you take this situation in all its aspects, and you couldn't ask for anything more hilarious. I'm going to have to stay sober so as not to miss any of it. I winked at you because you're in on it now, and you're going to be just as funny as all the rest."

"That won't worry me any, I always have been pretty ludicrous. Does Chapin get drunk with you?"

"He doesn't drink. He says it makes his leg hurt."

"Did you know that there's a reward of five thousand dollars for finding Andrew Hibbard?"

"No."

"Alive or dead."

It looked to me as if, just stabbing around, I had hit something. His face had changed; he looked surprised, as if confronted with an idea that hadn't occurred to him. He said, "Well, he's a valuable man, that's not too much to offer for him. At that, Andy's not a bad guy. Who offered the reward?"

"His niece. It'll be in the papers tomorrow."

"Good for her. God bless her." He laughed. "It is an incontrovertible fact that five thousand dollars is a hell of a lot of more money than a nickel. How do you account for that? I want a cigarette."

I got a packet out and lit us both up. His fingers weren't steady at all, and I began to feel sorry for him. So I said, "Just figure it out. Hibbard's home is up at University Heights. If you drove downtown somewhere—say around the Perry Street neighborhood, I don't know just where—and from there to One Hundred Sixteenth Street, ordinarily what would you get for it? Let's see—two, eight miles—that'd be around a dollar and a half. But if going uptown you happened to have your old classmate Andrew Hibbard with you—or just his corpse, maybe even only a piece of it, say, his head and a couple of arms—instead of a dollar-fifty you'd get five grand. As you see, it all depends on your cargo." So as not to take my eyes off him, I blew cigarette smoke out of the corner of my mouth. Of course, riding a guy who needed a drink bad and wouldn't take it was like knocking a cripple's crutch from under him, but I didn't need to remind myself that all's fair in love and business. Basic truths like that are either born right in a man or they're not.

At that he had enough grip on himself to keep his mouth shut. He looked at his fingers trembling holding the cigarette, so long that I finally looked at them too. Finally he let his hand fall to his knee, and looked at me and began to laugh. He demanded, "Didn't I say you were going to be funny?" His voice went harsh again. "Listen, you. Beat it. Come on, now, beat it. Go back in the house or you'll catch cold."

I said, "All right, how about that drink?"

But he was through. I prodded at him a little, but he had gone completely dumb and unfriendly. I thought of bringing out some rye and letting him smell it, but decided that would just screw him down tighter. I said to myself, anon, and passed him up.

Before going in the house I went around back of the taxi and got the license number.

I went to the kitchen. Wolfe was still there, in the wooden chair with arms where he always sat to direct Fritz and to eat when he was on a relapse.

I said, "Pitney Scott's out front. The taxi-driver. He brought her. He paid me a nickel for his share, and he says that's all it's worth. He knows something about Andrew Hibbard."

"What?"

"You mean what does he know? Search me. I told him about the reward Miss Hibbard, my client, is offering, and he looked like get thee behind me, Satan. He's shy, he wants to be coaxed. My surmise is that he may not exactly know where Hibbard or his remains has been cached, but he thinks he might guess. He's got about seven months to go to pink snakes and crocodiles. I tried to get him to come in for a drink, but he fought that off too. He won't come in. He may not be workable at the present moment, but I was thinking of suggesting that you go out and look at him."

"Out?" Wolfe raised his head at me. "Out and down the stoop?"

"Yeah, just on the sidewalk, you wouldn't have to step off the curb. He's right there."

Wolfe shut his eyes. "I don't know, Archie. I don't know why you persist in trying to badger me into frantic sorties. Dismiss the notion entirely. It is not feasible. You say he actually gave you a nickel?"

"Yes, and where's it going to get you to act eccentric with a dipsomaniac taxi-driver even if he did go to Harvard? Honest to God, sir, sometimes you run it in the ground."

"That will do. Definitely. Go and see if Mrs. Chapin has been made presentable."

I went. I found that Dr. Vollmer had finished with his patient in the bathroom and had her back in a chair in the office, with her neck bandaged so that she had to hold it stiff whether she wanted to or not. He was giving her instructions how to conduct herself, and Fritz was taking away basins and rags and things. I waited till the doc was through, then took him to the kitchen. Wolfe opened his eyes at him. Vollmer said:

"Quite a novel method of attack, Mr. Wolfe. Quite original, hacking at her from behind like that. He got into one of the posterior externals; I had to shave off some of her hair."

"He?"

The doctor nodded. "She explained that her husband, to whom she has been married three years, did the carving. With a little caution, which I urged upon her, she should be all right in a few days. I took fourteen stitches. Her husband must be a remarkable and unconventional man. She is remarkable too, in her way: the Spartan type. She didn't even clench her hands while I was sewing her; the fingers were positively relaxed."

"Indeed. You will want her name and address for your record."

"I have it, thanks. She wrote it down for me."

"Thank you, doctor."

Vollmer went. Wolfe got to his feet, pulled at his vest in one of his vain attempts to cover the strip of canary yellow shirt which encircled his magnificent middle, and preceded me to the office. I stopped to ask Fritz to clean off the inside of the furpiece as well as he could.

By the time I joined them Wolfe was back in his chair and she was sitting facing him. He was saying to her:

"I am glad it was no worse, Mrs. Chapin. The doctor has told you, you must be careful not to jerk the stitches loose for a few days. By the way, his fee—did you pay him?"

"Yes. Five dollars."

"Good. Reasonable, I should say. Mr. Goodwin tells me your cab is waiting. Tell the driver to go slowly; jolting is always abominable, in your present condition even dangerous. We need not detain you longer."

She had her eyes fixed on him again. Getting washed off and wrapped up hadn't made her any handsomer. She took a breath through her nose and let it out again so you could hear it.

She said, finally, "Don't you want me to tell you about it? I want to tell you what he did."

Wolfe's head went left and right. "It isn't necessary, Mrs. Chapin. You should go home and rest. I undertake to notify the police of the affair; I can understand your reluctant delicacy; after all, one's own husband to whom one has been married three years . . . I'll attend to that for you."

"I don't want the police." That woman could certainly pin her eyes. "Do you think I want my husband arrested? With his standing and position . . . all the publicity . . . do you think I want that? That's why I came to you . . . to tell you about it."

"But, Mrs. Chapin." Wolfe wiggled a finger at her. "You see, you came to the wrong place. Unfortunately for you, you came to the one man in New York, the

one man in the world, who would at once understand
what really happened at your home this morning. It
was unavoidable, I suppose, since it was precisely that
man, myself, whom you wished to delude. The devil of
it is; from your standpoint, that I have a deep aversion
to being deluded. Let's just call it quits. You really do
need rest and quiet, after your nervous tension and
your loss of blood. Go on home."

Of course, as had happened a few times before, I
had missed the boat; I was swimming along behind
trying to keep up. For a minute I thought she was
going to get up and go. She started to. Then she was
back again, looking at him. She said:

"I'm an educated woman, Mr. Wolfe. I've been in service, and I'm not ashamed of that, but I'm educated.
You're trying to talk so I won't understand you, but I do."

"Good. Then there is no need—"

She snapped at him suddenly and violently.
"You're a fat fool!"

Wolfe shook his head. "Fat visibly, though I prefer
Gargantuan. A fool only in the broader sense, as a
common characteristic of the race. It was not magnanimous of you, Mrs. Chapin, to blurt my corpulence at
me, since I had spoken of your fatuity only in general
terms and had refrained from demonstrating it. I'll do
that now." He moved a finger to indicate the knife
which still lay on the newspaper on the desk. "Archie,
will you please clean that homely weapon."

I didn't know, I thought maybe he was bluffing her.
I picked up the knife and stood there with it, looking
from her to him. "Wash off the evidence?"

"If you please."

I took the knife to the bathroom and turned on the
faucet, rubbed the blood off with a piece of gauze, and
wiped it. Through the open door I couldn't hear any
talking. I went back.

"Now," Wolfe instructed me, "grip the handle firmly in your right hand. Come towards the desk, so Mrs. Chapin can see you better; turn your back. So. Elevate your arm and pull the knife across your neck; kindly be sure to use the back of the blade, not to carry the demonstration too far. You noted the length and the position of the cuts on Mrs. Chapin? Duplicate them on yourself.—Yes. Yes, quite good. A little higher for that one. Another, somewhat lower. Confound you, be careful. That will do.—You see, Mrs. Chapin? He did it quite neatly, don't you think? I am not insulting your intelligence by hinting that you expected us to think the wounds could not have been self-inflicted in the position you chose for them. More likely, you selected it purely as a matter of precaution, knowing that the front, the neighborhood of the anterior jugular . . ."

He stopped, because he had no one to talk to except me. When I turned around after my demonstration she was already getting up from her chair, holding her head stiff and a clamp on her mouth. Without a word, without bothering to make any passes at him with her little gray glass eyes, she just got up and went; and he paid no attention, he went on with his speech until she had opened the office door and was through it. I noticed she was leaving her knife, but thought we might as well have it in our collection of odds and ends. Then all of a sudden I jumped for the hall.

"Hey, lady, wait a minute! Your fur!"

I got it from Fritz and caught her at the front door and put it around her. Pitney Scott got out of his cab and came over to help her down the stoop, and I went back in.

Wolfe was glancing through a letter from Hoehn and Company that had come in the morning mail. When he had finished he put it under a paperweight—a piece of petrified wood that had once been used to bust a guy's skull—and said:

"The things a woman will think of are beyond belief. I knew a woman once in Hungary whose husband had frequent headaches. It was her custom to relieve them by the devoted application of cold compresses. It occurred to her one day to stir into the water with which she wetted the compresses a large quantity of penetrating poison which she had herself distilled from an herb. The result was gratifying to her. The man on whom she tried the experiment was myself. The woman—"

He was just trying to keep me from annoying him about business. I cut in. "Yeah. I know. The woman was a witch you had caught riding around in the curl of a pig's tail. In spite of all that, it's time for me to brush up a little on this case we've got. You can give me a shove by explaining in long words how you knew Dora Chapin did her own manicuring."

Wolfe shook his head. "That would not be a shove, Archie; it would be a laborious and sustained propulsion. I shall not undertake it. I remind you merely: I have read all of Paul Chapin's novels. In two of them Dora Chapin is a character. He of course appears in all. The woman who married Dr. Burton, Paul Chapin's unattainable, seems to be in four out of five; I cannot discover her in the latest one. Read the books, and I shall be more inclined to discuss the conclusions they have led me to. But even then, of course, I would not attempt to place plain to your eyes the sights my own have discerned. God made you and me, in certain respects, quite unequal, and it would be futile to try any interference with His arrangements."

Fritz came to the door and said lunch was ready.

# Chapter 11

Sometimes I thought it was a wonder Wolfe and I got on together at all. The differences between us, some of them, showed up plainer at the table than anywhere else. He was a taster and I was a swallower. Not that I didn't know good from bad; after seven years of education from Fritz's cooking I could even tell, usually, superlative from excellent. But the fact remained that what chiefly attracted Wolfe about food in his pharynx was the affair it was having with his taste buds, whereas with me the important point was that it was bound for my belly. To avoid any misunderstanding, I should add that Wolfe was never disconcerted by the problem of what to do with it when he was through tasting it. He could put it away. I have seen him, during a relapse, dispose completely of a ten-pound goose between eight o'clock and midnight, while I was in a corner with ham sandwiches and milk hoping he would choke. At those times he always ate in the kitchen.

It was the same in business, when we were on a case. A thousand times I've wanted to kick him, watching him progress leisurely to the elevator on his way to monkey with the plants upstairs, or read a book tasting each phrase, or discuss with Fritz the best storage place for dry herbs, when I was running around barking my head off and expecting him to tell me where the right hole was. I admit he was a great man. When he called himself a genius he had a right to mean it whether he did or not. I admit that he never lost us a bet by his piddling around. But since I'm only human, I couldn't keep myself from wanting to kick him just because he was a genius. I came awful close to it sometimes, when he said things like, "Patience, Archie; if you eat the apple before it's ripe your only reward is a bellyache."

Well, this Wednesday afternoon, after lunch, I was sore. He went indifferent on me; he even went contrary. He wouldn't cable the guy in Rome to get into converse with Santini; he said it was futile and expected me to take his word for it. He wouldn't help me concoct a loop we could use to drag Leopold Elkus into the office; according to him, that was futile too. He kept trying to read in a book while I was after him. He said there were only two men in the case whom he felt any inclination to talk to: Andrew Hibbard and Paul Chapin; and he wasn't ready yet for Chapin and he didn't know where Hibbard was, or whether he was alive or dead. I knew Saul Panzer was going to the morgue every morning and afternoon to look over the stiffs, but I didn't know what else he was doing. I also knew that Wolfe had talked with Inspector Cramer on the phone that morning, but that was nothing to get excited about; Cramer had shot his bolt a week ago at Paul Chapin and all that was keeping him awake was the routine of breathing.

Saul had phoned around noon and Wolfe had talked to him from the kitchen while I was out with Pitney Scott. A little after two Fred Durkin phoned. He said that Paul Chapin had been to the barber and a drugstore, and that the town dick and the guy in the brown cap and pink necktie were still on deck, and he was thinking of forming a club. Wolfe went on reading. About a quarter to three Orrie Cather called up and said he had got hold of something he wanted to show us and could he come on up with it; he was at the Fourteenth Street subway station. I told him yes. Then, just before Orrie arrived, a call came that made Wolfe put down his book. It was from Farrell the architect, and Wolfe talked to him. He said he had had a nice lunch with Mr. Oglethrope, and he had had a tough argument but had finally persuaded him. He was phoning from the publisher's office. Paul Chapin had on several occasions found it convenient to make use of a typewriter there, but there was some disagreement as to which one or ones, so he was going to take samples from a dozen of them. Wolfe told him to be sure that the factory number of the machine appeared on each sample.

I said, after we hung up, "Okay, that one's turning brown. But even if you hang the warnings on him, you've just started. The Harrison demise is out, you'll never tie that up. And I'm telling you that the same goes for Dreyer, unless you get Leopold Elkus down here and perform an operation on him. You've got to find a hole in his story and open it up, or we've licked. What the hell are we waiting for? It's all right for you, you can keep occupied, you've got a book to read— what the devil is it, anyhow?"

I got up to take a squint at it, a dark gray cover stamped in gold: *The Chasm of the Mind*, by Andrew Hibbard. I grunted. "Huh, maybe that's where he is, maybe he fell in."

"Long ago." Wolfe sighed. "Poor Hibbard, he

couldn't exclude his poetic tendencies even from his title. Any more than Chapin can exclude his savagery from his plots."

I dropped back into my chair. "Listen, boss." There was nothing he hated more than being called boss. "I'm beginning to catch on. I suppose Dr. Burton has written books too, and Byron, and maybe Dreyer, and of course Mike Ayers. I'll take the roadster and drive out to Pike County for a little duck hunting, and when you get caught up with your reading just wire me care of Cleve Sturgis and I'll mosey back and we'll tackle this murder case. And take it easy, take your time; if you eat the apple after it is too ripe you'll get ptomaine poisoning or erysipelas or something, at least I hope to God you will." I was glaring at him, with no result except to make me feel like a sap, because he merely shut his eyes so as not to see me. I got up from my chair and glared anyhow. "Damn it, all I'm asking for is just a little halfway co-operation! One little lousy cablegram to that Roman wop! I ask you, should I have to work myself into turmoil—now what the hell do *you* want?"

The last was for Fritz. He had appeared in the door. He was frowning, because he never liked to hear me yell at Wolfe, and I frowned back at him. Then I saw someone standing behind him and I let the frown go and said:

"Come on in, Orrie. What's the loot?" I turned to Wolfe and smoothed my voice out and opened up the respect: "He phoned a while ago and said he had got hold of something he wanted to show us. I told you, but you were engrossed in your book."

Orrie Cather had a bundle about the size of a small suitcase, wrapped in brown paper and tied with heavy string.

I said, "I hope it's books."

He shook his head. "It's not heavy enough for books." He set it down on the desk and looked around, and I shoved up a chair for him.

"What is it?"

"Search me. I brought it here to open it. It may be just a lot of nothing at all, but I had a hunch."

I got out my pocketknife, but Wolfe shook his head. He said to Orrie, "Go on."

Orrie grinned. "Well, as I say, it may be a lot of nothing at all, but I'd got so fed up after a day and a half finding out nothing whatever about that cripple except where he buys his groceries and how often he gets his shoes shined, that when something came along that looked like it might be a little break I guess I got excited. I've just been following your instructions—"

"Yes. Let us arrive at the package."

"Right. This morning I dropped in at the Greenwich Bookshop. I got talking with the guy, and I said I supposed he had Paul Chapin's books in his circulating library, and he said sure, and I said I might like to get one, and he handed me one and I looked it over—"

I couldn't help it; I snorted and stopped him. Orrie looked surprised, and Wolfe moved his eyes at me. I sat down.

"Then I said Chapin must be an interesting guy and had he ever seen him, and he said sure, Chapin lived in that neighborhood and bought books there and came in pretty often. He showed me a photograph of Chapin, autographed, on the wall with some others. A woman with black hair was sitting at a desk in the back of the shop, and she called out to the guy that that reminded her, Mr. Chapin never had come for the package he had left there a couple of weeks ago, and with Christmas stuff coming in the package was in the way, and hadn't he better phone Mr. Chapin to send for it. The guy said maybe he would a little later, it was too early for Chapin to be up. I deposited my dollar and got my book and went down the street to a lunch counter and sat down with a cup of coffee to think."

Wolfe nodded sympathetically. Orrie looked at him suspiciously and went on: "I figured it this way. Two weeks ago was about the time the cops were warming up on Chapin. What if he got hep they would pull a search on him, and he had something in his place he didn't want them to see? There were a lot of things he might do, and one of them was to wrap it up and take it to his friends at the bookshop and ask them to keep it for him. It would be about as safe there as anywhere. Anyhow, I decided I liked Chapin well enough to do him the favor of taking a look at his package for him. I got an envelope and a piece of paper from a stationery store and went to a real estate office and bummed the use of a typewriter. I wrote a nice note to the bookshop. I had used my eyes on Chapin's signature on the autographed photograph and got it pretty good. But then I was afraid to send it, so soon after I'd been there and heard the package mentioned. I decided to wait until afternoon. So a while ago I got a boy and sent him to the bookshop with the note, and I'm telling you it worked and they gave it to him." Orrie nodded his head at the desk. "That's it."

I got up and got out my knife again. Wolfe said, "No. Untie it." I started to work at the knot, which was a lulu. Orrie wiped his hand across his forehead and said, "By God, if it's just fishing tackle or electric light bulbs or something, you'll have to give me a drink. This is the only break I've had."

I said, "Among other things, there's just a chance we might find a set of typewriter type-bars. Or love-letters from Mrs. Loring A. Burton, huh?— There's nothing doing on this knot. He didn't want me to untie it, or anybody else. Even if I do get it, I could never tie it back again the same." I picked up my knife again, and looked at Wolfe. He nodded, and I slashed the string.

I took off the paper, several thicknesses. It wasn't a suitcase, but it was leather, and not imitation. It was an oblong box made of light tan calfskin, a special job, beautifully made, with fine lines of tooling around the edges. It was a swell number. Orrie grunted:

"Jesus, I may be in for grand larceny."

Wolfe said, "Go on," but he didn't get up so he could see.

"I can't. It's locked."

"Well."

I went to the safe and got a couple of my bunches of keys, and went back and started trying. The lock was nothing remarkable; in a few minutes I had it. I laid the keys down and lifted the lid. Orrie stood up and looked in with me. We didn't say anything for a second, then we looked at each other. I never saw him look so disgusted.

Wolfe said, "Empty?"

"No, sir. We'll have to give Orrie a drink. It's not his, it's hers. I mean Dora Chapin's. It's her hand-and-foot box. Gloves and stockings and maybe other dainties."

"Indeed." To my surprise Wolfe showed interest. His lips pushed out and in. He was even going to get up. He did so, and I shoved the box across.

"Indeed. I suspect—yes, it must be. Archie. Kindly remove them and spread them on the desk.

Here, I'll help. No, Orrie, not unless you wash your hands first.—Ha, more intimate still! But mostly stockings and gloves.—Less roughly, Archie, out of respect for the dignity the race aspires to; what we are displaying on this desk-top is the soul of a man. Qualities may be deduced—for instance, do you notice that the gloves, varying as they do in color and material, are all of a size? Among twenty pairs or more, not one exception? Could you ask more of loyalty and fidelity? *O, that I were a glove upon that hand* . . . But with Romeo it was only rhetoric; for Paul Chapin the glove is the true treasure, with no hope beyond either of sweet or of bitter.— Again, let us not be carried away; it is a distortion to regard this or that aspect of a phenomenon to the exclusion of others. In the present case, for example, we cannot afford to forget that these articles are of expensive materials and workmanship, that they must have cost Dr. Burton something around three hundred dollars and that he therefore had a right to expect that they should get more wear. Some of them, indeed, are practically new. To strike a balance—"

Orrie was sitting down again staring at him. It was I who cut him off: "Where does Burton come in? I'm asking that in English."

Wolfe fingered the gloves some more, and held up a stocking to look through it at the light. To see him handling female hosiery as if he understood it gave me a new insight into the extent of his pretensions. He held up another one, dropped it back gently to the table, and took a handkerchief from his pocket and wiped his hands, carefully, fingers and palms. Then he sat down.

"Read your Anglo-Saxon poets, Archie. Romeo himself was English, in spite of geography. I am not trying to befuddle you, I am adhering to a tradition."

"All right. Where does Burton come in?"

"I have said, he paid the bills. He paid for these articles, his wife wore them, Dora Ritter, later Chapin, appropriated them, and Paul Chapin treasured them."

"How do you know all that?"

"How could I help but know it? Here are these worn things, kept by Paul Chapin in an elegant and locked receptacle, and in a time of crisis removed by him to a place of safety against unfriendly curiosity. You saw the size of Dora Chapin's hands, you see these gloves; they are not hers. You heard Monday evening the story of Chapin's infatuation with the woman who is now Dr. Burton's wife. You know that for years Dora Chapin, then Ritter, was Mrs. Burton's personal maid, and that she still attends her, to do something to her hair, at least once a week. Knowing these things, it would seem to me that only the most desperate stupidity—"

"Yes, sir. Okay on the stupidity. But why does it have to be that Dora took them? Maybe Chapin took them himself."

"He might. But most unlikely. Surely he did not strip the stockings from her legs, and I doubt if he was familiar with her dressing-room. The faithful Dora—"

"Faithful to who? Mrs. Burton, swiping her duds?"

"But, Archie. Having seen Dora, can you not grant her rarity? Anyone can be faithful to an employer; millions are, daily, constantly; it is one of the dullest and most vulgar of loyalties. We need not, even if we could, conjecture as to the first stirring of sympathy in Dora's breast on her perceiving the bitter torment in the romantic cripple's heart. I would like to believe it was a decent and honorable bargain, that Paul Chapin offered to pay her money, and did pay her, to get him a pair of gloves his unattainable beloved had worn, but I fear not. Having seen Dora, I suspect that it was the service of romance to which she dedicated herself; and that has been her faithfulness. It may even account for her continuing to visit Mrs. Burton when her marriage freed her from the practical necessity; doubtless, fresh specimens are added from time to time. What a stroke of luck for Chapin! The beloved odor, the intimate textile from the skin of his adored, is delivered to him as it may be required; more, the fingers which an hour ago played in his lady's hair are now passing him his dinner coffee. He enjoys, daily, all the more delicate associations with the person of his passion, and escapes entirely the enforced and common-place contacts which usually render the delights of dubious profit. So much for the advantage, the peculiar thirst called emotional, of the individual; it is true that the race of man cannot be continued without it. But the biological problem is another matter."

Orrie Cather said, "I knew a guy in the army that used to take out a girl's handkerchief and kiss it before he went to sleep. One day a couple of us sneaked it out of his shirt and put something on it, and you should have heard him when he stuck his snout against it that night. He burned it up. Later he laid and cried, he was like that."

I said, "It took brains to think up one as good as that." Wolfe looked at Orrie, shut his eyes for a few seconds, and opened them again. He said:

"There are no ubiquitous handkerchiefs in this collection. Mr. Chapin is an epicure.—Archie. Repack the box, with feeling, lock it, wrap it up, and find a place for it in the cabinet.—Orrie, you may resume; you know your instructions. You have not brought us the solution of our case, but you have lifted the curtain to another room of the edifice we are exploring. Telephone at five after six as usual."

Orrie went down the hall whistling.

# Chapter 12

I had a nice piece of leather of my own, not as big as Paul Chapin's treasure box, but fancier. Sitting at my desk around five o'clock that Wednesday afternoon, killing time waiting for a visitor who had phoned, I took it out of my inside breast pocket and looked at it; I had only had it a couple of weeks. It was brown, ostrich-skin, and was tooled in gold all over the outside. On one side the tooling was fine lines about half an inch apart, with flowers stemming out from them; the flowers were orchids; the workmanship was so good that you could tell Wolfe had given the guy a Cattleya to work from. The other side was covered with Colt automatics, fifty-two perfect little gold pistols all aiming at the center. Inside was stamped in gold: *A. G. from N. W.* Wolfe had given it to me on October 23rd, at the dinner-table, and I didn't even know he knew when my birthday was. I carried my police and fire cards in it, and my operator's license. I might have traded it for New York City if you had thrown in a couple of good suburbs.

When Fritz came and said Inspector Cramer was there I put it back in my pocket.

I let Cramer get eased into a chair and then I went

upstairs to the plant-rooms. Wolfe was at the potting-bench with Horstmann, spreading out some osmundine and leaning over to smell it; a dozen or so pots of Odontoglossums, overgrown, were at his elbow. I waited until he looked around, and I felt my throat drying up.

"Well?"

I swallowed. "Cramer's downstairs. The rugged Inspector."

"What of it? You heard me speaking to him on the telephone."

"Look here," I said, "I want this distinctly understood. I came up here only for one reason, because I thought maybe you had changed your mind and would like to see him. Yes or no will do it. If you give me a bawling out it will be nothing but pure childishness. You know what I think."

Wolfe opened his eyes a little wider, winked the left one at me, twice, and turned to face the potting-bench again. All I could see was his broad back that might have been something in a Macy Thanksgiving Day parade. He said to Horstmann:

"This will do. Get the charcoal. No sphagnum, I think."

I went back down to the office and told Cramer, "Mr. Wolfe can't come down. He's too infirm."

The Inspector laughed. "I didn't expect him to. I've known Nero Wolfe longer than you have, sonny. You don't suppose I thought I was going to tear any secrets out of him? Anything he would tell me he has already told you. Can I light a pipe?"

"Shoot. Wolfe hates it. To hell with him."

"What's this, you staging on me?" Cramer packed his pipe, held a match to it, and puffed. "You don't . . . need to. Did Wolfe tell you what . . . I told him on the phone?"

"I heard it." I patted my notebook. "I've got it down."

"The hell you have. Okay. I don't want George Pratt riding me, I'm too old to enjoy it. What went on here night before last?"

I grinned. "Just what Wolfe told you. That's all. He closed a little contract."

"Is it true that he nicked Pratt for four thousand dollars?"

"He didn't nick anybody. He offered something for sale, and they gave him the order."

"Yeah." He puffed. "You know Pratt? Pratt thinks that it's funny that he has to shell out to a private dick when the city maintains such a magnificent force of brave and intelligent men to cope with such problems. He said cope. I was there. He was talking to the Deputy Commissioner."

"Indeed." I bit my lip. I always felt like a sap when I caught myself imitating Wolfe. "Maybe he was referring to the Department of Health. That never occurred to me before, a cop coping."

Cramer grunted. He sat back and looked at the vase of orchids, and pulled at his pipe. Pretty soon he said:

"I had a funny experience this afternoon. A woman called up downtown and said she wanted Nero Wolfe arrested because he had tried to cut her throat. They put her onto me because they knew I had Wolfe in mind about this case. I said I'd send a man up to get the details and she gave me her name and address. You could have flipped me cold with a rubber band when I heard it."

I said, "That's a hot one. I wonder who it could have been."

"Sure you do. I'll bet you're puzzled. Then a couple of hours later a guy came to see me. By invitation. He was a taxi-driver. He said that no matter how much diversion it offered he didn't care to take the rap for perjury, and that he saw blood on her when she got in his cab on Perry Street. That was one of the things I was wanting to mention to Wolfe on the phone, but the picture in my mind's eye of him slicing a lady's gullet was so damn remarkable that I didn't get it out." He puffed at his pipe, lit a match, and got it going again. He went on, more forceful and rugged. "Look here, Goodwin. What the hell's the idea? I've tried that Chapin woman three times, and I couldn't get her to break down enough to tell me what her name was. She put on the clamp and left it. Wolfe gets in the case late Monday night, and here already, Wednesday morning, she's chasing up to his office to show him her operation. What the hell is it about him that gets them coming like that?"

I grinned. "It's his sympathetic nature, inspector."

"Yeah. Who carved her neck?"

"Search me. She told you, Wolfe. Pull him in and give him the works."

"Was it Chapin?"

I shook my head. "If I know that secret, it's buried here." I tapped my chest.

"Much obliged. Now listen to me. I'm being serious. Am I on the level?"

"Absolutely.

"I am?"

"You know damn well you are."

"Okay. Then I'm telling you, I didn't come here to lift the silver. I've been after Chapin more than six weeks, ever since Dreyer was croaked, and what I've got on him is exactly nothing. Maybe he killed Harrison, and I'm damn sure he killed Dreyer, and it looks like he got Hibbard, and he's got me feeling like a Staten Island flatfoot. He's as slick as a wet pavement. Right in a courtroom he confesses he committed murder, and the judge fines him fifty bucks for contempt of court! Later I find that he mentioned it beforehand to his publisher, as a publicity stunt! Covered everywhere. Is he slick?"

I nodded. "He's slick."

"Yes. Well, I've tried this and that. For one thing, I've got it figured that his wife hates him and she's afraid of him, and probably she knows enough about it to fill out a hand for us, if we could get her to spill it. So when I heard that she had dashed up here to see Wolfe, I naturally surmised that he had learned things. And I want to say this. You don't need to tell me a damn thing if you don't want to. I'm not trying to horn in. But whatever you got out of that Chapin woman, maybe you can make better use of it if you see whether it fits a few pieces I've got hold of, and you're welcome—"

"But, inspector. Wait a minute. If you think she came here friendly, to dump the can, how do you account for her calling up to get Wolfe arrested?"

"Now, sonny." Cramer's sharp eyes twinkled at me. "Didn't I say I've known Nero Wolfe longer than you have? If he wanted me to think she hadn't got confidential with him, that would be about exactly what he would tell her to do."

I laughed. While I was laughing it occurred to me that it wouldn't do any particular harm if Cramer continued to nurse that notion, so I laughed some more. I said, "He might, he sure might, but he didn't.

Why she phoned you to arrest him—wait till I get a chance to tell Wolfe about it—why she did that, she's psychopathic. So's her husband. They're both psychopathic. That's Park Avenue for batty."

Cramer nodded. "I've heard the word. We've got a department—oh, well . . ."

"And you're damn sure he killed Dreyer."

He nodded again. "I think Dreyer was murdered by Paul Chapin and Leopold Elkus."

"You don't say!" I looked at him. "That might turn out to be right. Elkus, huh?"

"Yeah. You and Wolfe won't talk. Do you want me to talk?"

"I'd love it."

He filled his pipe again. "You know about the Dreyer thing. Do you know who bought the nitroglycerin tablets? Dreyer did. Sure. A week before he died, the day after Elkus phoned him that the pictures were phony and he wanted his money back. Maybe he had ideas about suicide and maybe he didn't; I think he didn't; there's several things people take nitroglycerin for in small doses."

He took a drag at the pipe, pulled it in until I expected to see it squirt out at his belly-button, and went on leaving it to find its way by instinct. "Now, how did Chapin get the tablets out of the bottle that day? Easy. He didn't. Dreyer had had them for a week, and Chapin was in and out of the gallery pretty often. He had been there a couple of hours Monday afternoon, probably for a talk about Elkus's pictures. He could have got them then and saved them for an opening. The opening came Wednesday afternoon.— Wait a minute. I know what Elkus says. That Thursday morning a detective questioned Santini too, the Italian expert, and it checked, but of course at that

time it looked like nothing but routine. Since then I've
sent a request to Italy, and they found Santini in
Florence and had a good long talk with him. He says it
was like he told the detective in the first place, but
he forgot to mention that after they all left the office
Elkus went back for something and was in the office
alone for maybe half a minute. What if Dreyer's glass
was then maybe half full, and Elkus, having got the
tablets from Chapin, fixed it up for him?"

"What for? Just for a prank?"

"I'm not saying what for. That's one thing we're
working on now. For instance, what if the pictures
Dreyer sold Elkus were the real thing—it was six
years ago—and Elkus put them away and substituted
phonies for them, and then demanded his money back?
We're looking into that. The minute I get any evidence
what for, I'll arrange for some free board and room for
Elkus *and* Chapin."

"You haven't got any yet."

"No."

I grinned. "Anyway, you're working in a lot of nice
complications. I'll have to tell Wolfe about it; I hope to
God it don't bore him. Why don't you just decide to
believe it was suicide after all, and let it go at that?"

"Nothing doing. Especially since Hibbard disappeared. And even if I wanted to, George Pratt and
that bunch wouldn't let me. They got those warnings.
I don't blame them. Those things sound like business
to me, even if they are dolled up. I suppose you've
read them."

I nodded. He stuck his paw in his breast pocket
and pulled out some papers and began looking through
them. He said, "I'm a damn fool. I carry copies of them
around with me, because I can't get rid of a hunch that
there's a clue in them somewhere, some kind of a clue,

if I could find it. Listen to this one, the one he sent last Friday, three days after Hibbard disappeared:

> *One. Two. Three.*
> *Ye cannot see what I see:*
> *His bloody head, his misery, his eyes*
> *Dead but for terror and the wretched hope*
> *That this last blow, this finis, will not fall.*
>
> *One. Two. Three.*
> *Ye cannot hear what I hear:*
> *His moan for pity, now his desperate breath*
> *To suck the air in through the bubbling blood.*
>
> *And I hear, too, in me the happy rhythm,*
> *The happy boastful strutting of my soul.*
> *Yes! Hear! It boasts:*
> *One. Two. Three.*
> *Ye should have killed me.*

"I ask you, does that sound like business?" Cramer folded it up again. "Did you ever see a guy that had been beaten around the head enough so that things were busted inside? Did you ever notice one? All right, get this: *to suck the air in through the bubbling blood*. Does that describe it? I'll say it does. The man that wrote that was looking at it, I'm telling you he was looking right at it. That's why, as far as Andrew Hibbard is concerned, all I'm interested in is stiffs. Chapin got Hibbard as sure as hell, and the only question is where did he put the leavings. Also, he got Dreyer, only with that one Elkus helped him."

The Inspector stopped for a couple of pulls at his pipe. When that had been attended to he screwed his nose up at me and demanded, "Why, do *you* think it was suicide?"

"Hell no. I think Chapin killed him. And maybe Harrison, and maybe Hibbard. I'm just waiting to see you and Nero Wolfe and the Epworth League prove it on him. Also I'm annoyed about Elkus. If you get Elkus wrong you may gum it."

"Uh-huh." Cramer screwed his nose again. "You don't like me after Elkus? I wonder if Nero Wolfe will like it. I hope not to gum it, I really do. I suppose you know Elkus has got a shadow on Paul Chapin? What's he suspicious about?"

I lifted my brows a little, and hoped that was all I did. "No. I didn't know that."

"The hell you didn't."

"No. Of course you have one, and we have . . ." I remembered that I never had got hold of Del Bascom to ask him about the dick in the brown cap and pink necktie. "I thought that runt keeping the boys company down there was one of Bascom's experts."

"Sure you did. You didn't know Bascom's been off the case since yesterday morning. Try having a talk with the runt. I did, last night, for two hours. He says he's got a goddam legal right to keep his goddam mouth shut. That's the way he talks, he's genteel. Finally I just shooed him away, and I'm going to find out who he's reporting to."

"I thought you said, Elkus."

"That's my idea. Who else could it be? Do you know?"

I shook my head. "Hope to die."

"All right, if you do don't tell me, I want to guess. Of course you realize that I'm not exactly a boob. If you don't, Nero Wolfe does. I arrested a man once and he turned out to be guilty, that's why I was made an

inspector. I know Wolfe expects to open up this Mr.
Chapin and get well paid for it, and therefore if I
expected him to pass me any cards out of his hand I
*would* be a boob. But I'll be frank with you, in the past
six weeks I've made so many grabs at this cripple
without getting anything that I don't like him at all
and in fact I'd like to rip out his guts. Also, they're
giving me such a riding that I'm beginning to get
saddle-sores. I would like to know two things. First,
how far has Wolfe got?—Sure, I know he's a genius.
Okay. But has he got enough of it to stop that cripple?"

I said, and I meant it, "He's got enough to stop any
guy that ever started."

"When? I won't lose any sleep if he nicks Pratt for
four grand. Can you say when, and can I help?"

I shook my head. "No twice. But he'll do it."

"All right. I'll go on poking around myself. The
other thing, you might tell me this, and I swear to God
you won't regret it. When Dora Chapin was here this
morning did she tell Wolfe she saw nitroglycerin
tablets in her husband's pocket any time between
September eleventh and September nineteenth?"

I grinned at him. "There are two ways I could
answer that, inspector. One way would be if she had
said it, in which case I would try to answer it so you
couldn't tell whether she had or not. The other way is
the one you're hearing: she wasn't asked about it, and
she said nothing about it. She just came here to get
her throat cut."

"Uh-huh." Cramer got up from his chair. "And
Wolfe started working on her from behind. He would.
He's the damnedest guy at getting in the back
door . . . well. So-long. I'll say much obliged some
other day. Give Wolfe a Bronx cheer for me, and tell
him that as far as I'm concerned he can have the

money *and* the applause of the citizens in this Chapin case, and the sooner the better. I'd like to get my mind on something else."

"I'll tell him. Like to have a glass of beer?"

He said no, and went. Since he was an inspector, I went to the hall and helped him on with his coat and opened the door for him. At the curb was a police car, one of the big Cadillacs, with a chauffeur. Now, I thought, that's what I call being a detective.

I went back to the office. It looked dismal and gloomy; it was nearly six o'clock and the dark had come over half an hour ago and I had only turned on one light. Wolfe was still upstairs monkeying with the plants; he wasn't due down for seven minutes. I didn't feel like sitting watching him drink beer, and had no reason to expect anything more pertinent out of him, and I decided to go out and find a stone somewhere and turn it up to see what was under it. I opened a couple of windows to let Cramer's pipe-smoke out, got my Colt from the drawer and put it in my pocket from force of habit, went to the hall for my hat and coat, and beat it.

# Chapter 13

I didn't know Perry Street much, and was surprised when I walked up in front of number 203, across the street, having left the roadster half a block away. It was quite a joint, stucco to look like Spanish, with black iron entrance lamps and no fire escapes. On both sides were old brick houses. A few cars were parked along the block, and a couple of taxis. On my side of the street was a string of dingy stores: stationery, laundry, delicatessen, cigar store and so on. I moved along and looked in. At the delicatessen I stopped and went inside. There were two or three customers, and Fred Durkin was leaning against the end of the counter with a cheese sandwich and a bottle of beer. I turned around and went out, and walked back down to where the roadster was and got inside. In a couple of minutes Fred came along and climbed in beside me. He was still chewing and working his tongue in the corners. He asked me what was up. I said, nothing, I had just come down to gossip. I asked him:

"Where's the other club members?"

He grinned. "Oh, they're around. The city feller is probably in the laundry, I think he likes the smell. I suppose Pinkie is down at the next corner, in the

Coffee Pot. He usually deserts his post around this time to put on the nose bag."

"You call him Pinkie?"

"Oh, I can call him anything. That's for his necktie. What do you want me to call him?"

I looked at him. "You've had one or ten drinks. What's the big idea?"

"I swear to God I haven't, Archie. I'm just glad to see you. It's lonesome as hell around here."

"You chinned any with this Pinkie?"

"No. He's reticent. He hides somewhere and thinks."

"Okay. Go on back to your pickle emporium. If you see any kids scratching their initials on my car, pat 'em on the head."

Fred climbed out and went. In a minute I got out too, and walked down to the next corner, where if you was blind the smell would have told you Coffee Pot. I went in. There were three little tables along the wall, and half a dozen customers at the counter. Pinkie was there all right, along at one of the little tables, working on a bowl of soup, trying to get the spoon out of his mouth. He had his brown cap on, over one ear. I went over alongside his table and said to him, keeping my voice low:

"Oh, here you are."

He looked up. I said, "The boss wants to see you right away. I'll sit on the lid here a while. Make it snappy."

He stared at me a couple of seconds, and then squeaked so that I nearly jumped. "You're a goddam filthy liar."

The little runt! I could have reached down and jerked his gold teeth out. I slid the other chair back with my toe and sat down and put my elbows on the table and looked at him. "I said, the boss wants to see you."

"Oh, yeah?" He sneered at me with his mouth open, showing his gilded incisors. "You wouldn't string a guy, would you, mister? By God, I'll tell the goddam world you wouldn't. Who was I talking to a while ago on the goddam telephone?"

I grinned. "That was me. Listen here a minute. I can see you're tough. Do you want a good job?"

"Yeah. That's why I've got one. If you'd just move your goddam carcass away from my table . . ."

"All right, I will. Go on and eat your soup, and don't try to scare me with your bad manners. I might decide to remove your right ear and put it where the left one is, and hang the left one on your belt for a spare. Go on and eat."

He dropped his spoon in the soup-bowl and wiped his mouth with the back of his hand. "What the hell do you want, anyway?"

"Well," I said, "I was having tea with my friend, Inspector Cramer, this afternoon, and he was telling me how much he enjoyed his talk with you last night, and I thought I'd like to meet you. That's one story. Then another story might be that a certain guy whose name I needn't mention has got the idea that you're selling him out, and I'm supposed to find out, and I thought the quickest way was to ask you. How many people are you working for?"

"Of all the goddam curiosity!" He sucked something from between his teeth with his tongue. "Last night the goddam inspector, and now you. Hell, my soup's getting cold."

He got up from his chair and picked up the bowl and carried it ten feet to the table at the end. Then he came back for the bread and butter and glass of water and took them. I waited till he was through moving, then I got up and went to the end table and sat down across from him. I was sore because my nifty opening had gone wild. The counterman and the customers were watching us, but only to pass the time. I reached in my pocket and got out my roll and peeled off a pair of twenties.

"Look here," I said, "I could spot you in a day or two, but it would cost both money and time, and I'd just as soon you'd get it. Here's forty bucks. Half now if you tell me who's paying you, and the other half as soon as I check it. I'll find out, anyhow, this'll just save time."

I'll be damned if he didn't get up and pick up his soup again and start back for the first table. A couple of the customers began to laugh, and the counterman called out, "Hey, let the guy eat his soup, maybe he just don't like you." I felt myself getting sore enough to push in somebody's nose, but I knew there was no profit in that, so I swallowed it and put on a grin. I picked up the runt's bread and butter and water and took it down and set it in front of him. Then I went and tossed a dime on the counter and said, "Give him some hot soup and put poison in it." Then I left.

I walked the block back to the roadster, not in a hurry. Fred Durkin was in the cigar store as I passed by. I had a notion to see him and tell him to keep an eye on his friend Pinkie and maybe catch him on a phone call or something, but knowing how his mind worked I thought it would be better to let it stay on his main job. I got in the roadster and headed uptown.

I couldn't figure the runt at all. Was it possible that a dick that looked like that was as honest as that? Who was paying him enough to make him look at forty dollars like it was soap wrappers? Who was so partic-

ular about its not being known that he was having
Paul Chapin tailed? The inspector's idea didn't seem to
me to make sense, even if Leopold Elkus had helped
out that day with Dreyer's highball. Why would he put
a shadow on Chapin? Of course it was possible, but my
practice was to let the brain off easy on an idea until it
got a little better than possible. If it wasn't Elkus, who
was it? It might have been any one of the bunch who
was too scared for Wolfe's memorandum to quiet him
down and thought he needed his own reports of the
cripple's activities, but in that case why all the mystery? Driving uptown, I went over the list in my mind,
without any results.

I put the roadster in the garage and walked home.
It was nearly dinner time when I got there. Wolfe was
in the office, at his desk. He was doing something. His
beer tray had been pushed to one side, and he was
leaning over a piece of paper, inspecting it with a
magnifying glass, with the strong light turned on. He
looked up to nod at me, and then resumed. There was
a little pile of similar papers under a weight. The
typewriting on the paper began, *Ye should have killed
me, watched the last mean sigh.* It was the first
warning.

Pretty soon he looked up again, and blinked. He
put the magnifying glass on the table. I asked, "These
are Farrell's samples?"

"Yes. Mr. Farrell brought them ten minutes ago.
He decided to get a specimen from each machine in
Mr. Oglethorpe's office. I have examined two, and
discarded them—those marked with red pencil." He
sighed. "You know, Archie, it is remarkable how the
shortening of the days at this time of year, the early
darkness, seems to lengthen the period between lun-

cheon and dinner. I suppose I have made that comment before."

"Not very often, sir. Not more than once or twice a day."

"Indeed. It deserves more. You haven't washed."

"No, sir."

"There are two pheasants which should not be kept waiting."

I went upstairs.

After dinner we worked together at Farrell's samples; there were sixteen of them. He wasn't so good at the typewriter; he had exed out a good deal, but for our purpose that didn't matter. I brought a glass down from the plant-rooms and Wolfe went on with his. It didn't matter which of the originals we used, so long as it wasn't one of the carbons, since it had been definitely determined that they had all been written on the same machine. We did a thorough job of it, not finally eliminating one until we had both examined it. Wolfe loved that kind of work, every minute of it; when he had gone through a sample and made sure that the *a* wasn't off the line and the *n* wasn't cockeyed, he grunted with satisfaction. I liked it only when it got results. As we neared the bottom of the pile with the red pencil unanimous, I wasn't getting any gayer.

Around ten o'clock I got up and handed the last one across to him, and then went to the kitchen and got a pitcher of milk. Fritz, sitting there reading the French paper, giggled at me: "You drink milk looking like that, you curdle it." I stuck my tongue out at him and went back to the office. Wolfe had fastened the sheets together with a clip and was putting the originals back in the envelope.

I said, "Well. This has been a fine pregnant

evening. Huh?" I drank some milk and licked my lips.

Wolfe leaned back and got his fingers twined. He kept his eyes nearly open. He finally remarked, "We have sacrificed it to Mr. Chapin's adroitness, a tribute to him. And established a fact: that he did not type the warnings in his publisher's office. But he did type them, and doubtless holds himself in readiness to type another; so the machine exists and can be found. I have already another suggestion ready for Mr. Farrell—a little complicated, but worth the experiment."

"Maybe I could offer one. Tell him to get samples from the machines in Leopold Elkus's office."

Wolfe's brows went up. "Why particularly Elkus?"

"Well, for one thing Inspector Cramer got the idea of having someone in Italy get in touch with Mr. Santini. Dumb idea, of course, but he got it. Santini says that he has remembered that after they all left the office that day Elkus went back for something and was in there alone for maybe half a minute. Plenty of time to drop some tablets into a highball."

"But hardly enough to filch the bottle from Mr. Dreyer's pocket and return it again, not to mention the dexterity required."

"That's all right. Chapin did that himself some time previously, maybe the week before, and gave them to Elkus."

"Indeed. This was in the news reels?"

"It's in Cramer's bean. But it may also be in his bag one of these days. We would have to get a mirror and see how we look in it, if it turns out to be the dope and he bags it first. Another item is that Elkus has got a shadow on Chapin."

"That likewise is in Mr. Cramer's bean?"

"Yeah, likewise. But one of those dicks—"

"Archie." Wolfe wiggled a finger at me. "I think it would be as well to correct your perspective. You must not let the oddities of this case perplex you to the point of idiocy. For instance, Inspector Cramer. He is an excellent man. In nine murder cases out of ten his services would be much more valuable than mine; to mention a few points only, I need to keep regular hours, I could not function even passably where properly chilled beer was not continually available, and I cannot run fast. If I am forced to engage in extreme physical effort, such as killing a snake, I am hungry for days. But it is utterly futile, in this case or any other case in which we are interested, to give consideration to the contents of Mr. Cramer's bean. I supposed that in seven years you had learned that."

"Sure. His bean's out." I waved it out with my hand. "But what about his facts? Such as Elkus going back alone to the office?"

Wolfe shook his head. "You see, Archie? The dizzy revolutions of Mr. Chapin's cunning wheel of vengeance have hurled you off on a tangent. Consider what we have engaged to do under our memorandum: free our clients from fear of Paul Chapin's designs. Even if it were possible to prove that Dr. Elkus poisoned Mr. Dreyer's drink—which I strongly doubt—to what purpose should we attempt it? No; let us stick to the circumference of our own necessities and desires. Inspector Cramer might some day have a fact for us, as anyone might, there is no denying that, but he is welcome to this one. It is beyond our circle of endeavor."

"Still I don't see it. Look here. Say Elkus put the stuff in Dreyer's glass. Of course Chapin was in on it, look at the second warning. How are you going to prove Chapin guilty of Dreyer's murder unless you also prove how Elkus did his part?"

Wolfe nodded. "Your logic is impeccable. Your premise is absurd. I haven't the slightest expectation of proving Chapin guilty of Dreyer's murder."

"Then what the devil—"

I got that much out before I realized exactly what he had said. I stared at him. He went on:

"It could not be expected that you should know Paul Chapin as I know him, because you have not had the extended and intimate association that I have enjoyed—through his books. He is possessed of a demon. A fine old melodramatic phrase. The same thing can be said in modern scientific terms, but it would mean no more and its flavor would be much impaired. He is possessed of a demon, but he is also, within certain limits, an extraordinarily astute man. Emotionally he is infantile—he even prefers a vicar to a substitute, when the original object is unattainable, as witness his taking Dora Ritter to proxy for her mistress. But his intellectual competence is such that it is problematical whether factual proof could ever be obtained of any act of his which he intended to remain anonymous."

He stopped for some beer. I said, "If you mean you give up, you're wasting a lot of time and money. If you mean you're waiting for him to croak another one, and you're tailing him to watch him do it, and he's as smart as you say he is . . ."

I drank milk. Wolfe wiped his lips and went on: "Of course we have our usual advantage: we are on the offensive. And of course the place to attack the enemy is his weak spot; those are truisms. Since Mr. Chapin has an aversion to factual proof and has the intellectual equipment to preclude it, let us abandon the intellectual field, and attack him where he is weak. His emotions. I am acquainting you now with this decision which was made last Sunday. We are gathering what ammunition we may. Certainly facts are not to be sneered at; I need two more of them, possibly three, before I can feel confident of persuading Mr. Chapin to confess his guilt."

Wolfe emptied his glass, I said, "Confess, huh? That cripple?"

He nodded. "It would be simple. I am sure it will be."

"What are the three facts?"

"First, to find Mr. Hibbard. His meat and bone; we can do without the vital spark if it has found another errand. That, however, is more for the satisfaction of our clients and the fulfillment of the terms of our memorandum than for the effect on Mr. Chapin. That sort of fact will not impress him. Second, to find the typewriter on which he wrote the menacing verses. That I must have, for him. Third—the possibility—to learn if he has ever kissed his wife. That may not be needed. Given the first two, I probably should not wait for it."

"And with that you can make him confess?"

"I should think so. I see no other way out for him."

"That's all you need?"

"It seems ample."

I looked at him. Sometimes I thought I could tell how much he was being fanciful; sometimes I knew I couldn't. I grunted. "Then I might as well phone Fred and Bill and Orrie and the others to come up and check out."

"By no means. Mr. Chapin himself might lead us to the typewriter or the Hibbard meat and bone."

"And I've been useful too. According to you. Why

did you buy the gasoline I burned up yesterday and today if you decided Sunday night you couldn't get the goods on him? It seems as if I'm like a piece of antique furniture or a pedigreed dog, I'm in the luxury class. You keep me on for beauty. Do you know what I think? I think that all this is just your delicate way of telling me that on the Dreyer thing you've decided I'm a washout and you think I might try something else. Okay. What?"

Wolfe's cheeks unfolded a little. "Veritably, Archie, you are overwhelming. The turbulence of a Carpathian torrent. It would be gratifying if you should discover Mr. Hibbard."

"I thought so. Forget Dreyer?"

"Let him rest in peace. At least for tomorrow."

"A thousand dicks and fifteen thousand cops have been looking for Hibbard for eight days. Where shall I bring him when I find him?"

"If alive, here. If dead, he will care as little as I. But his niece will care, I presume, to her."

"Do you tell me where to look?"

"Our little globe."

"Okay."

I went upstairs. I was riled. We had never had a case, and I suppose never will have, without Wolfe getting cryptic about it sooner or later; I was used to it and expected it, but it always riled me. In the Fairmont-Avery thing he had deliberately waited for twenty-four hours to close in on Pete Avery after he had him completely sewed up, just for the pleasure of watching me and Dick Morley of the D.A.'s office play fox-and-goose with that old fool that couldn't find his ear trumpet. I suppose his awful conceit was one of the wheels that worked the machinery that got his results, but that didn't make it any more enjoyable when I was doing the worrying for both of us. That Wednesday night I nearly took the enamel off of my teeth with the brush, stabbing with it at Wolfe's conceit.·

The next morning, Thursday, I had had my breakfast and was in the office by eight o'clock, taking another good look at the photograph of her uncle which Evelyn Hibbard had given to us. Saul Panzer had phoned and I had told him to meet me in the McAlpin lobby at eight-thirty. After I had soaked in all I could of the photograph I made a couple of phone calls, one to Evelyn Hibbard and one to Inspector Cramer. Cramer was friendly. He said that on Hibbard he had spread the net pretty wide. If a body of a man was washed up on the sand at Montauk Point, or found in a coal mine at Scranton, or smelled in a trunk in a Village roominghouse, or pulled out of a turnip pit in south Jersey, he would know about it in ten minutes, and would be asking for specifications. That satisfied me that there was no sense in my wasting time or shoe leather looking for a dead Hibbard; I'd better concentrate on the possibility of a live one.

I went to the McAlpin and talked it over with Saul Panzer. He, with his wrinkled little mug not causing any stranger to suspect how cute he was, and he could be pretty damn cute—he sat on the edge of a tapestry chair, smoking a big slick light-brown cigar that smelled like something they scatter on lawns in the early spring, and told me about it to date. It was obvious from the instructions Saul had been following, either that Wolfe had reached the same conclusion that I had, that if Hibbard had been croaked the police routine was the best and quickest way of finding him,

or that Wolfe thought Hibbard was still alive. Saul had
been digging up every connection Hibbard had had in
and around the city for the past five years, every
degree of intimacy, man, woman, and child, and
calling on them. Since Hibbard had been an instructor
at a large university, and also a sociable man, Saul
hadn't made much more than a start. I supposed that
Wolfe's idea was that there was a possibility that
Chapin's third warning was a fake, that Hibbard had
just got too scared to breathe and had run off to hide,
and that in that case he was practically certain to get
in touch with someone he knew.

My heart wasn't really in it. For my part, I
believed the cripple, third warning and all. In the first
place, Wolfe hadn't said definitely that he didn't; and
secondly, I had known Wolfe to be wrong, not often,
but more than once. When the event proved that he
had been wrong about something, it was a delight to
see him handle it. He would wiggle his finger a little
more rapidly and violently than usual, and mutter
with his eyes nearly open at me, "Archie, I love to
make a mistake, to assume the burden of omniscience."

But although I believed the cripple and was perfectly comfortable with the notion that Hibbard wasn't
using up any more air, I couldn't see that there was
anything better to be done than to smell around places
where he had once been alive. I left the general
list—neighbors, friends, pupils and miscellaneous—to
Saul, and chose for myself the members of the League
of the White Feather.

The *Tribune* office was only seven blocks away, so
I called there first, but Mike Ayers wasn't in. Next I
went up on Park Avenue, to Drummond's florist shop,
and the little fat tenor was all ready for a talk. He

wanted to know many things, and I hope he believed what I told him, but he had nothing to offer in exchange that helped me any. From there I went back down to Thirty-ninth Street to see Edwin Robert Byron the editor, and that was also empty. For over half an hour about all he found time for was "Excuse me" as he was reaching for the telephone. I was thinking, with all that practice, if he should happen to get fired as an editor he could step right in anywhere as a telephone girl.

When I was out working I was supposed to phone in at eleven o'clock, at which time Wolfe got down from the plant-rooms, to ask if there were any new instructions. Leaving Edwin Robert Byron's office a little before eleven, I decided I might as well roll over to the house in person, since it was only a couple of blocks out of my way to the next call.

Wolfe wasn't down yet. I went to the kitchen and asked Fritz if anyone had left a corpse on the stoop for us, and he said he didn't think so. I heard the elevator and went to the office.

Wolfe was in one of his sighing moods. He sighed as he said good morning and he sighed as he got into his chair. It might have meant anything from one measly little orchid getting bugs on it up to a major relapse. I waited until he got his little routine chores done before trying to pass a couple of words.

Out of one of the envelopes in the morning mail he took some pieces of paper that looked familiar from where I stood. I approached. Wolfe looked up at me and back at the papers.

I asked, "What's that, Farrell's second edition?"

He handed me one of the sheets, a different size from the others. I read it:

*Dear Mr. Wolfe:*

*Here are two more samples which I failed to deliver with the others. I found them in another pocket. I am called suddenly to Philadelphia on a chance at a commission, and am mailing them to you so you will have them first thing in the morning.*

*Sincerely,*
*Augustus Farrell*

Wolfe had already got his magnifying glass and was inspecting one of the samples. I felt my blood coming up to my head, which meant a hunch. I told myself to hang onto the aplomb, that there was no more reason to expect it of these than of the others, and there were only two chances. I stood and watched Wolfe. After a little he pushed the sheet aside and shook his head, and reached for the other one.

One more, I thought. If it's that one he's got one of his facts. I looked for an expression on his face as he examined it, but of course I might as well have saved my eyes the strain. He moved the glass along, intent, but a little too rapidly for me not to suspect that he had had a hunch too. At length he looked up at me, and sighed.

"No."

I demanded, "You mean it's not it?"

"No, I believe, is negative. No."

"Let me see the damn things."

He pushed them across and I got the glass and gave them a look. I didn't need to be very thorough, after the practice I had had the night before. I was really almost incredulous, and sore as the devil, because in the detective business nothing is more important than to find your hunches good as often as possible. If you once get off of your hunches you might as well give up and go and get a job on the Homicide Squad. Not to mention that Wolfe had said that that typewriter was one of the two things he needed.

He was saying, "It is a pity Mr. Farrell has deserted us. I am not sure that my next suggestion should await his return; and he does not, by the way, mention his return." He picked up the note from Farrell and looked at it. "I believe, Archie, that you had best abandon the Hibbard search temporarily—"

He stopped himself; and said in a different tone:

"Mr. Goodwin. Hand me the glass."

I gave it to him. His using my formal handle when we were alone meant that he was excited almost beyond control, but I had no idea what about. Then I saw what he wanted the glass for. He was looking through it at the note from Farrell! I stared at him. He kept on looking. I didn't say anything. A beautiful suspicion was getting into me that you shouldn't ever ignore a hunch.

Finally Wolfe said, "Indeed."

I held out my hand and he gave me the note and the glass. I saw it at a glance, but I kept on looking, it was so satisfactory to see that *a* off the line and a little to the left, and the *n* cockeyed, and all the other signs. I laid it on the table and grinned at Wolfe.

"Old Eagle Eye. Damn me for missing it."

He said, "Take off your coat and hat, Archie. Whom can we telephone in Philadelphia to learn where an architect there in pursuit of a commission might possibly be found?"

# Chapter 14

I started for the hall to put my coat and hat away, but before I got to the door I turned and went back.

"Listen," I said, "the roadster needs some exercise. We might fool around with the phone all afternoon and not get anywhere. Why don't we do this: you phone Farrell's friends here and see if you can get a line on him. I'll roll down to Philly and call you up as soon as I arrive. If you haven't found out anything, I'll be on the ground to look for him. I can get there by two-thirty."

"Excellent," Wolfe agreed. "But the noon train will reach Philadelphia at two o'clock."

"Yeah, I know, but—"

"Archie. Let us agree on the train."

"Okay. I thought I might get away with it."

There was plenty of time to discuss a few probabilities, since it was only a five-minute walk to the Pennsylvania Station. I caught the noon train, had lunch on the diner, and phoned Wolfe from the Broad Street Station at two minutes after two.

He had no dope, except the names of a few friends and acquaintances of Farrell's in Philadelphia. I telephoned all I could get hold of, and chased around all afternoon, the Fine Arts Club, and an architectural magazine, and the newspaper offices to see if they knew who intended to build something and so on. I was beginning to wonder if an idea that had come to me on the train could possibly have anything in it. Was Farrell himself entangled somehow in the Chapin business, and had he written that note on that typewriter for some reason maybe to be discovered, and then beat it? Was there a chance that he hadn't come to Philadelphia at all but somewhere else, even perhaps on a transatlantic liner?

But around six o'clock I got him. I had taken to phoning architects. After about three dozen I found one who told me that a Mr. Allenby who had got rich and sentimental was going to build a library for a Missouri town that had been lucky enough to give birth to him and then lose him. That was a building project I hadn't heard of before. I phoned Allenby, and was told that Mr. Farrell was expected at his home at seven o'clock for dinner.

I snatched a pair of sandwiches and went out there, and then had to wait until he had finished his meal.

He came to me in Mr. Allenby's library. Of course he couldn't understand how I got there. I allowed him ten seconds for surprise and so forth, and then I asked him: "Last night you wrote a note to Nero Wolfe. Where's the typewriter you wrote it on?"

He smiled like a gentleman being bewildered. He said, "I suppose it's where I left it. I didn't take it away."

"Well, where was it? Excuse me for taking you on the jump like this. I've been hunting you for over five hours and I'm out of breath. The machine you wrote that note on is the one Paul Chapin used for his poems. That's the little detail."

"No!" He stared at me, and laughed. "By God, that's good. You're sure? After working so hard to get all those samples, and then to write that note—I'll be damned."

"Yeah. When you get around to it . . . "

"Certainly. I used a typewriter at the Harvard Club."

"Oh. You did."

"I did indeed. I'll be damned."

"Yeah. Where do they keep this typewriter?"

"Why, it's one—it's available to any of the members. I was there last evening when the telegram came from Mr. Allenby, and I used it to write two or three notes. It's in a little room off the smoking-room, sort of an alcove. A great many of the fellows use it, off and on."

"Oh. They do." I sat down. "Well, this is nice. It's sweet enough to make you sick. It's available to anybody, and thousands of them use it."

"Hardly thousands, but quite a few—"

"Dozens is enough. Have you ever seen Paul Chapin use it?"

"I couldn't say—I believe, though—yes, in that little chair with his game leg pushed under—I'm pretty sure I have."

"Any of your other friends, this bunch?"

"I really couldn't say."

"Do many of them belong to the club?"

"Oh, yes, nearly all. Mike Ayers doesn't, and I believe Leo Elkus resigned a few years ago . . . "

"I see. Are there any other typewriters in the alcove?"

"There's one more, but it belongs to a public

stenographer. I understand this one was donated by
some club member. They used to keep it in the library,
but some of the one-finger experts made too much
noise with it."

"All right." I got up. "You can imagine how I feel,
coming all the way to Philadelphia to get a kick in the
pants. Can I tell Wolfe when you're coming back, in
case he wants you?"

He said probably tomorrow, he had to prepare
drawings to submit to Mr. Allenby, and I thanked him
for nothing and went out to seek the air and a
streetcar to North Philadelphia.

The train ride back to New York, in a smoker filled
with the discard from a hundred pairs of assorted
lungs, was not what I needed to cheer me up. I
couldn't think up anything to keep me awake, and I
couldn't go to sleep. We pulled in at the Pennsylvania
Station at midnight, and I walked home.

The office was dark; Wolfe had gone to bed. There
was no note for me on my desk, so nothing startling
had happened. I got a pitcher of milk from the
refrigerator and went upstairs. Wolfe's room was on
the same floor as mine; mine overlooking Thirty-fifth
Street, and his in the rear. I thought possibly he was
still awake and would like to hear the joyous news, so
I went towards the back of the hall to see if there was
light under his door—not going close, for when he
went to bed there was a switch he turned on, and if
anyone stepped within eight feet of his door or
touched any of his windows a gong went off in my
room that was enough to paralyze you. The slit under
his door was dark, so I went on with my milk, and
drank it while I was getting ready for bed.

Friday morning, after breakfast, I was still sitting
in the office at eight-thirty. I sat there, first because I

was sour on the Hibbard search anyway, and second because I was going to wait until nine o'clock and see Wolfe as soon as he got to the plant-rooms. But at eight-thirty the inside phone buzzed and I got on. It was Wolfe from his bedroom. He asked me if I had had a pleasant journey. I told him that all it would have needed to make it perfect was Dora Chapin for company. He asked if Mr. Farrell had remembered what typewriter he had used.

I told him. "A thing at the Harvard Club, in a little room off the smoking-room. It seems that the members all play tunes on it whenever the spirit moves them. The good thing about this is that it narrows it down, it rules out all Yale men and other roughnecks. You can see Chapin wanted to make it as simple as possible."

Wolfe's low murmur was in my ear: "Excellent."

"Yeah. One of the facts you wanted. Swell."

"No, Archie. I mean it. This will do nicely. I told you, proof will not be needed in this case, facts will do for us. But we must be sure beyond peradventure of the facts. Please find someone willing to favor us who is a member of the Harvard Club—not one of our present clients. Perhaps Albert Wright would do; if not him, find someone. Ask him to go to the club this morning and take you as a guest. On that typewriter make a copy—no. Not that. There must be no hole for Mr. Chapin to squirm through, should he prove more difficult than I anticipate. In spite of his infirmity, he is probably capable of carrying a typewriter. Do this: after making arrangements for a host, purchase a new typewriter—any good one, follow your fancy—and take it with you to the club. Bring away the one that is there and leave the new one; manage it as you please, by arrangement with the steward, by prestidigitation, whatever suggests itself. With, however, the knowledge of your host, for he must be qualified to furnish corroboration, at any future time, as to the identity of the machine you remove. Bring it here."

"A new typewriter costs one hundred dollars."

"I know that. It is not necessary to speak of it."

"Okay."

I hung up and reached for the telephone book.

That was how it happened that at ten o'clock that Friday morning I sat in the smoking-room of the Harvard Club with Albert Wright, a vice-president of Eastern Electric, drinking vermouth, with a typewriter under a shiny rubberized cover on the floor at my feet. Wright had been very nice, as he should have been, since about all he owed to Wolfe was his wife and family. That was one of the neatest blackmailing cases . . . but let it rest. It was true that he had paid Wolfe's bill, which hadn't been modest, but what I've seen of wives and families has convinced me that they can't be paid for in cash; either they're way above any money price that could be imagined or they're clear out of sight in the other direction. Anyway, Wright had been nice about it. I was saying:

"This is it. It's that typewriter in there that I showed you the number of and had you put a scratch under it. Mr. Wolfe wants it."

Wright raised his brows. I went on:

"Of course you don't care why, but if you do maybe he'll tell you some day. The real reason is that he's fond of culture and he don't like to see the members of a swell organization like the Harvard Club using a piece of junk like that in there. I've got a brand new Underwood." I touched it with my toe. "I just bought it, it's a new standard machine. I take it in there and leave it, and bring away the junk, that's all. If anyone sees me I am unconcerned. It's just a playful lark; the club gets what it needs and Mr. Wolfe gets what he wants."

Wright, smiling, sipped his vermouth. "I hesitate chiefly because you had me mark the junk for identification. I would do about anything for Nero Wolfe, but I would dislike getting in a mess and having the club dragged in too, perhaps. I suppose you couldn't offer any guarantees on that score?"

I shook my head. "No guarantees, but knowing how Mr. Wolfe is arranging this charade I'd take you on a thousand to one."

Wright sat a minute and looked at me, and then smiled again. "Well, I have to get back to the office. Go on with your lark. I'll wait here."

There was nothing to it. I picked up the Underwood and walked into the alcove with it and set it down on the desk. The public stenographer was there only ten feet away, brushing up his machine, but I merely got too nonchalant even to glance at him. I pulled the junk aside and transferred the shiny cover to it, put the new one in its place, and picked up the junk and walked out. Wright got up from his chair and walked beside me to the elevator.

On the sidewalk, at the street entrance, Wright shook hands with me. He wasn't smiling; I guessed from the look on his face that his mind had gone back four years to another time we shook hands. He said, "Give Nero Wolfe my warmest regards, and tell him they will still be warm even if I get kicked out of the Harvard Club for helping to steal a typewriter."

I grinned. "Steal my eye, it nearly broke my heart to leave that new Underwood there."

I carried my loot to where I had parked the roadster on Forty-fifth Street, put it on the seat beside me, and headed downtown. Having it there made me feel like we were getting somewhere. Not that I knew where, but Wolfe either did or thought he did. I didn't very often get really squeamish about Wolfe's calculations; I worried, all right, and worked myself into a stew when it seemed to me that he was overlooking a point that was apt to trip us up, but down in my heart I nearly always knew that anything he was missing would turn out in the end to be something we didn't need. In this case I wasn't so sure, and what made me not so sure was that damn cripple. There was something in the way the others spoke about him, in the way he looked and acted that Monday night, in the way those warnings sounded, that gave me an uneasy idea that for once Wolfe might be underrating a guy. That wasn't like him, for he usually had a pretty high opinion of the people whose fate he was interfering with. I was thinking that maybe the mistake he had made in this case was in reading Chapin's books. He had definite opinions about literary merit, and possibly having rated the books pretty low, he had done the same for the man who wrote them. If he was rating Chapin low, I was all ready to fall in on the other side. For instance, here beside me was the typewriter on which the warnings had been written, all three of them, no doubt about it, and it was a typewriter to which Paul Chapin had had easy and constant access, but there was no way in the world of proving that he had done it. Not only that, it was a typewriter to which most of the other persons connected with the business had had access too. No, I thought, as far as writing those warnings went, nearly anything you might say about Chapin would be under-rating him.

When I got to the house it wasn't eleven o'clock

yet. I carried the typewriter to the hall and put it down on the stand while I removed my hat and coat. There was another hat and coat there; I looked at them; they weren't Farrell's; I didn't recognize them. I went to the kitchen to ask Fritz who the visitor was, but he wasn't there, upstairs probably, so I went back and got the typewriter and took it to the office. But I didn't get more than six feet inside the door before I stopped. Sitting there turning over the pages of a book, with his stick leaning against the arm of his chair, was Paul Chapin.

Something I don't often do, I went tongue-tied. I suppose it was because I had under my arm the typewriter he had written his poems on, though certainly he couldn't recognize it under the cover. But he could tell it was a typewriter. I stood and stared at him. He glanced up and informed me politely:

"I'm waiting for Mr. Wolfe."

He turned another page in the book, and I saw it was *Devil Take the Hindmost*, the one Wolfe had marked things in. I said:

"Does he know you're here?"

"Oh yes. His man told him some time ago. I've been here," he glanced at his wrist, "half an hour."

There hadn't been any sign of his noticing what I was carrying. I went over and put it down on my desk and shoved it to the back edge. I went to Wolfe's desk and glanced through the envelopes of the morning mail, the corner of my eye telling me that Chapin was enjoying his book. I brushed off Wolfe's blotter and twisted his fountain pen around. Then I got sore, because I realized that I wasn't inclined to go and sit at my desk, and the reason was that it would put me with my back to Paul Chapin. So I went there and got into my chair and got some plant records from the drawer and began looking at them. It was a damn funny experience; I don't know what it was about that cripple that got under my skin so. Maybe he was magnetic. I actually had to clamp my jaw to keep from turning around to look at him, and while I was trying to laugh it off ideas kept flashing through my mind such as whether he had a gun and if so was it the one with the hammer nose filed down. I had a good deal stronger feeling of Paul Chapin, behind me, than I've had of lots of people under my eyes and sometimes under my hands too.

I flipped the pages of the record book, and I didn't turn around until Wolfe came in.

I had many times seen Wolfe enter the office when a visitor was there waiting for him, and I watched him to see if he would vary his common habit for the sake of any effect on the cripple. He didn't. He stopped inside the door and said, "Good morning, Archie." Then he turned to Chapin and his trunk and head went forward an inch and a half from the perpendicular, in a sort of mammoth elegance. "Good morning, sir." He proceeded to his desk, fixed the orchids in the vase, sat down, and looked through the mail. He rang for Fritz, took out his pen and tried it on the scratch pad, and when Fritz came nodded for beer. He looked at me:

"You saw Mr. Wright? Your errand was successful?"

"Yes, sir. In the bag."

"Good. If you would please move a chair up for Mr. Chapin.—If you would be so good, sir? For either amenities or hostilities, the distance is too great. Come closer." He opened a bottle of beer.

Chapin got up, grasped his stick, and hobbled over to the desk. He paid no attention to the chair I placed for him, nor to me, but stood there leaning on his stick, his flat cheeks pale, his lips showing a faint movement like a race horse not quite steady at the barrier, his light-colored eyes betraying neither life nor death—neither the quickness of the one nor the glassy stare of the other. I got at my desk and shuffled my pad in among a pile of papers, ready to take my notes while pretending to do something else, but Wolfe shook his head at me. "Thank you, Archie, it will not be necessary.

The cripple said, "There need be neither amenities nor hostilities. I've come for my box."

"Ah! Of course. I might have known." Wolfe had turned on his gracious tone. "If you wouldn't mind, Mr. Chapin, may I ask how you knew I had it?"

"You may ask." Chapin smiled. "Any man's vanity will stand a pat on the back, won't it, Mr. Wolfe? I inquired for my package where I had left it, and was told it was not there, and learned of the ruse by which it had been stolen. I reflected, and it was obvious that the likeliest thief was you. You must believe me, this is not flattery, I really did come to you first."

"Thank you. I do thank you." Wolfe, having emptied a glass, leaned back and got comfortable. "I am considering—this shouldn't bore you, since words are the tools of your trade—I am considering the comical and tragical scantiness of all vocabularies. Take, for example, the procedure by which you acquired the contents of that box, and I got the box and all; both our actions were, by definition, stealing, and both of us are thieves; words implying condemnation and contempt, and yet neither of us would concede that he has earned them. So much for words—but of course you know that, since you are a professional."

"You said contents. You haven't opened the box."

"My dear sir! Could Pandora herself have resisted such a temptation?"

"You broke the lock."

"No. It is intact. It is simple, and surrendered easily."

"And . . . you opened it. You probably . . . " He stopped and stood silent. His voice had gone thin on him, but I couldn't see that his face displayed any feeling at all, not even resentment. He continued, "In that case . . . I don't want it. I don't want to see it.—But that's preposterous. Of course I want it. I must have it."

Wolfe, looking at him with half-closed eyes, motionless, said nothing. That lasted for seconds. All of a sudden Chapin demanded, suddenly hoarse:

"Damn you, where is it?"

Wolfe wiggled a finger at him. "Mr. Chapin. Sit down."

"No."

"Very well. You can't have the box. I intend to keep it."

Still there was no change on the cripple's face. I didn't like him, but I was admiring him. His light-colored eyes had kept straight into Wolfe's, but now they moved; he glanced aside at the chair I had placed for him, firmed his hand on the crook of his stick, and limped three steps and sat down. He looked at Wolfe again and said:

"For twenty years I lived on pity. I don't know if you are a sensitive man, I don't know if you can guess what a diet like that would do. I despised it, but I lived on it, because a hungry man takes what he can get. Then I found something else to sustain me. I got a measure of pride in achievement, I ate bread that I earned, I threw away the stick that I needed to walk

with, one that had been given me, and bought one of
my own. Mr. Wolfe, I was done with pity. I had
swallowed it to the extreme of toleration. I was sure
that, whatever gestures I might be brought, foolishly
or desperately, to accept from my fellow creatures, it
would never again be pity."

He stopped. Wolfe murmured. "Not sure. Not sure
unless you carried death ready at hand."

"Right. I learn that today. I seem to have acquired
a new and active antipathy to death."

"And as regards pity . . . "

I need it. I ask for it. I discovered an hour ago that
you had got my box, and I have been considering ways
and means. I can see no other way to get it than to
plead with you. Force"—he smiled the smile that his
eyes ignored—"is not feasible. The force of law is of
course, under the circumstances, out of the question.
Cunning—I have no cunning, except with words.
There is no way but to call upon your pity. I do so, I
plead with you. The box is mine by purchase. The
contents are mine by . . . by sacrifice. By purchase I
can say, though not with money. I ask you to give it
back to me."

"Well. What plea have you to offer?"

"The plea of my need, my very real need, and your
indifference."

"You are wrong there, Mr. Chapin. I need it too."

"No. It is you who are wrong. It is valueless to
you."

"But, my dear sir." Wolfe wiggled a finger. "If I
permit you to be the judge of your own needs you
must grant me the same privilege. What other plea?"

"None. I tell you, I will take it in pity."

"Not from me. Mr. Chapin. Let us not keep from
our tongues what is in our minds. There is one plea

you could make that would be effective.—Wait, hear me. I know that you are not prepared to make it, not yet, and I am not prepared to ask for it. Your box is being kept in a safe place, intact. I need it here in order to be sure that you will come to see me whenever I am ready for you. I am not yet ready. When the time comes, it will not be merely my possession of your box that will persuade you to give me what I want and intend to get. I am preparing for you. You said you have acquired a new and active antipathy to death. Then you should prepare for me: for the best I shall be able to offer you, the day you come for your box, will be your choice between two deaths. I shall leave that, for the moment, as cryptic as it sounds; you may understand me, but you certainly will not try to anticipate me.—Archie. In order that Mr. Chapin may not suspect us of gullery, bring the box please."

I went and unlocked the cabinet and got the box from the shelf, and took it and put it down on Wolfe's desk. I hadn't looked at it since Wednesday and had forgotten how swell it was; it certainly was a pip. I put it down with care. The cripple's eyes were on me, I thought, rather than on the box, and I had a notion of how pleased he probably was to see me handling it. For nothing but pure damn meanness I rubbed my hand back and forth along the top of it. Wolfe told me to sit down.

Chapin's hands were grasping the arms of his chair, as if to lift himself up. He said, "May I open it?"

"No."

He got to his feet, disregarding his stick, leaning on a hand on the desk. "I'll just . . . lift it."

"No. I'm sorry, Mr. Chapin. You won't touch it."

The cripple leaned there, bending forward, looking Wolfe in the eyes. His chin was stuck out. All of a sudden he began to laugh. It was a hell of a laugh, I thought it was going to choke him. He went on with it. Then it petered out and he turned around and got hold of his stick. He seemed to me about half hysterical, and I was ready to jump him if he tried any child's play like bouncing the stick on Wolfe's bean, but I had him wrong again. He got into his regular posture, leaning to the right side with his head a little to the left to even up, and from his light-colored eyes steady on Wolfe again you would never have guessed he had any sentiments at all.

Wolfe said, "The next time you come here, Mr. Chapin, you may take the box with you."

Chapin shook his head. His tone was new, sharper: "I think not. You're making a mistake. You're forgetting that I've had twenty years' practice at renunciation."

Wolfe shook his head. "Oh no. On the contrary, that's what I'm counting on. The only question will be, which of two sacrifices you will select. If I know you, and I think I do, I know where your choice will lie."

"I'll make it now. " I stared at the cripple's incredible smile; I thought to myself that in order to break him Wolfe would have to wipe that smile off, and it didn't look practical by any means I'd ever heard of. With the smile still working, fixed, Chapin put his left hand on the desk to steady himself, and with his right hand he lifted his stick up, pointing it in front of him like a rapier, and gently let its tip come to rest on the surface of the desk. He slid the tip along until it was against the side of the box, and then pushed, not in a hurry, just a steady push. The box moved, approached the edge, kept going, and tumbled to the floor. It bounced a little and rolled towards my feet.

Chapin retrieved his stick and got his weight on it

again. He didn't look at the box; he directed his smile at Wolfe. "I told you, sir, I had learned to live on pity. I am learning now to live without it."

He tossed his head up, twice, like a horse on the rein, got himself turned around, and hobbled to the door and on out. I sat and watched him; I didn't go to the hall to help him. We heard him out there, shuffling to keep his balance as he got into his coat. Then the outer door opening and closing.

Wolfe sighed. "Pick it up, Archie. Put it away. It is astonishing, the effect a little literary and financial success will produce on a spiritual ailment."

He rang for beer.

# Chapter 15

I didn't go out again that morning. Wolfe got loquacious. Leaning back with his fingers interlaced in front of his belly, with his eyes mostly shut, he favored me with one of his quiet endless orations, his subject this time being what he called bravado of the psyche. He said there were two distinct species of bravado: one having as its purpose to impress outside spectators, the other being calculated solely for an internal audience. The latter was bravado of the psyche. It was a show put on by this or that factor of the ego to make a hit with all the other factors. And so on. I did manage, before one o'clock, to make a copy of the first warning on the Harvard Club junk, and put it under the glass. It was it. Chapin had typed his poems of friendship on that machine.

After lunch I got in the roadster to hunt for Hibbard. The usual reports had come from the boys, including Saul Panzer: nothing. Fred Durkin had cackled over the phone, at a quarter to one, that he and his colleagues had made a swell procession following Paul Chapin to Nero Wolfe's house, and had retired around the corner, to Tenth Avenue, to await news of Wolfe's demise. Then they had trailed Chapin back home again.

I had about as much hope of finding Hibbard as of getting a mash note from Greta Garbo, but I went on poking around. Of course I was phoning his niece, Evelyn, twice a day, not in the expectation of getting any dope, since she would let us know if she got any kind of news, but because she was my client and you've got to keep reminding your clients you're on the job. She was beginning to sound pretty sick on the telephone, and I hardly had the heart to try to buck her up, but I made a few passes at it.

Among other weak stabs I made that Friday afternoon was a visit to the office of Ferdinand Bowen the stockbroker. Hibbard had an account with Galbraith & Bowen that had been fairly active fooling with bonds, not much margin stuff, and while I more or less took Bowen in my stride, calling on all the members of the league, there was a little more chance of a hint there than with the others. Entering the office on the twentieth floor of one of the Wall Street buildings, I told myself I'd better advise Wolfe to give a boost to Bowen's contribution to the pot, no matter what the bank report said. Surely they had the rent paid, and that alone must have been beyond the dreams of avarice. It was one of those layouts, a whole floor, that give you the feeling that a girl would have to be at least a duchess to get a job there as a stenographer.

I was taken into Bowen's own room. It was as big as a dance hall, and the rugs made you want to walk around them. Bowen sat behind a beautiful dark-brown desk with nothing on it but the *Wall Street Journal* and an ash tray. One of his little hands held a long fat cigarette with smoke curling up from it that smelled like a Turkish harlot—at least it smelled like what I would expect if I ever got close to one. I didn't like that guy. If I'd had my choice of pinning a murder on him or Paul Chapin, I'd have been compelled to toss a coin.

He thought he was being decent when he grunted to me to sit down. I can stand a real tough baby, but a bird that fancies himself for a hot mixture of John D. Rockefeller and Lord Chesterfield, being all the time innocent of both ingredients, gives me a severe pain in the sitter. I told him what I was telling all of them, that I would like to know about the last time he had seen Andrew Hibbard, and all details. He had to think. Finally he decided the last time had been more than a week before Hibbard disappeared, around the twentieth of October, at the theater. It had been a party, Hibbard with his niece and Bowen with his wife. Nothing of any significance had been said, Bowen declared, nothing with any bearing on the present situation. As he remembered it, there had been no mention of Paul Chapin, probably because Bowen had been one of the three who had hired the Bascom detectives, and Hibbard disapproved of it and didn't want to spoil the evening with an argument.

I asked him, "Hibbard had a trading account with your firm?"

He nodded. "For a long while, over ten years. It wasn't very active, mostly back and forth in bonds."

"Yeah. I gathered that from the statements among his papers. You see, one thing that might help would be any evidence that when Hibbard left his apartment that Tuesday evening he had an idea that he might not be back again. I can't find any. I'm still looking. For instance, during the few days preceding his disappearance, did he make any unusual arrangements or give any unusual orders regarding his account here?"

Bowen shook the round thing that he used to grow his hair on. "No. I would have been told . . . but I'll make sure." From a row on the wall behind him he pulled out a telephone, and talked into it. He waited a while, and talked some more. He pushed the phone back, and turned to me. "No, as I thought. There has been no transaction on Andy's account for over two weeks, and there were no instructions from him."

I bade him farewell.

That was a good sample of the steady progress I made that day in the search for Andrew Hibbard. It was a triumph. I found out as much from the other six guys I saw as I did from Ferdinand Bowen, so I was all elated when I breezed in home around dinner time, not to mention the fact that with the roadster parked on Ninetieth Street some dirty lout scraped the rear fender while I was in seeing Dr. Burton. I didn't feel like anything at all, not even like listening to the charming gusto of Wolfe's dinner conversation— during a meal he refused to remember that there was such a thing as a murder case in the world—so I was glad that he picked that evening to leave the radio turned on.

After dinner we went to the office. Out of spite and bitterness I started to tell him about all the runs I had scored that afternoon, but he asked me to bring him the atlas and began to look at maps. There were all sorts of toys he was apt to begin playing with when he should have had his mind on business, but the worst of all was the atlas. When he got that out I gave up. I fooled around a while with the plant records and the expense account, then I closed my affairs for the night and went over to his desk to look him over. He was doing China! The atlas was a Gouchard, the finest to be had, and did China more than justice. He had the folded map opened out, and with his pencil in one hand and his magnifying glass in the other, there he was buried in the Orient. Without bothering to say good night to him, for I knew he wouldn't answer, I picked up his copy of *Devil Take the Hindmost* and went upstairs to my room, stopping in the kitchen for a pitcher of milk.

After I had got into pajamas and slippers I deposited myself in my most comfortable chair, under the reading lamp, with the milk handy on the little tile-top table, and took a crack at Paul Chapin's book. I thought it was about time I caught up with Wolfe. I flipped through it, and saw there were quite a few places he had marked—sometimes only a phrase, sometimes a whole sentence, occasionally a long passage of two or three paragraphs. I decided to concentrate on those, and I skipped around and took them at random:

. . . *not by the intensity of his desire, but merely by his inborn impulse to act; to do, disregarding all pale considerations* . . .

*For Alan there was no choice in the matter, for he knew that the fury that spends itself in words is but the mumbling of an idiot, beyond the circumference of reality.*

I read a dozen more, yawned, and drank some milk. I went on:

*She said, "That's why I admire you. . . . I don't like a man too squeamish to butcher his own meat."*

. . . *and scornful of all the whining eloquence deploring the awful brutalities of war; for the true objection to war is not the blood it soaks into the grass and the thirsty soil, not the bones it crushes, not the flesh it mangles, not the warm nutritious viscera it exposes to the hunger of the innocent birds and beasts. These things have their beauty, to compensate for the fleeting agonies of this man and that man. The trouble with war is that its noble and quivering excitements transcend the capacities of our weakling nervous systems; we are not men enough for it; it properly requires for its sublime sacrifices the blood and bones and flesh of heroes, and what have we to offer? This little coward, that fat sniveler, all these regiments of puny cravens . . .*

There was a lot of that. I got through it, and went on to the next. Then some more. It got monotonous, and I skipped around. There were some places that looked interesting, some conversations, and a long scene with three girls in an apple orchard, but Wolfe hadn't done any marking there. Around the middle of the book he had marked nearly a whole chapter which told about a guy croaking two other guys by manicuring them with an axe, with an extended explanation of how psychology entered into it. I thought that was a pretty good job of writing. Later I came across things like this, for instance:

*. . . for what counted was not the worship of violence, but the practice of it. Not the turbulent and complex emotion, but the act. What had killed Art Billings and Curly Stephens? Hate? No. Anger? No. Jealousy, vengefulness, fear, enmity? No, none of these things. They had been killed by an axe, gripped by his fingers and wielded by the muscles of his arm . . .*

At eleven o'clock I gave up. The milk was all gone, and it didn't seem likely that I would catch up with where Wolfe thought he was if I sat up all night. I thought I detected a hint here and there that the author of that book was reasonably bloodthirsty, but I had some faint suspicions on that score already. I dropped the book on the table, stretched for a good yawn, went and opened the window and stood there looking down on the street long enough to let the sharp cold air make me feel like blankets and hopped for the hay.

Saturday morning I started out again. It was all stale bread to me, and I suppose I did a rotten job of it; if one of those guys had had some little fact tucked away that might have helped there wasn't much chance of my prying it loose, the way I was going about it. I kept moving anyhow. I called on Elkus, Lang, Mike Ayers, Adler, Cabot and Pratt. I phoned Wolfe at eleven o'clock and he had nothing to say. I decided to tackle Pitney Scott the taxi-driver. Maybe my wild guess that day had been right; there was a chance that he did know something about Andrew Hibbard. But I couldn't find him. I called up the office of his cab company, and was told that he wasn't expected to report in until four o'clock. They told me that his usual cruising radius was from Fourteenth to Fifty-ninth streets, but that he might be anywhere. I went down and looked around Perry Street, but he wasn't there. At a quarter to one I phoned Wolfe again, expecting to be invited home to lunch, and instead he handed me a hot one. He asked me to grab a bite somewhere and run out to Mineola for him. Ditson had phoned to say that he had a dozen bulbs of a new Miltonia just arrived from England, and had offered to give Wolfe a couple if he would send for them.

The only times I ever really felt like turning Communist were the occasions when, in the middle of a case, Wolfe sent me chasing around after orchids. It made me feel too damn silly. But it wasn't as bad this time as usual, since the particular job I was on looked like a washout anyhow. It was cold and raw that Saturday afternoon, and kept trying to make out that it was going to snow, but I opened both windows of the roadster and enjoyed the air a lot and the Long Island traffic not at all.

I got back to Thirty-fifth Street around three-thirty, and took the bulbs in the office to show them to Wolfe. He felt them and looked them over carefully, and asked me to take them upstairs to Horstmann and tell him not to snip the roots. I went up, and came back down to the office, intending to stop only a minute to enter the bulbs in the record book and then beat it again to get Pitney Scott. But Wolfe, from his chair, said:

"Archie."

I knew from the tone it was the start of a speech, so I settled back. He went on:

"Now and then I receive the impression that you suspect me of neglecting this or that detail of our business. Ordinarily you are wrong, which is as it should be. In the labyrinth of any problem that confronts us, we must select the most promising paths; if we attempt to follow all at once we shall arrive nowhere. In any art—and I am an artist or nothing—one of the deepest secrets of excellence is a discerning elimination. Of course that is a truism."

"Yes, sir."

"Yes. Take the art of writing. I am, let us say, describing the actions of my hero rushing to greet his beloved, who has just entered the forest. *He sprang up from the log on which he had been sitting, with his left foot forward; as he did so, one leg of his trousers fell properly into place but the other remained hitched up at the knee. He began running towards her, first his right foot, then his left, then his right again, then left, right, left, right, left, right . . .* As you see, some of that can surely be left out—indeed, must be, if he is to accomplish his welcoming embrace in the same chapter. So the artist must leave out vastly more than he puts in, and one of his chief cares is to leave out nothing vital to his work."

"Yes, sir."

"You follow me. I assure you that the necessity I have just described is my constant concern when we are engaged in an enterprise. When you suspect me of neglect you are in a sense justified, for I do ignore great quantities of facts and impingements which might seem to another intelligence—let it go without characterization—to be of importance to our undertaking. But I should consider myself an inferior workman if I ignored a fact which the event proved actually to have significance. That is why I wish to make this apology to myself, thus publicly, in your hearing."

I nodded. "I'm still hanging on. Apology for what?"

"For bad workmanship. It may prove not to have been disastrous, it may even turn out of no importance whatever. But sitting here this afternoon contemplating my glories and sifting out the sins, it occurred to me, and I need to ask you about it. You may remember that on Wednesday evening, sixty-five hours ago, you were describing for me the contents of Inspector Cramer's bean."

I grinned. "Yeah."

"You told me that it was his belief that Dr. Elkus was having Mr. Chapin shadowed."

"Yep."

"And then you started a sentence; I think you said, *But one of those dicks*—Something approximating that. I was impatient, and I stopped you. I should not have done so. My impulsive reaction to what I knew to be nonsense betrayed me into an error. I should have let you finish. Pray do so now."

I nodded. "Yeah, I remember. But since you've dumped the Dreyer thing into the ash can, what does it matter whether Elkus—"

"Archie. Confound it, I care nothing about Elkus; what I want is your sentence about a dick. What dick? Where is he?"

"Didn't I say? Tailing Paul Chapin."

"One of Mr. Cramer's men."

I shook my head. "Cramer has a man there too. And we've got Durkin and Gore and Keems, eight-hour shifts. This bird's an extra. Cramer wondered who was paying him and had him in for a conference, but he's tough, he never says anything but cuss words. I thought maybe he was Bascom's, but no."

"Have you seen him?"

"Yeah, I went down there. He was eating soup, and he's like you about meals, business is out. I waited on him a little, carried his bread and butter and so on, and came on home."

"Describe him."

"Well . . . he hasn't much to offer to the eye. He weighs a hundred and thirty-five, five feet seven. Brown cap and pink necktie. A cat scratched him on the cheek and he didn't clean it up very well. Brown eyes, pointed nose, wide thin mouth but not tight, pale healthy skin."

"Hair?"

"He kept his cap on."

Wolfe sighed. I noticed that the tip of his finger was doing a little circle on the arm of his chair. He said, "Sixty-five hours. Get him and bring him here at once."

I got up. "Yeah. Alive or dead?"

"By persuasion if possible, certainly with a minimum of violence, but bring him."

"It's five minutes to four. You'll be in the plant-rooms."

"Well? This house is comfortable. Keep him."

I got some things from a drawer of my desk and stuffed them in my pockets, and beat it.

# Chapter 16

I was not ever, in the Chapin case or any other case, quite as dumb as the prosecution would try to make you believe if I was on trial for it. For instance, as I went out and got into the roadster, in spite of all the preconceptions that had set up housekeeping in my belfry, I wasn't doing any guessing as to the nature of the fancy notion Wolfe had plucked out of his contemplation of his sins. My guessing had been completed before I left the office. On account of various considerations it was my opinion that he was cuckoo—I had told him that Cramer had had the dick in for a talk—but it was going to be diverting whether it turned out that he was or he wasn't.

I drove to Perry Street and parked fifty feet down from the Coffee Pot. I had already decided on my tactics. Considering what I had learned of Pinkie's reaction to the diplomatic approach, it didn't seem practical to waste my time on persuasion. I walked to the Coffee Pot and glanced in. Pinkie wasn't there; of course it was nearly two hours till his soup time. I strolled back down the street, looking in at all the chances, and I went the whole long block to the next corner without a sign either of Pinkie, Fred Durkin, or

anything that looked like a city detective. I went back
again, clear to the Coffee Pot, with the same result.
Not so good, I thought, for of course all the desertion
meant that the beasts of prey were out trailing their
quarry, and the quarry might stay out for a dinner and
a show and get home at midnight. That would be
enjoyable, with me substituting for Fred on the delicatessen sandwiches and Wolfe waiting at home to see
what his notion looked like.

I drove around the block to get the roadster into a
better position for surveying the scene, and sat in it
and waited. It was getting dark, and it got dark, and
I waited.

A little before six a taxi came along and stopped in
front of 203. I tried to get a glimpse of the driver,
having Pitney Scott on my mind, and made out that it
wasn't him. But it was the cripple that got out. He
paid, and hobbled inside the building, and the taxi
moved off. I looked around, taking in the street and
the sidewalk.

Pretty soon I saw Fred Durkin walking up from
the corner. He was with another guy. I climbed out to
the sidewalk and stood there near a street light as
they went by. Then I got back in. In a couple of
minutes Fred came along and I moved over to make
room for him.

I said, "If you and the town dick want to cop a little
expense money by pairing up on a taxi, okay. As long
as nothing happens, then it might be your funeral."

Durkin grinned. "Aw, forget it. This whole layout's
a joke. If I didn't need the money—"

"Yeah. You take the money and let me do the
laughing. Where's Pinkie?"

"Huh? Don't tell me you're after the runt again!"

"Where is he?"

"He's around. He was behind us on the ride just now—there he goes, look, the Coffee Pot. He must have gone down Eleventh. He takes chances. It's time for his chow."

I had seen him going in. I said, "All right. Now listen. I'm going to funny up your joke for you. You and the town dick are pals."

"Well, we speak."

"Find him. Do they sell beer at that joint on the corner?—Okay. Take him there and quench his thirst. On expense. Keep him there until my car's gone from in front of the Coffee Pot. I'm going to take Pinkie for a ride."

"No! I'll be damned. Keep his necktie for me."

"All right. Let's go. Beat it."

He climbed out and went. I sat and waited. Pretty soon I saw him come out of the laundry with the snoop, and start off in the other direction. I stepped on the starter and pushed the gear lever, and rolled along. This time I stopped right in front of the Coffee Pot. I got out and went in. I saw no cop around.

Pinkie was there, at the same table as before, with what looked like the same bowl of soup. I glanced at the other customers, on the stools, and observed nothing terrifying. I walked over to Pinkie and stopped at his elbow. He looked up and said:

"Well, goddam it."

Looking at him again, I thought there was a chance Wolfe was right. I said, "Come on, Inspector Cramer wants to see you," and took bracelets out of one pocket and my automatic out of another.

There must have been something in my eyes that made him suspicious, and I'll say the little devil had nerve. He said, "I don't believe it. Show me your goddam badge."

I couldn't afford an argument. I grabbed his collar and lifted him up out of his chair and set him on his feet. Then I snapped the handcuffs on him. I kept the gat completely visible and told him, "Get going." I heard one or two mutters from the lunch counter, but didn't bother to look. Pinkie said, "My overcoat." I grabbed it off the hook and hung it on my arm, and marched him out. He went nice. Instead of trying to hide the bracelets, like most of them do, he held his hands stuck out in front.

The only danger was that a flatfoot might happen along outside and offer to help me, and the roadster wasn't a police car. But all I saw was curious citizens. I herded him to the car, opened the door and shoved him in, and climbed in after him. I had left the engine running, just in case of a hurry. I rolled off, got to Seventh Avenue, and turned north.

I said, "Now listen. I've got two pieces of information. First, to ease your mind, I'm taking you to Thirty-fifth Street to call on Mr. Nero Wolfe. Second, if you open your trap to advertise anything, you'll go there just the same, only faster and more unconscious."

"I have no desire to call—"

"Shut up." But I was grinning inside, for his voice was different; he was already jumping his character.

The evening traffic was out playing tag, and it took long enough to get to West Thirty-fifth Street. I pulled up in front of the house, told my passenger to sit still, got out and walked around and opened his door, and told him to come on. I went behind him up the steps, used my key on the portal, and nodded him in. While I was taking off my hat and coat he started reaching up for his cap, but I told him to leave it on and steered him for the office.

Wolfe was sitting there with an empty beer glass, looking at the design the dried foam had left. I shut the office door and stood there, but the runt kept going, clear to the desk. Wolfe looked at him, nodded faintly, and then looked some more. He spoke suddenly, to me:

"Archie. Take Mr. Hibbard's cap, remove the handcuffs, and place a chair for him."

I did those things. This gentleman, it appeared, represented the second fact Wolfe had demanded, and I was glad to wait on him. He held his hands out for me to take the bracelets off, but it seemed to be an effort for him, and a glance at his eyes showed me that he wasn't feeling any too prime. I eased the chair up back of his knees, and all of a sudden he slumped into it, buried his face in his hands, and stayed that way. Wolfe and I regarded him, with not as much commiseration as he might have thought he had a right to expect if he had been looking at us. To me he was the finest hunk of bacon I had lamped for several moons.

Wolfe tipped me a nod, and I went to the cabinet and poured a stiff one and brought it over. I said:

"Here, try this."

Finally he looked up. "What is it?"

"It's a goddam drink of rye whiskey."

He shook his head and reached for the drink simultaneously. I knew he had some soup in him so didn't look for any catastrophe. He downed half of it, spluttered a little, and swallowed the rest. I said to Wolfe:

"I brought him in with his cap on so you could see him that way. Anyhow, all I ever saw was a photograph. And he was supposed to be dead. And I'm here to tell you, it would have been a pleasure to plug him, and no kinds of comments will be needed now or any other time."

Wolfe, disregarding me, spoke to the runt: "Mr. Hibbard. You know of the ancient New England custom of throwing a suspected witch into the river, and if she drowned she was innocent. My personal opinion of a large drink of straight whiskey is that it provides a converse test: if you survive it you can risk anything. Mr. Goodwin did not in fact plug you?"

Hibbard looked at me and blinked, and at Wolfe and blinked again. He cleared his throat twice, and said conversationally:

"The truth of the matter is, I am not an adventurous man. I have been under a terrible strain for eleven days. And shall be—for many more."

"I hope not."

Hibbard shook his head. "And shall. God help me. And shall."

"You call on God now?"

"Rhetorically. I am further than ever from Him, as a reliance." He looked at me. "Could I have a little more whiskey?"

I got it for him. This time he started sipping it, and smacked his lips. He said, "This is a relief. The whiskey is too, of course, but I was referring particularly to this opportunity to become articulate again. No; I am further than ever from a Deity in the stratosphere, but much closer to my fellow man. I have a confession to make, Mr. Wolfe, and it might as well be to you as anyone. I have learned more in these eleven days masquerading as a roughneck than in all the previous forty-three years of my existence."

"Harun-al-Rashid—"

"No. Excuse me. He was seeking entertainment, I was seeking life. First, I thought, merely my own life, but I found much more. For instance, if you were to say to me now what you said three weeks ago, that you would undertake to remove my fear of Paul Chapin by destroying him, I would say: certainly, by all means, how much do I owe you? For I understand now that the reason for my former attitude was nothing but a greater fear than the fear of death, the fear of accepting responsibility for my own preservation.—You don't mind if I talk? God, how I want to talk!"

Wolfe murmured, "This room is hardened to it." He rang for beer.

"Thank you. In these eleven days I have learned that psychology, as a formal science, is pure hocus-pocus. All written and printed words, aside from their function of relieving boredom, are meaningless drivel. I have fed a half-starved child with my own hands. I have seen two men batter each other with their fists until the blood ran. I have watched boys picking up girls. I have heard a woman tell a man, in public and with a personal application, facts which I had dimly supposed were known, academically, only to those who have read Havelock Ellis. I had observed hungry workingmen eating in a Coffee Pot. I have seen a tough boy of the street pick up a wilted daffodil from the gutter. It is utterly amazing, I tell you, how people do things they happen to feel like doing. And I have been an instructor in psychology for seventeen years! *Merde!* Could I have a little more whiskey?"

I didn't know whether Wolfe needed him sober, but I saw no warning gesture from him, so I went and filled the glass again. This time I brought some White Rock for a chaser and he started on that first.

Wolfe said, "Mr. Hibbard. I am fascinated at the prospect of your education and I shall insist on hearing it entire, but I wonder if I could interpose a question or two. First I shall need to contradict you by observing that before your eleven days' education began you had learned enough to assume a disguise simple and effective enough to preserve your incognito, though the entire police force—and one or two other people—were looking for you. Really an achievement."

The fizz had ascended into the psychologist's nose, and he pinched it. "Oh no. That sort of thing is rule of thumb. The first rule, of course, is, nothing that looks like disguise. My best items were the necktie and the scratch on my cheek. My profanity, I fear, was not well done; I should not have undertaken it. But my great mistake was the teeth; it was the very devil to get the gold leaf cemented on, and I was forced to confine my diet almost exclusively to milk and soup. Of course, having once made my appearance, I could not abandon them. The clothing, I am proud of."

"Yes, the clothing." Wolfe looked him over. "Excellent. Where did you get it?"

"A second-hand store on Grand Street. I changed in a subway toilet, and so was properly dressed when I went to rent a room on the lower West Side."

"And you left your second pipe at home. You have estimable qualities, Mr. Hibbard."

"I was desperate."

"A desperate fool is still a fool. What, in your desperation, did you hope to accomplish? Did your venture pretend to any intelligent purpose?"

Hibbard had to consider. He swallowed some whiskey, washed it off with fizz, and coated that with another sip of whiskey. He finally said, "So help me, I don't know. I mean I don't know now. When I left home, when I started this, all that I felt moving me was fear. The whole long story of what that unlucky episode, twenty-five years ago—of what it did to me, would sound fantastic if I tried to tell it. I was too highly sensitized in spots; I suppose I still am, doubtless it will show again in the proper surroundings. I am inclining now to the environmental school—you hear that? Atavism! Anyhow, fear had me, and all I was aware of was a desire to get near Paul Chapin and keep him under my eye. I had no plans, further than that. I wanted to watch him. I knew if I told anyone, even Evelyn—my niece, there would be danger of his getting onto me, so I made a thorough job of it. But the last few days I have begun to suspect that in some gully of my mind, far below consciousness, was a desire to kill him. Of course there is no such thing as a desire without an intention, no matter how nebulous it may be. I believe I meant to kill him. I believe I have been working up to it, and I still am. I have no idea what this talk with you will do to me. I see no reason why it should have any effect one way or another."

"You will see, I think." Wolfe emptied his glass. "Naturally you do not know that Mr. Chapin has mailed verses to your friends stating explicitly that he killed you by clubbing you over the head."

"Oh yes. I know that."

"The devil you do. Who told you?"

"Pit. Pitney Scott."

I gritted my teeth and wanted to bite myself. Another chance underplayed, and all because I had believed the cripple's warning. Wolfe was saying:

"Then you did keep a bridge open."

"No. He opened it himself. The third day I was around there I met him face to face by bad luck, and of course he recognized me." Hibbard suddenly stopped, and turned a little pale. "By heaven—ha, there goes another illusion—I thought Pit . . ."

"Quite properly, Mr. Hibbard. Keep your illusion; Mr. Scott has told us nothing; it was Mr. Goodwin's acuteness of observation, and my feeling for phenomena, that uncovered you.—But to resume: if you knew that Mr. Chapin had sent those verses, falsely boasting of murdering you, it is hard to see how you could keep your respect for him as an assassin. If you knew one of his murders, the latest one, to be nothing but rodomontade . . ."

Hibbard nodded. "You make a logical point, certainly. But logic has nothing to do with it. I am not engaged in developing a scientific thesis. There are twenty-five years behind this . . . and Bill Harrison, Gene Dreyer . . . and Paul that day in the courtroom . . . I was there, to testify to the psychological value of his book . . . It was on the day that Pit Scott showed me those verses about me sucking air in through my blood that I discovered that I wanted to kill Paul, and if I wanted it I intended it, or what the devil was I doing there?"

Wolfe sighed. "It is a pity. The back-seat driving of the less charitable emotions often makes me wonder that the brain does not desert the wheel entirely, in righteous exasperation. Not to mention their violent and senseless oscillations. Mr. Hibbard. Three weeks ago you were filled with horrified aversion at the thought of engaging me to arrange that Mr. Chapin should account legally for his crimes; today you are determined to kill him yourself. You do intend to kill him?"

"I think so." The psychological runt put his whiskey glass on the desk. "That doesn't mean that I will. I don't know. I intend to."

"You are armed? You have a weapon?"

"No. I . . . no."

"You what?"

"Nothing. I should have said, he. He is physically a weakling."

"Indeed." The shadows on Wolfe's face altered; his cheeks were unfolding. "You will rip him apart with your bare hands. Into quivering bloody fragments . . ."

"I might," Hibbard snapped. "I don't know whether you taunt me through ignorance or through design. You should know that despair is still despair, even when there is an intellect to perceive it and control its hysteria. I can kill Paul Chapin and still know what I am doing. My physical build is negligible, next to contemptible, and my mental equipment has reached the decadence which sneers at the blood that feeds it, but in spite of those incongruities I can kill Paul Chapin.—I think I understand now why it was such a relief to be able to talk again in my proper person, and I thank you for it. I think I needed to put this determination into words. It does me good to hear it.—Now I would like you to let me go. I can go on, of course, only by your sufferance. You have interfered with me, and frankly I'm grateful for it, but there is no reason—"

"Mr. Hibbard." Wolfe wiggled a finger at him. "Permit me. The least offensive way of refusing a request is not to let it be made. Don't make it.—Wait, please. There are several things you either do not know or fail to consider. For instance, do you know of an arrangement I have entered into with your friends?"

"Yes. Pit Scott told me. I'm not interested—"

"But I am. In fact I know of nothing else, at the moment, that interests me in the slightest degree; certainly not your recently acquired ferocity. Further, do you know that there, on Mr. Goodwin's desk, is the

typewriter on which Mr. Chapin wrote his sanguinary
verses? Yes, it was at the Harvard Club; we negotiated a trade. Do you know that I am ready for a
complete penetration of Mr. Chapin's defenses, in
spite of his pathetic bravado? Do you know that within
twenty-four hours I shall be prepared to submit to you
and your friends a confession from Mr. Chapin of his
guilt, and to remove satisfactorily all your apprehensions?"

Hibbard was staring at him. He emptied his whiskey glass, which he had been holding half full, and put
in on the desk, and stared at Wolfe again. "I don't
believe it."

"Of course you do. You merely don't want to. I'm
sorry, Mr. Hibbard, you'll have to readjust yourself to
a world of words and compromises and niceties of
conduct. I would be glad—well?"

He stopped to look at Fritz, who had appeared on
the threshold. Wolfe glanced at the clock; it was
seven-twenty-five. He said, "I'm sorry, Fritz. Three
of us will dine, at eight o'clock. Will that be possible?"

"Yes, sir."

"Good.—As I was saying, Mr. Hibbard, I would
like to help make the readjustment as pleasant as
possible for you, and at the same time serve my own
convenience. The things I have just told you are the
truth, but to help me in realizing the last one I shall
need your co-operation. I mentioned twenty-four
hours. I would like to have you remain here as my
guest for that period. Will you?"

Hibbard shook his head, with emphasis. "I don't
believe you. You may have the typewriter, but you
don't have Paul Chapin as I do. I don't believe you'll
get him to confess, ever in God's world."

"I assure you, I will. But that can be left to the

event. Will you stay here until tomorrow evening, and communicate with no one? My dear sir. I will bargain with you. You were about to make a request of me. I counter with one of my own. Though I am sure twenty-four hours will do, let us allow for contingencies; make it forty-eight. If you will agree to stay under this roof incommunicado until Monday evening, I engage that at that time, if I have not done as I said and closed the Chapin account forever, you will be free to resume your whimsical adventure without fear of any betrayal from us. Do I need to add a recommendation of our discretion and intelligence?"

As Wolfe finished speaking Hibbard unaccountably burst into laughter. For a runt he had a good laugh, deeper than his voice, which was baritone but a little thin. When he had laughed it out he said, "I was thinking that you probably have an adequate bathtub."

"We have."

"But tell me this. I am still learning. If I refused, if I got up now to walk out, what would you do?"

"Well . . . you see, Mr. Hibbard, it is important to my plans that your discovery should remain unknown until the proper moment. Certain shocks must be administered to Mr. Chapin, and they must be well timed. There are various ways of keeping a desired guest. The most amiable is to persuade him to accept an invitation; another would be to lock him up."

Hibbard nodded. "You see? What did I tell you? You see how people go ahead and do things they feel like doing? Miraculous!"

"It is indeed.—And now the bathtub, if we are to dine at eight. Archie, if you would show Mr. Hibbard the south room, the one above mine . . ."

I got up. "It'll be clammy as the devil, it hasn't been used . . . he can have mine . . ."

"No. Fritz has aired it and the heat is on; it has been properly prepared, even to Brassocattlaelias Truffautianas in the bowl."

"Oh." I grinned. "You had it prepared."

"Certainly.—Mr. Hibbard. Come down when you are ready. I warn you, I am prepared to demonstrate that the eighth and ninth chapters of *The Chasm of the Mind* are mystic nonsense. If you wish to repel my attack, bring your wits to the table."

I started out with Hibbard, but Wolfe's voice came again and we returned. "You understand the arrangement, sir; you are to communicate with no one whatever. Away from your masquerade, the desire to reassure your niece will be next to irresistible."

"I'll resist it."

Since it was two flights up, I took him to Wolfe's elevator. The door of the south room stood open, and the room was nice and warm. I looked around: the bed had been made, comb and brush and nail file were on the dresser, orchids were in the bowl on the table; fresh towels were in the bathroom. Not bad for a strictly male household. I went out, but at the door was stopped by Hibbard:

"Say. Do you happen to have a dark brown necktie?"

I grinned and went to my room and picked out a genteel solid-color, and took it up to him.

Down in the office Wolfe sat with his eyes shut. I went to my desk. I was sore as hell. I was still hearing the tone of Wolfe's voice when he said, "Sixty-five hours," and though I knew the reproach had been for himself and not for me, I didn't need a whack on the shins to inform me that I had made a bad fumble. I sat and considered the general and particular shortcomings of my conduct. Finally I said aloud, as if to myself, not looking at him:

"The one thing I won't ever do again is believe a cripple. It was all because I believed that damn warning. If it hadn't been imbedded in my nut that Andrew Hibbard was dead, I would have been receptive to a decent suspicion no matter where it showed up. I suppose that goes for Inspector Cramer too, and I suppose that means that I'm of the same general order as he is. In that case—"

"Archie." I glanced at Wolfe enough to see that he had opened his eyes. He went on, "If that is meant as a defense offered to me, none is needed. If you are merely rubbing your vanity to relieve a soreness, please defer it. There is still eighteen minutes before dinner, and we might as well make use of them. I am suffering from my habitual impatience when nothing remains but the finishing touches. Take your notebook."

I got it out, and a pencil.

"Make three copies of this, the original on the good bond. Date it tomorrow, November eleventh—ha, Armistice Day! Most appropriate. It will have a heading in caps as follows: CONFESSION OF PAUL CHAPIN REGARDING THE DEATHS OF WILLIAM R. HARRISON AND EUGENE DREYER AND THE WRITING AND DISPATCHING OF CERTAIN INFORMATIVE AND THREATENING VERSES. It is a concession to him to call them verses, but we should be magnanimous somewhere, let us select that for it. There will then be divisions, properly spaced and subheaded. The subheadings will also be in caps. The first one is DEATH OF WILLIAM R. HARRISON. Then begin . . . thus—"

I interrupted. "Listen, wouldn't it be fitting to type this on the machine from the Harvard Club? Of course it's crummy, but it would be a poetic gesture . . ."

"Poetic? Oh. Sometimes, Archie, the association of your ideas reminds me of a hummingbird. Very well, you may do that. Let us proceed." When he was giving me a document Wolfe usually began slow and speeded up as he went along. He began, "I, Paul Chapin, of 203 Perry Street, New York City, hereby confess that—"

The telephone rang.

I put my notebook down and reached for it. My practice was to answer calls by saying crisp but friendly, "Hello, this is the office of Nero Wolfe." But this time I didn't get to finish it. I got about three words out, but the rest of it was stopped by an excited voice in my ear, excited but low, nearly a whisper, fast but trying to make it plain:

"Archie, listen. Quick, get it, I may be pulled off. Get up here as fast as you can—Doc Burton's, Nine-tieth Street. Burton's croaked. The lop got him with a gat, pumped him full. They got him clean, I followed him—"

There were noises, but no more words. That was enough to last a while, anyway. I hung up and turned to Wolfe. I suppose my face wasn't very placid, but the expression on his didn't change any as he looked at me. I said, "That was Fred Durkin. Paul Chapin has just shot Dr. Burton and killed him. At his apartment on Ninetieth Street. They caught him red-handed. Fred invites me up to see the show."

Wolfe sighed. He murmured, "Nonsense."

"Nonsense hell. Fred's not a genius, but I never saw him mistake a pinochle game for a murder. He's got good eyes. It looks like tailing Chapin wasn't such a bad idea after all, since it got Fred there on the spot. We've got him—"

"Archie. Shut up." Wolfe's lips were pushing out and in as fast as I had ever seen them. After ten seconds he said, "Consider this, please. Durkin's conversation was interrupted?"

"Yeah, he was pulled off."

"By the police, of course. The police take Chapin for murdering Burton; he is convicted and executed, and where are we? What of our engagements? We are lost."

I stared at him. "Good God. Damn that cripple—"

"Don't damn him. Save him. Save him for us. The roadster is in front? Good. Go there at once, fast. You know what to do, get it, the whole thing. I need the scene, the minutes and seconds, the participants—I need the facts. I need enough of them to save Paul Chapin. Go and get them."

I jumped.

# Chapter 17

I kept on the west side as far as Eighty-sixth Street and then shot crosstown and through the park. I stepped on it only up to the limit, because I didn't want to get stopped. I felt pretty good and pretty rotten, both. She had cracked wide open and I was on my way, and that was all sweetness and light, but on the other hand Fred's story of the event decorated by Wolfe's comments looked like nothing but bad weather. I swung left into Fifth Avenue, with only five blocks to go.

I pulled up short of the Burton number on Ninetieth Street, locked the ignition and jumped to the sidewalk. There were canopies and entrances to big apartment houses all around. I walked east. I was nearly to the entrance I was headed for when I saw Fred Durkin. From somewhere he came trotting toward me. I stopped, and he jerked his head back and started west, and I went along behind him. I followed him to the corner of Fifth, and around it a few feet.

I said, "Am I poison? Spill it."

He said, "I didn't want that doorman to see you with me. He saw me getting the bum's rush. They caught me phoning you and kicked me out."

"That's too bad. I'll complain at headquarters. Well?"

"Well, they've got him, that's all. We followed him up here, the town dick and me, got here at seven-thirty. It was nice and private, without Pinkie. Of course we knew who lived here, and we talked it over whether we ought to phone and decided not to. We decided to go inside the lobby, and when the hall flunky got unfriendly Murphy—that's the town dick—flashed his badge and shut him up. People were going and coming, there's two elevators. All of a sudden one of the elevator doors bangs open and a woman comes running out popeyed and yells where's Dr. Foster, catch Dr. Foster, and the hall flunky says he just saw him go out, and the woman runs for the street yelling Dr. Foster, and Murphy nabs her by the arm and asks why not try Dr. Burton, and she looks at him funny and says Dr. Burton's been shot. He turns her loose and jumps for the elevator, and on the way up to the fifth floor discovers that I'm in it with him. He says—"

"Come on, for Christ's sake."

"Okay. The door of Burton's apartment is open. The party's in the first room we go into. Two women is there, one of them whining like a sick dog and jiggling a telephone, and the other one kneeling by a guy laying on the floor. The lop is sitting in a chair looking like he's waiting his turn in a barber shop. We got busy. The guy was dead. Murphy got on the phone and I looked around. A gat, a Colt automatic, was on the floor by the leg of a chair next to a table in the middle of the room. I went over and gave Chapin a rub to see if he had any more tools. The woman that was kneeling by the meat began to heave and I went and got her up and led her away. Two men came in, a doctor and a house guy. Murphy got through on the phone and came over and slipped some irons on Chapin. I stayed with the woman, and when a couple of precinct cops came loping in I took the woman out of the room. The woman that had gone for Dr. Foster came back, she came running through the place and took the other woman away from me and took her off somewhere. I went into another room and saw books and a desk and a telephone, and called you up. One of the precinct men came snooping around and heard me, and that's when I left. He brought me downstairs and gave me the air."

"Who else has come?"

"Only a couple of radios and some more precinct guys."

"Cramer or the D.A. office?"

"Not yet. Hell, they don't need to bother. A package like that, they could just have it sent parcel post."

"Yeah. You go to Thirty-fifth Street and tell Fritz to feed you. As soon as Wolfe has finished his dinner, tell him about it. He may want you to get Saul and Orrie—he'll tell you."

"I'll have to phone my wife—"

"Well, you got a nickel? Beat it."

He went downtown, towards Eighty-ninth, and I went around the corner and east again. I approached the entrance; I didn't see any reason why I couldn't crash it, though I didn't know anyone up there. Just as I was under the canopy a big car came along and stopped quick, and two men got out. I took a look, then I got in the way of one of them. I grinned at him:

"Inspector Cramer! This is luck." I started to walk along in with him.

He stopped. "Oh! You. Nothing doing. Beat it."

I started to hand him a line, but he got sharp.

"Beat it, Goodwin. If there's anything up there that belongs to you I'll save it for you. Nothing doing."

I fell back. People were gathering, there was already quite a crowd, and a cop was there herding them. In the confusion I was pretty sure he hadn't heard the little passage between Cramer and me. I faded away, and went to where I had parked the roadster. I opened up the back and got out a black bag I kept a few things in for emergencies; it didn't look just right, but good enough. I went back to the entrance and pushed through the line while the cop was busy on the other side, and got through the door. Inside was the doorman and another cop. I stepped up to them and said, "Medical Examiner. What apartment is it?" The cop looked me over and took me to the elevator and said to the boy, "Take this gent to the fifth floor." Inside, going up, I gave the black bag a pat.

I breezed into the apartment. As Durkin had said, the party was right there, the first room you entered, a big reception hall. There was a mob there, mostly flatfeet and dicks standing around looking bored. Inspector Cramer was by the table listening to one of the latter. I walked over to him and said his name.

He looked around, and seemed surprised. "Well, in the name of—"

"Now listen, inspector. Just a second. Forget it. I'm not going to steal the prisoner or the evidence or anything else. You know damn well I've got a right to curiosity and that's all I expect to satisfy. Have a heart. My God, we've all got mothers."

"What have you got in that bag?"

"Shirts and socks. I used it to bring me up. I'd just as soon have one of your men take it down to my car for me."

He grunted. "Leave it here on the table, and if you get in the way—"

"I won't. Much obliged."

Being careful not to bump anyone, I got back against the wall. I took a look. It was a room 17 × 20, on a guess, nearly square. One end was mostly windows, curtained. At the other end was the entrance door. One long wall, the one I was standing against, had pictures and a couple of stands with vases of flowers. In the other wall, nearly to the corner, was a double door, closed, leading of course to the apartment proper. The rest of that wall, about ten feet of it, had curtains to match those at the end, but there couldn't have been windows. I figured it was closets for wraps. The light was from the ceiling, indirect, with switches at the double door and the entrance door. There was one large rug, and a good-sized table in the middle. Near where I stood was a stand with a telephone and a chair.

There were only four chairs altogether. In one of them, at the end of the table, Paul Chapin was sitting. I couldn't see his face, he was turned wrong. At the other end of the table Doc Burton was on the floor. He just looked dead and fairly comfortable; either he had landed straight when he fell or someone had stretched him out, and his arms were neatly along his sides. His head was at a funny angle, but they always are until they're propped up. Looking at him, I thought to myself that Wolfe had had him down for seven thousand bucks, and now he'd never have that to worry about again along with a lot of other things. From where I was I couldn't see much blood.

A few details had happened since I arrived. There had been phone calls. One of the dicks had gone out and come back in a couple of minutes with an Assistant Medical Examiner; apparently there had been difficulty downstairs. I hoped he wouldn't take my bag by mistake when he went. They buzzed around. Inspector Cramer had left the room by the double door, to see the women I supposed. A young woman came in from outside and made a scene, but all in all she did pretty well with it, since it appeared that it was her father that had been croaked. She had been out somewhere, and she took it hard. I've often observed that the only thing that makes it a real hardship to have dealings with stiffs is the people that are still living. This girl was the kind that makes your throat clog up because you see how she's straining to fight it back in and you know she's licked. I was glad when a dick took her away, in to her mother.

I moseyed around to get a slant at the cripple. I went around the table and got in front of him. He looked at me, but there wasn't any sign of his being aware he had ever seen me before. His stick was on the table beside him, and his hat. He had on a brown overcoat, unbuttoned, and tan gloves. He was slouched over; his hands were resting on his good knee, fastened with the bracelets. There was nothing in his face, just nothing; he looked more like a passenger in the subway than anything else. His light-colored eyes looked straight at me. I thought to myself that this was the first piece of real hundred per cent bad luck I had ever known Nero Wolfe to have. He had had his share of bad breaks all right, but this wasn't a break, it was an avalanche.

Then I remembered what I was there for, and I said to myself that I had gone around for two days pretending to hunt Andrew Hibbard knowing all the time it was hopeless, and Hibbard was at that moment eating scallops and arguing psychology with Wolfe. And until Wolfe himself said finish for that case one way or the other, hopeless was out. It was up to me to dig up a little hope.

I got against the wall again and surveyed the field. The medical guy was done. There was no telling how long Cramer would be with the women, but unless their tale was more complicated than it seemed likely to be there was no reason why it should be very long. When he returned there would probably be no delay in removing the stiff and the cripple, and then there would be nothing to keep anybody else. Cramer wouldn't be apt to go off and leave me behind, he'd want me for company. Nor could I see any reason why he would leave anyone behind, except a dick out in the hall maybe and possibly one downstairs, to keep annoyance away from the family.

That was the way it looked. I couldn't go back to Wolfe with nothing but a sob story about a poor cripple and a dead man and a grief-stricken daughter. I wandered around again to the other side of the table, to the other wall where the curtains were. I stood with my back to the curtains. Then I saw my bag on the table. That wouldn't do, so I went over and got it, casually, and went back against the curtains again. I figured the chances were about fifty to one against me, but the worst I could get was an escort to the elevator. Keeping my eyes carelessly on the array of dicks and flatfeet scattered around, I felt behind me with my foot and found that back of the curtains the floor continued flush, with no sill. If it was a closet it was built into the wall and I had no idea how deep it was or what was in there. I kept my eyes busy; I had to pick an instant when every guy there had his face turned; at least not right on me. I was waiting for something, and luck came that time; it happened. The phone rang, on the stand by the other wall. Having nothing to occupy them, they all turned involuntarily. I had my hand behind me ready to pull the curtain aside, and back I went, and let the curtain fall again, with me behind.

I had ducked going in, in case there happened to be a hat shelf at the usual height, but the shelf was further back; the closet was all of three feet deep and I had plenty of room. I held my breath for a few seconds, but heard none of the bloodhounds baying. I eased the black bag onto the floor in a corner and got behind what felt like a woman's fur coat. One thing there had been no help for: the cripple had seen me. His light-colored eyes had been right at me as I backed in. If he should decide to open his trap I hoped he would find something else to talk about.

I stood there in the dark, and after a while wished I had remembered to bring an oxygen tank. To amuse me I had the voices of the dicks outside, but they were low and I couldn't pick out many words. Somebody came in, some woman, and a little later a man. It was all of half an hour before Cramer returned. I heard the double door opening, close to my curtain, and then Cramer handing out orders. He sounded snappy and satisfied. A dick with a hoarse voice told another one, right in front of me, to carry Chapin's stick and he'd help him walk; they were taking him away. There were noises, and directions from Cramer, about removing the corpse, and in a couple of minutes heavy feet as they carried it out. I was hoping to God that Cramer or someone else hadn't happened to hang his coat in my closet, but that wasn't likely; there had been three or four piled on the table. I heard a voice telling someone to go ask for a rug to put over the soiled place where Burton had been, and Cramer and others shoving off. It sounded like there were only two left, after the guy came back with the rug; they were kidding each other about some kind of a girl. I began to be afraid Cramer had spotted them to stay for some reason or other, but pretty soon I heard them going to the door, and it opened and closed.

I'd been in the closet long enough as far as my lungs were concerned, but I thought it was just possible one was still inside the main apartment, and I waited five minutes, counting. Then I pulled the edge of the curtain a little and took a slant. I opened it up and stepped out. Empty. All gone. The double doors were closed. I went over and turned the knob and pushed, and walked through. I was in a room about five times the size of the reception hall, dimly lit, furnished up to the hilt. There was a door at the far end and a wide open arch halfway down one side. I heard voices from somewhere. I went on in a ways and called:

"Hello! Mrs. Burton!"

The voices stopped, and there were footsteps coming. A guy appeared in the arch, trying to look important. I grinned inside. He was just a kid, around twenty-two, nice and handsome and dressed up. He said, "We thought you had all gone."

"Yeah. All but me. I have to see Mrs. Burton."

"But he said . . . the Inspector said she wouldn't be bothered."

"I'm sorry, I have to see her."

"She's lying down."

"Tell her just a few questions."

He opened his moth and shut it, looked as if he thought he ought to do something, and turned and beat it. In a minute he came back and nodded me along. I followed.

We went through a room and a sort of a hall and

into another room. This was not so big, but was better
lit and not so dolled up. A maid in uniform was going
out another door with a tray. A woman was sitting on
a couch, another woman in a chair, and the daughter I
had seen in the reception hall was standing behind the
couch. I walked over there.

I suppose Mrs. Loring A. Burton wasn't at her
best that evening, but she could have slipped a few
more notches and still have been in the money. A
glance was enough to show you she was quite a
person. She had a straight thin nose, a warm mouth,
fine dark eyes. Her hair was piled in braids at the
back, pulled back just right for you to see her temples
and brow, which maybe made most of the effect; that
and the way she held her head. Her neck knew some
artist's trick that I've seen many a movie star try to
copy without quite getting it. It had been born in her
spine.

With her head up like that I could see it would take
more than a murdered husband to overwhelm her into
leaving decisions to daughters and so on, so I disre-
garded the others. I told her I had a few confidential
questions to ask and I'd like to see her alone. The
woman in the chair muttered something about cruel
and unnecessary. The daughter stared at me with red
eyes. Mrs. Burton asked:

"Confidential to whom?"

"To Paul Chapin. I'd rather not . . ." I looked
around.

She looked around too. I saw that the kid wasn't
the son and heir after all, it was the daughter he was
interested in, probably had it signed up. Mrs. Burton
said, "What does it matter? Go to my room—you don't
mind, Alice?"

The woman in the chair said she didn't, and got up.

The kid took hold of the daughter's arm to steer her, by golly he wasn't going to let her fall and hurt herself. They went on out.

Mrs. Burton said, "Well?"

I said, "The confidential part is really about me. Do you know who Nero Wolfe is?"

"Nero Wolfe? Yes."

"Dr. Burton and his friends entered into an agreement—"

She interrupted me. "I know all about it. My husband . . ." She stopped. The way she suddenly clasped her fingers tight and tried to keep her lips from moving showed that a bust-up was nearer to coming through than I had supposed. But she soon got it shoved under again. "My husband told me all about it."

I nodded. "That saves time. I'm not a city detective. I'm private. I work for Nero Wolfe, my name's Goodwin. If you ask me what I'm here for there's lots of ways to answer you, but you'd have to help me pick the right one. It depends on how you feel." I had the innocence turned on, the candid eye. I was talking fast. "Of course you feel terrible, certainly, but no matter how bad it is inside of you right now, you'll go on living. I've got some questions to ask for Nero Wolfe, and I can't be polite and wait for a week until your nerves have had a chance to grow some new skin, I've got to ask them now or never. I'm here now, just tell me this and get rid of me. Did you see Paul Chapin shoot your husband?"

"No. But I've already—"

"Sure. Let's get it done. Did anybody see him?"

"No."

I took a breath. At least, then, we weren't floating with our bellies up. I said, "All right. Then it's a question of how you feel. How you feel about this, for instance, that Paul Chapin didn't shoot your husband at all."

She stared at me. "What do you mean—I saw him—"

"You didn't see him shoot. Here's what I'm getting at, Mrs. Burton. I know your husband didn't hate Paul Chapin. I know he felt sorry for him and was willing to go with the crowd because he saw no help for it. How about you, did you hate him? Disregard what happened tonight, how much did you hate him?"

For a second I thought I had carried her along; then I saw a change coming in her eyes and her lips beginning to tighten up. She was going to ritz me out. I rushed in ahead of it:

"Listen, Mrs. Burton, I'm not just a smart pup nosing around somebody's back yard seeing what I can smell. I really know all about this, maybe even some things you don't know. Right now, in a cabinet down in Nero Wolfe's office, there is a leather box. I put it there. This big. It's beautiful tan leather, with fine gold tooling on it, and it's locked, and it's full nearly to the top with your gloves and stockings. Some you've worn.—Now wait a minute, give me a chance. It belongs to Paul Chapin. Dora Ritter hooked them and gave them to him. It's his treasure. Nero Wolfe says his soul is in that box. I wouldn't know about that, I'm no expert on souls. I'm just telling you. The reason I want to know whether you hate Paul Chapin, regardless of his killing your husband, is this: what if he didn't kill him? Would you like to see them hang it on him anyway?"

She was looking at me, with the idea of ritzing me out put aside for the moment. She said, "I don't know what you're driving at. I saw him dead. I don't know what you mean."

"Neither do I. That's what I'm here to find out. I'm trying to make you understand that I'm not annoying you just for curiosity, I'm here on business, and it may turn out to be your business as well as mine. I'm interested in seeing that Paul Chapin gets no more than is coming to him. Right now I don't suppose you're interested in anything. You've had a shock that would lay most women flat. Well, you're not flat, and you might as well talk to me as sit and try not to think about it. I'd like to sit here and ask you a few things. If you look like you are going to faint I'll call the family and get up and go."

She unclasped her hands. She said, "I don't faint. You may sit down."

"Okay." I used the chair Alice had left. "Now tell me how it happened. The shooting. Who was here?"

"My husband and I, and the cook and the maid. One of the maids was out."

"No one else? What about the woman you called Alice?"

"That is my oldest friend. She came to . . . just a little while ago. There was no one else here."

"And?"

"I was in my room dressing. We were dining out, my daughter was out somewhere. My husband came to my room for a cigarette; he always . . . he never remembered to have any, and the door between our rooms is always open. The maid came and said Paul Chapin was there. My husband left to go to the foyer to see him, but he didn't go direct; he went back through his room and his study. I mention that because I stood and listened. The last time Paul had come my husband had told the maid to keep him in the foyer, and before he went there he had gone to his study and got a revolver out of the drawer. I had thought it was childish. This time I listened to see if he did it again, and he did, I heard the drawer opening. Then he called to me, called my name, and I answered what is it, and he called back, nothing, never mind, he would tell me after he had speeded his guest. That was the last . . . those were his last words I heard. I heard him walking through the apartment—I listened, I suppose, because I was wondering what Paul could want. Then I heard noises—not loud, the foyer is so far away from my room, and then shots. I ran. The maid came out of the dining-room and followed me. We ran to the foyer. It was dark, and the light in the drawing-room was dim and we couldn't see anything. I heard a noise, someone falling, and Paul's voice saying my name. I turned on the light switch, and Paul was there on his knee trying to get up. He said my name again, and said he was trying to hop to the switch. Then I saw Lorrie, on the floor at the end of the table. I ran to him, and when I saw him I called to the maid to go for Dr. Foster, who lives a floor below us. I don't know what Paul did then, I didn't pay attention to him, the first I knew some men came—"

"All right, hold it."

She stopped. I looked at her a minute, getting it. She had clasped her hands again and was doing some extra breathing, but not obtrusively. I quit worrying about her. I took out a pad and pencil, and said, "This thing, the way you tell it, needs a lot of fixing. The worst item, of course, is the light being out. That's plain silly.—Now wait a minute, I'm just talking about what Nero Wolfe calls a feeling for phenomena, I'm trying to enjoy one. Let's go back to the beginning. On his way to see Paul Chapin, your husband called to you from the study, and then said never mind. Have you any idea what he was going to say?"

"No, how could I—"

"Okay. The way you told it, he called to you after he opened the drawer. Was that the way it was?"

She nodded. "I'm sure it was after I heard the drawer open. I was listening."

"Yeah. Then you heard him walking to the foyer, and then you heard noises. What kind of noises?"

"I don't know. Just noises, movements. It is far away, and doors were closed. The noises were faint."

"Voices?"

"No. I didn't hear any."

"Did you hear your husband closing the foyer door after he got there?"

"No. I wouldn't hear that unless it banged."

"Then we'll try this. Since you were listening to his footsteps, even if you couldn't hear them any more after he got into the drawing-room, there was a moment when you figured that he had reached the foyer. You know what I mean, the feeling that he was there. When I say *Now*, that will mean that he has just reached the foyer, and you begin feeling the time, the passing of time. Feel it as near the same as you can, and when it's time for the first shot to go off, you say *Now.*—Get it? *Now.*"

I looked at the second hand of my watch; it went crawling up from the 30. She said, *"Now."*

I stared at her. "My God, that was only six seconds."

She nodded. "It was as short as that, I'm sure it was."

"In that case . . . all right. Then you ran to the foyer, and there was no light there. Of course you couldn't be wrong about that."

"No. The light was off."

"And you switched it on and saw Chapin kneeling, getting up. Did he have a gun in his hand?"

"No. He had his coat and gloves on. I didn't see a gun . . . anywhere."

"Did Inspector Cramer tell you about the gun?"

She nodded. "It was my husband's. He shot . . . it had been fired four times. They found it on the floor."

"Cramer showed it to you."

"Yes."

"And it's gone from the drawer in the study."

"Of course."

"When you turned on the light Chapin was saying something."

"He was saying my name. After the light was on he said—I can tell you exactly what he said. *Anne, a cripple in the dark, my dear Anne, I was trying to hop to the switch.* He had fallen."

"Yeah. Naturally." I finished scratching on the pad, and looked up at her. She was sitting tight. I said, "Now to go back again. Were you at home all afternoon?"

"No. I was at a gallery looking at prints, and then at a tea. I got home around six."

"Was your husband here when you got here?"

"Yes, he comes early . . . on Saturday. He was in his study with Ferdinand Bowen. I went in to say hello. We always . . . said hello, no matter who was here."

"So Mr. Bowen was here. Do you know what for?"

"No. That is . . . no."

"Now come, Mrs. Burton. You've decided to put up with this and it's pretty swell of you, so come ahead. What was Bowen here for?"

"He was asking a favor. That's all I know."

"A financial favor?"

"I suppose so, yes."

"Did he get it?"

"No. But this has no connection . . . no more of this."

"Okay. When did Bowen leave?"

"Soon after I arrived, I should say a quarter past six. Perhaps twenty after; it was about ten minutes before Dora came, and she was punctual at six-thirty."

"You don't say so." I looked at her. "You mean Dora Chapin."

"Yes."

"She came to do your hair."

"Yes."

"I'll be damned.—Excuse me. Nero Wolfe doesn't permit me to swear in front of ladies. And Dora Chapin got here at six-thirty. Well. When did she leave?"

"It always takes her three-quarters of an hour, so she left at a quarter past seven." She paused to calculate. "Yes, that would be right. A few minutes later, perhaps. I figured that I had fifteen minutes to finish dressing."

"So Dora Chapin left here at seven-twenty and Paul Chapin arrived at half past. That's interesting; they almost collided. Who else was here after six o'clock?"

"No one. That's all. My daughter left around half past six, a little before Dora came. Of course I don't understand—what is it, Alice?"

A door had opened behind me, and I turned to see. It was the woman, the old friend. She said:

"Nick Cabot is on the phone—they notified him. He wants to know if you want to talk to him."

Mrs. Burton's dark eyes flashed aside for an instant, at me. I let my head go sideways enough for her to see it. She spoke to her friend, "No, there is nothing to say. I won't talk to anyone. Are you folks finding something to eat?"

"We'll make out. Really, Anne, I think—"

"Please, Alice. Please—"

After a pause the door closed again. I had a grin inside, a little cocky. I said, "You started to say, something you don't understand . . ."

She didn't go on. She sat looking at me with a frown in her eyes but her brow smooth and white. She got up and went to a table, took a cigarette from a box and lit it, and picked up an ash tray. She came back to the couch and sat down and took a couple of whiffs. Then she looked at the cigarette as if wondering where it had come from, and crushed it dead on the tray, and set the tray down. She straightened up and seemed to remember I was looking at her. She spoke suddenly:

"What did you say your name is?"

"Archie Goodwin."

"Thank you. I should know your name. Strange things can happen, can't they? Why did you tell me not to talk to Mr. Cabot?"

"No special reason. Right now I don't want you to be talking to anybody but me."

She nodded. "And I'm doing it. Mr. Goodwin, you're not much over half my age and I never saw you before. You seem to be clever. You realized, I suppose, what the shock of seeing my husband dead, shot dead, has done to me. It has shaken things loose. I am doing something very remarkable, for me. I don't usually talk, below the surface. I never have, since childhood, except with two people. My husband, my dear husband, and Paul Chapin. But we aren't talking about my husband, there's nothing to say about him. He's dead. He is dead . . . I shall have to tell myself many times . . . he is dead. He wants to go on living in me, or I want him to. I think—this is what I am really saying—I think I would want Paul to.—Oh, it's impossible!" She jerked herself up, and her hands got clasped again. "It's absurd to try to talk about this— even    to    a    stranger—and    with    Lorrie dead—absurd . . ."

I said, "Maybe it's absurd not to. Let it crack open once, spill it out."

She shook her head. "There's nothing to crack open. There's no reason why I should want to talk about it, but I do. Otherwise why should I let you question me? I saw farther inside myself this evening than I have ever seen before. It wasn't when I saw my husband dead, it wasn't when I stood alone in my room, looking at a picture of him, trying to realize he was dead. It was sitting here with that police inspector, with him telling me that a plea of guilty is not accepted in first degree murder, and that I would have to talk with a representative of the District Attorney, and would have to testify in court so that Paul Chapin can be convicted and punished. I don't want him punished. My husband is dead, isn't that enough? And if I don't want him punished, what is it I want to hold onto? Is it pity? I have never pitied him. I have been pretty insolent with life, but not insolent enough to pity Paul Chapin. You told me that he has a box filled with my gloves and stockings which Dora stole for him, and that Nero Wolfe said it holds his soul. Perhaps my soul has been put away in a box too, and I didn't even know it . . ."

She got up, abruptly. The ash tray slid off the

couch to the floor. She stooped over, and with deliberate fingers that showed no sign of trembling picked up the burnt match stick and the cigarette and put them on the tray. I didn't move to help her. She went to the table with the tray and then came back to the couch and sat down again. She said:

"I have always disliked Paul Chapin. Once, when I was eighteen years old, I promised to marry him. When I learned of his accident, that he was crippled for life, I was delighted because I wouldn't have to keep my promise. I didn't know that then but I realized it later. At no time have I pitied him. I claim no originality in that, I think no woman has ever pitied him, only men. Women do not like him—even those who have been briefly fascinated by him. I dislike him intensely. I have thought about this; I have had occasion to analyze it; it is his deformity that is intolerable. Not his physical deformity. The deformity of his nervous system, of his brain. You have heard of feminine cunning, but you don't understand it as Paul does, for he has it himself. It is a hateful quality in a man. Women have been fascinated by it, but the two or three who surrendered to it—I not among them, not even at eighteen—got only contempt for a reward.

"He married Dora Ritter. She's a woman?"

"Oh yes, Dora's a woman. But she is consecrated to a denial of her womanhood. I am fond of her, I understand her. She knows what beauty is, and she sees herself. That forced her, long ago, to the denial, and her strength of will has maintained it. Paul understood her too. He married her to show his contempt for me; he told me so. He could risk it with Dora because she might be relied upon never to embarrass him with the only demand that he would find humiliating. And as for Dora—she hates him, but she would die for him. Fiercely and secretly, against her denial, she longed for the dignity of marriage, and it was a miracle of luck that Paul offered it under the only circumstances that could make it acceptable to her. Oh, they understand each other!"

I said, "She hates him, and she married him."

"Yes. Dora could do that."

"I'm surprised she was here today. I understood she had a bad accident Wednesday morning. I saw her. She seems to have some character."

"It could be called that. Dora is insane. Legally, I suppose not, but nevertheless she is insane. Paul has told her so many times. She tells me about it, in the same tone she uses for the weather. There are two things she can't bear the thought of: that any woman should suspect her of being capable of tenderness, or that any man should regard her as a woman at all. Her character comes from her indifference to everything else, except Paul Chapin."

"She bragged to Nero Wolfe that she was married."

"Of course. It removes her from the field.—Oh, it is impossible to laugh at her, and you can't pity her any more than you can Paul. A monkey might as well pity me because I haven't got a tail."

I said, "You were talking about your soul."

"Was I? Yes. To you, Mr. Goodwin. I could not speak about it to my friend, Alice—I tried but nothing came. Wasn't I saying that I don't want Paul Chapin punished? Perhaps that's wrong, perhaps I do want him punished, but not crudely by killing him. What have I in my mind? What is in my heart? God knows. But I started to answer your questions when you said something—something about his punishment—"

I nodded. "I said he shouldn't get more than is

coming to him. Of course to you it looks open and shut, and apparently it looks the same way to the cops. You heard shots and ran to the foyer and there it was, a live man and a dead man and a gun. And of course Inspector Cramer has already got the other fixings, for instance the motive all dressed up and its shoes shined, not to mention a willingness to even up with Chapin for certain inconveniences he has been put to. But as Nero Wolfe says, a nurse that pushes the perambulator in the park without putting the baby in it has missed the point. Maybe if I look around I'll find the baby. For example, Dora Chapin left here at seven-twenty. Chapin arrived at seven-thirty, ten minutes later. What if she waited in the hall outside and came back in with him? Or if she couldn't do that because the maid let him in, he could have opened the door for her while the maid was gone to tell Dr. Burton. She could have snatched the gun from Burton's pocket and done the shooting and beat it before you could get there. That might explain the light being out; she might have flipped the switch before she opened the outer door so if anyone happened to be passing in the outside hall they couldn't see in. You say she hates Chapin. Maybe to him it was entirely unexpected, he had no idea what she was up to—"

She was shaking her head. "I don't believe that. It's possible, but I don't believe it."

"You say she's crazy."

"No. As far as Dora could like any man, she liked Lorrie. She wouldn't do that."

"Not to make a reservation for Chapin in the electric chair?"

Mrs. Burton looked at me, and a little shudder ran over her. She said, "That's no better . . . than the other. That's horrible."

"Of course it's horrible. Whatever we pull out of this bag, it won't be a pleasant surprise for anyone concerned, except maybe Chapin. I ought to mention another possibility. Dr. Burton shot himself. He turned the light out so Chapin couldn't see what he was doing in time to let out a yell that might have given it away. That's horrible too, but it's quite possible."

That didn't seem to discompose her as much as my first guess. She merely said, calmly, "No, Mr. Goodwin. It might be barely conceivable that Lorrie wanted . . . had some reason to kill himself without my knowing it, but that he would try to put the guilt on Paul . . . on anyone . . . No, that isn't even possible."

"Okay. You said it yourself a while ago, Mrs. Burton; strange things can happen. But as far as that's concerned, anyone at all might have done it—anyone who could get into that foyer and who knew Chapin was there and that Dr. Burton would come.—By the way, what about the maid that's out this evening? Does she have a key? What's she like?"

"Yes, she has a key. She is fifty-six years old, has been with us nine years, and calls herself the housekeeper. You would waste time asking about her."

"I could still be curious about her key."

"She will have it when she comes in the morning. You may see her then if you wish."

"Thanks. Now the other maid. Could I see her now?"

She got up and went to the table and pushed a button, and took another cigarette and lit it. I noticed that with her back turned you could have taken her for twenty, except for the coil of hair. But she was slumping a little; as she stood her shoulders sagged.

She pulled them up again and turned and came back to the couch, as the inner door opened and the whole outfit appeared: cook, maid, friend Alice, daughter and boy friend. The cook was carrying a tray. Mrs. Burton said:

"Thank you, Henny, not now. Don't try it again, please don't, I really couldn't swallow. And the rest of you . . . if you don't mind . . . we wish to see Rose a few minutes. Just Rose."

"But, mother, really—"

"No, dear. Please, just a few minutes. Johnny, this is very nice of you. I appreciate it very much. Come here, Rose."

The kid blushed. "Aw, don't mention it, Mrs. Burton."

They faded back through the door. The maid came and stood in front of us and tried some swallowing which didn't seem to work. Her face looked quite peculiar because it intended to be sympathetic but she was too shocked and scared, and it would have been fairly peculiar at any time with its broad flat nose and plucked eyebrows. Mrs. Burton told her I wanted to ask her some questions, and she looked at me as if she had been informed that I was going to sell her down the river. Then she stared at the pad on my knee and looked even worse. I said:

"Rose. I know exactly what's in your mind. You're thinking that the other man wrote down your answers to his questions and now I'm going to do the same, and then we'll compare them and if they're not alike we'll take you to the top of the Empire State Building and throw you off. Forget that silly stuff. Come on, forget it.—By the way." I turned to Mrs. Burton: "Does Dora Chapin have a key to the apartment?"

"No."

"Okay. Rose, did you go to the door when Dora Chapin came this evening?"

"Yes, sir."

"You let her in and she was alone."

"Yes, sir."

"When she left did you let her out?"

"No, sir. I never do. Mrs. Kurtz don't either. She just went."

"Where were you when she went?"

"I was in the dining-room. I was there a long while. We weren't serving dinner, and I was dusting the glasses in there."

"Then I suppose you didn't let Mr. Bowen out either. That was the man—"

"Yes, sir, I know Mr. Bowen. No, I didn't let him out, but that was a long time before."

"I know. All right, you let nobody out. Let's get back to in. You answered the door when Mr. Chapin came."

"Yes, sir."

"Was he alone?"

"Yes, sir."

"You opened the door and he came in and you shut the door again."

"Yes, sir."

"Now see if you can remember this. It doesn't matter much if you can't, but maybe you can. What did Mr. Chapin say to you?"

She looked at me, and aside at Mrs. Burton, and down at the floor. At first I thought maybe she was trying to fix up a fake for an answer, then I saw that she was just bewildered at the terrible complexity of the problem I had confronted her with by asking her a question that couldn't be answered *yes* or *no*. I said, "Come on, Rose. You know, Mr. Chapin came in, and you took his hat and coat, and he said—"

She looked up. "I didn't take his hat and coat. He kept his coat on, and his gloves. He said to tell Dr. Burton he was there."

"Did he stand there by the door or did he walk to a chair to sit down?"

"I don't know. I think he would sit down. I think he came along behind me but he came slow and I came back in to tell Dr. Burton."

"Was the light turned on in the foyer when you left there?"

"Yes, sir. Of course."

"After you told Dr. Burton, where did you go?"

"I went back to the dining-room."

"Where was the cook?"

"In the kitchen. She was there all the time."

"Where was Mrs. Burton?"

"She was in her room dressing.—Wasn't you, madam?"

I grinned. "Sure she was. I'm just getting all of you placed. Did Dr. Burton go to the foyer right away?"

She nodded. "Well . . . maybe not right away. He went pretty soon. I was in the dining-room and heard him go by the door."

"Okay." I got up from my chair. "Now I'm going to ask you to do something. I suppose I shouldn't tell you it's important, but it is. You go to the dining-room and start taking down the glasses, or whatever you were doing after you told Dr. Burton. I'll walk past the dining-room door and on to the foyer. Was Dr. Burton going fast or slow?"

She shook her head and her lip began to quiver. "He was just going."

"All right, I'll just go. You hear me go by, and you decide when enough time has passed for the first shot to go off. When the time has come for the first shot, you yell *Now* loud enough for me to hear you in the foyer. Do you understand? First you'd better tell—"

I stopped on account of her lip. It was getting into high. I snapped at her, "Come on out of that. Take a look at Mrs. Burton and learn how to behave yourself. You're doing this for her. Come on now."

She clamped her lips together and held them that way while she swallowed twice. Then she opened them to say:

"The shots all came together."

"All right, say they did. You yell *Now* when the time comes. First you'd better go and tell the people inside that you're going to yell or they'll be running out here—"

Mrs. Burton interposed, "I'll tell them. Rose, take Mr. Goodwin to the study and show him how to go."

She was quite a person, that Mrs. Burton. I was getting so I liked her. Maybe her soul was put away in a box somewhere, but other items of her insides, meaning guts, were all where they ought to be. If I was the kind that collected things I wouldn't have minded having one of her gloves myself.

Rose and I went out. Apparently she avoided the bedrooms by taking me around by a side hall, for we entered the study direct from that. She showed me how to go, by another door, and left me there. I looked around; books, leather chairs, radio, smoke stands, and a flat-top desk by a window. There was the drawer, of course, where the gat had been kept. I went over to it and pulled it open and shut it again. Then I went out by the other door and followed directions. I struck a medium pace, past the dining-room door, across the central hall, through a big room and from that through the drawing-room; got my eye on my watch, opened the door into the foyer, went in and closed it—

It was a good thing the folks had been warned, for Rose yelling *Now* so I could hear it sounded even to me, away off in the foyer, like the last scream of doom. I went back in faster than I had come for fear she might try it again. She had beat it back to the room where Mrs. Burton was. When I entered she was standing by the couch with her face white as a sheet, looking seasick. Mrs. Burton was reaching up to pat her arm. I went over and sat down.

I said, "I almost didn't get there. Two seconds at the most. Of course she rushed it, but it shows it must have been quick.—Okay, Rose. I won't ask you to do any more yelling. You're a good brave girl. Just a couple more questions. When you heard the shots you ran to the foyer with Mrs. Burton. Is that right?"

"Yes, sir."

"What did you see when you got there?"

"I didn't see anything. It was dark."

"What did you hear?"

"I heard something on the floor and then I heard Mr. Chapin saying Mrs. Burton's name and then the light went on and I saw him."

"What was he doing?"

"He was trying to get up."

"Did he have a gun in his hand?"

"No, sir. I'm sure he didn't because he had his hands on the floor getting up."

"And then you saw Dr. Burton."

"Yes, sir." She swallowed. "I saw him after Mrs. Burton went to him."

"What did you do then?"

"Well . . . I stood there I guess . . . then Mrs. Burton told me to go for Dr. Foster and I ran out and ran downstairs and they told me Dr. Foster had just left and I went to the elevator—"

"Okay, hold it."

I looked back over my notes. Mrs. Burton was patting Rose's arm again and Rose was looking at her with her lip ready to sag. My watch said five minutes till eleven; I had been in that room nearly two hours. There was one thing I hadn't gone into at all, but it might not be needed and in any event it could wait. I had got enough to sleep on. But as I flipped the pages of my pad there was another point that occurred to me which I thought ought to be attended to. I put the pad and pencil in my pocket and looked at Mrs. Burton:

"That's all for Rose. It's all for me too, except if you would just tell Rose—"

She looked up at the maid and nodded at her. "You'd better go to bed, Rose. Good night."

"Oh, Mrs. Burton—"

"All right now. You heard Mr. Goodwin say you're a brave girl. Go and get some sleep."

The maid gave me a look, not any too friendly, looked again at her mistress, and turned and went. As soon as the door had closed behind her I got up from my chair.

I said, "I'm going, but there's one more thing. I've got to ask a favor of you. You'll have to take my word for it that Nero Wolfe's interest in this business is the same as yours. I'll tell you that straight. You don't want Paul Chapin to burn in the electric chair for killing your husband, and neither does he. I don't know what his next move will be, that's up to him, but it's likely he'll need some kind of standing. For instance, if he wants to ask Inspector Cramer to let him see the gun he'll have to give a better reason than idle curiosity. I can't quite see Paul Chapin engaging him, but how about you? If we could say we were acting on commission from you it would make things simple. Of course there wouldn't be any fee, even if we did something you wanted done. If you want me to I'll put that in writing."

I looked at her. Her head was still up, but the signs of a flop were in her eyes and at the corners of her mouth. I said to her, "I'm going, I won't stay and bark at you about this, just say yes or no. If you don't lie down somewhere and relax, let it go ahead and bust, you'll be doing another kind of relaxing. What about it?"

She shook her head. I thought she was saying no, to me, but then she spoke—though this didn't sound as if it was directed at me any more than the headshake: "I loved my husband, Mr. Goodwin. Oh yes, I loved him. I sometimes disapproved of things he did. He disapproved of things I did, more often—though he seldom said so. He would disapprove of what I am doing now—I think he would. He would say, let fate do her job. He would say that as he so often said it—gallantly—and about Paul Chapin too. He is dead . . . Oh yes, he is dead . . . but let him live enough to say that now, and let me live enough to say what I always said, I will not keep my hand from any job if I think it's mine. He would not want me to make any new concessions to him, dead." She rose to her feet, abruptly, and abruptly added, "And even if he wanted me to I doubt if I could. Good night, Mr. Goodwin." She held out her hand.

I took it. I said, "Maybe I get you, but I like plain words. Nero Wolfe can say he is acting in your behalf, is that it?"

She nodded. I turned and left the room.

In the foyer I took a glance around as I got my hat

and coat from the table and put them on. I took the black bag from the closet. When I opened the door I gave the lock an inspection and saw it was the usual variety in houses of that class, the kind where you can press a button countersunk in the edge of the door to free the cylinder. I tried it and it worked. I heard a noise in the hall and stepped out and shut the door behind me. There sitting in a chair, twisting the hide on his neck to see who had been monkeying with the door but not bothering to get up, was the snoop Cramer had left to protect the family from annoyance as I had suspected he would.

I started pulling on my gloves. I said to him friendly and brisk, "Thank you, my man. I assure you we appreciate this," and went on to the elevator.

# Chapter 18

At two o'clock that night—Sunday morning—I sat at my desk, in the office, and yawned. Wolfe, behind his own desk, was looking at a schedule I had typed out for him, keeping a carbon for myself, during one of the intervals in my report when he had called time out to do a little arranging in his mind. The schedule looked like this:

6:05   Mrs. Burton arrives home. Present in apartment: Burton, daughter, Bowen, maid, cook.
6:20   Bowen leaves.
6:25   Daughter leaves.
6:30   Dora Chapin arrives.
7:20   Dora leaves.
7:30   Paul Chapin arrives.
7:33   Burton is shot.
7:50   Fred Durkin phones.

I looked at my carbon and yawned. Fritz had kept some squirrel stew hot for me, and it had long since been put away, with a couple of rye highballs because the black sauce Fritz used for squirrel made milk taste like stale olive juice. After I had imparted a few of the prominent details without saying how I had got hold of them, Wolfe had explained to Hibbard that it is the same with detectives as with magicians, their primary and constant concern is to preserve the air of mystery which is attached to their profession, and Hibbard had gone up to bed. The development that had arrived over the telephone while he was taking his bath had changed his world. He had eaten no dinner to speak of, though the need to chaperon the gold leaf on his teeth had departed. He had insisted on phoning fifty or sixty people, beginning with his niece, and had been restrained only by some tall talk about his word of honor. In fact, that question seemed not entirely closed, for Wolfe had had Fritz cut the wire of the telephone which was in Hibbard's room. Now he was up there, maybe asleep, maybe doping out a psychological detour around words of honor. I had gone on and given Wolfe the story, every crumb I had, and there had been discussions.

I threw the carbon onto the desk and did some more yawning. Finally Wolfe said:

"You understand, Archie. I think it would be possible for us to go ahead without assuming the drudgery of discovering the murderer of Dr. Burton. I would indeed regard that as obvious, if only men could be depended upon to base their decisions on reason. Alas, there are only three or four of us in the world, and even we will bear watching. And our weak spot is that we are committed not to refer our success to a fact, we must refer it to the vote of our group of clients. We must not only make things happen, we must make our clients vote that they have happened. That arrangement was unavoidable. It makes it necessary for us to learn who killed Dr. Burton, so that if the vote cannot be sufficiently swayed by reason it can be bullied by melodrama. You see that."

I said, "I'm sleepy. When I have to wait until nearly midnight for my dinner and then it's squirrel stew . . ."

Wolfe nodded. "Yes, I know. Under those circumstances I would be no better than a maniac.—Another thing. The worst aspect of this Burton development, from our standpoint, is what it does to the person of Mr. Chapin. He cannot come here to get his box—or for anything else. It will be necessary to make arrangements through Mr. Morley, and go to see him. What jail will they keep him in?"

"I suppose, Centre Street. There are three or four places they could stick him, but the Tombs is the most likely."

Wolfe sighed. "That abominable clatter. It's more than two miles, nearer three I suppose. The last time I left this house was early in September, for the privilege of dining at the same table with Albert Einstein, and coming home it rained. You remember that."

"Yeah. Will I ever forget it. There was such a downpour the pavements were damp."

"You deride me. Confound it . . . ah well. I will not make a virtue of necessity, but neither will I whimper under its lash. Since there is no such thing as bail for a man charged with murder, and since I must have a conversation with Mr. Chapin, there is no escaping an expedition to Centre Street. Not, however, until we know who killed Dr. Burton."

"And not forgetting that before the night's out the cripple may empty the bag for Cramer by confessing that he did it."

"Archie." Wolfe wiggled a finger at me. "If you

persist . . . but no. King Canute tried that. I only say again, nonsense. Have I not made it clear to you? It is the fashion to say anything is possible. The truth is, very few things are possible, pitiably few. That Mr. Chapin killed Dr. Burton is not among them. We are engaged on a project. It is futile to ask you to exclude from your brain all the fallacies which creep, familiar worms, through its chambers, but I do expect you not to let them interfere with our necessary operations. It is late, past two o'clock, time for bed. I have outlined your activities for tomorrow—today. I have explained what may be done, and what may not. Good night, sleep well."

I stood up and yawned. I was too sleepy to be sore, so it was automatic that I said, "Okay, boss." I went upstairs to bed.

Sunday morning I slept late. I had been given three chores for that day, and the first one on the list probably wouldn't be practical at any early hour, so twice when I woke up to glance at the clock I burrowed in again. I finally tumbled out around nine-thirty and got the body rinsed off and the face scraped. When I found myself whistling as I buttoned my shirt I stopped to seek the source of all the gaiety, and discovered I probably felt satisfied because Paul Chapin was behind bars and couldn't see the sunshine which I was seeing on the front of the houses across the street. I stopped whistling. That was no way to feel about a guy when I was supposed to be fighting for his freedom.

It was Sunday morning in November, and I knew what had happened when I had called down to Fritz that I was out of the bathtub: he had lined a casserole with butter, put in it six tablespoons of cream, three fresh eggs, four Lambert sausages, salt, pepper, paprika and chives, and conveyed it to the oven. But before I went to the kitchen I stopped in the office. Andrew Hibbard was there with the morning paper. He said that he hadn't been able to sleep much, that he had had breakfast, and that he wished to God he had some of his own clothes. I told him that Wolfe was up on the top floor with the orchids and that he would be welcome up there if he cared to see them. He decided to go. I went to the phone and called up Centre Street and was told that Inspector Cramer hadn't shown up yet and they weren't sure when he would. So I went to the kitchen and took my time with the casserole and accessories. Of course the murder of Dr. Burton was front page in both papers. I read the pieces through and enjoyed them very much.

Then I went to the garage and got the roadster and moseyed downtown.

Cramer was in his office when I got there, and didn't keep me waiting. He was smoking a big cigar and looked contented. I sat down and listened to him discussing with a couple of dicks the best way to persuade some Harlem citizen to quit his anatomy experiments on the skulls of drugstore cashiers, and when they went I looked at him and grinned. He didn't grin back. He whirled his chair around to face me and asked me what I wanted. I told him I didn't want anything, I just wanted to thank him for letting me squat on the sidelines up at Doc Burton's last night.

He said, "Yeah. You were gone when I came out. Did it bore you?"

"It did. I couldn't find any clue."

"No." But still he didn't grin. "This case is one of those mean babies where nothing seems to fit. All we've got is the murderer and the gun and two witnesses. Now what do you want?"

I told him, "I want lots of things. You've got it, inspector. Okay. You can afford to be generous, and George Pratt ought to hand you two grand, half of what you saved him. I'd like to know if you found any fingerprints on the gun. I'd like to know if Chapin has explained why he planned it so amateur, with him a professional. But what I'd really like is to have a little talk with Chapin. If you could arrange that for me—"

Cramer was grinning. He said, "I wouldn't mind having a talk with Chapin myself."

"Well, I'd be glad to put in a word for you."

He pulled on his cigar, and then took it out and got brisk. "I'll tell you, Goodwin. I'd just as soon sit and chin with you, but the fact is it's Sunday and I'm busy. So take this down. First, even if I passed you in to Chapin you wouldn't get anywhere. That cripple is part mule. I spent four hours on him last night, and I swear to God he wouldn't even tell me how old he is. He is not talking, and he won't talk to anyone except his wife. He says he don't want a lawyer, or rather he don't say anything when we ask him who he wants. His wife has seen him twice, and they won't say anything that anyone can hear. You know I've had a little experience greasing tongues, but he stops them all."

"Yeah. Did you try pinching him, just between you and me?"

He shook his head. "Haven't touched him. But to go on. After what Nero Wolfe said on the phone last night—I suppose you heard that talk—I had an idea you'd be wanting to see him. And I've decided nothing doing. Even if he was talking a blue streak, not a chance. Considering how we got him, I don't see why you're interested anyhow. Hell, can't Wolfe take the short end once in his life?—Now wait a minute. You

don't need to remind me Wolfe has always been better
than square with me and there's one or two things I
owe him. I'll hand him a favor when I've got one the
right size. But no matter how tight I've got this
cripple sewed up, I'm going to play safe with him."

"Okay. It just means extra trouble. Wolfe will have
to arrange it at the D.A.'s office."

"Let him. If he does, I won't butt in. As far as I'm
concerned, the only two people that get to see Chapin
are his wife and his lawyer, and he's got no lawyer and
if you ask me not much wife.—Listen, now that you've
asked me a favor and I've turned you down, how about
doing one for me? Tell me what you want to see him
for? Huh?"

I grinned. "You'd be surprised. I have to ask him
what he wants us to do with what is left of Andrew
Hibbard until he gets a chance to tend to it."

Cramer stared at me. He snorted. "You wouldn't
kid me."

"I wouldn't dream of it. Of course if he's not talking
he probably wouldn't tell me, but I might find a way to
turn him on. Look here, inspector, there must be some
human quality in you somewhere. Today's my birthday. Let me see him."

"Not a chance."

I got up. "How straight is it that he's not talking?"

"That's on the level. We can't get a peep."

I told him much obliged for all his many kind-
nesses, and left.

I got in the roadster and headed north. I wasn't
downcast. I hadn't made any history, but I hadn't
expected to. Remembering the mask that Paul Chapin
had been using for a face as I saw him sitting in the
Burton foyer the night before, I wasn't surprised that
Cramer hadn't found him much of a conversationalist,

and I wouldn't have expected to hear anything even if I had got to see him.

At Fourteenth Street I parked and went to a cigar store and phoned Wolfe. I told him, "Right again. They have to ask his wife whether he prefers white or dark meat, because he won't even tell them that. He's not interested in a lawyer. Cramer wouldn't let me see him."

Wolfe said, "Excellent. Proceed to Mrs. Burton."

I went back to the roadster and rolled on uptown. When they telephoned from the lobby to the Burton apartment to say that Mr. Goodwin was there, I was hoping she hadn't got a new slant on this and that during the night. As Wolfe had said once, you can depend on a woman for anything except constancy. But she had stayed put; I was nodded to the elevator. Upstairs I was taken into the same room as the night before by a maid I hadn't seen—the housekeeper, Mrs. Kurtz, I surmised. She looked hostile and determined enough to make me contented that I didn't need to question her about a key or anything else.

Mrs. Burton sat in a chair by a window. She looked pale. If people had been with her she had sent them away. I told her I wouldn't sit down, I only had a few questions Nero Wolfe had given me. I read the first one from my pad:

"Did Paul Chapin say anything whatever to you last night besides what you have already told me, and if so, what?"

She said, "No. Nothing."

"Inspector Cramer showed you the gun that your husband was shot with. How sure are you that it was your husband's, the one he kept in the drawer of his desk?"

She said, "Quite sure. His initials were on it, it was a gift from a friend."

"During the fifty minutes that Dora Chapin was in the apartment last evening, was there any time when she went, or could have gone, to the study, and if so was there anyone else in the study at that time?"

She said, "No." Then the frown came into her eyes. "But wait—yes, there was. Soon after she came I sent her to the study for a book. I suppose there was no one there. My husband was in his room dressing."

"This next one is the last. Do you know if Mr. Bowen was at any time alone in the study?"

She said, "Yes, he was. My husband came to my room to ask me a question."

I put the pad in my pocket, and said to her, "You might tell me what the question was."

"No, Mr. Goodwin. I think not."

"It might be important. This isn't for publication."

Her eyes frowned again, but the hesitation was brief. "Very well. He asked me if I cared enough for Estelle Bowen—Mr. Bowen's wife—to make a considerable sacrifice for her. I said no."

"Did he tell you what he meant?"

"No."

"All right. That's all. You haven't slept any."

"No."

Ordinarily I've got as much to say as there's time for, but on that occasion no more observations suggested themselves. I told her thank you, and she nodded without moving her head, which sounds unlikely but I swear that's what she did, and I beat it. As I went out through the foyer I paused for another glance at one or two details, such as the location of the light switch by the double door.

On my way downtown I phoned Wolfe again. I told

him what I had gathered from Mrs. Burton, and he told me that he and Andrew Hibbard were playing cribbage.

It was twenty minutes past noon when I got to Perry Street. It was deserted for Sunday. Sidewalks empty, only a couple of cars parked in the whole block, and a taxi in front of the entrance to 203. I let the roadster slide to the curb opposite, and got out. I had noted the number on the taxi's license plate and had seen the driver on his seat. I stepped across to the sidewalk and went alongside; his head was tilted over against the frame and his eyes were closed. I put a foot on the running-board and leaned in and said:

"Good morning, Mr. Scott."

He came to with a start and looked at me. He blinked. "Oh," he said, "it's little Nero Wolfe."

I nodded. "Names don't bother me, but mine happens to be Archie Goodwin. How's tips?"

"My dear fellow." He made noises, and spat out to the left, to the pavement. "Tips is copious. When was it I saw you, Wednesday? Only four days ago. You keeping busy?"

"I'm managing." I leaned in a little further. "Look here, Pitney Scott. I wasn't looking for you, but I'm glad I found you. When Nero Wolfe heard how you recognized Andrew Hibbard over a week ago, but didn't claim the five grand reward when it was offered, he said you have an admirable sense of humor. Knowing how easy it is to find excuses for a friendly feeling for five grand, I'd say something different, but Wolfe meant well, he's just eccentric. Seeing you here, it just occurred to me that you ought to know that your friend Hibbard is at present a guest up at our house. I took him there yesterday in time for dinner. If it's all the same to you, he'd like to stay under cover for another couple of days, till we get this whole thing straightened out. If you should happen to turn mercenary, you won't lose anything by keeping your sense of humor."

He grunted. "So. You got Andy. And you only need a couple of days to straighten it all out. I thought *all* detectives were dumb."

"Sure, we are. I'm so dumb I don't even know whether it was you that took Dora Chapin up to Ninetieth Street last evening and brought her back again. I was just going to ask you."

"All right, ask me. Then I'll say it wasn't." He made noises and spat again—another futile attack on the imaginary obstruction in the throat of a man with a constant craving for a drink. He looked at me and went on, "You know, brother—if you will pardon the argot, I'm sore at you for spotting Andy, but I admire you for it too because it was halfway smart. And anyway, Lorrie Burton was a pretty good guy. With him dead, and Mr. Paul Chapin in jail, the fun's gone. It's not funny any more, even to me, and Nero Wolfe's right about my sense of humor. It is admirable. I'm a character. I'm sardonic." He spat again. "But to hell with it. I didn't drive Mrs. Chapin to Burton's last night because she went in her own coupé."

"Oh. She drives herself."

"Sure. In the summertime she and her husband go to the country on picnics. Now that was funny, for instance, and I don't suppose they'll ever do that again. I don't know why she's using me today, unless it's because she doesn't want to park it in front of the Tombs—there she comes now."

I got off the running-board and back a step. Dora Chapin had come out of the 203 entrance and was headed for the taxi. She had on another coat and another furpiece, but the face was the same, and so were the little gray eyes. She was carrying an oblong package about the size of a shoebox, and I supposed that was dainties for her husband's Sunday dinner. She didn't seem to have noticed me, let alone recognize me; then she stopped with one foot on the running-board and turned the eyes straight at me, and for the first time I saw an expression in them that I could give a name to, and it wasn't fondness. You could call it an inviting expression if you went on to describe what she was inviting me to. I stepped into it anyway. I said:

"Mrs. Chapin. Could I ride with you? I'd like to tell you—"

She climbed inside and slammed the door to. Pitney Scott stepped on the starter, put the gear in, and started to roll. I stood and watched the taxi go, not very jubilant, because it was her I had come down there to see.

I walked to the corner and phoned Wolfe I wouldn't be home to lunch, which I didn't mind much because the eggs and cream and sausages I had shipped on at ten o'clock were still undecided what to do about it; bought a *Times* and went to the roadster and made myself comfortable. Unless she had some kind of pull that Inspector Cramer didn't know about, they wouldn't let her stay very long at the Tombs.

At that I had to wait close to an hour and a half. It was nearly two o'clock, and I was thinking of hitting up the delicatessen where Fred Durkin had been a tenant for most of the week, when I looked up for the eightieth time at the sound of a car and saw the taxi slowing down. I had decided what to do. With all that animosity in Dora's eyes I calculated it wouldn't pay to try to join her downstairs and go up with her; I would wait till she was inside and then persuade Pitney Scott to take me up. With him along she might let me in. But again I didn't get the break. Instead of stopping at the entrance Scott rolled down a few yards, and then they both got out and both went in. I stared at them and did a little cussing, and decided not to do any more waiting. I got out and entered 203 for the first and last time, and went to the elevator and said fifth floor. The man looked at me with the usual mild and weary suspicion but didn't bother with questions. I got out at the fifth and rang the bell at 5C.

I can't very well pretend to be proud of what happened that afternoon at Paul Chapin's apartment. I pulled a boner, no doubt of that, and it wasn't my fault that it didn't have a result that ended a good deal more than the Chapin case, but the opinion you have of it depends entirely on how you use it. I can't honestly agree that it was quite as dumb as one or two subsequent remarks of Wolfe's might seem to indicate. Anyway, this is how it happened.

Dora Chapin came to the door and opened it, and I got my foot inside the sill. She asked me what I wanted, and I said I had something to ask Pitney Scott. She said he would be down in half an hour and I could wait downstairs, and started to shut the door, and got it as far as my foot. I said:

"Listen, Mrs. Chapin. I want to ask you something too. You think I'm against your husband, but I'm not, I'm for him. That's on the level. He hasn't got many friends left, and anyway it won't hurt you to listen to me. I've got something to say. I could say it to the police instead of you, but take it from me you wouldn't like that nearly as well. Let me in. Pitney Scott's here."

She threw the door wide open and said, "Come in."

Maybe the shift in her welcome should have made me suspicious, but it didn't. It merely made me think I had scared her, and also made me add a few chips to the stack I was betting that if her husband hadn't croaked Dr. Burton, she had. I went in and shut the door behind me, and followed her across the hall, and through a sitting-room and dinning-room and into the kitchen. The rooms were big and well furnished and looked prosperous; and sitting in the kitchen at an enamel-top table was Pitney Scott, consuming a hunk of brown fried chicken. There was a platter of it with four or five pieces left. I said to Dora Chapin:

"Maybe we can go in front and leave Mr. Scott to enjoy himself."

She nodded at a chair and pointed to the chicken: "There's plenty." She turned to Scott: "I'll fix you a drink."

He shook his head, and chewed and swallowed. "I've been off for ten days now, Mrs. Chapin. It wouldn't be funny, take my word for it. When the coffee's ready I'd appreciate that.—Come on—you said Goodwin, didn't you?—come on and help me. Mrs. Chapin says she has dined."

I was hungry and the chicken looked good, I admit that, but the psychology of it was that it looked like I ought to join in. Not to mention the salad, which had green peppers in it. I got into the chair and Scott passed the platter. Dora Chapin had gone to the stove to turn the fire down under the percolator. There was still a lot of bandage at the back of her neck, and it looked unattractive where her hair had been shaved off. She was bigger than I had realized in the office that day, fairly hefty. She went into the dining-room for something, and I got more intimate with the chicken after the first couple of bites and started a conversation with Scott. After a while Dora Chapin came back, with coffee cups and a bowl of sugar.

Of course it was in the coffee, she probably put it right in the pot since she didn't drink any, but I didn't notice a taste. It was strong but it tasted all right. However, she must have put in all the sleeping tablets and a few other things she could get hold of, for God knows it was potent. I began to feel it when I was reaching to hand Scott a cigarette, and at the same time I saw the look on his face. He was a few seconds ahead of me. Dora Chapin was out of the room again. Scott looked at the door she had gone through, and tried to get up out of his chair, but couldn't make it. That was the last I really remember, him trying to get out of his chair, but I must have done one or two things after that, because when I came out of it I was in the dining-room, halfway across to the door which led to the sitting-room and the hall.

When I came out of it, it was dark. That was the first thing I knew, and for a while it was all I knew, because I couldn't move and I was fighting to get my eyes really open. I could see, off to my right, at a great distance it seemed, two large oblongs of dim light, and I concentrated on deciding what they were. It came with a burst that they were windows, and it was dark in the room where I was, and the street was lit. Then I concentrated on what room I was in.

Things came back but all in a jumble. I still didn't know where I was, though I was splitting my head fighting for it. I rolled over on the floor and my hand landed on something metal, sharp, and I shrunk from it; I pulled myself to my knees and began to crawl. I bumped into a table and a chair or two, and finally into the wall. I crawled around the wall with my shoulder against it, detouring for furniture, stopping every

couple of feet to feel it, and at last I felt a door. I tried
to stand up, but couldn't make it, and compromised by
feeling above me. I found the switch and pushed on it,
and the light went on. I crawled over to where there
was some stuff on the floor, stretching the muscles in
my brow and temples to keep my eyes open, and saw
that the metal thing that had startled me was my ring
of keys. My wallet was there too, and my pad and
pencil, pocketknife, fountain pen, handkerchief—
things from my pockets.

I got hold of a chair and pulled myself to my feet,
but I couldn't navigate. I tried, and fell down. I looked
around for a telephone, but there wasn't any, so I
crawled to the sitting-room and found the light
switch by the door and turned it on. The phone was on
a stand by the further wall. It looked so far away that
the desire to lie down and give it up made me want to
yell to show I wouldn't do that, but I couldn't yell. I
finally got to the stand and sat down on the floor
against it and reached up for the phone and got the
receiver off and shoved it against my ear, and heard
a man's voice, very faint. I said the number of
Wolfe's phone and heard him say he couldn't hear me,
so then I yelled it and that way got enough steam
behind it. After a while I heard another voice and I
yelled:

"I want Nero Wolfe!"

The other voice mumbled and I said to talk louder,
and asked who it was, and got it into my bean that it
was Fritz. I told him to get Wolfe on, and he said
Wolfe wasn't there, and I said he was crazy, and he
mumbled a lot of stuff and I told him to say it again
louder and slower. "I said, Archie, Mr. Wolfe is not
here. He went to look for you. Somebody came to get

him, and he told me he was going for you. Archie, where are you? Mr. Wolfe said—"

I was having a hard time holding the phone, and it dropped to the floor, the whole works, and my head fell into my hands with my eyes closed, and I suppose what I was doing you would call crying.

# Chapter 19

I haven't the slightest idea how long I sat there on the floor with my head laying in my hands trying to force myself out of it enough to pick up the telephone again. It may have been a minute and it may have been an hour. The trouble was that I should have been concentrating on the phone, and it kept sweeping over me that Wolfe was gone. I couldn't get my head out of my hands. Finally I heard a noise. It kept on and got louder, and at last it seeped into me that someone seemed to be trying to knock the door down. I grabbed the top of the telephone stand and pulled myself up, and decided I could keep my feet if I didn't let go of the wall, so I followed it around to the door where the noise was. I got my hands on it and turned the lock and the knob, and it flew open and down I went again. The two guys that came in walked on me and then stood and looked at me, and I heard remarks about full to the gills and leaving the receiver off the hook.

By that time I could talk better. I said I don't know what, enough so that one of them beat it for a doctor, and the other one helped me get up and steered me to the kitchen. He turned the light on. Scott had slewed off of his chair and curled up on the floor. My chair was turned over on its side. I felt cold air and the guy said something about the window, and I looked at it and saw the glass was shattered with a big hole in it. I never did learn what it was I had thrown through the window, maybe the plate of chicken; anyway it hadn't aroused enough curiosity down below to do any good. The guy stooped over Scott and shook him, but he was dead to the world. By working the wall again, and furniture, I got back to the dining-room and sat on the floor and began collecting my things and putting them in my pockets. I got worried because I thought something was missing and I couldn't figure out what it was, and then I realized it was the leather case Wolfe had given me, with pistols on one side and orchids on the other, that I carried my police and fire cards in. And by God I started to cry again. I was doing that when the other guy came back with the doctor. I was crying, and trying to push my knuckles into my temples hard enough to get my brains working on why Dora Chapin had fed me a knockout so she could frisk me and then took nothing but that leather case.

I had a fight with the doctor. He insisted that before he could give me anything he'd have to know just what it was I had inside of me, and he went to the bathroom to investigate bottles and boxes and I went after him with the idea of plugging him. I was beginning to have thoughts and they were starting to bust in my head. I got nearly to the bathroom when I forgot all about the doctor because I suddenly remembered that there had been something peculiar about Scott curled up on the floor, and I turned around and started for the kitchen. I was getting overconfident and fell down again, but I picked myself up and went on. I looked at Scott and saw what it was: he was in his shirt-sleeves. His gray taxi-driver's jacket was gone. I was trying to decide why that was important when the doctor came in with a glass of brown stuff in his hand. He said something and handed me the glass and watched me drink it, and then went over and knelt down by Scott.

The stuff tasted bitter. I put the empty glass on the table and got hold of the guy who had gone for the doctor—by this time I recognized him as the elevator man—and told him to go downstairs and switch the Chapin phone in, and then go outside and see if Scott's taxi was at the curb. Then I made it through the dining-room again into the sitting-room and got into a chair by the telephone stand. I got the operator, and gave her the number.

Fritz answered. I said, "This is Archie. What was it you told me a while ago about Mr. Wolfe?"

"Why . . . Mr. Wolfe is gone." I could hear him better, and I could tell he was trying not to let his voice shake. "He told me he was going to get you, and that he suspected you of trying to coerce him into raising your pay. He went—"

"Wait a minute, Fritz. Talk slow. What time is it? My watch says a quarter to seven."

"Yes. That's right. Mr. Wolfe has been gone nearly four hours. Archie, where are you?"

"To hell with where I am. What happened? Someone came for him?"

"Yes. I went to the door, and a man handed me an envelope."

"Was it a taxi-driver?"

"Yes, I think so. I took the envelope to Mr. Wolfe, and pretty soon he came to the kitchen and told me he was going. Mr. Hibbard helped him into his coat, the brown one with the big collar, and I got his hat and stick and gloves—"

"Did you see the taxi?"

"Yes, I went out with Mr. Wolfe and opened the door of the cab for him. Archie, for God's sake, tell me what I can do—"

"You can't do anything. Let me talk to Mr. Hibbard."

"But Archie—I am so disturbed—"

"So am I. Hold the fort, Fritz, and sit tight. Put Hibbard on."

I waited, and before long heard Hibbard's hello. I said to him:

"This is Archie Goodwin, Mr. Hibbard. Now listen, I can't talk much. When Nero Wolfe gets home again we want to be able to tell him that you've kept your word. You promised him to stay dead until Monday evening. Understand?"

Hibbard sounded irritated. "Of course I understand, Mr. Goodwin, but it seems to me—"

"For God's sake forget how it seems to you. Either you keep your word or you don't."

"Well . . . I do."

"That's fine. Tell Fritz I'll call again as soon as I have anything to say."

I hung up. The brown stuff the doctor had given me seemed to be working, but not to much advantage; my head was pounding like the hammers of hell. The elevator man had come back and was standing there. I looked at him and he said Scott's taxi was gone. I got hold of the phone again and called Spring 7-3100.

Cramer wasn't in his office and they couldn't find him around. I got my wallet out of my pocket and with some care managed to find my lists of telephone numbers, and called Cramer's home. At first they said he wasn't there, but I persuaded them to change their

minds, and finally he came to the phone. I didn't know
a cop's voice could ever sound so welcome to me. I told
him where I was and what had happened to me, and
said I was trying to remember what it was he had said
that morning about doing a favor for Nero Wolfe. He
said whatever it was he had meant it. I told him:

"Okay, now's your chance. That crazy Chapin bitch
has stole a taxi and she's got Nero Wolfe in it taking
him somewhere. I don't know where and I wouldn't
know even if my head was working. She got him four
hours ago and she's had time to get to Albany or
anywhere else.—No matter how she got him, I'll
settle for that some other day. Listen, inspector, for
God's sake. Send out a general for a brown taxi, a
Stuyvesant, MO 29-6342. Got it down? Say it back.—
Will you put the radios on it? Will you send it to
Westchester and Long Island and Jersey? Listen, the
dope I was cooking up was that it was her that croaked
Doc Burton. By God, if I ever get my hands on her—
What? I'm not excited.—Okay. Okay, inspector,
thanks."

I hung up. Someone had come in and was standing
there, and I looked up and saw it was a flatfoot
wearing a silly grin, directed at me. He asked me
something and I told him to take his shoes off to rest
his brains. He made me some kind of a reply that was
intended to be smart, and I laid my head down on the
top of the telephone stand to get the range, and
banged it up and down a few times on the wood, but it
didn't seem to do any good. The elevator man said
something to the cop and he went towards the kitchen.

I got up and went to open a window and damn near
fell out. The cold air was like ice. The way I felt I was
sure of two things: first, that if my head went on like
that much longer it would blow up, and second, that
Wolfe was dead. It seemed obvious that after that

woman once got him into that taxi there was nothing
for her to do with him but kill him. I stood looking out
onto Perry Street, trying to hold my head together,
and I had a feeling that all of New York was there in
front of me, between me and the house fronts I could
see across the street—the Battery, the river fronts,
Central Park, Flatbush, Harlem, Park Avenue, all of
it—and Wolfe was there somewhere and I didn't know
where. Something occurred to me, and I held on to the
window jamb and leaned out enough so I could see
below. There was the roadster, where I had parked it,
its fender shining with the reflection from a street
light. I had an idea that if I could get down there and
get it started I could drive it all right.

I decided to do that, but before I moved away from
the window I thought I ought to decide where to go.
One man in one roadster, even if he had a head on him
that would work, wouldn't get far looking for that taxi.
It was absolutely hopeless. But I had a notion that
there was something important I could do, somewhere
important I could go, if only I could figure out where
it was. All of a sudden it came to me that where I
wanted to go was home. I wanted to see Fritz, and the
office, and go over the house and see for myself that
Wolfe wasn't there, look at things . . .

I didn't hesitate. I let go of the window jamb and
started across the room, and just as I got to the hall
the telephone rang. I could walk a little better. I went
back to the telephone stand and picked up the receiver
and said hello. A voice said:

"Chelsea-two three-nine-two-four? Please give me
Mr. Chapin's apartment."

I nearly dropped the receiver, and I went stiff. I
said, "Who is this?" The voice said:

"This is someone who wishes to be connected with Mr. Chapin's apartment. Didn't I make that clear?"

I let the phone down and pressed it against one of my ribs for a moment, not wanting to make a fool of myself. Then I put it up to my mouth again: "Excuse me for asking who it is. It sounded like Nero Wolfe. Where are you?"

"Ah! Archie. After what Mrs. Chapin has told me, I scarcely expected to find you operating an apartment house switchboard. I am much relieved. How are you feeling?"

"Swell. Wonderful. How are you?"

"Fairly comfortable. Mrs. Chapin drives staccato, and the jolting of that infernal taxicab . . . ah well. Archie. I am standing, and I dislike to talk on the telephone while standing. Also I would dislike very much to enter that taxicab again. If it is practical, get the sedan and come for me. I am at the Bronx River Inn, near the Woodlawn railroad station. You know where that is?"

"I know. I'll be there."

"No great hurry. I am fairly comfortable."

"Okay."

The click of his ringing off was in my ear. I hung up and sat down.

I was damn good and sore. Certainly not at Wolfe, not even at myself, just sore. Sore because I had phoned Cramer an SOS, sore because Wolfe was to hell and gone up beyond the end of the Grand Concourse and I didn't really know what shape he was in, sore because it was up to me to get there and there was no doubt at all about the shape I was in. I felt my eyes closing and jerked my head up. I decided that the next time I saw Dora Chapin, no matter when or where, I would take my pocketknife and cut her head off, completely loose from the rest of her. I thought of going to the kitchen and asking the doctor for another shot of the brown stuff, but didn't see how it could do me any good.

I picked up the phone and called the garage, on Tenth Avenue, and told them to fill the sedan with gas and put it at the curb. Then I got up and proceeded to make myself scarce. I would rather have done almost anything than try walking again, except go back to crawling. I made it to the hall, and opened the door, and on out to the elevator. There I was faced by two new troubles: the elevator was right there, the door standing wide open, and I didn't have my hat and coat. I didn't want to go back to the kitchen for the elevator man because in the first place it was too far, and secondly if the flatfoot found out I was leaving he would probably want to detain me for information and there was no telling how I would act if he tried it. I did go back to the hall, having left the door open. I got my hat and coat and returned to the elevator, inside, and somehow got the door closed, and pulled the lever, hitting down by luck. It started down and I leaned against the wall.

I thought I was releasing the lever about the right time, but the first thing I knew the elevator hit bottom like a ton of brick and shook me loose from the wall. I picked myself up and opened the door and saw there was a dark hall about two feet above my level. I climbed out and got myself up. It was the basement. I turned right, which seemed to be correct, and for a change it was. I came to a door and went through, and through a gate, and there I was outdoors with nothing between me and the sidewalk but a flight of concrete steps. I negotiated them, and crossed the street and found the roadster and got in.

I don't believe yet that I drove that car from Perry Street to Thirty-sixth, to the garage. I might possibly have done it by caroms, bouncing back from the buildings first on one side of the street and then on the other, but the trouble with that theory is that next day the roadster didn't have a scratch on it. If anyone is keeping a miracle score, chalk one up for me. I got there, but I stopped out in front, deciding not to try for the door. I blew my horn and Steve came out. I described my condition in round figures and told him I hoped there was someone there he could leave in charge of the joint, because he had to get in the sedan and drive me to the Bronx. He asked if I wanted a drink and I snarled at him. He grinned and went inside, and I transferred to the sedan, standing at the curb. Pretty soon he came back with an overcoat on, and got in and shoved off. I told him where to go and let my head fall back in the corner against the cushion, but I didn't dare to let my eyes shut. I stretched them open and kept on stretching them every time I blinked. My window was down and the cold air slapped me, and it seemed we were going a million miles a minute in a swift sweeping circle and it was hard to keep up with my breathing.

Steve said, "Here we are, mister."

I grunted and lifted my head up and stretched my eyes again. We had stopped. There it was, Bronx River Inn, just across the sidewalk. I had a feeling it had come to us instead of us to it. Steve asked, "Can you navigate?"

"Sure." I set my jaw again, and opened the door and climbed out. Then after crossing the sidewalk I tried to walk through a lattice, and set my jaw some more and detoured. I crossed the porch, with cold bare tables around and no one there, and opened the

door and went inside to the main room. There some of
the tables had cloths on them and a few customers
were scattered here and there. The customer I was
looking for was at a table in the far corner, and I
approached it. There sat Nero Wolfe, all of him, on a
chair which would have been economical for either
half. His brown greatcoat covered another chair,
beside him, and across the table from him I saw the
bandages on the back of Dora Chapin's neck. She was
facing him, with her rear to me. I walked over there.

Wolfe nodded at me. "Good evening, Archie. I am
relieved again. It occurred to me after I phoned you
that you were probably in no condition to pilot a car
through this confounded labyrinth. I am greatly
relieved.—You have met Mrs. Chapin.—Sit down.
You don't look as if standing was very enjoyable."

He lifted his glass of beer and took a couple of
swallows. I saw the remains of some kind of a mess on
his plate, but Dora Chapin had cleaned hers up. I
moved his hat and stick off a chair and sat down on it.
He asked me if I wanted a glass of milk and I shook my
head. He said:

"I confess it is a trifle mortifying, to set out to
rescue you and end by requesting you to succor me,
but if that is Mr. Scott's taxicab he should get new
springs for it. If you get me home intact—and no
doubt you will—that will not be your only triumph for
this day. By putting me in touch with Mrs. Chapin in
unconventional circumstances, though it seems inadvertently, you have brought us to the solution of our
problem. I tell you that at once because I know it will
be welcome news. Mrs. Chapin has been kind enough
to accept my assurances—"

That was the last word I heard. The only other
thing I remembered was that a tight wire which had

been stretched between my temples, holding them together, suddenly parted with a twang. Wolfe told me afterwards that when I folded up my head hit the edge of the table with a loud thud before he could catch me.

# Chapter 20

**M**onday morning when I woke up I was still in bed. That sounds as if I meant something else, but I don't. When I got enough awake to realize where I was I had a feeling that I had gone to bed sometime during Lent and here it was Christmas. Then I saw Doc Vollmer standing there beside me.

I grinned at him. "Hello, doc. You got a job here as house physician?"

He grinned back. "I just stopped in to see how it went with what I pumped into you last night. Apparently—"

"What? Oh. Yeah. Good God." It struck me that the room seemed full of light. "What time is it?"

"Quarter to twelve."

"No!" I twisted to see the clock. "Holy murder!" I jerked myself upright, and someone jabbed a thousand ice-picks into my skull. "Whoa, Bill." I put my hands up to it and tried moving it slowly. I said to Vollmer, "What's this I've got here, my head?"

He laughed. "It'll be all right."

"Yeah. You're not saying when. Wowie! Is Mr. Wolfe down in the office?"

He nodded. "I spoke to him on the way up."

"And it's noon." I slid to my feet. "Look out, I might run into you." I started for the bathroom.

I began soaping up, and he came to the bathroom door and said he had left instructions with Fritz for my breakfast. I told him I didn't want instructions, I wanted ham and eggs. He laughed again, and beat it. I was glad to hear him laugh, because it seemed likely that if there really were ice-picks sticking in my head he, being a doctor, would be taking them out instead of laughing at me.

I made it as snappy as I could with my dizziness, cleansing the form and assuming the day's draperies, and went downstairs in pretty good style but hanging onto the banister.

Wolfe, in his chair, looked up and said good morning and asked me how I felt. I told him I felt like twin colts and went to my desk. He said:

"But, Archie. Seriously. Should you be up?"

"Yeah. Not only should I be up, I should have been up. You know how it is, I'm a man of action."

His cheeks unfolded. "And I, of course, am supersedentary. A comical interchange of roles, that you rode home last evening from the Bronx River Inn, a matter of ten miles or more, with your head on my lap all the way."

I nodded. "Very comical. I told you a long while ago, Mr. Wolfe, that you pay me half for the chores I do and half for listening to you brag."

"So you did. And if I did not then remark, I do so now—but no. We can pursue these amenities another time, now there is business. Could you take some notes, and break your fast with our lunch?—Good. I spoke on the telephone this morning with Mr. Morley, and with the District Attorney himself. It has been arranged that I shall see Mr. Chapin at the Tombs at two-thirty this afternoon. You will remember that on Saturday evening I was beginning to dictate to you the confession of Paul Chapin when we were interrupted by news from Fred Durkin which caused a postponement. If you will turn to that page we can go on. I'll have to have it by two o'clock."

So as it turned out I not only didn't get to tie into the ham and eggs I had yearned for, I didn't even eat lunch with Wolfe and Hibbard. The dictating wasn't done until nearly one, and I had the typing to do. But by that time the emptiness inside had got to be a vacuum, or whatever it may be that is emptier than emptiness, and I had Fritz bring some hot egg sandwiches and milk and coffee to my desk. I wanted this typed just right, this document that Paul Chapin was to sign, and with my head not inclined to see the importance of things like spelling and punctuation I had to take my time and concentrate. Also, I wasted three minutes phoning the garage to tell them to bring the sedan around, for I supposed of course I would take Wolfe in it; but they said they already had instructions from Wolfe, and that the instructions included a driver. I thought maybe I ought to be sore about that, but decided not to.

Wolfe ate a quick lunch, for him. When he came into the office at a quarter to two I barely had the thing finished and was getting the three copies clipped into brown folders. He took them and put them in his pocket and told me to take my notebook and started on the instructions for my afternoon. He explained that he had asked for a driver from the garage because I would be busy with other things. He also explained that on account of the possibility of visitors he had procured from Hibbard a promise that he would spend the entire afternoon in his room, until dinner time. Hibbard had gone there from the lunch-table.

Fritz came to the door and said the car was there, and Wolfe told him he would be ready in a few minutes.

What gave me a new idea of the dimensions of Wolfe's nerve was the disclosure that a good part of the arrangements had been completed for a meeting of the League of the White Feather, in the office that evening at nine o'clock. Before he had seen Chapin at all! Of course I didn't know what Dora might have told him, except a couple of details that had been included in the confession, but it wasn't Dora that was supposed to sign on the dotted line, it was her little crippled husband with the light-colored eyes; and that was a job I was glad Wolfe hadn't bestowed on me, even if it did mean his sashaying out of the house twice in two days, which was an all-time record. But he had gone ahead and telephoned Boston and Philadelphia and Washington, and six or eight of them in New York, after we got home Sunday evening and from his room early that morning, and the meeting was on. My immediate job was to get in touch with the others, by phone if possible, and ensure as full an attendance as we could get.

He gave me another one more immediate, just before he left. He told me to go and see Mrs. Burton at once, and dictated two questions to ask her. I suggested the phone, and he said no, it would be better if I saw the daughter and the maids also. Fritz was standing there holding his coat. Wolfe said:

"And I was almost forgetting that our guests will be thirsty. Fritz, put the coat down and come here, and we shall see what we need.—Archie, if you don't mind you had better start, you should be back by three.—Let us see, Fritz. I noticed last week that Mr. Cabot prefers Aylmer's soda—"

I beat it. I walked to the garage for the roadster, and the sharp air glistened in my lungs. After I got the roadster out into the light I looked it over and couldn't find a scratch on it, and it was then I reflected on miracles. I got back in and headed uptown.

I was worried about Wolfe. It looked to me like he was rushing things beyond reason. It was true that Andrew Hibbard's parole was up that evening, but probably he could have been persuaded to extend it, and besides it certainly wasn't vital to produce him at the meeting as a stunt. But it was like Wolfe not to wait until the confession was actually in the bag. That sort of gesture, thumbing his nose at luck, was a part of him, and maybe an important part; there were lots of things about Wolfe I didn't pretend to know. Anyhow, there was no law against worrying, and it didn't make my head feel any better to reflect on the outcome of the meeting that evening if Paul Chapin stayed mule. So that was what I reflected on, all the way to Ninetieth Street.

Wolfe had said that both of the questions I was to ask Mrs. Burton were quite important. The first was simple: *Did Dr. Burton telephone Paul Chapin between 6:50 and 7:00 o'clock Saturday evening and ask him to come to see him?*

The second was more complicated: *At 6:30 Saturday evening a pair of gray gloves was lying on the table in the Burton foyer, near the end towards the double doors. Were the gloves removed between then and 7:20 by anyone in the apartment?*

I got a break. Everybody was home. The housekeeper had me wait in the drawing-room and Mrs. Burton came to me there. She looked sick, I thought, and had on a gray dress that made her look sicker, but the spine was still doing its stuff. The first question took about nine seconds; the answer was no, definitely. Dr. Burton had done no telephoning after 6:30 Saturday evening. The second question required more time. Mrs. Kurtz was out of it, since she hadn't been there. The daughter, having left before 6:30, seemed out of it too, but I asked Mrs. Burton to call her in anyhow, to make sure. She came, and said she had left no gloves on the foyer table and had seen none there. Mrs. Burton herself had not been in the foyer between the time she returned home and around six, and 7:33 when the sound of the shots had taken her there on the run. She said she had left no gloves on that table, and certainly had removed none. She sent for Rose. Rose came, and I asked her if she had removed a pair of gloves from the foyer table between 6:30 and 7:20 Saturday evening.

Rose looked at Mrs. Burton instead of me. She hesitated, and then she spoke: "No, ma'am, I didn't take the gloves. But Mrs. Chapin—"

She stopped. I said, "You saw some gloves there."

"Yes, sir."

"When?"

"When I went to let Mrs. Chapin in."

"Did Mrs. Chapin take them?"

"No, sir. That's when I noticed them, when she picked them up. She picked them up and then put them down again."

"You didn't go back later and get them?"

"No, sir, I didn't."

That settled that. I thanked Mrs. Burton, and left. I wanted to tell her that before tomorrow noon we would have definite news for her that might help a

little, but I thought Wolfe had already done enough
discounting for the firm and I'd better let it ride.

It was after three when I got back to the office, and
I got busy on the phone. There were eight names left
for me, that Wolfe hadn't been able to get. He had told
me the line to take, that we were prepared to mail our
bills to our clients, the signers of the memorandum,
but that before doing so we would like to explain to
them in a body and receive their approval. Which
again spoke fairly well for Wolfe's nerve, inasmuch as
our clients knew damn well that it was the cops who
had grabbed Chapin for Burton's murder and that we
had had about as much to do with it as the lions in
front of the library. But I agreed that it was a good
line, since the object was to get them to the office.

I was doing pretty well with my eight, having
hooked five of them in a little over half an hour, when,
at a quarter to four, while I was looking in the book for
the number of the Players' Club, on the trail of Roland
Erskine, the phone rang. I answered, and it was
Wolfe. As soon as I heard his voice I thought to
myself, uh-huh, here we go, the party's up the flue.
But it didn't appear that that was the idea. He said to
me:

"Archie? What luck at Mrs. Burton's?"

"All negatives. Burton didn't phone, and nobody
took any gloves."

"But perhaps the maid saw them?"

"Oh, you knew that too. She did. She saw Mrs.
Chapin pick them up and put them down again."

"Excellent. I am telephoning because I have just
made a promise and I wish to redeem it without delay.
Take Mr. Chapin's box from the cabinet, wrap it
carefully, and convey it to his apartment and deliver it

to Mrs. Chapin. I shall probably be at home by your return."

"Okay. You got any news?"

"Nothing startling."

"I wouldn't expect anything startling. Let's try a plain straightforward question. Did you get the confession signed or didn't you?"

"I did."

"It's really signed?"

"It is. But I forgot to say: before you wrap Mr. Chapin's box take out a pair of gloves, gray leather, and keep them. Please get the box to Mrs. Chapin at once."

"Okay."

I hung up. The fat devil had put it over. I had no idea what items of ammunition he had procured from Dora Chapin, and of course he had the advantage that Chapin was already in the Tombs with a first degree murder charge glued on him, but even so I handed it to him. I would say that that cripple was the hardest guy to deal with I had ever run across, except the perfume salesman up in New Rochelle who used to drown kittens in the bathtub and one day got hold of his wife by mistake. I would have loved to see Wolfe inserting the needle in him.

Wolfe had said without delay, so I let the last three victims wait. I wrapped the box up and drove down to Perry Street with it, removing a pair of gloves first in accordance with instructions and putting them in a drawer of my desk. I parked across the street from 203 and got out. I had decided on the proper technique for that delivery. I went across to where the elevator man was standing inside the entrance and said to him:

"Take this package up to Mrs. Chapin on the fifth

floor. Then come back here and I'll give you a quarter."

He took the package and said, "The cop was sore as a boil yesterday when he found you'd gone. How're you feeling?"

"Magnificent. Run ahead, mister."

He went, and came back, and I gave him a quarter. I asked him, "Did I break anything on your vertical buggy? The lever wouldn't work."

He grinned about a sixteenth of an inch. "I'll bet it wouldn't. Naw, you didn't break it."

So I kept Wolfe's promise for him and got the package delivered without running any unnecessary risk of being invited in for tea, and all it cost me was two bits, which was cheap enough.

Wolfe returned before I got back home. I knew that in the hall, seeing his hat and coat there. Since it was after four o'clock he would of course be upstairs with the plants, but all of his traipsing around had me nervous, and before going to the office I went up the three flights. I had hardly seen the orchids for more than brief glances for nearly a week. Wolfe was in the tropical room, going down the line looking for aphids, and from the expression on his face I knew he had found some. I stood there, and pretty soon he turned and looked at me as if I was either an aphid myself or had them all over me. There was no use attempting any conversation. I beat it downstairs to resume at the telephone.

I only got two of the remaining three, couldn't find Roland Erskine anywhere. As it was, we had done pretty good. A telegram had come from Boston saying that Collard and Gaines would be there, and Mollison was coming down from New Haven. I suspected that

Wolfe would have handled the long distance babies himself even if I hadn't been in bed.

Wolfe didn't come to the office directly from the plant-rooms at six o'clock as usual. Apparently he had stopped in his room, for when he appeared around six-thirty he was lugging a stack of books and I saw they were Paul Chapin's novels. He put them on his desk and sat down and rang for beer.

I told him Mrs. Chapin had the box, and read him the notes of my afternoon call on Mrs. Burton. He gave me some instructions for the evening, which I made notes of because he liked to have everything down, and then he got playful. He made a lot of random remarks and I took them like a gentleman, and then because it was getting on towards dinner I observed that it was about time I got acquainted with the mystery of the pair of gloves on the foyer table. To my surprise he agreed with me.

He said: "That was the contribution of Mrs. Chapin. She furnished other information too, but nothing as interesting as that. She arrived at the Burton apartment, as you know, at six-thirty. The maid called Rose let her in. As she passed through the foyer she saw a pair of gloves on the table, and she stopped to pick them up. She says she intended to take them in to Mrs. Burton, but it would not be charitable to surmise that she had in mind starting a new treasure box for her husband; and that it is supported by the reasons she gives for returning the gloves to the table. She gives two reasons: that the maid had turned and was looking at her, and that the gloves seemed a little heavier than any she had known Mrs. Burton to wear. At any rate, she left them there. But when she went through the foyer, alone, on the way out, she thought to look at them again to satisfy herself whether they were Mrs. Burton's or not. The gloves were gone. She even looked around for them. They were gone."

"I see. And that proves she didn't croak Burton."

"It does. And it identifies the murderer. If it should turn out that factual corroboration is needed of Mrs. Chapin's innocence, which seems unlikely, it can be established that at half past seven she was receiving a summons from a policeman at Park Avenue and Fiftieth Street for passing a red light. Not to mention the probability that the hallman and doorman saw her leaving the building before the event occurred. But none of that should be needed."

"Uh-huh. I suppose you got her confidence by giving her some orchids."

"No. But as a matter of fact, I promised her some. Make a note of that for tomorrow. I got her confidence by telling her the truth, that the conviction of her husband for murder would cost me many thousands of dollars. You see, what happened—what time is it?— Good. She was convinced, as was Chapin himself, that I was responsible for his predicament. Not knowing the nature of my agreement with his friends, he thought I had framed him. Having seen me, he could not of course suppose that I myself had performed the acrobatics in the foyer. Do you know who did that? You. Yes, indeed, you did the killing, I merely devised it. Mrs. Chapin, believing that, seized an opportunity. With you and Pitney Scott fast asleep, she went through your pockets, took his cap and jacket, sat down and wrote a note, and drove the taxicab here. She handed the envelope to Fritz at the door and returned to the cab. The note was brief and quite clear, I can quote it verbatim: *Archie Goodwin will be dead in two hours unless you get in my taxi and go where I drive you.* And it was signed with her name, Dora Chapin. Admirably forthright. What persuaded me that some sort of action was called for was the presence in the envelope of the leather case you had seemed to like."

He paused for a glass of beer. I grunted, and thought I ought to say something, but all I could think of was, "Yeah, I liked it. And you've still got it."

He nodded, and resumed. "The only aspect of the episode that was really distressing came from Mrs. Chapin's romantic idea of what constitutes a remote and secluded spot. Since I was committed to follow her, a bush in a corner of Central Park would have done her just as well, but that infernal female ass bounced that cab far beyond the limits of the city. I learned subsequently that she had in mind an isolated wood somewhere on the edge of Long Island Sound where she and her husband had gone last summer to have a picnic. It became unendurable. I lowered the glass between us and shouted at the back of her ear that if she did not stop within three minutes I would call for help at every passing car and every visible human being. I convinced her. She turned into a byroad and soon stopped under a clump of trees.

"This will amuse you. She had a weapon. A kitchen knife!—By the way, that carving she exhibited to us last Wednesday was done on her own initiative; her husband disapproved. At that time the game was still on of establishing Mr. Chapin in the minds of his friends as a dangerous and murderous fellow, without involving him in any demonstrable guilt. He already suspected that I might uncover him, and his wife's bloody neck was a red herring, though her own idea.—Well. She could not very well have expected to kill me with a knife, since none could be long enough to reach a vital spot; I suppose no gun was available, or perhaps she mistrusts them as I do. Perhaps she meant merely to hack me into acquiescence; and of course she had in reserve my anxiety as to the peril of your situation. At all events, her purpose was to force me to reveal the skulduggery by which her husband had been entrapped. I was to write it. She had pen and paper with her. That attention to detail endeared her to me."

"Yeah. And?"

He drank beer. "Nothing much. You know my fondness for talking. It was an excellent opportunity. She was calm from the outset. She and I have much in common—for instance, our dislike of perturbation. It would have been instructive to see her using the knife on the back of her neck that day, I would wager she did it much as one trims a chop. After I had explained the situation to her, we discussed it. The moment arrived when it seemed pointless to continue our conference in that cold, dark forbidding spot, and besides, I had learned what had happened to you. She seemed so uncertain as to what she had used to flavor your coffee that I thought it best to reach a telephone with as little delay as possible.—Ah! Mr. Hibbard, I trust the long afternoon has been fairly tolerable."

Hibbard walked in, looking a little groggy, still wearing my brown necktie. Behind him came Fritz, to announce dinner.

# Chapter 21

They piled in early. By nine o'clock ten of them had already arrived, checked off on my list, and I was doing the honors. Four of them I hadn't seen before: Collard and Gaines from Boston, Irving from Philadelphia and Professor Mollison of Yale. Mike Ayers, stony sober on arrival, helped me get drinks around. At nine sharp Leopold Elkus joined the throng. I had no idea what Wolfe had told him to get him there; anyway there he was, and what he wanted to drink was a glass of port, and I restrained an impulse to tell him there was no nitroglycerin in it. He recognized me and acted gracious. Some more came, among them Augustus Farrell, who had phoned on Saturday that he was back from Philadelphia and had landed the commission for Mr. Allenby's library. Wolfe, surmising that what he was really phoning about was the twenty bucks due him for Wednesday's work, had had me mail him a check.

They didn't seem as subdued as they had a week before. They took to the drinks with more gusto, and gathered in groups and talked, and two or three of them even came up to me and got impatient. Collard, the Boston textile man who owned the cliff that Judge

Harrison had fallen off of, told me he hoped to see the last act of the opera, and I said I was sorry but I myself had had to give up that hope long ago. I overheard Elkus telling Ferdinand Bowen that it appeared likely that Nero Wolfe was in an advanced stage of megalomania, and tried to get Bowen's reply but missed it.

There were fifteen of them present at a quarter past nine, which was the time Wolfe had told me he would make his entrance.

It was a good entrance all right. He did it in perfect style. I was watching for him, not to miss it. He came in, three paces in, and stood there, until they had all turned to look at him and the talking had stopped. He inclined his head and used his resonance: "Good evening, gentleman." Then he faced the door and nodded at Fritz, who was standing on the threshold. Fritz moved aside, and Andrew Hibbard walked in.

That started the first uproar. Pratt and Mike Ayers were the quickest to react. They both yelled "Andy!" and jumped for him. Others followed. They encircled him, shouted at him, grabbed his hands and pounded him on the back. They had him hemmed in so that I couldn't see any of him, to observe what kind of psychology he was taking it with. It was easy to imagine, hearing them and looking at them, that they really liked Andy Hibbard. Maybe even Drummond and Bowen liked him; you've got to take the bitter along with the sweet.

Wolfe had eluded the stampede. He had got to his desk and lowered himself into his chair, and Fritz had brought him beer. I looked at him, and was glad I did, for it wasn't often he felt like winking at me and I wouldn't have wanted to miss it. He returned my look and gave me the wink, and I grinned at him. Then he drank some beer.

The commotion went on a while longer. Mike Ayers came over to Wolfe's desk and said something which I couldn't hear on account of the noise, and Wolfe nodded and replied something. Mike Ayers went back and began shooing them into chairs, and Cabot and Farrell helped him. They subsided. Pratt took Hibbard by the arm and steered him to one of the big armchairs, and then sat down next to him and took out his handkerchief and wiped his eyes.

Wolfe started the ball rolling. He sat pretty straight, his forearms on the arms of his chair, his chin down, his eyes open on them.

"Gentlemen. Thank you for coming here this evening. Even if we should later come to disagreement, I am sure we are in accord as to the felicitous nature of our preamble. We are all glad that Mr. Hibbard is with us. Mr. Goodwin and I are gratified that we were able to play the Stanley to his Livingstone. As to the particular dark continent that Mr. Hibbard chose to explore, and the method of our finding him, those details must wait for another occasion, since we have more pressing business. I believe it is enough at present to say that Mr. Hibbard's disappearance was a venture on his own account, a sally in search of education. That is correct, Mr. Hibbard?"

They all looked at Hibbard. He nodded. "That's correct."

Wolfe took some papers from his drawer, spread them out, and picked one up. "I have here, gentlemen, a copy of the memorandum of our agreement. One of my undertakings herein was to remove from you all apprehension and expectation of injury from the person or

persons responsible for the disappearance of Andrew
Hibbard. I take it that that has been accomplished? You
have no fear of Mr. Hibbard himself?—Good. Then that
much is done." He paused to look them over, face by
face, and went on. "For the rest, it will be necessary to
read you a document." He put the memorandum down
and picked up another paper, sheets clipped to a brown
paper jacket. "This, gentlemen, is dated November
twelfth, which is today. It is signed with the name of
Paul Chapin. At the top it is headed, CONFESSION OF PAUL
CHAPIN REGARDING THE DEATHS OF WILLIAM R. HARRISON AND
EUGENE DREYER AND THE WRITING AND DISPATCHING OF CERTAIN
INFORMATIVE AND THREATENING VERSES. It reads as
follows—"

Cabot the lawyer butted in. He would. He interrupted: "Mr. Wolfe. Of course this is interesting, but
in view of what has happened do you think it's
necessary?"

"Quite." Wolfe didn't look up. "If you will permit
me:

> "*I, Paul Chapin, of 203 Perry Street, New
> York City, hereby confess that I was in no way
> concerned in the death of Judge William R.
> Harrison. To the best of my knowledge and
> belief his death was accidental.*
>
> *I further confess that I was in no way con-
> cerned in the death of Eugene Dreyer. To the
> best of my knowledge and belief he committed
> suicide.*
>
> *I further confess—*"

There was an explosive snort from Mike Ayers,
and mutterings from some of the others. Julius Adler's

mild sarcastic voice took the air: "This is drivel. Chapin has maintained throughout—"

Wolfe stopped him, and all of them. "Gentlemen! Please. I ask your indulgence. If you will withhold comments until the end."

Drummond squeaked, "Let him finish," and I made a mental note to give him an extra drink. Wolfe continued:

*"I further confess that the verses received by certain persons on three separate occasions were composed, typed and mailed by me. They were intended to convey by inference the information that I had killed Harrison, Dreyer and Hibbard, and that it was my purpose to kill others. They were typed on the typewriter in the alcove of the smoking-room at the Harvard Club, a fact which was discovered by Nero Wolfe. That ends my confession. The rest is explanation, which I offer at Nero Wolfe's request.*

*The idea of the verses, which came to me after Harrison's death, was at first only one of the fantasies which occupy a mind accustomed to invention. I composed them. They were good, at least for one purpose, and I decided to send them. I devised details as to paper, envelopes and typing which would leave no possibility to proving that they had been sent by me. They worked admirably, beyond my expectations.*

*Three months later the death of Dreyer, and the circumstances under which it occurred, offered another opportunity which of course was irresistible. This was more risky than the first, since I had been present at the gallery*

*that afternoon, but careful consideration con-
vinced me that there was no real danger. I
typed the second verses, and sent them. They
were even more successful than the first ones. I
need not try to describe the satisfaction it gave
me to fill with trepidation and terror the insolent breasts which for so many years had
bulged their pity at me. They had called themselves the League of Atonement—Oh yes, I
knew that. Now at last atonement had in fact
begun.*

*I supplemented the effect of the verses ver-
bally, with certain of my friends, whenever a
safe opportunity offered, and this was more
fertile with Andrew Hibbard than with anyone
else. It ended by his becoming so terrified that
he ran away. I do not know where he is; it is
quite possible that he killed himself. As soon as
I learned of his disappearance I decided to take
advantage of it. Of course if he reappeared the
game was up, but I had not supposed that I
could continue the business indefinitely, and
this was too good a chance to be missed. I sent
the third verses. The result was nothing short of
magnificent, indeed it proved to be too magnificent. I had never heard of Nero Wolfe. I went
to his office that evening for the pleasure of
seeing my friends, and to look at Wolfe. I saw
that he was acute and intuitive, and that my
diversion was probably at an end. An attempt
was made by my wife to impress Wolfe, but it
failed.*

*There are other points that might be touched
upon, but I believe none of them require explanation. I would like to mention, though, that*

*my testimony on the witness-stand regarding
my reason for writing my novel* Devil Take the
Hindmost, *was in my opinion a superlative bit
of finesse, and Nero Wolfe agrees with me.*

*I will add that I am not responsible for the
literary quality of this document. It was written by Nero Wolfe.*

*Paul Chapin."*

Wolfe finished, dropped the confession on the
table, and leaned back. "Now, gentlemen. If you wish
to comment."

There were mumblings. Ferdinand Bowen, the
stockbroker, spoke up: "It seems to me Adler has
commented for all of us. Drivel."

Wolfe nodded. "I can understand that viewpoint.
In fact, I suppose that under the circumstances it is
inevitable. But let me expound my own viewpoint. My
position is that I have met my obligations under the
memorandum and that the payments are due."

"My dear sir!" It was Nicholas Cabot. "Preposterous."

"I think not. What I undertook to do was to remove
your fear of Paul Chapin. That's what it amounts to,
with the facts we now have. Well: as for Andrew
Hibbard, here he is. As for the deaths of Harrison and
Dreyer, it should have been obvious to all of you, from
the beginning, that Chapin had nothing to do with
them. You had known him all his mature life. I had
merely read his books; but I was aware last Monday
evening, when you gentlemen were here, that Chapin
could not possibly commit a premeditated murder, and
not even an impromptu one unless suddenly de-
mented. And you, Mr. Hibbard, a psychologist! Have

you read Chapin's books? Why are they so concerned with murder and the delight of it? Why does every page have its hymn to violence and the brute beauty of vehement action? Or, to change heroes, why did Nietzsche say, *Thou goest to woman, forget not thy whip*? Because he had not the temerity to touch a woman with the tip of a goose-feather. The truth is that Paul Chapin did murder Harrison and Dreyer, and all of you. He has murdered you, and will doubtless do so again, in his books. Let him, gentlemen, and go on breathing.

"No. Harrison and Dreyer and Hibbard are out of it. Consult the memorandum. There remains only the matter of the warnings. Chapin admits he sent them, and tells you how and why and where. The trilogy is done. There will be no sequels, and even if there were I should not suppose they would alarm you. If he should desire to use the same typewriter again he would have to come to this office for it, for it rests there on Mr. Goodwin's desk."

They all looked, and I moved out of the way so they could see it. Wolfe drank beer, and wiped his lips. He resumed:

"I know, of course, where the trouble lies. Paul Chapin is in the Tombs charged with the murder of Dr. Burton. If that had not happened, if Dr. Burton were here with us this evening alive and well, I have no doubt that all of you would acquiesce in my position. I have done the work I was engaged for. But as it is, you are confused; and what confuses you is this, that whereas you formerly had no security at all against Paul Chapin's injurious designs, you now have more than you need. I offer you the security I undertook to get for you, but you are no longer interested in it because you already have something just as good:

namely, that Chapin is going to be electrocuted and
can no longer murder you even in books.—Mr. Cabot,
I ask you as a lawyer, is that exposition of the
situation correct? What do you think of it?"

"I think . . ." Cabot pursed his lips, and after a
moment went on, "I think it is remarkably ingenious
rubbish."

Wolfe nodded. "I would expect you to. I take it,
gentlemen, that Mr. Cabot's opinion is approximately
unanimous. Yes?—So it becomes necessary for me to
introduce a new consideration. This: that Chapin did
not kill Dr. Burton, that I can establish his innocence,
and that if tried he will be acquitted."

That started the second uproar. It began as a
muttering of incredulity and astonishment; it was
Leopold Elkus that put the noise in it. He jumped out
of his chair and ran around Wolfe's desk to get at him
and grabbed his hand and began pumping it. He
seemed to be excited; he was yelling at Wolfe something about justice and gratitude and how great and
grand Wolfe was; I didn't hear anything about megalomania. The others, busy with their own remarks,
didn't pay any attention to him. Mike Ayers, roaring
with laughter, got up and went to the table for a drink.
I got up too, thinking I might have to go and haul
Elkus off of Wolfe, but he finally trotted back to the
others, gesticulating and still talking. Wolfe lifted his
hand at them:

"Gentlemen! If you please. I seem to have startled
you. Similarly, I suppose, the police and the District
Attorney will be startled, though they should not be.
You of course expect me to support my statement with
evidence, but if I do that I must ask you for more
impartiality than I observe at the moment on most of
your faces. You cannot be at the same time juridical

and partisan, at least not with any pretense at competence.

"I offer these items. First, at a few minutes before seven on Saturday evening Paul Chapin answered the telephone in his apartment. It was Dr. Burton, who asked Chapin to come to see him immediately. A little later Chapin left to go to Ninetieth Street, arriving there at seven-thirty. But there was something wrong with that telephone call, namely, that Dr. Burton never made it. For that we have the word of his wife, who says that her husband telephoned no one around that time Saturday. It seems likely, therefore, that there was somewhere a third person who was taking upon himself the functions of fate.—I know, Mr. Adler. And I think I perceive, Mr. Bowen, that your face carries a similar expression. You would ask if I am gullible enough to believe Mr. Chapin. I am not gullible, but I believe him. He told his wife of the telephone call, and she told me; and there is the switchboard operator at the Chapin apartment house.

"Item two. Consider the details of what is supposed to have happened in the Burton foyer. Dr. Burton took the pistol from his desk and went to the foyer. Chapin, there waiting for him, took the pistol from him, shot him four times, turned out the light, threw the pistol on the floor and then got down on his hands and knees to look for it in the dark. What a picture! According to the story of Mrs. Burton and of the maid, Dr. Burton had been in the foyer not more than six seconds, possibly less, when the shots were fired. Burton was a good-sized man, and powerful. Chapin is small and is handicapped by a major deformity; he cannot even walk without support. Well . . . I am going to count six seconds for you. One . . . two . . . three . . . four . . . five . . .

six. That was six seconds. In that space of time, or less, the crippled Chapin is supposed to have got the gun from Burton's pocket, God knows how, shot him, dropped the gun, hobbled to the switch to turn off the light, and hobbled back to the table to fall to the floor. In your juridical capacity, gentlemen, what do you think of that?"

Leopold Elkus stood up. His black eyes were not floating back into his head now; he was using them for glaring. He let the bunch have the glare, right and left, saying loudly and clearly, "Anyone who ever believed that is no better than a cretin." He looked at Wolfe. "I shall have apologies for you, sir, when this kindergarten is over." He sat down.

"Thank you, Dr. Elkus.—Item three, for what conceivable reason did Chapin turn out the light? I shall not take your time by listing conjectures only to have you reject them as I have done. Make your own when you have leisure for it, if it amuses you. I only say, the actions even of a murderer should be in some degree explicable, and to believe that Chapin shot Burton and then hobbled to the wall to turn out the light is to believe nonsense. I doubt if any of you believe that. Do you?"

They looked at one another as if, having no opinions of their own, they would like to borrow one. Two or three shook their heads. George Pratt spoke up, "I'll tell you what I believe, Wolfe. I believe we hired you to get Paul Chapin into trouble, not out of it." Drummond giggled and Mike Ayers laughed. Nicholas Cabot demanded:

"What does Chapin have to say? Did he shoot or didn't he? Did he turn out the light or didn't he? What does he say happened during those six seconds?"

Wolfe shook his head and his cheeks unfolded a

little. "Oh no, Mr. Cabot. It is possible that Mr. Chapin will have to tell his story on the witness-stand in his own defense. You can hardly expect me to disclose it in advance to those who may consider themselves his enemies."

"What the hell, no one would believe him anyway." It was Ferdinand Bowen relieving himself. "He'd cook up a tale, of course."

Wolfe turned his eyes on Bowen, and I had mine there too. I was curious to see if he would take it. I didn't think he would, but he did; he kept his gaze steady back at Wolfe.

Wolfe sighed. "Well, gentlemen, I have presented my case. I could offer further points for your consideration: for instance, the likelihood that if Chapin intended to kill Dr. Burton as soon as he set eyes on him he would have gone provided with a weapon. Also, Chapin's constitutional incapacity for any form of violent action, which I discovered through his novels, and which all of you must be acquainted with as a fact. And in addition, there are items of evidence which I cannot divulge to you now, out of fairness to him, but which will certainly be used should he come to trial. Surely, surely I have offered enough to show you that if your minds have been cleared of any fear of injury from Paul Chapin, it is not because a policeman found him sitting in Dr. Burton's foyer, stunned by an event he could not have foreseen; it is because I have laid bare the purely literary nature of his attempt at vengeance. The question is this, have I satisfactorily performed my undertaking? I think I have. But it is you who are to decide it, by vote. I ask you to vote yes.—Archie. If you will please call the names."

They began to talk. Bowen muttered to his neighbor, Gaines of Boston, "Pretty slick, he's a damn fool if he thinks we'll fall for it." Elkus glared at him. I caught a few other observations. Cabot said to Wolfe, "I shall vote no. In case Chapin does get an acquittal, and evidence is presented—"

Wolfe nodded at him. "I am aware, Mr. Cabot, that this vote is not the last dingdong of doom. As you shall see, if I lose." He nodded at me, and I started the roll call. On the list I was using they were alphabetical.

"Julius Adler."

"No. I would like to say—"

Wolfe cut him off. "The no is sufficient. Proceed, Archie."

"Michael Ayers."

"Yes!" He made it emphatic. I thought, good for him, with two weeks' wages up.

"Ferdinand Bowen."

"No."

"Edwin Robert Byron."

"Yes." That evened it up.

"Nicholas Cabot."

"No."

"Fillmore Collard."

"Yes." Wowie. Nine thousand berries. I paused because I had to look at him.

"Alexander Drummond."

"No." Sure, the damn canary.

"Leopold Elkus."

"Yes!" And it was even again, four and four.

"Augustus Farrell."

"Yes."

"Theodore Gaines."

"No."

"L. M. Irving."

"No."

"Arthur Kommers."

"No." Three out-of-town babies, three noes in a row, and I hoped Wolfe was proud of his long-distance phoning.

"Sidney Lang."

"Yes."

"Archibald Mollison."

"Yes."

It was even again, seven and seven, and just one more to go, but I knew what it would be before I called it. It was George Pratt, the Tammany bird who had tried to get Inspector Cramer worried about his four grand. I said it:

"George R. Pratt."

"No."

I counted them over to make sure, and turned to Wolfe: "Seven yeses and eight noes."

He didn't look at me. They all began talking. Wolfe had rung for another bottle of beer, and now he opened it, poured a glass, watched the foam go down in front of him, but he didn't look at it. He drank some more beer, and wiped his lips with his usual care. Then he leaned back and shut his eyes. They were all talking, and two or three of them directed questions or remarks at him, but he kept his eyes closed and paid no attention. Leopold Elkus walked to the desk and stood and looked at him a minute, and then went back again. They were getting louder, and the arguments were warming up.

Finally Wolfe came to. He opened his eyes, and saw that a fresh bottle of beer had arrived, which I had attended to, and opened it and drank some. Then he picked up a paperweight and rapped on the desk. They looked around, but went on talking. He rapped again, and they began to quiet down.

He spoke. "Gentlemen. I must again ask your indulgence—"

But Cabot was feeling his oats. He broke in, snappy: "We have voted. According to the memorandum, that settles it."

Wolfe got snappy too. "It settles that vote, sir. It does not settle the destiny of the human race. If you wish to leave us, of course you may, but we would still have a quorum without you.—Good. I have two appeals to make. First, to those eight who voted no. Please heed me. I appeal to each and all of you—you understand, to each one of you—to change your vote to yes. I have a specific reason to hope that one of you will decide to change. Well, gentlemen? I shall give you one minute."

They shook their heads. One or two spoke, but mostly they were silent, gazing at Wolfe. There had been a new tone in his voice. He had taken out his watch and kept his eyes on it. At the end of the minute he returned it to his pocket and looked up.

He sighed. "Then I must proceed to my second appeal. This time, Mr. Bowen, it is to you alone. I ask you to vote yes. You of course know why. Will you vote yes?"

They all looked at the stockbroker. Including me. He was still taking it, but not so good. He damn near stuttered, shooting it back at Wolfe. I would say he did just fair with it: "Certainly not. Why should I?" His mouth stayed open; he thought he would talk some more, and then he thought he wouldn't.

Wolfe sighed again. "Mr. Bowen, you are a simpleton.—Gentlemen, I would like to explain briefly why I have not done sooner what I am going to do now. There were two reasons: because I am not fond of interfering in affairs that are not my concern, and

because it would be expensive for me. To be exact, it
will cost me twelve hundred dollars, the amount of Mr.
Bowen's payment under the memorandum. Besides
that, as I have said, it was none of my business. If any
person is suspected of having committed a crime, and
if I am offered a sufficient sum of money to catch him
up, I will do it. That is my business. I understand that
there are individuals who will undertake to apprehend
wrongdoers, especially murderers, without being paid
for it. They do it, I presume, for amusement, which is
not astonishing when you consider what odd diver-
sions have been sought by various members of our
race. I myself have other means of escaping boredom,
but this is the only one I have developed of avoiding
penury. I will hunt anyone down if you pay me
enough. But no one has offered to pay me for discovering the murderer of Dr. Burton. By exposing him
and delivering him to justice I shall lose twelve
hundred dollars, but I shall ensure the collection of a
larger sum.—Now. Mr. Farrell, would you mind moving to another chair? If you please. And you, Archie,
take the seat Mr. Farrell is vacating, next to Mr.
Bowen."

I moved. My eye hadn't left Bowen since Wolfe had
asked him to vote yes, and now all eyes were on him.
Nobody was saying a word. The stockbroker was up
against it. By skating all around him with inference
and insinuation but not directly accusing him, and
prolonging it, Wolfe had him plenty perplexed. The
others staring at him didn't help him any. I suppose he
was trying to decide whether it was time for him to
jump up and begin resenting things. He didn't glance
at me as I sat down by him; he was looking at Wolfe.

Wolfe was on the phone. He kept his usual tempo,
taking his time, though he had to try three numbers

before he reached the man he wanted. He finally got him. Nobody on the chairs moved by a hair while he was talking.

"Inspector Cramer? This is Nero Wolfe. That's right. Good evening, sir.—Inspector, I would like you to do me a favor. I have guests in my office, and no leisure at present for long explanations. I believe you know how much reliance may be placed in any positive statement I may make. Well. Will you send a man to my office—perhaps two would be better—for the murderer of Dr. Loring A. Burton? I have him here.— No. No, indeed. I beg you, explanations can come later.—Of course, proof; what good is certainty without proof.—By all means, if you wish to come yourself. Certainly."

He pushed the phone back, and Bowen jumped up. His knees were trembling, and so were his little lady-hands, which I was watching to see that he didn't make a pass. I took advantage of his being up to feel his rear for a gun; and my hands on him startled him. He forgot what he was going to say to Wolfe and turned on me, and by God he hauled off and kicked me on the shin. I got up and grabbed him and pushed him back into his chair and observed to him:

"You try another friendly gesture like that and I'll paste you one."

Drummond, who had been sitting next to Bowen, on the other side, moved away. Several others got up. Wolfe said:

"Sit down, gentlemen.—I beg you, there is no occasion for turmoil.—Archie, if you will kindly bring Mr. Bowen closer; I would like to see him better while talking to him. If it is necessary to prod him, you may do so."

I stood up and told the stockbroker to find his feet.

He didn't move and he didn't look up; his hands were in his lap twisting in a knot and there were various colors distributed over his face and neck and I was surprised not to see any yellow. I said, "Get a move on or I'll move you." From behind me I heard George Pratt's voice:

"You don't have to prove you're tough. Look at the poor devil."

"Yeah?" I didn't turn because I didn't care to take my eyes off of Bowen. "Was it your shin he kicked? Speak when you're spoken to."

I grabbed Bowen's collar and jerked him up, and he came. I admit he was pitiful. He stood for a second trying to look around at them, and he tried to keep the quaver out of his voice: "Fellows. You understand why . . . if I don't say anything now to . . . to this ridiculous . . ."

He couldn't finish it anyhow, so I hauled him away. I put a chair up and sat him in it, then I perched on the edge of Wolfe's desk so as to face him. Two or three of the bunch got to their feet and approached us. Wolfe turned to face the stockbroker:

"Mr. Bowen. It gives me no pleasure to prolong your discomfiture in the presence of your friends, but in any event we must wait until the police arrive to take you away. Just now you used the word ridiculous; may I borrow it from you? You are the most ridiculous murderer I have ever met. I do not know you well enough to be able to say whether it was through vast stupidity or extraordinary insouciance; however that may be, you planned the most hazardous of all crimes as if you were devising a harmless parlor game.

"I am not merely taunting you; I am depriving you of your last tatters of hope and courage in order to break you down. You stole a large sum from Dr.

Burton through his account with your firm. I know nothing of the mechanism of your theft; that will be uncovered when the District Attorney examines your books. You found that Dr. Burton had discovered the theft, or suspected it, and on Saturday you went to his apartment to appeal to him, but already you had arranged an alternative in case the appeal failed. You were with Burton in his study. He went to his wife's room to ask her if she cared enough for Estelle Bowen to make a big sacrifice for her, and his wife said no. Burton returned to the study and you got your answer; but during his absence you had got his automatic pistol from the drawer of his desk and put it in your pocket. Since you were his close friend, you had probably known for a long time that he kept a gun there; if not, you heard him in this room a week ago tonight telling all of us that on the occasion of Paul Chapin's last visit to him he had got the gun from the drawer before he went to see Chapin in the foyer. Would you like a drink?"

Bowen made no reply or movement. Mike Ayers went to the table and got a shot of rye and came over with it and offered it to him, but Bowen paid no attention. Mike Ayers shrugged his shoulders and drank it himself. Wolfe was going on:

"Soon you left, at twenty minutes past six. No one went to the foyer with you; or if Burton did go, you pushed the button on the edge of the door as you went out, so it would not lock, and in a moment re-entered. At all events, you were alone in the foyer and the Burtons thought you had gone. You listened. Hearing no one, you went to the telephone. You had your gloves in your hand, and not to be encumbered with them while phoning, you laid them on the table. But before your call had gone through you were interrupted by the sound of someone approaching in the drawing-room. Alarmed, you ran for the concealment which you had already decided on: the curtained closet next to the light switch and the double doors. You got behind the curtain in time, before Miss Burton, the daughter of the house, came through, leaving the apartment.

"You realized that you had left your gloves lying on the table, and that concerned you, for you would need them to keep fingerprints from the gun—and, by the way, did it occur to you that the phone would show prints? Or did you wipe them off? No matter. But you did not at once dash out for the gloves, for you needed a little time to collect yourself after the alarm that the daughter had given you. You waited, and probably congratulated yourself that you did, for almost at once you heard the double door opening again, and footsteps, and the opening of the entrance door. It was Dora Chapin, arriving to do Mrs. Burton's hair.

"Mr. Paul Chapin was out Saturday afternoon and did not return until rather late. This morning on the telephone, the switchboard operator at 203 Perry Street told me that there was a phone call for Mr. Chapin some fifteen or twenty minutes before he arrived home. So it seems likely that about six-forty you emerged from your hiding place, got the gloves, and tried the phone again, but there was no answer from the Chapin apartment. You returned to the closet, and fifteen minutes later tried again. Of course you did not know that the last phone call of yours, at about five minutes to seven, happened to coincide with Mr. Chapin's entrance into the hall of 203 Perry Street; the switchboard operator called to him, and he answered that call at the switchboard itself, so the operator heard it. Apparently you imitated Dr. Burton's voice with some success, for Mr. Chapin was deceived. He went upstairs to his apartment for a few minutes, and then came down to take a cab to Nine- tieth Street.

"After phoning Chapin you returned again to the closet and waited there, with an accelerated pulse, I presume, and an emergency demand on your supply of adrenaline. Indeed, you seem practically to have ex- hausted the latter. I imagine that it seemed quite a while before Chapin arrived, and you were surprised to find that it had been only thirty-five minutes since your phone call. At all events, he came, was admitted by the maid, and sat down. In your closet, you kept your ears keen to learn if he took a chair that would turn his back to you; you had your gloves on, and the gun in your right hand ready for action. Still you strained your ears, to hear the approach of Dr. Burton. You heard his steps crossing the drawing- room, and the instant the sound came of his hand on the doorknob, you moved. Here, I confess, you showed efficiency and accuracy. Your left arm shot out past the edge of the curtain, your fingers found the light switch and pushed it, and the foyer was in darkness except for the dim light that wandered through the door from the drawing-room after Dr. Burton had opened it. With the light off, you jumped from the closet, found Chapin in his chair, and shoved him off onto the floor—not difficult with a cripple, was it, Mr. Bowen? By that time Dr. Burton had ap- proached the commotion and was quite close when you shot him, and there was enough light from the drawing-room door for you to tell where his middle was. You pulled the trigger and held it for four shots, then threw the gun to the floor—and made your exit, after closing the double door. In the hall you ran to the stairs, and ran down them. There were only four flights, and one more to the basement, and a short stretch of hall to the service entrance. You calculated that even if you encountered someone, there would be no great danger in it, for the guilt of Paul Chapin would be so obvious that no questions would be asked of anyone outside of the apartment.

"Now, Mr. Bowen, you made many mistakes, but none so idiotic as your sole reliance on Chapin's obvious guilt, for that one was the father of all the others. Why in the name of heaven didn't you turn on the light again as you went out? And why didn't you wait until Chapin and Burton had talked a minute or two before you acted? You could have done just as well. Another inexcusable thing was your carelessness in leaving the gloves on the table. I know; you were so sure that they would be sure of Chapin that you thought nothing else mattered. You were worse than a tyro, you were a donkey. I tell you this, sir, your exposure is a credit to no one, least of all to me. Pfui!"

Wolfe stopped, abruptly, and turned to ring for Fritz, for beer. Bowen's fingers had been twisting in and out, but now they had stopped that and were locked together. He was shaking all over, just sitting in his chair shaking, with no nerve left, no savvy, no nothing; he was nothing but a gob of scared meat.

Leopold Elkus came up and stood three feet from Bowen and stood staring at him; I had a feeling that he had a notion to cut him open and see what was inside. Mike Ayers appeared with another drink, but this time it wasn't for Bowen, he held it out to me and I took it and drank it. Andrew Hibbard went to my desk and got the telephone and gave the operator the number of his home. Drummond was squeaking something to George Pratt. Nicholas Cabot passed around

Bowen's chair, went up to Wolfe and said to him in a tone not low enough for me not to hear:

"I'm going, Mr. Wolfe. I have an appointment. I want to say, there's no reason why you shouldn't get that twelve hundred dollars from Bowen. It's a legal obligation. If you'd like me to handle the collection I'd be glad to do it and expect no fee. Let me know."

That lawyer was tough.

# Chapter 22

Three days later, Thursday around noon, we had a caller. I had just got back from taking a vast and voluminous deposit to the bank, and was sitting at my desk bending my thoughts towards a little relaxation in the shape of an afternoon movie. Wolfe was in his chair, leaning back with his eyes shut, still and silent as a mountain, probably considering the adequacy of the plans for lunch.

Fritz came to the door and said: "A man to see you, sir. Mr. Paul Chapin."

Wolfe opened his eyes to a slit, and nodded. I whirled my chair around, and stood up.

The cripple hobbled in. It was a bright day outside, and the strong light from the windows gave me a better look at him than I had ever had. I saw that his eyes weren't quite as light-colored as I had thought; they were about the shade of dull aluminum; and his skin wasn't dead pale, it was more like bleached leather, it looked tough. He gave me only half a glance as he thumped across to Wolfe's desk. I moved a chair around for him.

"Good morning, Mr. Chapin." Wolfe nearly opened his eyes. "You won't be seated? I beg you . . .

thanks. It gives me genuine discomfort to see people stand. Allow me to congratulate you on your appearance. If I had spent three days in the Tombs prison, as you did, I would be nothing but a wraith, a tattered remnant. How were the meals? I presume, unspeakable?"

The cripple lifted his shoulders, and dropped them. He didn't appear to be settling down for a chat; he had lowered himself onto the edge of the chair I had placed for him, and perched there with his stick upright in front and both his hands resting on the crook. His aluminum eyes had the same amount of expression in them that aluminum usually has. He said:

"I sit for courtesy. To relieve you of discomfort. For a moment only. I came for the pair of gloves which you removed from my box."

"Ah!" Wolfe's eyes opened the rest of the way. "So your blessings are numbered. Indeed!"

Chapin nodded. "Luckily. May I have them?"

"Another disappointment." Wolfe sighed. "I was thinking you had taken the trouble to call to convey your gratitude for my saving you from the electric chair. You are, of course, grateful?"

Chapin's lips twisted. "I am as grateful as you would expect me to be. So we needn't waste time on that. May I have the gloves?"

"You may.—Archie, if you please. To me."

I got the gloves from a drawer of my desk and handed them across to Wolfe. He came forward in his chair to place them in front of him on his own desk, one neatly on top of the other, and to smooth them out. Chapin's gaze was fastened on the gloves. Wolfe leaned back and sighed again.

"You know, Mr. Chapin, I never got to use them. I retained them, from your box, to demonstrate a point

Monday evening by showing how nearly they fitted Mr. Bowen, thus explaining how Dora Chapin—your wife—could mistake Mr. Bowen's gloves for a pair of Mrs. Burton's; but since he wilted like a Dendrobium with root-rot there was no occasion for it. Now"— Wolfe wiggled a finger—"I don't expect you to believe this, but it is nevertheless true that I halfway suspected that your knowledge of the contents of your box was intimate enough to make you aware of the absence of any fraction of the inventory; so I did not return these. I kept them. I wanted to see you."

Paul Chapin, saying nothing, took a hand from his walking-stick and reached out for the gloves. Wolfe shook his head and pulled them back a little. The cripple tossed his head up.

"Just a morsel of patience, Mr. Chapin. I wanted to see you because I had an apology to make. I am hoping that you will accept it."

"I came for my gloves. You may keep the apology."

"But, my dear sir!" Wolfe wiggled a finger again. "Permit me at least to describe my offense. I wish to apologize for forging your name."

Chapin lifted his brows. Wolfe turned to me:

"A copy of the confession, Archie."

I went to the safe and got it and gave it to him. He unfolded it and handed it across to the cripple. I sat down and grinned at Wolfe, but he pretended not to notice; he leaned back with his eyes half closed, laced his fingers at his belly, and sighed.

Chapin read the confession twice. He first glanced at it indifferently and ran through it rapidly, then took a squint at Wolfe, twisted his lips a little, and read the confession all over again, not nearly so fast.

He tossed it over to the desk. "Fantastic," he

declared. "Set down that way, prosaically, baldly, it sounds fantastic. Doesn't it?"

Wolfe nodded. "It struck me, Mr. Chapin, that you went to a great deal of trouble for a pitifully meager result. Of course, you understand that I required this document for the impression it would make on your friends, and knowing the impossibility of persuading you to sign it for me, I was compelled to write your name myself. That is what I wish to apologize for. Here are your gloves, sir. I take it that my apology is accepted."

The cripple took the gloves, felt them, put them in his inside breast pocket, grabbed the arms of his chair and raised himself. He stood leaning on his stick.

"You knew I wouldn't sign such a document? How did you know that?"

"Because I had read your books. I had seen you. I was acquainted with your—let us say, your indomitable spirit."

"You have another name for it?"

"Many. Your appalling infantile contumacy. It got you a crippled leg. It got you a wife. It very nearly got you two thousand volts of electricity."

Chapin smiled. "So you read my books. Read the next one. I'm putting you in it—a leading character."

"Naturally." Wolfe opened his eyes. "And of course I die violently. I warn you, Mr. Chapin, I resent that. I actively resent it. I have a deep repugnance for violence in all its forms. I would go to any length in an effort to persuade you—"

He was talking to no one; or at least, merely to the back of a cripple who was hobbling to the door.

At the threshold Chapin turned for a moment, long enough for us to see him smile and hear him say: "You will die, sir, in the most abhorrent manner conceivable to an appalling infantile imagination. I promise you."

He went.

Wolfe leaned back and shut his eyes. I sat down. Later I could permit myself a grin at the thought of the awful fate in store for Nero Wolfe, but for that moment I had my mind back on Monday afternoon, examining details of various events. I remembered that when I had left to call on Mrs. Burton Wolfe had been there discussing soda water with Fritz, and when I returned he had gone, and so had the sedan. But not to the Tombs to see Paul Chapin. He had never left the house. The sedan had gone to the garage, and Wolfe to his room, with his coat and hat and stick and gloves, to drink beer in his easy chair. And at a quarter to four it was from his room that he had telephoned me to take the box to Mrs. Chapin, to give him a chance to fake a return. Of course Fritz had been in on it, so he had fooled me too. And Hibbard shooed off to the third floor for the afternoon . . .

They had made a monkey of *me* all right.

I said to Wolfe: "I had intended to go to a movie after lunch, but now I can't. I've got work ahead. I've got to figure out certain suggestions to make to Paul Chapin for his next book. My head is full of ideas."

"Indeed," Wolfe's bulk came forward to permit him to ring for beer. "Archie." He nodded at me gravely. "Your head full of ideas? Even my death by violence is not too high a price for so rare and happy a phenomenon as that."

# Rex Stout

REX STOUT, the creator of Nero Wolfe, was born in Noblesville, Indiana, in 1886, the sixth of nine children of John and Lucetta Todhunter Stout, both Quakers. Shortly after his birth, the family moved to Wakarusa, Kansas. He was educated in a country school, but by the age of nine he was recognized throughout the state as a prodigy in arithmetic. Mr. Stout briefly attended the University of Kansas, but left to enlist in the Navy, and spent the next two years as a warrant officer on board President Theodore Roosevelt's yacht. When he left the Navy in 1908, Rex Stout began to write free-lance articles and worked as a sightseeing guide and as an itinerant bookkeeper. Later he devised and implemented a school banking system which was installed in four hundred cities and towns throughout the country. In 1927 Mr. Stout retired from the world of finance and, with the proceeds of his banking scheme, left for Paris to write serious fiction. He wrote three novels that received favorable reviews before turning to detective fiction. His first Nero Wolfe novel, *Fer-de-Lance*, appeared in 1934. It was followed by many others, among them *Too Many Cooks, The Silent Speaker, If Death Ever Slept, The Doorbell Rang* and *Please Pass the Guilt*, which established Nero Wolfe as a leading character on a par with Erle Stanley Gardner's famous protagonist, Perry Mason. During World War II, Rex Stout waged a personal campaign against Nazism as chairman of the War Writers' Board, master of ceremonies of the radio program "Speaking of Liberty," a member of several national committees. After the war he turned his attention to mobilizing public opinion against the wartime use of thermonuclear devices, was an active leader in the Authors' Guild, and resumed writing his Nero Wolfe novels. Rex Stout died in 1975 at the age of eighty-eight. A month before his death, he published his seventy-second Nero Wolfe mystery, *A Family Affair*. Ten years later, a seventy-third Nero Wolfe mystery was discovered and published in *Death Times Three*.